DRAGONBOUND

DRAGONBOUND

BOOK TWO OF THE SOULMIST SERIES

HELEN GARRAWAY

Published by Jerven Publishing

Cover designed by MiblArt

eBook ISBN: 978-1-915854-03-2

Paperback ISBN: 978-1-915854-04-9

Hardcover ISBN: 978-1-915854-05-6

A CIP catalogue record for this book is available from the British Library.

Sign up to my mailing list to join my magical world and for further information about forthcoming books and latest news at: www. helengarraway.com

First Edition

For my Daughter, Jennifer
Love You xx

ALSO BY HELEN GARRAWAY

<u>Sentinal Series</u>

Sentinals Awaken

Sentinals Rising

Sentinals Justice

Sentinals Recovery

Sentinals Across Time

Sentinals Banished

Sentinals Destiny (Fall 2023)

<u>SoulMist series</u>

SoulBreather

DragonBound

CONTENTS

ANGELICUS
PURONIA
CITADEL
CHECKPOINT
SERAPHIM CASTLE
MINE
INN
SHANDRA'S DEN
CROSSROADS
RENSOR
DESTINE
BASRIL
JINNEL
TYRAL
FALLIR
MERAPOL
EIDOLON

1

SOLANJI, CITADEL, PURONIA

A soft snore woke Solanji, and she slowly flexed her fingers against the luxuriously comfortable bed, inhaling the gentle scent of violets from the bedsheets. Warm skin slid under her touch, and the arms wrapped around her tightened.

A hard body was glued to her back, long legs entwined with hers, and wherever his bare skin touched her, a spark of fire ignited, tightening her core as she realised she had fallen asleep in Mav's bed, with him. He was wrapped around her as if he was never letting go, and Solanji smiled as she luxuriated in his heat, his breath hot on the back of her neck.

After rescuing him from the cells under the citadel, Felather had helped her steer Mav back to his rooms. He had been a sorry sight, bruised and bleeding, but Felather had dosed him up, and numbed out of his mind, with Felather and Solanji under an arm each, they had half carried, half dragged him through the corridors. Servants averted their eyes, though Solanji had no doubt they thought he was inebriated, another slur to add to his already blackened name. As an archdeus, he was one step away from a god, but he wasn't treated as one.

The golden dragon tattoo on her forearm watched her. Its golden snout lifted off her skin momentarily, cocked its head, and hissed a few brilliant sparks before merging back onto Solanji's arm. A reminder that her life had changed beyond all recognition. As a SoulBreather, one who could return souls to the soulless, she had gained the SoulBreather's dragon. Not that she knew how to summon or control it. The burning need to learn how to be a proper SoulBreather flashed through her. Her brother's life depended on it. Banished to Eidolon, her nine-year old brother was cast out and soulless. Punished for a crime she was sure he hadn't committed.

Rubbing away sudden tears, she glared at the tattoo glowing on her forearm. It was a brilliant gold against her brown skin. Would the dragon become more active as she learnt what it meant to be a SoulBreather? It hadn't been very helpful so far. How was she supposed to learn? There was no one to teach her. Athenia, the last SoulBreather, had been an Archangel, supposedly immortal, and yet she had still died. Solanji was…nobody.

Sliding exploratory fingers up Mav's bare arm, she gently kissed his pale skin. Mottled yellow bruises were fading from where the guards had viciously attacked him. She wondered how his ribs were faring. Felather had said they were cracked when he'd healed them.

Carefully turning in his arms, she inspected his face. Winged black eyebrows curved over his currently closed amber eyes. Purple bruising still surrounded one of them, darkening across the ridge of his cheek. A firm face even so, with a stubborn chin, covered with a close-cut beard. Threads of silver streaked his shoulder-length black hair, greying prematurely under all the stresses he had been through. Lines creased the skin around his eyes, and she smoothed them with a gentle finger as she kissed him on his lips, still swollen from his recent beating. The citadel guards had used him as a punching bag before incarcerating him in a cell. Again.

Gritting her teeth, she snuggled into his embrace as she reviewed the previous day's events. Inhaling the comforting aroma of his slightly damp skin, she tried to figure out where they had gone so tragically wrong. She had led Mav through the tunnel under the divide and brought him out in the city of Puronia, fifty years after he had left it, and then taken him to her home. They had collapsed in exhaustion and been awoken by the guards of the Heavenly Host kicking in her door. She scowled. They had better repair the damage.

Nothing ever goes the way you expect, she thought, ruminating on how their plans had gone so awry before they had even started. Had someone been watching her rooms? But why? How did they know they would be returning to Puronia that day? Yes, she had sent the note to Kyrill stating that she was trying to persuade Mav to cross the divide but that he was resistant. They should have been watching the crossing not her home. She hadn't said *when* they would cross, and that was before she had realised she couldn't betray Mav. Was it her fault? Kyrill had made out that she was his spy, feeding him information. She supposed she had, but only to a limited degree. After all, her brother's life hung in the balance.

Tensing, she remembered there was some question as to whether Mav would survive the night. He had to be present for the session of Apologia, where he had to prove he had a soul, amongst other accusations.

Heavy curtains covered the window, though enough light bled around the edges to let her see the room. Peering at the timepiece on the mantle, she couldn't see what time it was.

Was it still the same day? Had he slept through the deadline or was it still looming?

Her chest tightened and her stomach churned with fear. She slid her arms around him and hugged him tight, suddenly afraid she was going to lose him. As she kissed his bare chest, Mav stirred, hugging her back and inhaling deeply. She studied his face as his eyelashes fluttered. If his shadowsoul wasn't truly a soul, then after one full day, he would expire and he would descend into the waiting embrace of Kaenera, the Keeper of the Oblivion Gate. The God of the soulless didn't offer redemption or let you go again.

His eyes opened and she was snared by his amber gaze. "Good morning," she whispered against his lips as she kissed him.

He smiled and kissed her back, deepening the kiss as she tried to pull away. He held her tight for a moment before releasing her. "It is when you get woken by a beautiful woman in your bed," he said, his voice husky with the last vestiges of sleep.

Solanji grinned back at him. They were in Mav's bedchamber, surrounded by his long-forgotten belongings. She knew he had never expected to see them again, had given up on returning to Puronia, but they seemed untouched as far as she could tell. No doubt his scribe, Felather, had something to do with that.

As soon as she thought of Mav's scribe, Felather opened the door and peered in. The slender man looked weary. His normally youthful face was showing signs of his true age, with lines and wrinkles. Felather smiled as he saw they were awake, his shadowed face lightening, and he entered, two mugs of bannoe in hand.

"How long?" Mav asked.

"How long what?" Felather said as he placed a mug on the table next to him.

"How long have I been out?"

"A few turns, just enough time to get you back here. I suggest you bathe and soak your muscles; I know you're hurting." Felather overrode his attempted protest. "Take the time, Mav. Who knows when you'll get another chance? You're safe in here, but as soon as you step out your door, you'll become a target again."

Mav scowled and Solanji smiled. Mav had complained about how independent and more determined his oathsworn had become in his absence. Not surprising, since they would've had to learn to be self-sufficient if they wanted to survive. And they had survived. All four of his oathsworn. The only ones who had believed in his innocence.

"Where's Adriz?" he asked as he shuffled upright. Solanji sat up and leaned against his side as she accepted the mug of bannoe from Felather. Adriz was his cherubim. His bodyguard. Solanji was surprised Adriz had let Mav out of her sight, but then Adriz peered through the doorway, her large bulk blocking out the light, and Solanji realised Adriz had been guarding his sleep. She was sure it would be months, if not years, before Adriz relaxed now that she had got him back.

Mav waved her in. No one could enter his private chambers unless he allowed them. Guarding him here was a waste of time.

"I'm safe here," was all he said. "We need to make plans. There are too many undercurrents to navigate this easily. What has been the reaction in the citadel to my incarceration?"

"Uncertainty, suspicion as to why you've returned now," Felather replied.

"And in the city?"

"Shock, surprise, horror," Felather admitted. "Though more in the vein of 'how could he?', than 'isn't it terrible how he's been treated?'."

"Not surprising, I suppose. A whole new generation has grown up in my absence. No one remembers me except for whatever the citadel has been saying."

A tap at the outer chamber door had Adriz stiffening and marching out of the room. After a low murmur of voices, Adriz returned with Sero fluttering beside her.

The baby-faced cherub had dispensed with his bow and arrow and instead wore a frown. He dropped onto the end of the bed, folded his golden wings, and smoothed his tunic over his chubby legs. "You don't have time to be lazing about."

Mav smiled. "And hello to you, Sero. What's this? Twice in one day. People will begin to think you like me."

Sero snorted and leaned against Mav's leg. "Have you decided what you will say?" He shifted, his hand hovering above the blankets. His gaze swivelled to Felather. "Haven't you healed him yet?"

Felather shrugged. "The knee joint is smashed beyond repair. All I can do is ease the swelling and help with pain management."

Solanji's lips tightened as Mav waved the words away. He had to be hurting after the beating, and it must have aggravated his previous injury. "There are more important things to worry about. In fact, there are so many I'm not even sure where to start."

"Before you do," Felather said, and pinned Sero with a piercing scowl. "What are *your* intentions here? Why did you come down to the cells to find Mav? You were not a supporter of his previously."

"I don't think you can afford to be picky," Sero snapped.

"There seems to be a lack of people knocking on your door offering to help."

"Sero already stated his concerns about the citadel, Felather," Mav said.

"Do you usually hold meetings in your bed chamber?" Solanji asked, sipping her bannoe and relieved she at least still wore her shirt, if nothing else.

Mav chuckled. "No, but these are unusual times. I'm surprised Ryvalin hasn't turned up. We'd have a full house then."

Solanji eyed him over the rim of her mug. Ryvalin was the rider of the dragon, Xylvin. Both were oathsworn to Archdeus Demavrian, as was she. "What about Xylvin? She won't like being left out."

Clapping his hands, Sero drew their attention back to him. "Enough. How many times do I need to say you don't have time for this?"

"You mean you haven't decided on a plan already?" Mav asked as he raised his arm so Solanji could snuggle into his side. He hugged her tighter and sighed out his breath. She knew what she'd rather be doing, but Sero was right. Mav needed to focus. He dropped a kiss on her head and then asked, "How long have we got before we have to prove I'm still alive?"

Felather glanced at the timepiece. "About three turns. Apologia recommences at nine. By then you will have been here for a day. In fact, I'd say you're already past any deadline, so you can relax."

"If he relaxes any further, he'll slither off the bed," Sero said.

"So I use the first count of lacking a soul to find out who is trying to undermine me," Mav said, ignoring Sero. "They will have to state who is making the accusation. When we return, I can request an audience with Serenia and

Amaridin, see what they have to say for themselves, and then Solanji can help me search my memories to see if we can discover any clues that I've buried for some reason." Mav scowled at Sero. "What do you think has happened to the citadel? I can't feel anything. I'm not sure if that's because I've been absent for so long or something else."

"The citadel is silent; it's not just you," Sero replied.

"What should you feel?" Solanji asked.

"There should be a sense of welcome, or rejection, and a constant heartbeat. But there was nothing when I entered. Even now, I hear nothing. There is no connection."

"I've never felt anything," Felather said thoughtfully.

"And Amaridin's never mentioned it?" Mav asked.

"Not that I am aware of. Do you think Serenia would know?"

Mav stared into the distance for a moment and then flicked his gaze back to Sero. "It's not something that was ever discussed. It just was. I never thought to question it. The citadel's been here since before I was born. But I'm not fully fit, so it could be me."

"I think it all changed when you left," Sero said. "What-ever happened with Athenia and you affected the citadel as well."

"So if the heart of the citadel has been absent for fifty years, there has been nothing to prevent the corruption of the assembly," Mav said.

"That would explain why the real murderer has never been expelled," Felather added.

"Could it have been deliberate?" Solanji asked, tensing as everyone stared at her. She continued, "Disabling the citadel, I mean. Who would understand how the citadel works?"

"What an interesting question," Sero murmured, switching his attention to Mav. "Were you and the citadel the target and not Athenia? Was she an unfortunate casualty?"

Solanji stroked Mav's arm as it tightened around her and then hugged him as he paled, staring at the cherub. He visibly forced himself to speak. "What?"

The idea that it was supposed to have been Mav lying on those steps chilled Solanji to the bone, and she shivered.

"What made you go into the halls in the middle of the night?" Felather asked.

Mav ran a shaking hand through his hair. "I don't remember. I had been in a meeting with my father and Athenia. I left first, and she stayed behind because my father wanted to discuss some other things. By the time I returned from visiting Xylvin it was late. I took the shortest route back to my rooms."

"Talking about time, you need to have a bath and prepare. We'll continue this discussion later. I'll have something ready to eat when you're finished." Felather shooed a protesting Sero out of the bedchamber, along with Adriz.

"Can't you do something about the bruising? He looks like a battered rainbow." Sero's complaining voice was cut off as the door thudded shut.

Mav caressed Solanji's back as he gazed up at the ceiling, trying to build up the energy to move. Her warm embrace was comforting. He didn't deserve her, not after how she had been treated by the guards of the Heavenly Host and the angels at the citadel.

Grinding his teeth, he scowled as Archangel Serenia's voice echoed in his mind. She had called Solanji a whore. How dare she. And Kyrill, the bastard who had tortured him for months, had tried to claim her as his fledgling. That wasn't happening.

"I'm sorry you got caught up in my problems," he said, caressing her shoulder.

Solanji lifted her head from where she had been nuzzling his neck and looked at him in surprise. "Don't go blaming yourself for Kyrill's actions. He was the one who dragged me into your affairs, and anyway, you should be grateful. We might never have met otherwise."

"True."

Solanji paused a moment as if choosing her words carefully.

"What?" Mav asked as the silence extended.

"Kyrill said I was his fledgling. Can he make that claim stick?"

Mav huffed. "He could try. But he can't force you. That would be slavery."

"Which I wouldn't put passed him."

"He can't break our personal oaths."

"But no one knows we swore them. How do they become official?"

"Normally, I would make a public declaration, but I would prefer not to draw attention to you at the moment. We don't want anyone discovering you are my wife and a SoulBreather just yet. And to be honest," Mav heaved a sigh, "until Apologia is declared null and void, people would start asking questions we don't want to answer."

"I'm worried he might try and grab me in a corridor or something. He seemed pretty determined to claim me as his. Though…" Solanji hesitated again.

Mav raised an eyebrow. "Though?"

"I wondered if it was an opportunity to get someone inside his organisation."

"Not an option." Mav's heart rate spiked, an uncomfortable flutter in his chest. "You know what he is capable of. There is no way he is getting his hands on you. You're my wife. I'm not allowing anyone else to threaten you."

"I didn't realise you would be so possessive!" Solanji said with a smile as she kissed his chin. "I like it, but he is your only lead into what's happening in the citadel. And we don't have any proof of what he is up to."

"Felather will find out. That's what he is good at."

"You need him focused on Apologia. That's your priority. If we can't prove your innocence, then there is no point doing anything else. And I can't help with any of that; it all happened before my time."

"That is a last resort." Mav scowled. The idea was preposterous and dangerous. Kyrill wouldn't hesitate to kill her if he caught her snooping in his office.

"My love, it is the most likely outcome. Be realistic. Kyrill claimed me in front of the assembly; he will demand you return me to him when he realises I left the cells with you. We don't want to give him more reason to target you. We need to take advantage of the opportunity. I can spy on him during the day, and Sero can teach me what he knows about soulbreathing in the evening while *you* prove your innocence." She emphasised her point by kissing him on the lips and Mav kissed her back. Reluctantly, he let her go.

"We haven't been back a day yet. Apologia will only take four days, and then we can focus on discovering how your soulbreathing works and find your brother." He hugged her tight as her beautiful eyes gleamed with unshed tears. "We will find him," he murmured into her hair.

Mav still couldn't believe she had thrown her lot in with him and risked losing her younger brother, now banished to Eidolon, soulless and no doubt terrified. How could the citadel justify treating a child in such an inhumane manner, stripping a nine-year-old of his soul and condemning him to an unknown future in the grim depths of Eidolon.

Mav would stop it the minute he had the chance. But the long list of problems he needed to resolve first meant he had to park that desire and focus on his more immediate life-threatening issues.

Apologia. That his brother had agreed to accuse him of four counts. Burning fury rushed through him, and he tensed again at the sense of betrayal.

"You are thinking horrible thoughts again," Solanji said and reached up to kiss his nose. Her body slid against his, and he groaned. A small smile curved her lips as she hovered above him. "I know something that will help you stop thinking." She kissed him again, forcing his mouth open, and he surrendered to her demands. The kiss deepened and Mav chased after her tongue.

Solanji lifted her face and arched her neck as Mav continued kissing down her smooth skin to her chest, the heat between them building. He tugged her shirt up her body, his fingers grazing her ribs, and she raised her arms so he could slide it over her head.

"Felather said you mustn't do anything strenuous; your ribs were cracked, and they are still healing."

That explained the ache. "He wasn't serious, was he?" Mav mumbled against the base of her throat, revelling in her scent as he moistened her skin. She tasted divine and smelt even better. A vibration of desire stirred deep inside him. "Not with you in my bed."

Solanji chuckled and straddled him. "If, and only if, you let me do all the work."

Mav stopped kissing her long enough to lift an eyebrow. "Is that a trick question?" he asked.

Leaning over him, her unruly curls tumbling over her shoulder as she slid her hands up his chest, Solanji ground against him, sparking an ache in his groin that she'd better be prepared to quench. His fingers drifted up over her ribs and caressed her breasts, unable to resist the instinctive thrust of his hips as she shuddered.

"At least it's much more comfortable than cold stone," she murmured as she dove back in, not giving him time to respond. Solanji raised herself over him and guided him into the exquisite heat, which enveloped him as he thrust deeper. A deep groan rumbled through his chest as he slid his fingers up her bare back, revelling in the silky-soft sensation. They moved together, desire tingling through his body and making his toes curl.

He kissed her throat, nipping at the pulse beating at the base, and she writhed. His need increased, as did his rhythm as he held her close; skin slid against skin, heated and slick. Flipping her over onto her back, he ignored her protests and the ache in his side and his knee, and sliding back inside her, exulted as she arched up to meet him, they shuddered in unison as the climax burst through them, leaving them boneless heaps of sensitised skin.

With a shuddering sigh, he raised himself off her and kissed her lips. "You are amazing, you do know that, don't you?" he asked when he was able to think coherently.

"And you never listen. You'll do yourself more damage," Solanji replied against his skin, dropping light kisses that belied her nagging tone.

"It was worth it, though," he murmured as he rolled to the side.

Solanji followed him, smoothing her hand over his sweaty chest, brushing her fingers through his soft chest hair as if reluctant to stop touching him. "Well, it is something we're very good at." She continued to kiss him.

"Mmm…" Mav mumbled, melting under her touch.

Solanji raised herself on one arm and looked down at him. The smile in her voice caressed him. "We have to bathe, otherwise Felather will be storming in and catching us at it again."

Mav huffed, but he knew she was right. He cracked open an eye and smiled up at her. "How fortunate the bath is big enough for two."

2

DEMAVRIAN

The corridors were crowded with wide-eyed staff and red-robed administrators. Mav didn't pause, he just kept moving, confident in his destination, Adriz and Felather behind him and Solanji trailing, lost and worried.

Mav searched for the heart of the citadel as he strode through the hallways. His fingertips trailed along the marble walls, the cool sensation stirring long forgotten memories. He found nothing, no heartbeat, no welcome, and he sighed out his breath in resignation. Why was he so surprised? His soul had been severed from him and the citadel, and he had no idea how to fix that. Maybe Solanji would be able to help.

They reached a wider corridor flanked with marble columns interspersed with busts of ancient personages. None had wings, only serene expressions, but their gaze followed Mav down the passageway. They came to an abrupt halt at the end of the passage where a central fountain graced an open courtyard and a rank of armoured soldiers blocked the way.

"By what right do you impede an archdeus?" Mav

demanded, stiffening as he met the derisive glare of the guards. Someone had shoved a stick up their arse and set them off. They had condemned him as guilty without a second thought. He wondered who.

He was answered as his once best friend, Julius, pushed his way through his men, his face stiff, his blue eyes glinting with fury and retribution. Mav stepped forward, leaning on his stick as he gazed around the courtyard. His robes hid the injury to his knee and his general debilitation, though the bruising on his face was in full bloom. He was in no condition for a fight, but he couldn't back down. Easing his weight off his bad knee for a moment, Mav met Julius' glare.

"How dare you…" Julius began.

Mav didn't give him a chance to finish his sentence. He whipped his stick up, cracked Julius over the head, jabbed it forward, and swept his feet out from under him. As Julius fell backwards, he balanced his weight briefly on the stick and then smacked it across Julius' chest, all so quick no one really saw what happened. Mav stood over him, negligently resting on his support. "Satisfied?" he asked, looking around the galleries. He twirled his stick and walked out as the Heavenly Host stared at him in shock.

Once out of the courtyard he paused, leant against the wall, and caught his breath, visible shudders threatening to overwhelm him. Felather rushed to his side, hands fluttering. "Julius is out cold. We should get you into the hall before they revive him." Felather glanced down the empty hallway. "That he dared to delay your appearance before Apologia."

"It is to be expected. Let us not be delayed further." Mav pushed off the wall, and limping heavily, he allowed Felather to escort him towards the audience chamber. The guards reluctantly parted as he approached, their unforgiving eyes boring into his back as he passed through the doors.

The chamber fell silent as he stalked down the central

aisle. The benches on either side rose in tiers and were filled with seraphim, administrators, and officials. Red-robed councillors to the left, grey-robed angels to the right. White marble lined the floor and walls, interspersed with ornately carved golden columns that held up the vaulted ceiling. Mav's reflection flickered in the polished stone as he passed, and he ignored the fact that he didn't look very angelic, battered and bruised as he was. Maybe that was their intent, to keep him off-balance from the beginning.

"You are too late, Archdeus Demavrian. You have missed your opportunity. And anyway...you can't speak unless you flare, and we both know you can't do that, now don't we?"

Mav halted and turned to face the blond-haired seraphim sneering down at him from his seat in the ranks. He held Kyrill's eyes until he looked away.

Mav continued to walk through the marble hall, flanked by Adriz and trailed by Felather and Solanji. Vast crystal chandeliers hung from the cavernous ceiling, and Mav spotted Sero and some other cherubs perched in them as he passed. His footsteps echoed in the silence until he stopped just before the dais, where the most beautiful and serene angel waited. The angel's sheer wings swept up either side of her, glittering in an incandescent rainbow of colours in the candlelight.

A sense of peace and calm pervaded the room as she gazed at them.

"Archdeus Demavrian Deusson. You are late," she said, her melodious voice caressing the air they breathed.

"The reason I am late is because I was attacked without cause on my way here, with obvious intent to delay my arrival, and as such, for an unprovoked attack, I am granted one turn of the glass." Mav strived to remain calm as he gestured at the huge timepiece on the wall and then inspected Serenia properly for the first time in nearly five decades. The last audience, he had spent most of it pressed face-first into the marble floor. An echoing silence followed his words, along with the agitated ruffling of wings. His breath fluttered in his chest as she caught his eye, conveying a message he couldn't interpret, and a chill spread through him. Uncertainty of her regard for him another worry undermining his confidence.

"Is there anyone here wishing to speak in rebuttal?" Serenia's melodious voice grew cold, and Mav regretted the sharp edge that marred it. And then his stomach plummeted as Kyrill replied.

"The host was assisting me in rescuing my fledgling that the archdeus was holding against her will." He snapped his fingers and pointed at Solanji and then at the floor before him. "Here."

Adriz hissed, but Mav raised a hand and she fell silent.

"Solanji?" Mav asked. He tried to keep his face expressionless. He hadn't expected Kyrill to act so fast even though Solanji had predicted he would. Her beautiful eyes were anguished and uncertain, and she clenched her fingers so tight they cracked. She opened her mouth but few words left them.

"Mav, I-I…"

Kyrill continued, waving a piece of paper. "Here is her note advising me they were travelling to the crossing. That Demavrian attempted to purchase a false soul to cross the divide, as he has no soul of his own."

Voices rose in shock. Adriz hissed her breath out, behind Mav's shoulder.

"Prove it," Mav snapped, deepening his voice. A shiver rippled through him. Kyrill was showing his hand much earlier than he had anticipated. He had said Kyrill couldn't force her to serve him. He had been wrong and over confident. There was nothing he could say to refute Kyrill without putting Solanji more at risk. If they knew she was a Soul-Breather, he doubted she would last the night. They hadn't agreed that Solanji would join Kyrill's retinue, but maybe it was meant to be. He didn't like it, though in his current position, there was little he could do to prevent it. He so wished he could mind speak to reassure her.

"What?"

"Prove your claim or defend your honour."

Kyrill descended from his seat in the tiers to the floor. "She's a SoulSucker; she can prove it."

"And yet you dragged her off the streets of Puronia and didn't report her. Instead, you forced her to go to Eidolon, promised to redeem her brother and return him to her family."

Kyrill waved his hand, his jaw tightening. "I needed to confirm my suspicions before reporting her."

"Do you lie about others things as well? Do you lie about what you get up to in Eidolon? Do you deny that you have a castle in the north of Eidolon? Captain Teravin can confirm. After all, he dragged me there and allowed me to be incarcerated in your torture chamber. Do you deny that?"

"Enough," Serenia interrupted, a scowl marring her exquisite face. "This has nothing to do with the first count."

Mav coldly inspected the hall, seeing some doubt on confused faces. He almost lost his stern demeanour when Solanji defiantly raised her chin. God, she was beautiful. His gaze lingered, and he met her eyes and saw the determination. She had made her own decision, and he gave her the slightest of nods. Her shoulders stiffened, and he looked back at the seraphim who dared to challenge him.

"Are you the accuser for the first count?"

"Flare your wings," Kyrill demanded.

Mav stared him down. Since when had this seraphim become so sure of himself? So confident that he would openly confront an archdeus in the citadel? Mav's breath stuttered. He supposed torturing an archdeus near to death might make him believe he had the upper hand. Was that Kyrill's plan all along? Get Mav to the citadel and denounce him in full view of the council? "The claim was 'no soul'. You cannot prove it, therefore your claim is invalid. The word of a mere seraphim," Mav speared him with a look of pure disdain, and Kyrill licked his lips as he glanced around his shocked peers; the brethren were watching him with wide-eyed expectation, "does not supersede that of an archdeus. My scribe will expect your reparation." Mav lifted his chin. "Now, who else here claimed I don't have soul?"

He struggled to remain calm as Kyrill dragged a resistant Solanji back to his seat.

Serenia cleared her throat, her gaze encompassing the room and demanding silence. Her expression hardened as she glared at Mav. He held her stare. This confrontation had not been his choice, and Serenia's lips tightened.

"We are gathered here today to finally lay to rest the accusations against Archdeus Demavrian Deusson. I declare Apologia is in session. A reminder of the counts, in case you had forgotten. "First count, the murder of Archangel Athenia Demois, our one and only SoulBreather; second count, the murder of Deus Veradeus; third count, lack of a soul; fourth count, inability to flare wings and therefore no longer a divine, blessed angel." The hall was silent. "First count, lack of a soul." Serenia turned to face him. "Failure of any count forfeits your life." Serenia returned to her seat. "Proceed."

Mav's lips peeled back in a vicious grin as fury flashed through him. He suddenly understood how innocent people could be driven to terrible actions, behaviour typically beyond their capabilities. The ferocity of his anger at the injustice of this whole situation astonished him. He knew he was innocent, therefore someone else was lying. He stored his feelings away to explore later. And they'd had the temerity to change one of the counts. He was now accused of murdering his father? That they would believe him capable of such a thing took his breath away. He inhaled and exhaled, trying to calm his riotous pulse. Once he was sure he could speak calmly, he said, "Count one, lack of a soul," and after hooking his stick on his belt, he walked towards the steps.

When he reached the bottom of the marble stairs, he spread his arms and rotated, demonstrating his complete dearth of weapons as his trousers swirled around him. A statement of vulnerability that he knew would have Adriz in a panic, but he had to make it to demonstrate his belief in his innocence.

"Who accuses?" Mav demanded. By right he could identify his accuser, and if he was proved innocent of the charge then the accuser would be found guilty.

'I-I do," a shaky voice said from the lower tier. A skinny angel rose to his feet, his eyes fearful and his face as pale as his grey robes. Throat bobbing, he cast about for support from the ranks of his companions, but they all drew away from him, leaving him exposed.

Mav scowled at him. "And who might you be?"

"D-Dalruan."

Mav was not enlightened. He turned to his scribe, and Felather sauntered towards him.

"Seraphim Dalruan is newly appointed. Maybe his ascension has gone to his head," Felather said in his silky-soft voice as he stopped beside Mav.

Dalruan threw a desperate glance at the dais and gulped. "Th-the accused has been involved in attempting to buy a soul on the black market. I have a signed statement from a trusted source that he was retained to carry a soul across the divide to the crossroads and there to hand it over to you in return for six halos." A ripple of murmurs spread around the hall. "The only reason to make such an exchange would be because he, Archdeus Demavrian, needs a soul."

Mav inspected the man. "And you are prepared to stake your life on it?"

Gulping, Dalruan paled. "My life is not the one in question."

"Apologia is in session. Each count demands my life in forfeit. Each count proved false rebounds that forfeit on the accuser. Each count demands a justification and the death of the false party before we can declare the charge proven or defended and we can move on to the next one. Maybe you should all check the rules and your proof before you stand forward and make your accusations."

Mav crossed his arms and watched the horror dawn on the faces of the angels. Maybe they were not so certain in their accusations after all. Wondering who was orchestrating it all, Kyrill wasn't senior enough to be in charge, he let his gaze travel over the senior angels and archangels.

Golaran was sitting on his designated bench, calmly watching him as if he was some rare species, and raised a bushy white eyebrow when Mav caught his eye. Mav dipped his head slightly, which Golaran returned, and Mav moved on. He had never thought Golaran was the culprit, though a meeting would not go amiss with the portly archangel.

"I need to speak to Golaran after this debacle," Mav said.

"Noted," Felather replied.

"What time were we dragged to the citadel yesterday?"

"You've got about half a turn to go."

"Do we have proof of our arrival time?"

"I can call the duty guard here as witness."

"Call him forward to make his statement."

Mav endured Felather's searching inspection before he nodded. Taking a deep breath, Mav climbed the first few steps. He would demand his chair for the next count. They had no right to remove it, nor his father's. Shortly after, Felather returned with the stocky soldier who had logged all entrances into the citadel. This was all such a farce. Everyone in this hall knew when he had arrived in Puronia the previous day. That time had long passed and he hadn't expired on the spot.

The soldier stood beside the scribe in the middle of the hall, and Felather raised his voice. "Silence for the rebuttal of Apologia count one by Archdeus Demavrian Deusson. No Soul. Accuser Seraphim Dalruan.

"First witness, corporal of the citadel guard. On duty ninth turn yesterday morning." Felather paused and then raised his voice. "I said, SILENCE!" He waited, glowering at the tiers until the hall fell silent. "Thank you. You can discuss today's events in your own time. NOT during Apologia. If you are unable to abide by the rules of Apologia, leave now. I do not expect to request silence a second time. If I do, the citadel forfeits a charge."

The swish of the timepiece intruded on the unnatural silence, a sibilant echo that reminded Mav of better times.

"As I said. First witness, corporal of the citadel guard. On duty ninth turn yesterday morning. The duty log confirms his shift." Felather held the book out and waited until a scribe dashed out from his seat and grabbed it.

"Duty log accepted as evidence," the man squeaked and scuttled back to his seat.

"Corporal. Did you see the accused, Archangel Demavrian Deusson, enter the citadel yesterday?"

"Yes sir."

"And at what time did he enter?"

"Just before the half bell of the ninth turn, sir."

"And did the citadel reject him?"

"No sir, he entered without issue."

"Thank you." Felather looked across at Dalruan. "Your witness."

Dalruan rose. "You are sure it was before ninth turn half bell?"

"Yes, sir. You can ask anyone; you were all here."

"That will not be necessary. The half bell approaches. Time will confirm or deny his innocence." Dalruan stared at the large timepiece on the wall. A golden mosaic of cogs and chains whirred and clicked, driving a slender pointer that marked the turn and a smaller pointer that spun on its axis, releasing a silver ball to swish down the rail and hit the bell as it marked the passage of time. Once the receiving basin was full, the weight triggered the release and the turn pointer moved another notch.

Everyone in the room stared at it as the hand moved inexorably towards the midpoint between the ninth and tenth digit. Sweat gleamed on Dalruan's face as his gaze flicked between the time piece and Mav. A mass exhale marked the moment the hand moved passed the half way point and Mav remained standing on the steps.

Mav breathed. In and out. Anger stirred, and he tamped it down. That they would waste his time like this. He walked up the remaining steps and turned to face the hall and waited.

"I claim falsehood," Dalruan shouted in desperation. "Call a SoulSinger to confirm he has a soul."

"The charge is resolved. The claim that Archdeus Demavrian has no soul is proved false and is closed." Serenia rose from her seat, her face expressionless. "Seraphim Dalruan is charged with false accusation and pays the price. Take him away." Serenia nodded at Mav, ignoring the seraphim's cries and pleas. "Second count is tomorrow, same time, same place." And she descended the stairs and left the hall, her scribe close behind her.

3

KERRIS, EIDOLON

Kerris rose early and quickly dressed in the freezing morning air. Peering out of the door, he scanned the yard and surrounding fields. Everything was still and quiet. A thin mist lay over the ground, hiding the muddy fields and gorse bushes. Shivering, he pulled another shirt over the top of the one he was wearing and grabbed a cloak.

Shandra was before him, a steaming mug of soup in her hand. "You'll need something to get you to the market," she said, proffering the mug.

Kerris grimaced, but took it. "Thanks. You didn't have to get up." He inhaled the fragrant steam and sighed in appreciation. Bailey had a magic touch in the kitchen, but Shandra was the mothering type. She was not much older than him, young for the responsibilities on her shoulders, always making sure everyone had what they needed. None of them were older than fifteen; the majority of the kids were less than ten.

Sometimes he wondered who made sure she got what *she* needed, but she wouldn't appreciate him saying as much.

Slim and ethereal, a tangle of blond hair escaping the bun she tied it in, she ruled the house with determined efficiency. Kerris knew she thrived on it.

Over the last few days, the kids had helped to harvest the squashes, most of which they had stored in the hay loft, but today Kerris was going to the nearest village in the hopes of trading some of them for flour and oats. They couldn't grow grains themselves; the land around their house was too heavy and wet.

Bailey made do with various root vegetables for soups and stews, but he had finally admitted he had run out of anything that he could use to make his flat breads.

He handed the empty mug back to Shandra and, as an afterthought, leaned in to kiss her cheek before turning to leave.

"Be careful," Shandra said, her blue eyes wide as her fingers touched where he had kissed her cheek.

"Always," Kerris replied.

Stretching, Kerris took one last glance across the yard and strode over to the barn. He would load their one mule with the sacks of squashes and walk the five miles to the nearest village, which he knew had a grain mill. He had traded there before, so he was hopeful that it wouldn't take too long. Leaving Shandra and Muntra on their own with twenty youngsters to protect felt wrong, but they also needed to eat.

Shandra's Den, as their home had been named, was a dilapidated house that Mav, an angel who had fallen on hard times, had helped them set up. Kerris had stumbled across Mav a few years back, when he was starving and desperate, and Mav had shared his food and his clothes with him and the other kids travelling with him.

Mav had been the first person to offer him anything expecting nothing in return. Kerris scowled as he loaded the mule. He wished Mav had never left. He may be one man, but he made you feel safe. There was something about him that melted your fears away.

The last time he had seen Mav, he had been injured. Kerris worried that it would get worse, even though, as an angel Mav should be able to heal himself. The fact that he hadn't, and that the injury had become infected, was concerning.

Staring down at his hands, Kerris wondered why he was able to heal minor injuries. Inspecting his palms, he frowned at how callused his skin had become. Ingrained dirt darkened his already brown skin; he found it impossible to stay clean. Mav had begun to explain how healing worked and to help him hone his ability, but he hadn't been able to stay long. Kerris knew he should have insisted that he travel with Mav and Solanji, at least to the Divide, but again Mav had said he was needed here. Shandra and the kids needed him. Their house drew abandoned children like a lone light in the dark.

It made little difference. Mav was gone and they were on their own. Leading the mule out of the barn, he started up the track that led to the wider road. It would take him most of the day to reach the village. He'd be lucky to get back before the sun set.

Brennan huddled in the corner of the cart and covered his ears. It didn't help as the piercing shrieks of terrified people still penetrated, and he tried to make himself as small as possible.

This shadowed land of Eidolon petrified him, as did the looming men who dragged him from one place to another without explanation. No one cared if he lived or died. They only wanted to use him for their own purposes.

For weeks now, he had been hauled around like a sack of grain, becoming more lost and afraid as they took him further from home. Why had no one listened to him? He didn't understand how he had ended up here. Accused and sentenced without a shred of evidence against him. All he remembered was being grabbed on the street and a voice saying he was too young and another saying he was old enough, and that was it. Old enough for what?

The Justicers had terrified him. He had stood in absolute silence as a grey-haired man, wearing spectacles, had observed him and then scowled before he scribbled on his pad and sent him into another room. There he had been instructed to lie down, and then a woman had placed a cloth over his mouth and nose, and he didn't remember anything after that.

When he awoke, something was wrong. He hadn't realised what at the time, only that he felt off, unbalanced, as if he had lost something. Something wasn't right but the answer was just out of reach. A constant wave of nausea turned his stomach, keeping him unsettled and uncomfortable.

It wasn't until they bundled him into a cart and descended the trail down the escarpment and into Eidolon that he understood. The guards called him a soulless bastard. The unsettled, empty feeling was explained; they had taken his soul, and now he was destitute and homeless. Banished to live in the shadows until he died and passed through the Oblivion Gate. His guts churned, and he hugged himself tight as he shuddered. If only they would leave him somewhere quiet, but no, the shouts and screams continued, and he tried to block them out.

Images of his mother and his home by the clear, blue seas of Bruatra teased him, and his eyes stung. Sniffing, he used his sleeve to rub away the tears; he had done his crying.

One person after another had sneered at him as they pushed him into another locked room as if he was some dangerous murderer. He was only nine. What did they expect him to do? Even if he did escape, where would he go? He had no idea how to survive on his own. He knew his sister, Solanji, had a home in the city somewhere, but the city was huge and he didn't know where she lived.

The man who had collected him from the staging house had called him a freller, after the timid creatures that hid in burrows in the fields. Always hiding from the night predators. How apt was that? Brennan snorted and curled tighter. He didn't even have his own name anymore. He was just a frightened creature hiding from the next threat.

A tremor shook him as silence fell outside, and the canvas was pulled aside. Children smaller than him were lifted into the wagon, and they scrabbled away from the men threatening them, snuffling into their ragged shirts, eyes wide with fear.

"Unhand him, you brute," a young girl shouted, and there was a heavy thud against the side of the cart.

More shouts followed, and the sound of a scuffle preceded a high-pitched scream, which was suddenly cut off.

"Enough," a man snapped. "Either get in or we'll kill him now. He looks too fragile to be of use anyway."

"You have no right to take of any us." A boy's voice, trembling with anger.

"Bailey, don't make it worse. Just get in the cart," the girl said.

"If we go with them, it won't get any better," the boy snapped. "They hurt Muntra. They'll hurt all of us."

"They'll hurt him more if we don't do as they say," the girl replied.

More kids were lifted onto the wagon, followed by a slender boy and a young girl. The boy peered around him and smiled at the children, and Brennan caught his breath. The boy's smile lit up his face, and his soft blond curls glowed like a halo in the weak light. "That's right, stay together. It will be warmer." He turned and peered out the canvas awning. "Shandra, don't let them leave Muntra behind."

"Wake him up," the man snapped. The sound of water being splashed on someone was followed by a low groan. The cart rocked as more people climbed in, and then a heavyset boy was shoved over the lip, and he rolled onto his back and groaned again as the tarpaulin was pulled down and blocked the light. Brennan shrank into his corner, trying to disappear.

"Muntra, you idiot. Why did you try and fight?" Bailey asked as he knelt beside the boy.

"Mav said I was to protect you."

"Not when you are outnumbered ten to one. Where's Shandra?"

"She went in the other wagon. She was trying to calm the youngsters."

"What do we do?" Bailey asked.

Muntra groaned in response. "There's nothing we can do until we find out where they are taking us."

"Nowhere good."

"I think they busted my ribs," Muntra said, wincing as the cart rocked as it began to move.

"We need Kerris."

"Shhh. At least he is out of this mess."

"He won't know what's happened or where we're going. He's not due back for ages."

Muntra huffed. "I'm sure it won't take him long to figure it out. It's not like we all go out on some trek together every day, is it?" He peered into the dim cart. "Kiara? Are you alright?"

"I'm fine. We need to pay attention to the road and see

where they take us," Kiara replied, trying to peek out between the canvas and the wooden boards. "Otherwise we'll have no chance of finding our way home."

"Great idea. You and Bailey do that while I lie here and die."

Some of the smallest kids began crying, and Kiara hushed them. "He isn't going to die. You know what a big baby Muntra is. Try and get comfortable. I imagine we're going to be stuck in here for a while."

Brennan curled tighter as the boy moved amongst the little kids, patting shoulders, kissing cheeks, a constant murmuring, a soothing litany of endearments, which drew closer and closer. He flinched when a gentle hand touched his shoulder.

"Hey, my name is Bailey. What's yours?"

Brennan could only stare at him in wide-eyed terror. As much as he wanted to answer, to be embraced by this boy's goodwill, he couldn't. His throat constricted, and he began to shake.

"Shhh, it's alright. You can stay with us. We'll look after you." Soft arms hugged him and then gently began to rock, but Brennan remained stiff and unresponsive, unable to even meet the boy half way.

4

SOLANJI, CITADEL

Kyrill almost jerked Solanji off her feet as he dragged her out of the hall. When she had first seen him, she had thought he was the most beautiful person she had ever met. She had been wrong. His beauty was superficial, only skin deep. The archdeus glowed from within; even Mav, damaged as he was.

The day her fingers had trailed through Kyrill's soulmist was the worst day of her life. She should have handled it better, disseminated quicker. What was a seraph doing in the city streets, anyway? Only the fledglings and administrators mingled with the peasants as he called them.

How had Kyrill found out who she was? Discovered where she was vulnerable and been quick to use it against her, along with the threat of public humiliation and incarceration. Her shoulders dropped. She should have let them humiliate her. Her pride had led her to this, thinking she could save her family by betraying a stranger.

She should have asked more questions; if she had known who Mav was…sneering at herself, she knew it wouldn't have made any difference with what hung in the balance. Her family's safety was more important than any friendship. It was only as she had grown to know Mav and understood what he had suffered that she'd realised she couldn't betray him. Mav was the only person fighting for the soulless in Eidolon, and her brother was now one of them.

Kyrill jerked her forward again, almost pulling her arm out of its socket as he stomped down the corridor, his elegance misplaced or just a sham. Mav hadn't needed to pretend, it was innate. She should have trusted him from the beginning. Told him everything. An archdeus could have helped her out of this mess, even an angel as badly damaged as he was. How *had* Kyrill managed to get his hands on Mav in the first place?

There was a way to find out if she had the courage to take the risk. She extended her soul fingers and grazed his soulmist. Skimming the surface, she shivered in delight as the trails curled around her ephemeral fingers. Feather light, like Felather. As the memory of the stark worry in Felather's eyes intruded, she almost let go. No, concentrate, that's right. What does he want?

Hazy images swirled, out of sequence and time, and then she lost the connection as Kyrill slammed open a door and shoved her into a darkened room. He snapped his fingers and candles lit, illuminating a pleasant study. Ornate mouldings were accented in gold, framing large gilt mirrors. Everything was gilt and white, much like the seraphim.

"Well, you failed spectacularly," he snarled as he paced. "It's unfortunate your family isn't around to see how you let them down."

Solanji hugged herself, watching him pace. Icy cold shivers shuddered through her at the mention of her family. "I did as you bid. I rescued him and brought him to you. You promised if I did that, you'd help my brother."

Kyrill swirled on her. "You do not speak unless I give you

permission. Not one word." He continued to pace, the chords in his neck rigid as his anger grew. "Fucking Demavrian. Always thinks he's one step ahead. He shouldn't be standing, let alone defeating Apologia." He paced again. "You said he was crippled. His knee pulverised."

"You did it; you should know," she replied.

Hissing his breath out, he struck her across the face. "For that I will make your mother scream."

"No, please, forgive me, I spoke out of turn." The tang of blood filled her mouth as she held her aching cheek. *Keep calm*, she chanted, *don't rile him*. Protecting her family came first.

"I don't want your apologies; I want information. How did he do it?" He grabbed her hair and yanked her head back and then smoothed his hand down her neck. "Such a pretty throat. If you want to keep it, tell me everything that's happened since you escaped the dungeon. I made it easy enough for you."

"He was badly hurt, unable to move until I pulled the spears out. When I suggested we fly, he said he couldn't. So we had to steal a couple of your calope. He couldn't heal his knee. He could hardly walk."

"He walked today."

"We've been three weeks on the road, if not longer. He trained every day, with…with his cherubim, working on regaining some flexibility."

"What powers does he still have?"

"I don't know. I don't know what he's supposed to be capable of," she added hurriedly as his eyes narrowed.

"Mind speech."

Solanji shook her head. "I never saw any sign of it." Unless of course, he had camouflaged it in his comments. How pretty her hair was, her beautiful eyes. Had he been disguising his conversations with the others? Had he been suspicious of her? She didn't think so, not at any point, not even when she had confessed to him. She shivered.

"Healing," Kyrill snapped.

"That's definitely not working properly. He said he was drained."

Kyrill nodded. "Flight."

"He said he couldn't fly."

All of which she had already told him; she wasn't revealing anything new. What if she took his soul? Could she take his soul? He seemed to think she could take Mav's. But she didn't know where her family was. She couldn't. Not yet. She fluttered her fingers through his agitated soulmist, skimming his thoughts until her fingers snagged on a knot.

His soulmist was different, twisted, as if it was all tangled in on itself. Solanji frowned, trying to make sense of it. His soulmist no longer trailed as it once had. His uppermost thoughts were of taking Mav's power, killing him, and stepping into his shoes. He was so frustrated, he wanted to kill something. Like her for instance. She stilled, keeping out of his way. His thoughts and emotions swirled through her. He had been so close; he had felt it at the tips of his fingers. The power flaring through him, and then it had been snatched away again. So close.

Kyrill snarled, his fist striking out again. "Don't you try your shenanigans on me, girl. You stay out of my head. You try and I'll kill you."

"I-I can't mind read," Solanji stuttered from the floor. Her ears were ringing, a sharp ache jabbed behind her eyes, and blood dripped from a cut under her eye. Shuddering her breath out, she scrambled to her knees and gritting her teeth, pretended to cower before him. Oh, how she would like to shove her knife through his arrogant ribs, but she restrained herself with an effort and remained silent.

"How did he get out of the cell?"

"His scribe, Felather, got him out, and me too."

"For now, you stay away from him. Avoid his cherubim if you want to live; she'll kill you if she has the chance, and my name won't protect you. He wasn't supposed to make it this far. He wasn't supposed to reconnect with his oathsworn. You'll pay for your failure."

"I did what was asked of me. You have to save my brother. Please."

"You think you can tell me, a seraphim, what to do? I think not." Kyrill loomed over her, his fists clenching. "You have to redeem yourself. Otherwise, I'll kill you myself." He swung round, clearing the expression on his face as his assistant, Carna, entered the room, trailed by another older man.

"Ah yes, Lormin, we have a new fledgling for you to manage." Lormin wore simple dark grey robes, belted by a red corded rope. He was heavyset, stocky, nothing like the elegant seraphim, and he fidgeted with the tassel as he listened to Kyrill's instructions. His gaze skittered around the room until he found Solanji. He scowled, and she gave him a faint smile, which faded as Kyrill turned back to her, his golden eyebrows pinched low over his eyes.

"You will go with Lormin. He will explain your duties."

Scrambling to her feet, Solanji kept Kyrill in her sight as she shuffled nearer to Lormin. Kyrill wasn't old; his beauty just seemed faded and cheap against the simple purity of the archdeus. Not that she would have said Mav was simple, but his beauty was clean and graceful, unforced. Unconscious, she thought, as she watched Kyrill deliberately position himself in a ray of sunlight and tilt his head. Mav wouldn't be seen dead posing like that.

She wondered what Mav and his...friends were doing. An archdeus, a cherubim, and his scribe; how could she have misjudged them so badly? The care and concern they showed for Mav were above and beyond any form of servitude. She was glad he had them, for he needed them. He only found trouble when he was alone.

Watching the golden soulmist emanating from the men, Solanji considered how different they were; Carna's and Lormin's trailed loosely behind them, in stark contrast to the tangled mess of Kyrill's, instead of wrapped tightly as Adriz's and Felather's were. Not as Mav had clasped his altered soul around him, with reverence, as if it was to be treasured, even though it wasn't a true soul. He had made it his, and it had subverted itself willingly.

Mav was more vibrant than any soul-endowed person she had met. Admittedly, she had tried to give him what she thought was his soul back, but the shadows hadn't accepted it, or at least not all of it. She wasn't sure what he did have, even if it acted like a soul.

These souls looked like they didn't care if they stayed or left. There was no connection with its host. She pondered that. Why did some people control their souls and others didn't? Whatever the reason, it made it simple for her to trail her fingers through the loose strands.

Kyrill stopped and pointed an imperious finger at her. "Get her cleaned up and get her some clothes. Bring her back in one turn. Don't be late." He strode towards his desk, an abrupt dismissal, and the fledgling scowled at her and jerked his head.

Not knowing what else to do, Solanji followed him out the door. She sighed out a breath, glad to be away from Kyrill. The fledgling glared at her. He was older than she had first thought, and he was still a fledgling?

"What is a fledgling?" she asked before he could tell her to be silent.

The man raised his chin. "An angel or seraphim may tap

a student from each year's academy intake to support his or her endeavours. It is an honour to be tapped."

"How long have you been a fledgling?"

"None of your business. You are the newest so you do what we say and will run the errands."

"How many fledglings does the seraphim have?"

"As many as he needs." He veered down a plain hallway with grey painted walls. "Where possible you use the back corridors. Don't get caught in the main passageways or another seraphim may order you to do something for them."

"Can any seraphim command us?" Maybe she could find a way to cross Mav's path.

"They can command all fledglings until they are elevated, and all fledglings must obey the seraphim."

"All? Aren't you a fledgling?"

"I am in charge of the seraphim's fledglings. You are his fledgling," the man said pompously, though he glanced around quickly to make sure no one had overheard him.

Solanji hovered her fingers over his soulmist. If he was lying, she would soon find out. "But we look to Seraphim Kyrill, don't we?"

"Yes. And don't forget it. He'll expect a report of any errands you run for the others. It's a game they play, trying to get one over each other."

"And the angels?"

"Stay away from them. If you value your life, you won't go near them." He shivered as if in fear, but she knew he felt her caress. His thoughts shimmered into her, uppermost his disgust at having to show her around, next his worry that she would supplant him. Interesting idea.

Lormin indicated a door. "This is where we sleep. There is a bathing room out back, hurry up and wash. You are a disgrace. I'll get you some clean clothes."

When Solanji ventured back out of the bathing room,

the antechamber was empty, and she hurried to dress in the pile of folded clothes waiting for her on the bench before anyone came in. They turned out to be a tunic and trousers made of a coarse cloth, nothing like her leathers. She was rubbing her hair dry when Lormin returned.

"Aren't you ready yet?" he snapped.

Solanji ran her fingers through her hair, the fledgling not having left her a comb. Her hair would dry into a wild mop, and she shrugged, giving up. She watched the fledgling thoughtfully. He thought he knew everything, when he actually knew nothing. He was an insignificant cog in the machinations of the upper echelons of the citadel. She was more concerned with what was happening to Mav and how she could find out. How long had they been in the citadel?

As Solanji followed Lormin through the corridors, she caught a glimpse of the brilliant orange sky as the sun set. Mav had about another twelve turns before he would have to face the second count.

They skirted the main chamber hall, and Solanji's steps slowed as she gaped at the massive glass chandeliers being tended by the citadel staff. One of the giant golden branches had been lowered to the ground, and the crystal drops were being polished as the candles were replaced and relit.

"What are we expected to do?" she asked as she sifted through his thoughts.

"Whatever the seraphim ask us to. Run messages, collect things, deliver things." Carna was remembering a visit he had made into the city. To some obscure shop to collect a package. He was annoyed because he didn't know what was in it.

"Do you know why he hates Demavrian so much?" she asked. And his thoughts spiked as if in a panic.

"If you want to live, you won't say his name. The seraph

is determined to prove he is the root of all the citadel's troubles."

"What troubles?"

"You ask too many questions."

"If I don't ask, I don't know what to avoid."

"Don't say anything unless you are spoken to first. That is safest. You won't be punished then."

"Punished?" Dark thoughts swirled through his soulmist, and Solanji shivered. "Aren't angels supposed to be good? Why would they want to punish us?"

Lormin came to a halt and thrust his face into hers. "If you want to live, you keep your mouth shut and do as you're told."

5

DEMAVRIAN

M av's scribe and his cherubim were fairly bristling by the time they reached his quarters and threw open the door. They had been ready to bite the head off any person who so much as looked at them wrong, and if Mav hadn't been with them, he thought they might have.

He limped through the door behind them, Sero darting in just before the door swung shut as candles lit all around them, and the long-missed familiarity of his sanctuary embraced him. Dropping into a chair, he rested his head against the back and tried to remember when he had last been here. It had been decades. He rolled his head and watched his friends as they vented their anger, against the citadel, against Kyrill, against him for not protesting against Kyrill's claim on Solanji.

They had been so frantic to find him. They had never given up on him, and he still hadn't explained himself. "When were we last here?" he asked, his quiet voice breaking through their angry tirade. They were so furious they were not making sense.

Felather stared at him, halting mid-rant. "What?"

"When was the last time we were here? I can't remember." Mav could. He remembered it exactly.

"Don't give us that shit. You remember perfectly well. And if you ever disappear like that again, I'll personally kill you myself," Adriz growled.

Sero chuckled. "Line up and join the queue."

"Ah, that's right. The day before I found Athenia. The night before my father told me that I had to go into Eidolon and find out who was scheming against his plan to reunite Angelicus and Eidolon and remove the Divide."

"He told you what?" Felather said, his blue eyes wide as Adriz dragged her breath in.

"How many years ago was that? How long has my father been absent?"

"Forty-nine years and seventy-two days," Felather replied.

"I think I was in shock. One of my best friends had just died in my arms, and Julius was accusing me of her murder; I was all over the place. Did you never wonder why my father disappeared the day I fell? No? Plenty of others wondered where I'd gone. And why. All those conspiracy theories. Did you never doubt me? Not once?"

"Whatever you're getting at, spit it out," Adriz growled.

"When I regained consciousness in Eidolon, I knew something had changed. At the time I wasn't sure what. I was confused, battered. No idea how I had ended up there, nor how much time had passed." He fingered the blue stone around his neck. "I had intended on faking my fall, but everything happened so fast. When I woke in Eidolon, I knew nothing, not who I was nor why I was there. It took many years before I pieced my shattered memories back together, before I figured out that someone had planned my downfall. I don't believe my father abandoned me, not when he had asked me to help him. So, I began the search for the shadow within the shadows."

They stilled, those friends of his. Mav had lied to them repeatedly. Lied to keep them safe, to keep them as far away from trouble as he could. He hadn't wanted to involve them, but they wouldn't see it like that. They would see it as a betrayal of their trust, their trust in him.

"It all happened at once; I couldn't think straight. I didn't have time to tell you, and I never saw you after Julius knocked me out…"

"They wouldn't let us near you," Adriz said, her eyes narrowed but her angry demeanour softened.

"At first, I didn't realise my father had disappeared as well." Mav huffed his breath out. "When I woke, I didn't even know where I was." His fingers drifted back to the stones around his neck. Realising what he was doing, he dropped his hand. Adriz had followed his movement, and he knew she would ask the question—Why did he have two vendetta stones?

"Where were you?" Adriz asked.

"In the depths of southern Eidolon. About two leagues east of Misserin."

Adriz's eyes bored into him, but he didn't look away from her growing concern. "And where did you get those?" she asked, nodding at the vendetta stones.

"I don't know. When I woke, they were around my neck."

"But you know what they are for?"

Mav slowly nodded. Deep in his bones he knew. A vendetta stone was a curse, a life sentence, and they couldn't be removed by anyone until the oath was fulfilled. He knew that Athenia had tasked him to find her murderer with her dying breath, though his father's vendetta stone, he was sure was more complex. "The red one is for Athenia; the blue is my father's."

"And you are telling us now because?" Adriz asked.

"Because you need to understand that there are bigger things at play here than Kyrill's petty games. Solanji knew Kyrill would try and claim her and she was determined to use his actions to our advantage." He rubbed his face, worry gnawing at him. "I just didn't expect him to act so fast."

"We can't leave her in his clutches." Adriz flexed her fingers as if she wanted to grab Kyrill's neck. "He is dangerous."

"I know," Mav held Adriz's worried gaze for a moment. "She is a SoulBreather, and we need her if I'm to save the people of Eidolon." He shrugged. "Unless, of course, you'd rather tell me to shove it and end your service to me."

"If you weren't already so banged up, I swear I'd do it myself," Adriz growled as she started pacing.

"I wondered why you had a mortal trailing about after you," Sero said. "You're sure she is a SoulBreather?"

"Positive," Mav replied. "And she needs your help to understand what that means."

"Bit difficult when you let the enemy take her without putting up a fight."

"Tactical decision," Mav said with a grim smile. "It won't be for long."

Felather's eyes widened as he finally sat. "You mean she's spying for us?"

"She suggested it to begin with, but I didn't like the idea."

"Unsurprisingly," Sero murmured from his perch on the back of a chair. He crossed his legs and rested his chin on his hand. "It's the first time you've let her out of your sight. Now I understand why, but I'm still surprised. The only Soul-Breather in the world and you let her go."

Mav rubbed his temples. "I don't own her, you know."

"How do we rescue her? Kyrill won't put up with her for

long. There's no way he'll trust her when he realises she misled him over when you were crossing," Felather said.

"I don't know. She was, and still is, in an impossible situation."

"She's trying to rescue her brother," Felather murmured as he leaned forward, a frown creasing his face. "Does she really think Kyrill will know anything about her brother's location?"

"Unlikely. But she's chosen to assist me, to help me so I can help her. I wish I could mind speak her, but it's not working. The only voice I can hear is Xylvin, and that's all her, I think."

"You need to reconnect to the citadel. I think that needs to be your priority," Sero stated, sitting upright. "You're showing signs of wear and tear."

"Is that what you call it?" Felather muttered, and Sero grinned at him.

"No doubt, a result of not being connected to the citadel. I think if you reconnect, you'll find your abilities get stronger."

"Return, you mean. They are non-existent at the moment," Mav said with a sigh.

"Do not say that outside of this room," Sero said, his expression serious.

"I have no intention of doing so, but as you say, I'm aging. It won't take people long to figure out something is wrong."

"Then we keep them busy talking about something else," Felather said.

Mav's gaze wandered around his room as Felather and Sero talked strategy, reacquainting himself with the shelves of leather-bound books, his desk still littered with quills and notebooks and his favourite inkwell. His weapons neatly stacked in the rack, sleek steel gleaming in the candle light. If only he'd had the use of such weapons a few times in Eidolon. He flexed his hand, suddenly eager to grasp his sword.

Even so, he realised he hadn't missed his rooms as much as he'd thought, not as much as he missed his young fledglings, Kerris and Shandra. Worry for them niggled away in the back of his mind, shelved for the moment as he couldn't do anything about it. Adriz finally stopped pacing and collapsed into the chair opposite, holding her head in her hands.

"I'm sorry," he said.

"Sorry doesn't cut it," Adriz said, her voice tinged with concern.

"I promise I'll never lie to you again," he said, making sure his hands were visible.

"And you'll never leave us out of any decision. We're a team." Adriz faltered. "We're family. Swear it. Never ever again."

"I swear."

She stared at him, the hurt clear in her eyes.

"If I could have told you, I would have. But I never had time. And then it was too late."

"But for fifty years," she whispered, "you let us search for you. No message; no explanation. You let us think you were dead, you let them think the worst of you. You've let the rumours entrench, and we've done nothing to stop the rot."

"Ah no, they've become complacent and impatient. Kyrill has shown his hand." Mav wasn't touching the other part of her complaint. She was right, and he had no answer that she would accept.

A precious turn of the timepiece passed as he told them everything he could think of about his father's plans to reunite Eidolon. How he had narrowed down the shadowy resistance to a seraphim he could now name as Kyrill and, as much as he hated to say it, Julius. He skimmed over the torture chamber and his latest incarceration, though in complete honesty, he mentioned Kaenera's visit and how he wasn't sure if his uncle's visit was real or a dream. Then he finally sat back and waited.

"I suppose it's not surprising that Kaenera is involved. He swore vengeance on your father when he tossed him out. I'm only surprised it took so long," Felather murmured.

"If Kaenera is involved, it's only for his own personal reasons. It has nothing to do with the unification of Eidolon and Angelicus," Mav said.

"How do you know that?" Adriz asked in suspicion. "I am sure he would love to have all of it under his control, much like your father, but for more selfish reasons."

"I got the impression his interest was only in me. He wants me."

"What for?" Felather asked, his frown firmly in place.

"I don't know."

"And that's everything?" Adriz asked.

"You want more? Isn't that enough?" Felather said as he stared at his hands.

"It's everything that I can think of that's pertinent. There may be some other stuff, like I hate that blue cheese they always serve at the gatherings, the smell makes me want to vomit, or…"

"Alright, smartass," Adriz laughed, and Mav sighed in relief.

"Kyrill isn't smart enough to manage this on his own. He looks to Golaran, who has had more responsibility since you've been gone. Your brother, Amaridin, has leaned on the others in your absence. He may be older than you, but he doesn't have your…" Felather faltered, and then changed what he was going to say. "Do you think Goloran would be that obvious?" he asked, instead.

"Maybe he isn't satisfied as a mere archangel and he wants to make the next step, to be an archdeus," Adriz suggested.

"Whoever it was removed Averdeus, his general, and his SoulBreather in one move," Sero said. "And then they waited."

"For what?" Felather asked.

Mav shifted in his chair. Exhaustion dragged at him, his body's aches throbbing unrelenting, and they hadn't even begun to unravel whatever was happening in the citadel. "For my return."

"Why now?"

Mav exhaled slowly, calming the anxious flutter in his chest. He rose, limped over to the tall window, and gazed down over the sunlit gardens, once a preferred retreat. Taking a deep breath, he turned back to his oathsworn. "The only thing I can think of is they want to discredit me completely, send me through Kaenera's hands to the Gate. Free up my seat with no possible contention, allowing another to step up to Archangel."

"Then they are fools. You can't change what you are. You are the son of a god. How do they think you can change that?" Adriz asked, a snarl rasping her voice.

"Who pushed Amaridin to support the motion to remove my position?"

Felather stared at his hands.

Adriz filled the silence. "No one. Amaridin proposed it."

"What was his reason?"

"He said he couldn't continue on his own and he needed someone to share the responsibility with him."

Mav raised an eyebrow. "And who did he propose? Serenia? Golaran?"

Felather snorted. "Both of them. But they have to follow the process and pick their successors from the seraphim before they can step up, so the seraphim are in a scramble to prove their worth. It's a mess."

"I'm not surprised. The whole citadel must be in turmoil with everyone trying for a power grab, and I walk in and scupper all their plans."

"Why did Kyrill capture you? Why now? Amaridin has already set the changes in motion," Felather asked.

"Maybe he has his own agenda. His hand was forced when he couldn't get what he wanted. He tried to weaken me as much as he could and then sent Solanji to rescue me so he would know where I was at all times." Mav grimaced. "He didn't want to lose track of me again."

"This is all conjecture." Felather threw his hands up in the air.

"It's all we've got. It has to be a power move. They can only make it if they remove me. I need to speak with Amaridin."

"Eodan won't let you near him," Sero said. "I know *I* wouldn't if Amaridin were trying to see you."

"Eodan? Since when is he Amaridin's scribe? Where's Valerian?" Mav asked. The two had been inseparable.

"He left, years ago. They went their separate ways."

"I don't believe it. Valerian would never leave Amaridin." Mav was positive the two men would never part. They had been so devoted to each other, to the extent that one would have died for the other. "What happened?"

"They never said," Felather replied.

Mav shook his head in disbelief and then moved towards his desk, his fingers trailing over the smooth wood as he tried to disguise his awkwardness.

"Don't waste your energy." Felather said, rolling his eyes. "We know you are suffering, and there's no point hiding it. You promised."

Mav groaned. "Give me a little slack, it's instinctive. I've been fending for myself for far too long."

"And whose fault is that?" Adriz snapped back without hesitation.

"Please, just…please?" Mav spread his hands in supplication. He thought he might cry. His throat was tight, his eyes welling. He was so tired; of living, of the uncertainty, if he was honest.

Strong hands gripped his shoulders. "You are not alone now, nor will you ever be. Just don't shut us out. We're here for you, Mav. Always."

Mav was definitely going to cry. His eyes stung, and his vision blurred. Adriz's voice was full of tears too, and then his face was mashed against her chest and he inhaled the comforting scent of lavender that Adriz always used. He could have stayed there, in the safety of her embrace, forever, but there was a knock at the door and Adriz released him. She gently wiped the tears from his cheek.

"Always," she murmured. He nodded and then sank down into his chair, exhausted. He covered his eyes with his hand. Sero tutted and then fluttered behind him. "I'll keep an eye on your SoulBreather for you," he said, patting Mav's shoulder.

Felather cast them a concerned look and went to answer the door. He spoke briefly and shut the door. He held up an envelope. "Amaridin wishes to speak to you later this evening."

Mav raised his head. "Well, that's a good sign."

"Is it?" Adriz asked, watching him.

"I'll have a chance to find out where his head is at."

"We're going with you," Adriz said, her tone uncompromising.

Mav winced but was quick to agree. He hadn't intended on going anywhere without them.

"You need to rest," Felather said. "Just half a turn. Amaridin isn't expecting you until later."

Mav didn't have a choice with his cherubim and scribe bearing down on him, and he took the path of least resistance and lay down on his bed and soon fell asleep.

When he awoke, a whole turn later and not the promised half, his mind was full of Solanji. His stomach churned at the thought of her in Kyrill's hands, and the urge to go and claim her was overwhelming. He would only relax when she was in his arms. Concern rippling through him, he glared at Adriz. "Kyrill wasn't happy when he left. He's likely to strike out, so we need to watch him. You need to help Sero keep an eye on Solanji. Try to intervene if needed. She's one of mine and she's been dragged into this situation through no fault of her own. Felather, her brother is at risk in Eidolon. Keep hounding your contacts to trace his journey. We need to find him." His cherubim and scribe nodded; their faces determined. He knew they would protect Solanji wherever possible.

Sero was a boon he hadn't expected. That the little cherub had chosen to support him was more of a relief than he had realised. That there was one angel in the citadel who supported him meant there might be others.

"You know..." Felather paused as if wondering if he should vocalise whatever he had just thought.

"What?" Mav asked as he carefully swung his legs over the side of the bed.

"You need to use your stick. Solanji was right about that."

"I can't be seen to be weak."

"Falling flat on your face will do you a load of good," Adriz said as she rolled her eyes.

Felather knelt beside him, his hands hovering over Mav's knee. He flicked a glance at his face. "You are still burning up."

"I don't doubt it," Mav replied.

Felather supported him as he limped into his study and dropped into a chair. Pulling over a stool, Felather lifted his leg. Mav hissed as a white-hot pain flashed through him. He resisted the urge to pant.

Felather scowled at him. "You should have said. Suffering like this helps no one. I told you if you didn't take care, you'd do more damage."

"You can only draw the pain away so many times. I was trying to hold out until I was desperate."

Felather's face grew grimmer. "Well don't. Desperation won't help any of us. You promised not to be a hero."

Mav's lips twitched. "I did? When was that?" Though he visibly relaxed as Felather drew the heat away and eased his pain.

"When you promised not to lie," Adriz growled.

Mav ignored her and pointed at Felather. "What were you going to say?"

Felather sat back on his heels. "What do you think happened to the citadel? Do you think you can reconnect to it?"

Adriz hissed her breath out. "Is that a possibility? And what if it rejects Mav?"

"Solanji returned my soul. It may not be what it was originally, but she is adamant she returned it. There is no reason for the citadel to reject me."

"If you reconnected, the citadel should identify the murderer," Felather said.

"What is involved in reconnecting?" Adriz asked in concern

"That's the problem, I don't know. The citadel was

always there. It wasn't something I ever thought about. All I know is that something's missing now. But no one else seems to have noticed the citadel's absence or seems concerned."

Adriz raised her hands. "Until we know more then, that is not even an option. We are not risking Mav's life. I veto it. It's off the table. We have enough problems."

Mav raised his eyebrows. "Since when did you have a veto?"

"Since you demonstrated such a poor lack of judgement," she snapped and then crossed her arms.

Mav swallowed his retort. He had a long, long way to go before she forgave him. "We might not have a choice. Felather, ask Sero if he remembers anything about how the citadel works."

Felather nodded in agreement, and Mav knew he would begin researching to see what he could find out about the citadel.

Mav struggled to gather his thoughts. "Time is passing. Adriz and I will go and speak with Amaridin," he said rubbing his temples. He already had a headache. Amaridin wasn't going to make it any better.

"You deserve everything you get," Adriz said brutally, though she did stand and pour a glass of water, into which she emptied a sachet of powder and stirred. She handed him the glass.

He swirled the liquid. He had never had a use for pain relief before. Usually, he could heal himself.

"Drink it." Adriz stood over him until he did.

"I'll get addicted," he complained as the relief flooded through him and he relaxed bonelessly into his chair. The absence of pain made everything around him sharpen, including the expressions on his friend's faces. Hesitating for a moment as if the chains of pain being released made him feel lighter, he drifted. The urge to flare his wings consumed him and…he stiffened. It had been so long since he hadn't felt any pain.

"You are a fool," Adriz said. "I won't let you get addicted."

"Thank you." Mav rose and limped over to the gilt-framed mirror. He stared at himself. His hair was frosted with silver, more grey than black. His wings were mere shadow, nothing he could use. He didn't recognise himself. He had done so much damage. As he stared, Adriz moved behind him and met his amber eyes in the reflection. The only part of him that was unchanged.

"Once more," she murmured and gripped his shoulder.

He clasped her hand. "Thank you," he said, not breaking her gaze until the knock on the door announced a herald with the expected summons.

6

DEMAVRIAN

Golden sunlight enticed Mav to stare out the window, absorbing the view of the beautiful gardens, the sparkling fountains throwing out shimmering rainbows; such colour, such vibrancy, it took his breath away while he waited for his brother, Amaridin. He had missed the sun, the sunlit buildings, the domes and spires of the skyline. They soothed an empty corner of his heart, a sense of familiarity of being home. And yet he knew Eidolon occupied the same amount of space. No, not Eidolon, the *people* of Eidolon.

The angels of Puronia had deserted them. For centuries, left to die and pass through the Gates of Oblivion without any chance of redemption. Why were Serenia and Amaridin still removing souls, knowing that they could never restore them? Mav didn't understand the rationale, nor the cold-hearted disdain for human life.

He needed to find time to speak to one of the Soul-Singers, a much nicer name than SoulSucker, to see what they believed was happening. Maybe they weren't aware they were destroying people's lives? When Athenia had been alive, removing someone's soul had been seen as a just punishment as there was a chance they could earn it back. But with Athenia's death, anyone divested of a soul was sentenced to walk through the Oblivion Gate, through Kaenera's hands.

Mav stiffened. Kaenera guarded the Oblivion Gate. He decided who could pass through the gate and embrace the final release and who he retained to serve him. Those he kept became his dybbuks, bound to his will. Their only purpose to obey his every whim. Was he behind Athenia's death? So he could get more dybbuks? And if so, why did he need more?

Mav's head ached with the confused thoughts swirling around his brain. He was surprised the people of Eidolon hadn't descended into a state of anarchy, of complete self-destruction and despair, encouraged by Kaenera. His uncle would be hovering at the gates ready to influence whomever he could. Fortunately, the door opened behind him before he could start the coil of endless questioning again.

Mav sensed Adriz and Felather stiffening to attention. His oathsworn ready to leap to his defence if needed. He was no longer sure he deserved them.

Mav was surprised to see that Amaridin had also aged. Silver highlights adorned his temples, though only the sunlight revealed their presence in his thick blonde hair. It was the lines on his forehead and around his eyes and mouth, grooved into a permanent frown, that marred his perfect face.

Eodan, Amaridin's captain, hovered behind him. A tall, lean predator, his sharp green eyes locked on Mav as soon as he entered the room. Eodan was beautiful. Blond like Amaridin but with a supple strength that exuded dominance. He looked down on everyone in his presence, even Amaridin, though he pretended he didn't. Eodan was the power behind Amaridin that made his apparent softness acceptable. Once,

Eodan's steel had been tempered by Valerian's compassion, but Valerian was a notable absence.

Mav knew that Amaridin could be as cruel as any other person, but he preferred to project an image of a benevolent god. One who could forgive, if he wanted to, not that he had ever seemed to do so. His decisions were always in the best interest of the citadel and had typically been backed up by Valerian.

The extended silence trickled into Mav's awareness as he and his brother inspected each other. They were an estranged family reacquainting. What they had once known about each other may no longer be true. Mav was sure that Eodan's influence must have stiffened some of Amaridin's more benevolent intentions, but then his brother had always been too malleable, swayed too easily by whoever was strongest.

Amaridin cleared his throat and gestured to the chairs. "Please, we understand it is better that you sit." His gaze sharpened as he observed Mav cross the room.

"Thank you, though I'm fine," Mav replied as he sat and crossed his left leg over his knee in a semblance of relaxation. No matter what rumours flew around the citadel about his health, he would not show weakness to his brother.

"I am glad to hear it," Amaridin said as he sat opposite Mav. He hesitated for a moment and then dived straight in. "Where have you been, Mav? We've missed you."

"I woke up in the Eidolon hinterland, and I have no idea how I got there," Mav replied.

Eodan stiffened behind Amaridin. Mav raised an eyebrow as he stared at the captain of the Heavenly Host. "Do you know how I ended up there, Eodan?" he asked.

"Why would Eodan know?" Amaridin asked, an edge to his voice.

Mav shrugged, holding the captain's eyes. "You tell me."

"You've been gone for fifty years, and as soon as you return you begin accusing everyone around you of being conspirators in your downfall?" Amaridin said.

Mav stifled a laugh. Was his brother serious? "I am doing no such thing. I was answering your question. It looked like Eodan had something to say."

"I can assure you I have nothing to say about your downfall," Eodan replied, and then he clenched his jaw as if he regretted speaking.

"Good to know," Mav said and looked at his brother and took a deep breath. "I found Athenia dying on the steps. I did what I could to help her, but she died in my arms. When help arrived, Julius attacked me before I was able to say anything."

"Understandable seeing as you were the one holding the body of his dearest in your arms."

"Does everyone jump to conclusions without finding out the facts first?" Mav demanded with some heat.

"You were the one caught holding the body."

"Why is it you all want to believe me guilty?"

"We don't," Amaridin hurried to reassure him. "Where is Averdeus?"

Mav inhaled. "I have no idea. I thought you might know, seeing as I was knocked unconscious and then carted off to Eidolon without so much as a by your leave."

"Mav, it won't go well with the council if you don't have a good reason for our father being missing."

"His disappearance has nothing to do with me."

"Of course it does. He disappeared the same day."

"Have you not found any clues as to who might have killed Athenia?"

"It's not Athenia you should be worrying about. We need to find Father."

Mav uncrossed his legs and leaned forward. "You don't think

it is suspicious that in one day, Averdeus, Athenia, and I were all wiped from the board? Do you not think these events might have been connected? Did you not even try to discover why?"

Amaridin stiffened. "I had my hands full with keeping the citadel together. You were still alive and the suspected killer of Athenia. My immediate concern was covering for Father before anyone else thought to stand in for him.

"And did anyone try?" Mav asked, barely able to keep the bite out of his voice.

"Of course not. Everyone rallied round. It was quite comforting how everyone tried to help."

"Even Kaenera?"

"Kaenera? I haven't heard anything from him."

"And you didn't try to find out who might have wanted to kill Athenia?"

Eodan stepped forward and gripped Amaridin's shoulder. "Amaridin was distraught at his friend's death. Serenia offered to handle the investigation."

Adriz shifted behind him. Mav was sure she was furious at Amaridin's lack of concern for him.

"And what about me? Weren't you concerned when I went missing?"

"You escaped. You ran. That was your choice."

"What if it wasn't my choice?"

"There was no evidence to suggest that."

"I was unconscious in a cell and yet I escaped all on my own?"

Amaridin didn't meet his gaze and shifted in his seat. "You were known to be… competent," he replied.

"Competent?" Mav gasped.

"You were the Archdeus General. No one could keep you restrained, if you decided not to be," Amaridin protested.

Mav was rendered silent. He had no rebuttal to voice.

Who or what did they think he was? Did everyone believe he was invincible? And yet at the same time so corrupt?

Adriz moved closer and rested her hand on Mav's shoulder. "Will you accept that Demavrian did not leave of his own free will?"

Amaridin gaped at her, and Eodan's eyes widened as if this was a completely new concept.

"But if you didn't kill her, that would mean the killer is still on the loose and has been for the last fifty years," Amaridin gasped.

"You don't say?" Mav ground out.

Eodan scowled. "There were no other suspects and no one else was seen near the great hall."

"Don't you think that odd?" Felather asked from his position by the door. "The great hall is usually teeming with people. Why was it empty at that exact time?"

"The citadel didn't cast anyone else out," Amaridin said as if in justification.

"How do you know that? The killer could have been a hired thug, brought in from Eidolon for the day. Once he or she died, there would be no one for the citadel to expel," Felather argued.

Eodan hissed his breath out. "There was no evidence to suggest that anyone from Eidolon was involved."

Mav glared at his brother. It was easier to fix the blame on him; a nice neat solution, except for the fact that Mav had no reason to kill Athenia. "Why?" he whispered. "Why would I kill Athenia?"

"You were jealous of her and Julius," Amaridin immediately replied.

"Mav and Julius have been friends for years; they grew up together. And you know that is ridiculous. Mav would never harm Athenia," Adriz growled.

Amaridin had the grace to blush. "Letters were found in Athenia's rooms. Letters from you, Mav."

Mav frowned. "What letters?"

"Letters written in your hand, saying you would always be there for her. I saw them; I verified they were in your handwriting."

"I sent those years ago, before Julius ever displayed an interest. I was consoling her when her sister died. She was my friend!"

Amaridin shrugged. "Athenia kept them. They were presented as proof against you. That was when the host was sent to track you down. There was nothing I could do. You hadn't confided in me. The evidence was strong enough against you."

Mav was appalled. That his friends and family had been so quick to accuse him left him breathless. Adriz squeezed his shoulder again in silent support. He needed to get out. Out of this room before he tore his brother to shreds. Eodan must have seen something in his expression as he suddenly moved in front of Amaridin.

"I think that is enough for today. Archdeus Amaridin has another appointment he needs to prepare for."

Mav rose. His muscles were coiled, ready to lash out, and Eodan stepped back. "I hope," Mav said, his voice like ice, "that if you ever find yourself in a similar predicament to me, your supposed family and friends do not leap to accuse and desert you as quickly as mine seem to have done."

Amaridin sprang to his feet and shoved Eodan out of his way. "Mav," he said, anguish in his expression, but Mav spun and marched to the door, which Felather only just managed to open before him. He blanched at whatever expression he saw on Mav's face. Mav didn't stop but kept walking, barely holding himself together.

No one stopped him, and if anyone had tried, he didn't

see them. He strode through the corridors, his face like flint, eyes flashing, his feet automatically finding the way back to his rooms, his sanctuary. He stormed into his bedchamber and slammed the door behind him. Striding back and forth, he tried to temper his breathing. He was about to hyperventilate he was so angry. The betrayal sliced through him, burning through his fragile control.

"Mav."

He spun and staggered, and Felather was there, embracing him, murmuring reassurance, belief, and love in his ear. He was not abandoned, he had supporters, his oathsworn believed in him. Felather forced him into a chair and knelt before him.

"Mav," he said firmly. "You are not alone and you never will be. I am yours, my life and my soul, now and forever. You are a good man. Your compassion, your honesty, your loyalty is unquestioned by those who truly know you. Only those with ulterior motives would ever suggest otherwise."

Mav stared at him, slowly bringing his breathing under control. The roaring in his ears died away and exhaustion swept through him. "I can't do this," he said, the shake in his voice making Felather grip his forearms.

"Yes, you can. We will help you, as will others." Adriz's voice came from the doorway. "You have more support than you realise, Mav. There are many who do not believe you guilty, and they are glad you are returned."

"Not that you would notice," Mav replied as he sank his face into his hands.

7

SOLANJI

Solanji silently followed Lormin back to the fledgling quarters and dumped the pile of dreary, grey clothes she had collected from the stores room on the bed. There were two other beds squashed into the small chamber. One narrow window allowed a slither of sun to illuminate the crowded space.

"How many fledglings does Seraphim Kyrill have?" she asked as she inspected the room. The lack of any trinkets or personal items was telling.

"Three females, including you, and five males."

"Is that typical?" Solanji wondered if Mav had ever had any fledglings. He had never mentioned any.

"You don't know when to stop asking questions, do you?"

Solanji shrugged. "How else am I supposed to learn what I'm meant to do?"

"By watching what your betters do," Lormin snapped and stomped out of the room, his grey robes flaring behind him.

Sighing, Solanji put her clothes away, scowling at the coarse material that scratched her skin. Fledglings were nothing more than slaves by another name. She wondered where the other girls were and whether they would be more forthcoming. Tying her hair back off her face with a leather lace, she set to work searching the room, but there was nothing to identify any of the occupants.

Huffing out her breath, she sat on a bed. She didn't have a lot of time. Apologia would only take three more days. She must have been mad to think she could find something to help Mav before then. There had to be evidence of Kyrill's business dealings in Eidolon somewhere. Something to incriminate him.

She would wait until the others were asleep and then search the seraphim's study. From the thoughts she had skimmed from Lormin, it seemed he was basically an errand boy, collecting and delivering packages. She wondered what the girls did for Kyrill. Twisting her lips, it probably wasn't too hard to guess. The question was, what did he want with her?

Solanji didn't know what to do or where to go. With Mav she had been part of his team, included, accepted. But here…she was at a loss. She poked her nose out of the door and found Lormin seated at his desk.

"What am I supposed to do?" she asked as she stopped in front of him.

The man heaved a big sigh and screwed up his face as if he had just sucked a sour lemon. It didn't suit him and made him look a lot older than she had first thought. "Wait until you receive instructions from the Seraphim."

"And until then?" Solanji trailed her fingers through his brilliant soulmist. He was frustrated with having to look after her. An image of Carna flitted by, Kyrill's aide. Ah, that was the job he was after.

"I told you. Wait. Stay out of his way, if you know what's good for you."

"Why? Is he not a nice master?" Solanji already knew that, but the spike of fear that flashed through Lormin's thoughts surprised her.

"All seraphim are task masters. It's how you learn."

"But by your expression, Kyrill is especially nasty. Archdeus Demavrian is nicer. Why don't you change masters?"

Lormin curled his lip. "Just try it. Once claimed, you have no choice. And anyway, if you liked Demavrian so much, why did you lead him by the nose to his slaughter?"

"What does that mean?" This time the fear flashed through Solanji.

"It's obvious, isn't it? Demavrian's days are numbered. Less than three to be exact." Lormin huffed out his breath. "Seraphim Kyrill has been very vocal about how he brought Demavrian back to face his crimes. This is the best place to be. He is highly valued by the archangels and the archdeus. He will rise through the ranks fast and bring us along with him."

"Based on his ability to bring down an archdeus? I bet he hasn't talked about his methods. What about his torture chamber where I found *Archdeus* Demavrian a bloodied mess? Has he mentioned that?" Solanji gritted her teeth against saying more.

Lormin rested his chin on his fist, his thoughts swirling into images of men being held down and whipped. He had seen someone being tortured! Before Solanji could phrase a question, he spoke. "I wonder what he wants you for. I can't say that I've seen any potential in you, except maybe for trouble." He lurched to his feet as the door opened, and the blood drained from his face as Seraphim Kyrill entered. "Sir! I wasn't expecting you." His ugly thoughts scattered, leaving a grey haze overlaying his agitated soulmist.

Kyrill tossed a package tied up in string on the desk.

"Take that to Councillor Gineray and wait for a reply. Tell him it's his final chance, after this, the price doubles."

"Yes sir." Lormin grabbed the package and left.

Solanji stiffened under Kyrill's inspection. She bit her lip and then blurted, "Have you had news of Brennan? My brother? Is he still in Puronia?"

"He'll be fine." Kyrill waved his hand. "I've requested he be returned home to your mother."

A chill stole over Solanji's skin. Kyrill had done no such thing. According to Felather, Bren was already in Eidolon. He couldn't return until Solanji found him and restored his soul. Mav had been right. Kyrill had absolutely no intention of honouring his promise.

Forcing a bright smile on her face, Solanji slowly exhaled. "That is good news. I'll write a note to my mother. She'll be so relieved."

"Come with me. I want a complete report on your journey here." Kyrill led her across the hall and into his study. Relaxing in his chair, he pointed to a spot in front of his desk. "I want every detail, every thought you skimmed, every word Demavrian said."

Solanji glanced around her. His study was bare, empty of the warmth and character that filled Mav's, even with him being absent for fifty years. There were a few pictures on the wall, scenes of the citadel at sunset, a great waterfall falling over the divide. Impersonal, if beautiful.

Clearing her throat, she started speaking, describing how she had released Mav and their escape. She paused, frowning at him as he smiled genially at her to continue. "Why did you need me to bring him to Eidolon if you had already captured him?"

"Hope."

"Hope?"

Kyrill leaned forward, his face alight. "The loss of hope

is even more destructive than hope itself. The possibility of saving himself being snatched away will force him into despair faster."

Despair? Why did he need Demavrian spiralling into despair? Solanji swallowed and didn't ask the question. Kyrill's golden soulmist undulated with anticipation, straying around the desk and reaching for Solanji.

"We escaped from the castle. He was unable to heal his knee; the joint is smashed beyond repair, so we stole the calopes as he couldn't walk."

"He's walking fine now."

"Only because his scribe is healing it on a daily basis." Solanji tried to hide her flinch as an image of Felather strung up and beaten flittered across her mind. Was Kyrill seriously thinking of abducting him?

She hurriedly continued. "It took weeks to travel to the crossroads. We camped most of the time. He tried to heal himself, but I could see it wasn't working as he expected."

"How did he react to that?"

"He said it would take time. He was tired, drained."

Kyrill nodded. "Did he admit to not having a soul?"

"He never mentioned it. But he doesn't have a golden soulmist like you do."

"That old hound," he murmured under his breath. He looked up, his brilliant blue eyes flickering for a moment. "How did he get around entering the citadel?"

Solanji shrugged. "I don't know. I know he was nervous. He was expecting something that never happened. What does the citadel usually do?"

"No one knows. It hasn't reacted to anything for years. Not since Demavrian left."

Solanji caught her breath. Was that what Kyrill was after? Had Mav taken something with him when he left?

"How did you escape Teravin?"

"Teravin?"

"Julius Teravin, the Captain of the Heavenly Host you managed to knock out, while his men stood around and watched," Kyrill said with a twist of his lips.

"Didn't you get a report?" Solanji asked. "Archdeus Demavrian did it again when he was delayed from entering the citadel assembly. He is faster than you realise. I suppose that's not surprising seeing as he used to be the General of the Heavenly Host."

"Don't underestimate him, is that what you are saying? I know that already. What does he know?"

"About what?"

Kyrill steepled his fingers as he observed Solanji. "What was he thinking? What thoughts, images did you see? How is he feeling?"

"He's in pain," Solanji replied. "Uppermost, his thoughts have been about the torture you inflicted on him."

Kyrill waved his hand, dismissing her comment. "What were his memories of what happened the day he left? Returning to the citadel must have reminded him of those events.

"He was apprehensive about returning. He wasn't sure of his welcome."

"Why not?"

"Without a soul, he wasn't supposed to be able to enter the citadel. Anyone would be concerned. He never mentioned anything about the day he left. His memories of being banished to Eidolon are hazy. I couldn't pick up any thoughts. He was knocked out by Julius and awoke in Eidolon. He doesn't know how he got there."

"He must do." Kyrill tensed. His eyes darkened to a deeper blue, a glimpse of shadows in the depths. "I need to know how he gained..." he bit off his comment. "He tried to reconnect to the citadel. The citadel let him in and responded to him, therefore he has a soul, even though you stated he didn't. It is only a matter of time before he tries again. I need to know how he is doing it. If he can…"

Solanji watched him as he snapped his mouth tight. Kyrill was tense, anxious. What had he intended to say? Did he know how Mav had lost his soul? How would he know unless he'd been there when it had happened or spoken to the person who had taken it? "He was angry at his treatment. After all, he is an Archdeus." There! Kyrill's mouth tightened. Was he *jealous* of Mav? Was that it? "But he is determined to prove his innocence."

"He would be, but he won't find a way out of this one. He'll be proven guilty and he'll have to take the consequences. Kaenera's arms will be open wide, and he won't be able to avoid them. Demavrian no longer has the support he once had. Times have changed."

Solanji hesitated. Kyrill seemed to change before her as he spoke, his uncertainty fading, his body straightening, his expression hardening. He was so confident. So sure of himself. What did he know that they didn't? She shivered as a chill crept over her skin.

8

KERRIS, EIDOLON

Kerris tugged the mule down the road, eager to get home before darkness descended. Trade had gone well, and the beast was laden with sacks of flour, grain, and a few treats he had managed to find. Bailey would bake them up some amazing cakes with the pouch of powdered sweet cane he had traded his final sack of squashes for. The littlest kids had never tasted sweet cake before. He couldn't wait to see the expression on their faces.

Skirting the large puddle dominating the middle of the track, he climbed on the raised verge only to slip on the muddy slope. Cold water seeped through the holes in his shoes. He had hoped to find some leather at the market, because he wasn't the only one with worn out shoes, but the leather on display wouldn't have lasted to the next full moon, so he hadn't wasted his goods.

The mule slogged through the puddles, undeterred, and they turned onto the narrow, muddy trail that led to their farmstead. He frowned at the sight of deep gouges in the mud either side of the track and the broken foliage in the hedgerow as if a large wagon had passed by.

His gut tightened at the possibility that someone had found their hideaway. Wagons and carts didn't usually bother with this overgrown trail. They chose not to cut it back so no one would visit.

He quickened his pace and hurried the mule down the trail. More evidence of visitors surrounded him, as the mud was churned up by hooves and the bracken hacked. Someone had deliberately cleared a path. As the farmstead came into sight, he dropped the leading rein and ran.

It was too quiet.

He scuttled into the barn and pulled the warning cord. The barn was empty and there was no response from the house. Skirting the yard, Kerris peered through the window of the front room. Nothing moved. Entering the house, he knew it was deserted. The deadened air stirred as he passed, but the subtle signs of other people were absent. No low voices murmuring, no children's shouts as they played, no clatter from Kiara tinkering on her latest project.

A chair was overturned, but other than that, there was no sign of anything amiss.

Pulling back the rug, Kerris tugged up the trapdoor, but deep in his gut, he knew it was pointless. "Shandra? Muntra?" he called down into the depths. Only silence greeted him.

A neigh from the yard had him running back out of the house, but it was only his mule protesting about being left behind.

Suddenly afraid, Kerris rubbed the mule's nose. "Where is everyone?" he whispered into the ear that the animal flicked in his face. Mind spinning, Kerris led the mule into the barn and unloaded him. The mule had worked hard. The least he could do was relieve his burden while he tried to figure out what he should do. There was no way Shandra would have taken every child out on a hike. They would have been way too obvious. So someone must have taken them. And those someones had wagons to conceal them.

He struggled to unknot the ropes and paused, shaking out his trembling fingers. A shudder rippled through him. He had never felt so bereft and alone before, and he no idea what to do. Resting his head against the mule's neck, he squeezed his eyes shut against the sudden tears. His family had been abducted and he didn't know how to get them back.

The mule shifted beneath him, and he straightened, sniffing back the rising tears. Taking a deep breath, he concentrated on untying the ropes and stacked the sacks in the barn. Adding a scoop of grain to the bucket, he left the mule munching as he went to check the other animals.

The chicken coops were empty and the nanny goats were missing. Whoever had taken the kids had cleared out their animal stock as well.

A growing wave of anger rushed through him. How dare they? Shandra had worked so hard to build this home, and someone had waltzed in and stolen it all. Anguish burned away his fear, and he returned to the house.

A quick search revealed that there were no hidden messages or signs; everything must have happened too fast. Stuffing a spare shirt and a blanket in a sack, along with their precious flint and the candles they had saved for deepest winter, Kerris hunted for the kitchen knife Bailey hid from curious fingers. Wrapping it in a cloth, he considered what else he would need. Shandra's healing kit, just the basics, but if anyone was hurt it would help. His healing skills were limited and he didn't really know how they worked. Best not to rely on them.

He raided the cupboards for foodstuff that would last,

some dried out strips of meat, and a hunk of cheese was followed by a small pan to cook them in. The pan would do for a bowl as well. He wasn't fussy, and the mule could only carry so much. A spoon might help. He would grab a sack of beans and one of gruel from the stores in the barn.

Shaking his head, Kerris grimaced. He was so unprepared for any type of journey. He had no idea how to fend for himself. He had grown too comfortable under Shandra's guidance and Bailey's good cooking. Once his gruel ran out, he would starve.

No, that was defeatist. He knew how to set a snare. He had caught their dinner before; he could do it again.

After loading up the mule, he went to fill a canteen with water from the tiny brook at the back of the house, Kerris paused and scanned the surrounding hills. Home. Would he ever return here? He suddenly doubted it.

Returning to the barn, he shrugged into the only warm jacket they possessed between them and took one last look around the deserted yard. He shoved his hands deep into the pockets as he slowly rotated, inspecting his home as if to commit the final image to memory.

His fingers snagged on a crunched-up piece of paper, and Kerris pulled it out and then smoothed it flat. Mav had left him the name of someone who could help them in need, and he had forgotten all about it, thinking he would never need it.

He stared at the bold slashes of the letters. Mav's handwriting. Just the sight of the words filled Kerris with hope. He was not alone. *They* were not alone. Mav would move mountains to help save them. He had promised as much.

Did he have the courage to cross the divide and find Mav's contact? He had no idea how. Carefully memorising the letters, he folded the piece of paper and slipped it back into the pocket. He knew the patterns the lines made and could replicate them if necessary.

First though, he needed to track those wagons as far as he could. At least discover if they went north or south. Then he would worry about finding a way to cross the divide.

9

DEMAVRIAN, CITADEL

Mav rolled his neck, ignoring the crunching as he tried to relieve some of the tension.

"Let me," Felather murmured as he moved behind him and began massaging his shoulders. "This is where you belong, Mav. The citadel needs you. You have to clear your name."

"I am not what I once was."

"No. I'm sure you are more. You said you wanted to speak with Archangel Golaran?"

"Yes, he at least would tell me his opinion."

"You don't think he will side with the council?"

"I don't know, but he was always my father's most trusted supporter. I don't see him deviating from his course now."

"Serenia will have primed him."

"Then I need to unprime him. Go request a meeting. I can go to him, or he can come here, or a neutral location, if that is preferred."

"Discretion will be key. I doubt he will want to show his hand openly, if that is what he is prepared to do."

Mav sighed, his thoughts tumbling in a mass of confusion. "Which count next? Do you think we can defend against the murder charge? Sow enough doubt?"

"Is it true that Kyrill took your wings? Have you tried flaring them? Isn't that the simplest count to get off the table?" Felather suggested.

"That may not be possible."

"What? Mav, no!"

Rotating his shoulders, Mav relished the warm burn left from Felather's ministrations. According to Solanji, he had shadows. He had flared them once, but never in flight. They felt like wings, and to him they had looked like wings. Ever since he had entered the citadel, the pull of their weight had straightened his posture as he compensated, not realising that was what he was doing. Unconsciously, he had acknowledged he had wings. He just wasn't sure what anyone else would see.

"I'm not sure whether whatever's left will be classed as wings." Mav spoke to the floor. "I was afraid to accept they were gone for good."

Felather knelt before him. His voice was gentle when he said, "Wouldn't it be better to know one way or the other?"

"Not yet. I-I can't. It would be one more thing I've lost, and I'm worried it might be one thing too many."

Mav kept his head bowed, conscious of Felather's gaze boring into him. His eyes teared and he blinked furiously.

"I'll go see if Golaran will speak to you. If I can, I'll bring him here."

"Thank you." Once the door snicked shut, Mav heaved himself out of the chair with a deep sigh and went to sit at his desk. Pulling a piece of paper towards him, he stared at it for a moment before listing the charges. The words blurred as he tried to identify who would accuse him of such things. Who would know he had lost his soul or that he lacked wings? He shivered as the memory of his wings going up in flames flashed through his mind. Kyrill and his men knew. The loss burned as hot as his wings had. Pinching his lips, he shoved the memory back in its box and tried to concentrate on his list.

A turn later, he was still seated behind his desk, trying to think of reasons why anyone would want to remove him from the citadel, because ultimately that was what it boiled down to. Who would see him as a threat and what did they gain by removing him? He was grieved to find his list was growing quite long. He hadn't thought he had any enemies, well except his uncle Kaenera. Not an enemy as such, but he had certainly staked his claim.

The soft tap at the door had him rising as he called for them to enter, and Mav limped around the desk to shake Golaran's hand as he crossed the room. "Thank you for agreeing to speak to me, sir."

"Least I could do, my boy. I have the feeling you were blind-sided."

"You could say that," Mav agreed with a twist of his lips.

Golaran nodded. "Thought as much," he said as he sat in the chair opposite Mav. Golaran was a grey-haired, ruddy-cheeked angel. He tugged his golden robes around his rotund stomach and accepted the goblet of wine Felather offered before he discreetly left. Mav observed Golaran for a moment. He was unchanged since the last time he had seen him across the council chambers fifty years ago. He had a few more frown lines, but his blue eyes were just as sharp as he remembered.

The lines on Golaran's face deepened as he scowled at Mav. "You have found yourself a heap of trouble, boy. And may I say quite bluntly, I've seen you in better shape."

"I'm glad to say you seem unchanged, sir," Mav replied with a wry smile. His eyebrows rose. "You did not bring your scribe?"

Golaran shook his head. "There is much to discuss, and it needs to be off the record. I only agreed to come if your scribe left us alone."

"With the current climate, I doubt neither of our scribes will be pleased."

Snorting, Golaran raised his glass. "They're paid to worry. But you, my boy, have bigger problems than me."

Mav smiled. "What do you see as my problems, sir?"

"Someone wants you dead."

"I've come to a similar conclusion," Mav admitted as he picked up the glass Felather had left for him. After a sip, he carefully placed it back on the table. His oathsworn had spiked his wine with a draught of something. He hoped it was for pain, because his knee was throbbing and his neck was so tight it ached. "Though having been absent for five decades, I have no idea of what threat I pose to whom."

"I've been watching," Golaran said slowly. "But before I tell you what I've observed, I need you to tell me what really happened to Athenia."

Mav spread his hands. "I don't know. I found her on the steps to the grand chamber already bleeding out. The hall was empty, and I didn't hear anyone running away and those halls echo." Mav hesitated. "There was nothing I could do, and she had passed the point of being able to heal herself. All I could do was hold her as she died."

"She didn't say anything? Do anything?"

Mav gave the man a sharp glance. "She kept telling me to go. By the time I found her, she was unable to say anything else, though she did give me this." Mav pulled out the red vendetta stone.

Golaran hissed his breath out. "Serenia was adamant you killed her. She has been reinforcing her accusation for so long that everyone believes her. Julius, the poor man, was so distraught, he just accepted whatever he was told. She wound him up and set him off searching for you, also removing the one person who, once he got over his grief, may have realised that there was actually no proof against you." Golaran sipped his wine and then cleared his throat. "Why did you run, lad?"

"I didn't."

Golaran laughed. "What do you mean, you didn't? You escaped from that cell and never came back. That sealed your guilt for everyone. Case closed."

Mav rubbed his eyes and took another sip of his spiked wine in the hope that it would start working soon. "You have to understand that a lot of this I have only just found out. It was a series of disasters. One after the other. Did Amaridin or Serenia ever mention my father's plan to reunite Angelicus and Eidolon?"

Goloran sat up. "What? No! Why did he never tell me? He knows I would have supported him."

"I don't know. I think he meant to, only I think he fell afoul of the same hand that I did before he had a chance. When I last spoke to him, he was going to send me to Eidolon to see how the people really lived. A last-minute change was that he decided it would be best if I went without my soul so I would fit in better, and he told Athenia to take it and hold it for me until I returned."

"What?"

"Even though our plans were going awry, Athenia still took it, just before she died. And then Julius came along and knocked me out while I was still dazed from losing her and my soul and all over the place. When I awoke, I was in Eidolon, and I was in a state. I was confused, didn't know who I was, and didn't understand what had happened.

"Fortunately, a couple took me in until I recovered; well, physically recovered. I still didn't know who I was or why I was there. They said I'd had a bad transition from losing my soul. So I knew I didn't have a soul but not why."

Golaran grunted and leaned forward. "But how did you get out of the cells? Who helped you?"

"I don't know."

"But why didn't Averdeus intervene?"

"I don't know that either. I don't know where he went or what happened to him."

"So in one evening someone removed you, Athenia, and Averdeus," Golaran said.

"I would call that a coup," Mav said.

Pursing his lips, Golaran nodded in thought. "But they didn't execute the final step. Why not?"

"They must have been missing something, but I don't know what. I've been wracking my brain, but I've come up with nothing. If it was to overthrow my father, then Amaridin and Serenia are the only ones left, and yet they haven't claimed his throne. Why not?"

"I think they have to know your father is still alive some-where and they daren't make a move until they complete whatever is needed. You need to figure out where your father is, lad, and how to get him back."

"I didn't even know he was missing until…" Mav's voice faded. He tried again. "I don't understand why they kept hunting me down. Surely, I wasn't a threat…no memory, no power. Julius was persistent, keeping me moving, only I didn't know why he was trying to kill me. When he finally did catch me, he didn't kill me, he handed me over to your seraphim, Kyrill, and he took me to a dungeon in the depths of Eidolon."

"You must be mistaken. Kyrill would never do such a thing, and nor would Julius."

"Doesn't it seem odd how belligerent Kyrill is towards me? He openly challenged me in front of the full assembly.

Few would have the guts to do so, but he did. He is bolstered by the fact that he had me at his mercy and is over confident."

"Kyrill is my most trusted seraphim. There is no reason for him abduct you."

"And yet he did."

"Do you have proof of this?"

"Only my word against his and the word of his newest fledgling who helped rescue me, but in light of Apologia, I doubt many will believe me, much like yourself."

"I'm sorry, lad. It's just so far-fetched. Kyrill would not behave so. I don't believe it."

"Maybe you should ask him why he held me for nearly a year and didn't hand me over to the citadel?"

"I will."

Mav didn't think it would make any difference. Kyrill would not admit to any such crime. "They were after my soul. I believed I had already lost it, but they thought I still had one."

"So they didn't know Athenia had taken it?"

"Apparently not."

"I don't understand, Demavrian. How did you survive that first day if you don't have a soul?"

"I don't know. None of it makes sense." Mav wasn't going to talk about his shadow soul to anyone. He had no idea who he could trust. "Maybe Athenia didn't take my soul, but then why was I so confused when I woke in Eidolon?"

Golaran sat back in his chair and stared at Mav. "You have something they need to finish what they started," he said after a moment. "And it sounds like it is your soul."

"Amaridin would never..." Mav began.

"People do the strangest things under pressure," Golaran said gently. "Did you notice Valerian's absence? Amaridin changed the day he left. I never thought I would see the day those two would part company, but they did. Maybe his priorities changed. You should speak to him, find out what happened."

"I did, but Eodan was a restricting presence."

"Try again," Golaran advised. "Which count are you going to face next?"

"Does it matter?"

"I think the order is acutely important, for more things may come to light as each one is refuted, giving you further evidence to defend yourself."

"You think I'll be able to negate them all?"

"If you do it in the right order."

"The right order," Mav breathed. "Why do you believe me innocent when no others do?"

"You are in error, my boy. Many believe you innocent but are swayed by the guile of others. The question is who is doing the swaying and why." Goloran stroked his chin as he observed Mav. "I think you need to challenge Serenia and Amaridin."

Mav raised an eyebrow. "Challenge them?"

"You've allowed them to put you on the defensive. You have not been proven guilty. You are still an archdeus, the son of Averdeus. They cannot take that from you. You should be treated as such."

"A little difficult when they dragged me in like a common criminal."

"Is that what you are?"

Mav straightened his shoulders, feeling the long absent pull of his wings. No, he wasn't. He had handed his power over without a fight. Goloran was right; it was time to take it back.

"Let me share a story your mother once told me."

Mav relaxed back in chair as Golaran recounted a story

he had heard many times—how his father couldn't resist a challenge and how his mother constantly came up with impossible puzzles to confound a god.

"But what does that have to do with anything?" Mav asked when he had finished.

"Think about it, lad. What is the one thing your father would have accepted without a second's thought? The one thing that would remove him from this plane until the challenge was complete?"

"But who would challenge him, and for what?"

"You need to find out," Golaran said. "I think your life may depend on it."

"Why have you never mentioned this before?"

Golaran shrugged. "No one knew there was a conspiracy happening. They still don't. Why would anyone ask? Your father often absents himself for decades at a time. Amaridin is still in his seat. The citadel glitters, though its heart is subdued. As there is no heartbeat, people speculate its existence is just a myth. You should reconnect to the citadel, if you can. No one thinks anything is wrong. No one questions your father's absence." He hesitated a moment. "I believe with your connection disrupted, there is even more at stake. Everyone is ageing."

"What?" Mav realised he had risen out of his chair and was pacing. He came to halt. "I thought it was just me."

"We are all ageing. It is not yet obvious, but it is happening. I believe the citadel is what sustains our immortality. And with both the citadel and your father absent, we are all suffering."

"Why haven't you mentioned it to Serenia or Amaridin? Neither of them seem concerned."

"As I said, it's not noticeable. No one will believe me. They don't think the citadel is important."

"And you think they would believe me?" Mav stared at

him in disbelief. Would Serenia or one of the others put all angels at risk to gain the golden throne? Who else would benefit from removing Averdeus, Athenia, and him all at the same time? Could Kaenera have infiltrated the citadel? And why did they still want to remove him? Trying to ease the tension in his shoulders, he rolled his head. "I'm sorry, Golaran, I'm not sure you've helped."

"No, *I'm* sorry, lad. You've given me more to think about as well. But be careful. I don't think they just want to kill you; they need you for something."

10

SOLANJI

Not knowing what else to do, Solanji claimed one of the empty beds and lay down. Staring up at the ceiling, she scrunched up her face as she reviewed her conversation with Kyrill.

"Your face will stay like that," a light voice said from above her.

Solanji jerked upright in surprise and gaped at the little cherub hovering in the doorway. "Are you supposed to be in here?" she whispered.

Sero inspected Solanji thoughtfully. "No reason not to be." He fluttered over and dropped onto the end of her bed. Gazing around the room, he wrinkled his brow. "Kyrill doesn't provide much in the way of comfort, does he?"

"You'll get caught! What if one of the others return?"

"Kyrill is keeping them occupied. We're safe for a turn or two."

"How's Mav?"

"He's fine."

"And…?"

Sero quirked an eyebrow at her. "And what? He's fine." He smirked. "Missing him already?"

Swallowing, Solanji nodded as sudden tears gathered in her eyes.

Sero leaned forward and patted her knee. "He's fine. Missing you as well, I'm sure. I can give him a message if you want?"

And tell him what? That she loved him? He knew that. No, something that would help him. "Kyrill is frustrated. He thought he had Mav where he wanted, with Mav's powers at his fingertips. I'm not sure why he believes he can take Mav's power. Is it even transferable?"

"Interesting," Sero murmured.

"He wanted to know what Mav could do; mind speak, healing, flight, all things he knew Mav had lost when he had him in that torture chamber." Solanji stared at her hands. "Will he get them back do you think?"

"My belief is that his power is linked to his connection with the citadel. When his bond was severed, his abilities were diminished. I would never say Demavrian is without power; he is the son of Averdeus, after all, but he has obviously been affected. He has aged when he shouldn't, which is the most telling sign."

"What is the citadel?"

"Many things. Depends who you speak to."

"What do you believe it is?"

"A sanctuary. For lost souls and for our future. The citadel guides our steps on the path to peace and prosperity."

"And yet it has been dormant since Mav left, and no one has been concerned?"

"As I said, it depends on who you speak too. Most people just think it is a building and nothing more."

"But they expected the citadel to reject Mav. How could a building do that?"

Sero chuckled. "I never said angels were logical. The sentience of the citadel has always been more a myth than a reality. After all, it has been inanimate for years. Its lack of response to Demavrian has reinforced their belief that it is a myth." He observed Solanji for a moment. "I think you should try and connect to the citadel."

"Me?" Solanji's heart stuttered.

"Yes, you. You're a SoulBreather. You should connect, if only to check on the souls that the citadel harbours. We need to figure out how you can retrieve them if you are going to be able to return them to their hosts."

"I have no idea how."

"Athenia always said it was as natural as breathing, which makes me think you must inhale them. How did you get the spare soul you have?"

"It was just hovering in the air, waiting. I-I just spooled the strands into me."

Sero nodded. "Inhaled them. Can you manipulate it? Maybe pass it from hand to hand?"

Solanji pulled the golden soulmist out of her body and tossed it from one hand to the other. "What does this prove?" she asked after a moment.

"That I can't see souls," Sero replied, his eyes following her hand movements but obviously not seeing anything. "But at least you know you *can* manipulate them. Shame we haven't got a soulless here. You could weave a soul back in and take it out again for practice."

"Wouldn't that be a bit mean on the soulless one? They would feel it returning and being removed again."

Sero sighed. "I suppose so. Maybe we can get you in with the SoulSingers and you could remove a few souls?"

"Eww, no! And we don't want anyone knowing what I can do."

"Well, I thought you could then return them afterwards and no one would know."

Now that was an interesting idea, and Solanji wrinkled her nose as she considered it. "Wouldn't the SoulSingers know?"

"The SoulSingers don't see their victims again, so no one would know except the person."

"Why don't I practice on you? You have soulmist," Solanji suggested, wincing as he yelped and rose into the air out of reach, his wings fluttering in panic.

"Don't you dare."

Hesitantly, Solanji spread her hands. "I was only teasing. You can come back down. I would never touch your soul without permission."

Sero was slow to return, and he watched Solanji cautiously. Solanji suddenly realised why SoulSingers were so feared. They could take a soul before the person even realised it, and there was nothing they could do to stop it from happening.

"I promise, Sero, I would never take your soul," she said earnestly, and the little cherub relaxed and rubbed his face.

"Maybe we should search the library, see if we can find any books on SoulBreathing. A safer option," he mumbled.

"Didn't Athenia tell you anything else?"

Sero twisted his lips. "We weren't best friends, you know. It was just a passing conversation, and I never saw her history. She had died by the time I found out she had been attacked, and it was too late to even try."

"What about the other cherubs? There are more within the citadel, aren't there?"

"I've been sounding the others out but none of them know much about Athenia or SoulBreathing. They are well aware something is awry, they are just not sure what it is.

Demavrian's return has at least stimulated conversation and questions."

"Is there anyone else who would know about Soul-Breathing?"

"The most likely person to have some knowledge would be Julius, Captain Teravin, as he was betrothed to Athenia, but as you know, he is not going to help us. Did Demavrian not say anything? He was close to Athenia."

"We never had a chance to talk about it. The memory of Athenia was painful and upsetting. We never really got passed her death."

Tutting, Sero fluttered above her and flew over to the door. "Until then, let's try the library."

"Now?"

"Yes, now. We have at least one turn before anyone returns. Let's see what the library can tell us. There must be something in there."

Solanji hurriedly dressed in her fledgling robes and absently rubbed her skin as the tattoo itched. "What do we even look for?"

Sero grinned and pointed at her arm. "Maybe your dragon will guide us."

Glancing down, Solanji gasped as the glowing tattoo morphed into a tiny dragon, its slender wings fluttering much like Sero's. "You can see it? Only Mav has seen the tattoo before. No one else does."

Sero tilted his head as he watched the little dragon. "I remembered you have a tattoo, so I must have seen it some-where." He snapped his fingers. "I saw it in Demavrian's memories when I touched him, remember?"

A golden glow emanated from the dragon's body. At times it seemed transparent, and then its shimmering skin would ripple and the light would dim as it solidified. It fluttered over beside

Sero and stared at her. Obeying its unspoken command, she opened the door and peeked out into the silent hallway. Sero and the dragon flew out the door. "Come on." Sero's voice echoed eerily down the empty corridor, and she hurried after them.

White marble lined the walls and the floors, tinged by a fleeting golden glimmer as the dragon passed overhead. Solanji was soon lost as they ducked into alcoves to avoid guards and darted down narrow back corridors before returning to the main marble-lined thoroughfares.

The library was hidden behind tall ornate wooden doors. Carvings of cherubs, angels, and the stars above covered the wood panelling, and Solanji ran the tips of her fingers over them in wonder.

"Quick, open the door before anyone passes by," Sero hissed and Solanji lifted the heavy iron latch and swung the door inwards. The air was thick, and the aroma of musty books and old parchment lingered, along with the slight tang of ink.

Shutting the door behind her, Solanji hesitated, straining to see the wooden desks in the dark. "Where do we start?" she whispered. Oppressive silence deadened the sound of her voice.

"Well, if your dragon could illuminate the room for us, we'll have a looksee before I fly into a chandelier and knock myself out," Sero said from somewhere above her.

"You mean you can't see in the dark?" Solanji asked.

There was a short silence before Sero said, with a slight edge to his voice, "I am not a demora."

Solanji chuckled, though she had no idea how to speak to the dragon. She rubbed the faint ridges of the tattoo on her skin as she stared up at the dragon. "Can you give us some light?"

The little dragon began to glow more brightly, its body

flickering as the sturdy wooden desks and book shelves appeared out of the gloom.

"Oof!" Sero said as he pirouetted away from a large crystal chandelier, the glass drops tinkling as he passed by. "That was close. Right, let's check the alchemy and augury section first."

"Alchemy? What does SoulBreathing have to do with alchemy?"

"Probably nothing but I'm working through the alphabet."

"Maybe it would better to start with witchcraft or sorcery."

"No such thing," Sero replied as he began running his fingers across the spines of the books in the shelves opposite the main doors. Flying back and forth, he worked his way down to the floor. He moved onto the next bookcase.

"Then what would you call SoulBreathing?"

"Hmmm, manipulation? Out of body experience?"

"Very funny, and not particularly helpful."

"Why don't you follow your dragon? She may have more ideas."

"She?" Solanji breathed as she followed his suggestion and skirted the solid wooden desk in the centre of the room then ventured deeper into the bookstacks following the golden glow. The dragon was hovering before a large ceiling-to-floor oil painting, and Solanji squinted up at it and then choked as her breath caught in her throat.

The man in the painting was Demavrian, in the full regalia of the Archdeus General. He stood on the steps of the citadel assembly hall. A white fur cloak descended from his shoulders, where golden clasps held it in place. Underneath he wore a smartly cut uniform in a deep blue, which moulded to his muscular body. A gleaming sword nestled at his waist, along with ornate daggers. He looked so young. His black hair glinted with blue highlights, not silver. His amber eyes were bright, so vibrant and alive, though that could just be a result of the dragon's glow. Was that what he was supposed to look like? The ever youthful general?

He looked calm, like he was in complete control, and he held his hand out to the most exquisite young woman dressed in the glimmering golden robes of an archangel. Her strawberry blonde hair fell around her shoulders like rivulets of liquid gold, and her expression was joyful as she reached for his hand. For a moment, it seemed as though the woman was staring at Solanji, and their eyes met, a message deep in the woman's gaze, and then she was staring at Mav. The painting was so vibrant and full of life it was almost as if they both stood in the room with her.

She must be Athenia, the SoulBreathing archangel. Solanji swallowed, her throat tight. She was so inadequate in comparison to this exquisite, angelic woman. Where Athenia was all things light, Solanji was all things dark. *Maybe that's a good thing*, a small voice in the back of her mind said. Mav was all shadows and darkness as well. Maybe she was what he needed. Feeling a little reassured at the thought, she turned as she heard Sero fluttering towards her.

"You do know there are thousands of books in this library, don't you?" Sero said as he approached, and then he saw the painting and came to a stop, hovering. "Ah. Demavrian and Athenia. I always thought those two would make a lovely couple. They did love each other, but Athenia said it was more like brother and sister. They told each other everything, which is why I think he is probably our best source of information."

"Then you must speak to him tomorrow before the next count."

"I must, must I?"

Solanji peered at the spines of the books in the bookstack

in front of her. "Botany," she said, running her finger down one.

"There's going to be nothing in the botany section."

"Flowers. Trailing flowers engraved in the walls. They conceal much," Solanji murmured, ignoring him. Sero sighed and began running his fingers over the spines. He had just dropped to the floor when he stopped. "That's weird," he said, crouching down.

"What's weird?"

"This book is fairly humming with Athenia's presence as if she read it often." He pulled it out and handed it to Solanji.

She flipped through the pages as the dragon hovered beside her, providing some light. Pages and pages of exquisite ink drawings of flowers, exotic and more mundane, all annotated. "She was an amazing artist," Solanji murmured and then gasped as she came across a blank page save for one short paragraph.

"SoulBreathing is twofold: first, accepting you are a conduit for a person's life force and second, that the connection to the citadel is sacrosanct and should never be disclosed." Solanji stared at the elegant writing. Even Athenia's handwriting was beautiful. "This is it." She stumbled to a small alcove framed by red velvet curtains tied back with golden cord and sat at the desk. Laying the book flat on the table, she began flipping through the pages. "See if you can find any similar books that reek of Athenia," Solanji said and stilled when she found another nearly blank page.

"The citadel is a haven for souls until they can be returned to their hosts. SoulBreathing is a blessing providing those less fortunate a second chance."

She continued searching and frowned at the next sentence she came across. *"The archdeus is the cornerstone to all.*

What does that mean? The archdeus. There's more than one. Did she mean Amaridin or Demavrian?"

Sero's chuckle was faint as he hovered in front of a book stack deeper in the library. "In Athenia's eyes there was only ever one."

"So Demavrian, then. Why Demavrian? What was so special about him?"

"You haven't figured that out yet?" Sero's tone was suggestive, and Solanji's cheeks grew heated as she concentrated on the pages.

"Soulbreathing is also a curse as the burden can only be carried by the one with the marque." What burden? What marque? Was that the tattoo? She rubbed the faint ridges on her arm and then turned the page and she softly read it out loud. *"The citadel knows all. Connect at your peril."*

Darkness descended as the dragon disappeared, and the door rattled as it opened. Solanji stiffened. Hairs rose on the back of her neck as she held her breath. A chill shivered down her spine as she carefully leaned behind the drape of the red velvet curtain. Silently cursing herself for not releasing the cord to allow the curtain to hide her better, she strained to hear who had entered.

The soft glow of a lantern lit the main desk, and two men seemed to be arguing.

"Enough!" one of the men snapped. "Now is the time. No one will be checking the requests; they are all distracted by Apologia. This is our chance to get it through without questions."

"But what if they do check? Our names are on it. A claim for land in Eidolon is not insignificant." The other man's voice quavered with fear.

"They won't. Eidolon is up for grabs anyway, no one will care. Golaran wants our support. He'll smooth the way." The man's voice was sharp.

"But…"

One of the men slammed a hand down on the wooden desk, and Solanji jumped, dropping her quill with a slight clatter.

"What was that?" the nervy man asked.

"Stay here," the bolder man muttered, and the glow of the candle moved towards the book stacks. Solanji shrank in her chair. The man didn't venture far before he paused, listening intently, and then he huffed out his breath and retraced his steps. "Rats, I expect. I'm not arguing any further. This is our only chance. I will submit the proposal tomorrow during Apologia. Be ready to approve it." The door opened and the men left.

"Shh. Stay still," Sero's whisper came from on top of the stack next to her, and Solanji crouched in her chair. Minutes passed and Solanji wanted to bite her nails. Tension shivered through her, making her neck and shoulders ache. She thought she might scream from sheer terror.

A few minutes later, the door opened again and there was silence as the person stuck their head through the door and listened and then left again. Sero exhaled and fluttered down to the floor. "I think it's time we got out of here."

"Me too," Solanji agreed as she picked up the book with shaking hands. "Should we put Athenia's book back?"

"Yes, keep it safe." Sero took the book and slotted it back in its place. "I didn't find any other books. We'll come back another night and you can finish it."

"Do we have to?"

Sero snorted. "Yes, you do." And then, after listening intently at the door for a moment, he led the way out of the library and back to her room. Solanji crept into the dormitory, surprised and relieved, that none of the other girls had returned yet. She quickly got ready for bed and snuggled under the blanket. The words from Athenia's book ran through her mind. Mav was the cornerstone? How? Why? Did she need to reconnect him to the citadel? Should *she* try and connect to the citadel? She didn't know. She fell asleep dreaming about trailing vines of exotic flowers that seemed vaguely familiar as they climbed up a stone tower wall.

11

DEMAVRIAN

Mav stirred from his slump over his desk at the soft tap on his door. He had fallen asleep trying to make sense of all the associations of the new seraphim. Rubbing his stiff neck, he frowned blearily around the room trying to identify what had woken him.

A knock on the door gave him the probable cause. "Come," he croaked and cleared his throat, ready to repeat his command, but the door opened anyway and Ryvalin peered in. Her expression relaxed as she saw Mav. "Thank goodness," she murmured, slipping in through the door and closing it behind her. "Can we talk?"

"Of course," Mav replied, indicating the chair opposite and trying to look awake.

"You look like shit," Ryvalin said as she perched on the edge of the seat.

"So kind of you to notice," Mav murmured, observing his old friend for a moment. He could have returned the compliment; she looked as tired as he felt. Fine lines creased her skin, puffy bags lingered under her vivid blue eyes, and her grey uniform was crumpled and worn.

Huffing out her breath on a laugh, Ryvalin leaned forward. "What happened to you, Mav? You've been gone for so long."

"I am beginning to think I fell foul of someone's plan to take over the world," Mav said with a wry grin.

Ryvalin stiffened. "You may not be far wrong," she said.

"I was joking."

"Well don't. Because nothing has been right since you and your father disappeared. In fact, it's all wrong. Everything is out of kilter." She hesitated a moment. "You need to speak to Xylvin. She is upset about something, but she won't tell me what."

Mav's eyebrows rose. "And you think she'll tell me? I've not even been back a day. What makes you think she'll tell me?"

"It is only since you returned that she's been acting strange. If I didn't know better, I would say she is feeling guilty about something, but dragons never regret anything." Her lips quirked. "They are never wrong!"

"Certainly not Xylvin," Mav agreed.

"Will you come?"

"Now? It's the middle of the night." Mav glanced around for his stick, knowing he would go. He wasn't even sure why he was protesting. If Xylvin knew something, then he needed to know what it was. He was already rising as Ryvalin opened her mouth to persuade him. She snapped her mouth shut and twisted her lips.

Ryvalin was waiting with the door open before Mav had got his balance. Aware of her acute observation, he tried to disguise his limp. A sharp pain flashed through his knee each time his foot touched the floor, and he couldn't help tensing. Shutting the door, she leaned against it, her eyes wide. "You are carrying an injury? Mav! Why haven't you healed yourself?"

"Long story. My healing ability is not working properly right now."

"You can't let them see you like this. They will know you're vulnerable."

"Can't be helped. Either I use the stick or I fall flat on my face. Which would make me look more vulnerable?"

Ryvalin swallowed. "What is going on, Mav?" Her expression tightened as she scanned his face, not liking what she saw.

"I believe that whatever has been going on is about to come to a head. And it all seems to be about proving me guilty of murder. So, if you or Xylvin know anything that can help me, now would be the time to tell me."

She cupped his cheek for a moment, then nodded, her face firming with determination. "Xylvin knows something, I'm sure of it."

"Let's go then."

Ryvalin led the way down the corridor, her shoulders square, chin raised. After a few steps, she shortened her stride and flashed a sideways glance at Mav.

"I'm going as fast as I can," he muttered under his breath.

"Aren't you supposed to be in your prime?"

"I could ask the same of you. Anyway, why are you still working at this time of night? Haven't you gone off duty?"

Ryvalin snorted. "They think dragons don't need rest. They have us running all over the place. We are a glorified delivery service."

"Who is they?" Mav asked as he halted at the top of a flight of stairs. He had been hoping to avoid stairs for the rest of his life. He began descending one step at a time. "You know, if I had one wish in life, it would be to remove every stair in existence."

Ryvalin turned to look up at him, her eyes twinkling as she grinned. Her expression morphed into horror as she stared over his shoulder. "Mav, look out!"

A hard shove against his back sent him tumbling down the stairs. He twisted, trying to save his knee, and whipping his stick around as he fell, he managed to parry the knife that followed. He had time to be thankful that they hadn't led with the blade as his shoulder hit the step. Pain blossomed through his back as he crashed down the rest of the steps. Stunned, he lay still for a moment, a heap of bruised and battered muscle. His shoulder twinged, his back ached, but his knee was a burning ball of flame and it subsumed every other pain that existed.

Sweat dewed his skin as he tried to sit up, and Mav shivered as dizziness made him sway. Swallowing down the rising bile, he groped for his stick but came up empty-handed. Ryvalin fought on the steps above him. Who, he didn't know. A vibrating roar echoed down the corridor, and a crash soon followed, and then another. The building trembled.

Guards came running, and Mav stiffened. Any one of them could just run him through, and that would be the end. He would not be able to heal himself. Another crash echoed down the hallway, and Ryvalin clattered down the stairs and stood over Mav. Breathing a sigh of relief, he realised he had never felt so vulnerable, not even in all the years he had survived in Eidolon. At least then he had been able to heal himself. Fear had kept him frozen, relief made him go limp, and he remembered to breathe.

"What is going on here?" one of the guards demanded, peering down at Mav.

"We were attacked," Ryvalin replied. "You'd be better off chasing the culprits; they ran that way." She pointed back up the stairs.

With a sharp command, two men pelted up the steps, and after a keen glance at the remaining guards, Ryvalin crouched beside Mav. "Can you get up?"

"Not sure," Mav said as another crash reverberated through the building and raised voices grew shriller.

"You need to control your dragon before she destroys the citadel," the officer said, casting a nervous glance over his shoulder.

"I'll control my dragon when I know Archdeus Demavrian is alright. If anyone looks at him wrong, she will eat you for breakfast."

"There is no need for threats."

"There is when it is not safe to walk through the corridors of the citadel," Ryvalin snarled. Her expression gentled as she helped Mav upright. "Shit, Mav, you never said someone wanted you dead."

Mav groaned as she straightened him out.

"He's just a bit battered. Even archangels need a moment to recover from falling down the stairs," she said to the officer.

Under Ryvalin's stern gaze, Mav leant against the wall and just breathed. His shoulder burned with the same heat as his knee. Adriz was going to kill him. After a moment, he limped down the passageway surrounded by suspicious guards.

Silence fell as they approached the entrance hall. Xylvin's head and her sinewy neck took up most of the open space, having forced her way through the doors. They hung drunkenly either side of her, hinges torn away, glass windows smashed, and Ryvalin winced as she saw the damage. Citadel staff shrank back against the wall, afraid to move as Xylvin's head swayed back and forth, searching. Her eyes blazed red, and her razor-sharp teeth looked ready to bite.

Ryvalin hissed a curse under her breath, and Xylvin swung her head round. *"Mav, you're hurt, again?"*

"Again?" Mav thought that was a bit unfair. But he allowed Ryvalin to hurry him across the hall towards Xylvin.

Smoke drifted from her nostrils as she watched. *"Who dared?"*

Staff scuttled away as the dragon focused on Mav, and her huge jaws snapped shut. Her eyes calmed down to a more soothing pink and gradually faded to lilac. She offered her snout and Mav leaned against her nose and breathed in ashy warmth as his shoulders and back throbbed. *"Hold on,"* she murmured as she gently wrapped her jaws arounds him. She lifted him off the ground and shuffled back out of the building. One of the teetering doors crashed to the marble floor, glass shards tinkling on the stone tiles.

Mav relaxed into her soft thrum as she lulled him into a semi doze and carried him to her lair, a roughly hewn out cavern in the cliff which rose behind the citadel. Ryvalin climbed up on Xylvin's bent leg, grabbed a leather strap, and hung on as the dragon vaulted into the air, flapped her wings, and glided to her ledge. Ryvalin stepped off as Xylvin landed and hovered as the dragon shuffled in deeper and laid Mav on the cot by the wall, which was Ryvalin's bed when she stayed in the cavern.

"Is he alright?" Ryvalin asked, gently smoothing Mav's hair off his face.

"Not really, your assessment that he's a bit banged up is an under-statement."

"He did just get pushed down the stairs."

"Hmmm, he's broken his collarbone."

"Can you fix it?"

"Easier than his knee, which is a lost cause."

"I can hear you both, you do know that, don't you?" Mav asked

as he drifted in the warm embrace that Xylvin was creating for him.

"*Just relax, Mav, we'll talk in a moment,*" Xylvin said, increasing her thrum, and Mav slid deeper into slumber before he could protest that he didn't have time to sleep.

12

DEMAVRIAN

Mav opened his eyes to a stone ceiling and a soft rumbling vibration that slowly died away as he catalogued his body's woes. He felt revitalised, all except his knee of course, but then if Xylvin couldn't fix it, he was stuck with it. At least it was no longer a burning ball of flame, just a simmering ache that reminded him all was not well.

Sitting up, he glanced around the cavern, empty except for coils of an iridescent dragon's tail and frothy veined wings. The dry rustle of scales drew his gaze, and he met the gleaming facets of Xylvin's eyes, flashing in the dim light.

"How are you feeling?" she asked.

"Much better, thank you." He swung his legs over the side of the cot and paused for a moment resting his weight on the floor. *"Where is Ryvalin?"*

"I told her to go to bed. She needs to sleep. Who did that to you?"

Mav didn't ask what she referred to. He knew Xylvin had seen all that he was and wasn't, but she wouldn't say it unless he did. *"I don't know. Nor do I know why, and I think I have had enough of living in the dark. Someone knows. My father for one, wher-*

ever he has retreated to." Mav rose and walked over to her, and resting his palm on her cheek, he asked, *"Xylvin. What do you know? Where is Averdeus?"*

Hot breath wafted over him, warm and comforting, and he leaned into her. He felt her smile as if he had seen it. *"You should have bonded with a dragon,"* she murmured. *"You always knew what we were thinking."*

"Indeed, and I know when you are avoiding the subject. What did my father tell you to do?"

Xylvin's sigh was long and deep. *"To take you to Eidolon and hide you. He said you needed time to rebalance and accept the changes wrought in your life."*

"Why didn't you tell anyone?"

"I did, as did Ryvalin, but no-one would listen. I am one of yours, so my word was suspect and no one would believe us."

"What else?" Mav asked, an ice-cold shiver flashed through him at the confirmation that his oathsworn had been disregarded so quickly and that his father had been behind his initial downfall.

"That I was to be your conduit to the citadel and advise you what was happening. But Mav, you disappeared and I couldn't find you. I searched. I've been searching ever since. That's why I agreed to be their delivery service. I was looking for you. Where did you go? Your father said you would be unbalanced once you realised Athenia took your soul, but she wasn't supposed to die; she was supposed to give it back to you." The anguish in Xylvin's voice cut through him. *"It's all my fault. I took you to Eidolon and left you there without you knowing why."*

"It's not your fault. You did what my father asked of you. The fault is his for not planning properly and for not protecting those in his care." Mav took a deep calming breath as the steel grey dawn lifted the shadows in the cavern entrance. He was running out of time. *"Do you know where Averdeus is?"*

"I have my suspicions. Just as I am sure you have yours."

"Do you really think he would accept a challenge? A challenge that would remove him from our plane until it was won or lost?"

"Maybe he thought it would be worth it if his challenger was taken out of the frame as well. I think he would if he thought it would give you a free hand."

"Xylvin, start at the beginning and explain what my father told you."

"Averdeus said that he wanted to reunite Angelicus and Eidolon. That his original intention had been twisted for other purposes and hadn't provided the path to redemption that he had hoped for."

Mav nodded. *"I remember him saying something similar to me. He wanted me to experience Eidolon and report back when I saw what had gone wrong. I didn't expect the journey to be so extreme. I don't understand why Athenia had to take my soul. Nor why she still took it, when she knew she was dying."*

Xylvin pondered for a moment. *"Your father had great hopes that you would find a way for those in Eidolon to be redeemed without restoring their soul. Averdeus believed a soul was not the element that determined whether you were good or bad, whether you deserved to live in light or shadow. He didn't believe it was so simple, so clearly delineated. He saw much good in those who lived in Eidolon and wanted them to have the same opportunities as those in Angelicus, even though they couldn't return."*

Mav rubbed his temples. His brain was struggling to keep up. *"I was supposed to go and find out how the people of Eidolon were really living, not delve into the pros and cons of a soul. In fact, my father never mentioned souls. I certainly didn't expect to be dumped in Eidolon without mine."*

"I'm so sorry, Mav. I don't think that is what your father intended. I should never have left you there."

Mav screwed up his face as he tried to make sense of it all, and then he exhaled. *"It was just a major fuck up, wasn't it?"*

Xyvin's breath rumbled out. *"Even gods can make mistakes."*

"Yeah, but they are not the ones who suffer," Mav replied.

"At least you know that, Mav. You can make a difference."

There was a short silence. *"And how am I supposed to do that?"*

Smoke drifted through the cavern as Xylvin huffed. Her coils rustled as they shifted and curled around him, smooth and warm, comforting and secure. *"Be who you are, Demavrian. Who you have become. You are not the man I left in the shadows of Eidolon."*

Mav snorted. *"I am much less."*

Xylvin's angular head tilted, her sparkling eyes snaring him as a rumbling growl began deep in her chest. *"You know that is not true."*

"It is. Anyone could knock me over with their little finger. I can't heal myself. I can't hear my oathsworn or sense anything else. I-I no longer have wings, let alone a soul."

"You may have lost some abilities, but you have gained so much more. And you know perfectly well you do have wings and a soul. They may not be the same as what you had before, but they exist. There is a weight, a knowledge you didn't have before. They cannot dismiss you if you don't allow it."

Mav rolled his eyes, but she was only reinforcing what Golaran had said. His power was his to take back. And he would. He needed to speak to Felather and Sero. Neither of them would get much sleep tonight.

"Don't underestimate who you are, Demavrian, or the difference you can make. I think that may be what your father was relying on."

"Since when have you been so wise, Xylvin?"

More tendrils of smoke curled around him, an ashy embrace reminding him of his childhood when he would retreat to Xylvin's lair to escape Serenia's critical gaze. His shoulders dropped as his tension bled out, and he relaxed against Xylvin's warm scales as he considered her words without the pressure of celestial expectations.

He did know a lot more than he realised. He had many

years of embracing the Eidolon way of life, minus a few years he would prefer to forget. Well, more than a few years, but he needed to let them go. They were done; he couldn't change what had happened.

He stilled.

Xylvin's tail slithered around him, a comforting embrace. *"What have you remembered?"* she asked, her voice a husky whisper in his head.

"Ryvalin will get jealous," he murmured out loud.

Her laugh was a flush of heat through his body. *"No, she won't. Though I will say again, you should have bonded with a dragon."*

"There aren't any dragons to bond with."

"There is still time," she replied, unconcerned.

Mav swivelled to meet her eye. *"What do you know?"*

Xylvin's faceted eye winked at him. *"Dragon's come in many forms,"* she said. *"And don't change the subject. What was your epiphany?"*

"Epiphany? I wouldn't say that. But you are right. Maybe I do know more than I thought."

"I would hope so," she murmured. *"I doubt you would have wasted your time."*

Mav huffed his breath out. He hoped not.

A commotion at the cavern entrance revealed Adriz. "Mav, why did you leave your rooms without me?" she demanded as she stormed into Xylvin's lair, closely followed by a panting Felather.

"You promised that you would be sensible," Felather said as he bent over his knees, trying to catch his breath.

Sero fluttered in behind him. "We've been hearing all sorts of strange stories about you falling down the stairs."

"Trust the host to only share that bit," Mav replied with a wry twist of his lips. "Felather, I want you to reinstate my seat in the assembly hall."

Felather straightened and stared at him in horror. "We don't have time for that. Your next appearance is only a few turns away. We need to finalise your defence."

"I'll do that. I am the son of Averdeus. Make sure I am treated as such."

Sero clapped his hands together. "Yes! It's about time you acted like an archdeus."

13

SHANDRA, EIDOLON

As the wagon rattled to a halt, Shandra hushed the rising wails coming from the smaller children. Her heart twisted at the sight of their drawn faces and cringing bodies. She wrinkled her nose at the stench of urine and fear. No matter how often she had yelled and pleaded, they had refused to stop for the children to relieve themselves. The kiddies were crying as much from embarrassment and shame as fear. She was not much better. Her stomach ached with the effort of holding it in.

Shandra needed to remain calm. Breathe deep and slow her racing heart. She needed to be sensible and look after the little ones as best she could. The others were older and would have to fend for themselves. There was only so much she could do.

As if she could ignore the plight of a single one of her brood. They were all hers, and they all looked to her to protect them. Concern for Muntra rushed through her, tightening her already aching gut. He had looked rough when they had tossed him into the other cart. Hopefully, he was only suffering a slight concussion. They were unlikely to get any access to a healer wherever it was the dybbuks had taken them.

Kerris was their only hope, and he had no idea what had happened to them. He would return to a deserted farm and there was nothing she could leave him to explain where they had gone. She didn't know herself.

The carts had travelled all day and late into the night, not stopping once, not even to rest or feed the horses. The dybbuks were relentless and unfeeling.

Shandra braced herself as the back board rattled and then was lowered. The canvas parted and she peered into the gloom. Dark shadows rose around them, buildings of some sort.

"Out," the dybbuk snapped.

Shandra jumped down, and her boots sank into thick, cold mud. Damp air and the turgid aroma of rotting vegetation assailed her. Shuddering, she turned to help the smaller kids, trying to swing them over onto firmer ground. They huddled in a forlorn group like tiny chicks searching for warmth.

Her stomach fluttered as she searched for the other wagon; the thought that they might be taken to different places hadn't even crossed her mind. Quelling the stirrings of panic, she herded the children towards one of the buildings.

"The children need food and clean clothes," she said, halting before the door.

"In," the dybbuk replied.

"Not without food and clothes." Shandra glared at him. He was a stocky man, roughly dressed in a mismatched uniform which couldn't be his, as they hung off him. Only his sword belt kept his trousers up. His blank face morphed into a snarl, and Shandra struggled not to flinch at his fierce expression. *Don't show fear, don't show fear.* The words were a litany running through her head. "If you'd stopped when I asked, they wouldn't be soiled."

The dybbuk sniffed and then sniffed again before wrinkling his nose.

"Exactly, clean clothes and food."

"Clean clothes. In." The dybbuk shoved her against the door.

Rubbing her arm, she opened it and led the way inside. "Is there any light?" she asked, spinning around just as the door slammed shut and the lock clicked.

Straining to see in the dark, she reached out in front of her and stubbed her fingers on a wooden pole. She grabbed it, something solid and strangely reassuring. Resting her head against it for a moment, she closed her eyes and just breathed.

A whimper reminded her of her responsibilities. "Is there anyone in here?" she called.

"Yeah, and we're tryin' to sleep. You should too," a hoarse voice replied.

"Where are we?"

A low creak from the far corner preceded the thump of feet on the ground. "The depths of hell," a woman said as a flame flared at the strike of a match and the small yellow glow illuminated the woman's worn features. Deep lines creased her face, and her brown hair straggled around sunken cheeks. She raised her candle. "What do we have here, then?"

"They're just kids, hungry and cold," Shandra replied.

"Them dybbuks getting desperate or summat?" the hoarse voice asked.

"If you want a bed, you'll have to earn it. Each bed comes with a price. You pay the tithe, you get to sleep in it. Each bowl of muck they provide, you pay a tithe. No tithe, no food."

"What is a tithe?" Shandra asked.

"You work, you get paid. You use your pay for the tithe. You choose, food or bed."

"What about clothes or washing?"

"You pay."

"What is this place? Where are we?"

"We are nowhere. No one will find us, no one is coming to save you. You work in the mines or the factory. You earn."

One of the little ones tugged her sleeve, and she bent down to hear the quiet whisper. Hugging the child, she straightened. "Where can the kids relieve themselves?"

The woman laughed, though it was not a kind laugh. "There's a bucket in the corner."

"They've not been all day. The dybbuks wouldn't stop. They need to wash."

"Empty your head of all niceties, girl. Washing is a luxury. Don't waste your money when you won't have enough for food." The woman raised the candle and peered at the huddled children. "How many of 'em you got?"

"Twelve with me. There are more in another wagon."

The woman tutted. "What is this world coming to?" She shook her head. "The bunks near the door are empty. Top and tail 'em. Then they only got to pay half each. Then get some sleep. You'll need it." The woman thrust the candle at Shandra. "You owe me for the candle." The woman shuffled back to her cot in the back of the room.

Shandra quickly sorted the children into pairs and allocated them to a bunk. The stench from the corner informed her where the bucket was, but her kids smelt no better. Holding the candle, she waited until each child paid a visit and hurried them back to the bunks. Lumpy straw mattresses, likely filled with bugs, greeted them, and Shandra lifted those who needed help into the upper bunks. "Sleep as best you can," she whispered, kissing soft cheeks and stroking their heads.

With the kids settled, Shandra visited the bucket. Steeling herself to the indignity, she was glad it was dark. She had no doubt who would have the job of emptying it in the morning. As the latest arrivals, she was sure they would get the worst of everything. Her bed was right next to the door. At least the cold blast of air that rushed in each time it opened cleared the stench lingering over them.

She squirmed to get comfortable on the lumpy mattress on the floor. They would have to get past her to get to the kids. She stared at the joyfully flickering flame and prayed that Kerris would find them and that Muntra and the others were alright wherever they may be. She blew out the candle and huddled under the thin blanket.

Lurching upright, a cold blast of air woke Shandra from the exhausted sleep she had fallen into. A lantern flared in her face and a bundle of cloth landed with a soft thump beside her. "Clothes," a deep voice said, and the door slammed shut. Muffled complaints rose from the dark, but Shandra ignored them as she hugged the clean-smelling linen close. She wasn't letting anyone else steal anything from her.

The next morning, a loud clanging jerked her awake. Her stomach growled with hunger, and she knew the kids would be just as starving. Dim, grey light crept in through the cracks in the walls and ceilings. Shandra's lips tightened at the sight; this building would not keep out the winter storms.

They would fall ill from chills and colds, if they didn't starve first. She had nothing to prevent it. No warm blankets, no reassuring fires, no soothing soup. There had been no time to even consider stashing away a flint or a knife. Her concern had been the children.

Realising she was still hugging the bundle of cloth as if her life depended on it, she relaxed her grip and sat up.

The door swung open, the fresh air blasting away the stale overnight odours. A tall man stood in the doorway, his bulk blocking most of the light.

He scowled into the room. "Everyone out." And then he stepped back.

"They'll want to see what the dybbuks brought them," the woman said. "You'll be given jobs. That's all you do, work and sleep. Nothing else. All we're good for." She ran an appraising eye over Shandra. "Though you might be lucky. They are just as desperate for distractions from this shit hole. Pretty girl, pretty boy. They're not fussy. Extra money goes a long way in a place like this. Especially for one with twelve kids to look after. You have some decisions to make, girl."

Shandra stared after her, but at the shout from outside, she hurriedly spread out the cloth and found thin grey shifts and trousers. She doled them out to children who needed it and doubled up where possible. The kids would freeze otherwise. She collected the dirty clothes, determined to find a way to wash them.

Stumbling out into the grey dawn, Shandra and the children stood in a line as the man inspected them. Relief flooded her as she saw Muntra, Bailey, and the others lined up opposite, along with some youngsters she didn't know. Muntra was battered and bruised and held his side, but the sight of them chased away the fear of being on her own.

The man sorted them into sizes. The smallest were led away, and it broke her heart to see their scared little faces. "Where are you taking them?" Shandra scuttled after them.

The tall man grabbed her arm and jerked her back. "They will work, just as you will."

"They are just kids. You can't expect them to mine rock."

"They fit where others can't. You'll see." He inspected

her, and a grim smile spread over his face. "You, however, will fit just fine." He shoved her over next to Bailey, who wrapped his arm around her waist and tugged her close. Shandra felt the slight tremor running through him as the man added, "Both of you will."

14

SOLANJI, CITADEL

The next morning, Solanji squeezed into a seat beside Lormin up in the highest tiers and stared wide-eyed at the dais with the ornate thrones.

Her gaze wandered around the elegantly vaulted hall with the curving ceilings adorned by sparkling chandeliers. Golden branches held slender ivory candles, causing the crystal to glisten and glitter in a rainbow of colours across the marble walls. The sight was spectacular and more beautiful than anything she had ever seen.

Silence fell as Amaridin escorted Serenia down the hall. Both had their pure white wings flared, and they nodded regally at the angels seated in the wooden tiers on one side and the councillors on the other. Solanji pursed her lips as she observed them. They really thought they were something.

As she watched, Serenia slowed as she glared towards the dais. Solanji followed her gaze to the three golden chairs positioned in front of the larger throne. They were backless to cater for the archangel's wings, but the arms were covered in elaborate scrollwork, as were the legs. The red velvet material of the cushion was vibrant against the gold frame.

Voices rose as the angels discussed her reaction, though Solanji didn't know what was wrong.

"What's happened?" she asked Lormin.

"There's an extra seat on the dais, and it doesn't look like Archangel Serenia requested it."

Solanji watched with eager interest as Serenia mounted the steps and turned before her chair, her mauve gown swirling around her legs, leaving a short train rippling down the marble. *She planned that,* Solanji thought. Now Serenia did look angelic, even with the frown marring her perfect features. A halo of golden hair was plaited around her head, and artful strands escaped to soften her exquisite face.

The sudden rise in whispered conversations drew Solanji's gaze back to the floor to see Mav enter the chamber. God, he was handsome. Not in an ethereal angelic way, but in a masculine sight-for-sore-eyes way. He looked so good. Some of her tension relaxed as she watched him walk the length of the hall. His slight limp was unnoticeable if you didn't know to look for it and he had dispensed with his stick. His expression was carefully neutral, though the stiff way he held himself betrayed his exhaustion.

His leather tunic was crisscrossed with the straps and belts that typically held his weapons but were now empty. His wide-legged, dark grey trousers flowed around him like swirling shadows; an apt image she thought.

Silence fell and the angels all turned to watch his progress up the hall to the seat to the right of the golden throne. Amaridin sat to the left, with Eodan behind his shoulder. Serenia sat on a chair situated in front of Averdeus' throne, neither of them quite prepared to sit in the seat of the Almighty. Julius stood behind her shoulder, his face hard and unyielding.

Solanji watched as Mav adjusted his stance as if he was compensating for his wings, and she smiled as his shadows formed above his shoulders even though she was sure no one else could see them.

Lifting his chin, he sat in the golden chair to the right and stared down the hall. His reputation would precede him, and even with their suspicions, they would not be able to ignore his presence. Solanji drank in the sight of him seated in his rightful place. He would take the upper hand and leave them to try and take it away.

Adriz and Felather entered the chamber and marched under the crystal chandeliers in unison. The candle light reflected off their dress uniforms, gold and red, polished to perfection. Adriz's golden wings glistened and sparkled, small but strong, and flared to their full extent they were exquisite. Solanji's breath caught in her throat.

That they would do this for him.

Perfectly in step and immaculate.

A statement.

In support of their archdeus.

Mav's demeanour softened for a moment as he accepted his oathsworn's public declaration. One they had probably made many times before but never so poignantly, and she watched as it almost undid him.

It must have been the martial light in Adriz's eye that made him hold it together as he inhaled and exhaled and ignored their approach. They stopped at the base of the dais and in unison knelt, heads bent. They waited for a count of five as he stared down the room, and then they rose, mounted the steps, and took their positions behind his shoulder. The hall was silent.

Solanji bit her knuckles, holding back the tears. It was so moving, the absent son returning home and claiming his seat, supported by his oathsworn. It hardened her resolve to find out what Kyrill was up to. That these people, these angels, could sit here and accuse Mav. It made her stomach twist.

When Ryvalin entered, the murmur of voices rose again, accentuated by gasps as the audience took in her uniform. Iridescent dragon scales covered her arms and chest, rising to a peak on either shoulder. A declaration of support from the citadel's dragon and her rider.

Silence fell as she strode up the hall, looking neither left or right, her eyes on Mav. Ignoring Serenia and Amaridin, she knelt before Mav and waited.

Solanji gasped as she heard Xylvin's voice in her mind. *"She won't rise until you give her permission. It is a sign of respect to the Archdeus General."*

Mav managed to disguise his surprise as he cleared his throat and said, "Rise, Dragonair Xylvin and her rider Ryvalin. It is my honour to accept your allegiance."

"Nicely said," Xylvin said, and Ryvalin's lips twitched as she rose and nodded at Mav, before moving to stand on the step below and to his left. Murmurs started immediately as she stood in the position of the captain of his Heavenly Host, if he had one.

His triumvirate of protectors. Solanji wished she were one of them, welcomed back into the fold and cherished as much as they cherished each other.

"Mav? Can you hear me?" Solanji asked.

Tensing, Mav's gaze rose to the flickering candles and sparkling crystal. *"Solanji? Are you alright?"*

"Yes, though I have little to report except that he still wants something from you. He believes he can step into your shoes."

"Well, he'll find out that is a little more difficult than he realises. Stay safe, my dear."

"And you."

Mav gazed into the distance, ignoring the gossiping angels.

His amber eyes flickered like the candle flames burning in the sconces, and Solanji wondered what he was thinking about.

"Count two, Demavrian. Which is it to be?" Serenia said without any preamble. Pale blue eyes, like chips of ice, were the only hard element of her perfect ensemble, and they glared at Mav as if he was some intruder spoiling her party.

Mav rose and descended the steps to the stand in the centre of the hall. "Second count. Defence against the accusation that I am behind my father's disappearance."

"Against the murder of Averdeus," Serenia corrected coldly as the galleries rustled with hushed discussions.

"Changing the rules, Serenia?" Mav's voice was derisive but he didn't wait for her answer. "Who accuses?" he demanded.

One of Archdeus Amaridin's scribes stood forward, and Mav froze in shock. He tried to hide it, but Solanji watched the blood recede from his already pale face as he licked his lips. His own brother accused him? Solanji's heart clenched as Mav fought to keep his composure. He was being assaulted from all directions.

His brother was accusing him? Mav's brain shut down and he struggled to breathe. Muffled words penetrated his confusion, and he held up his hand. "A moment," he rasped. Felather approached and squeezed his arm as he placed a glass of water in his hand, and Mav took a long sip before handing it back to Felather and giving his brother an incredulous glare. "My apologies, please continue."

"Count two, the murder of our dear lord, Averdeus who disappeared from Angelicus the same day as the accused, his son Demavrian. Not only did Demavrian have motive and ability, he also murdered Archangel Athenia—"

"Objection," Felather snapped into the silence. "That has not been proven nor is it the count in question."

"Sustained," Serenia said. "Continue."

Felather's jaw tightened but he stepped back and gestured for the man to continue.

"As I was saying, Demavrian was the last person to see his father alive—"

"Objection," Felather stood forward hand raised.

Serenia raised an eyebrow. "For what?"

"That is an assumption. It is possible someone else saw Veradeus after Demavrian left, when his father was very much alive."

"It was the middle of the night. No one else visited Veradeus. Demavrian was the last person to see him, continue."

Mav touched Felather's arm and shook his head. Lips tight, Felather stepped back.

"It is well known that Demavrian is a skilled soldier, he was the Archdeus General—"

"Objection! Archdeus Demavrian is still the Archdeus General." Felather glared at the scribe. "Only Veradeus has the power to remove that title."

Serenia sighed. "Scribe Felather! Are you going to interrupt every sentence Scribe Roland says?"

"If he keeps making unsubstantiated statements, then yes."

"They are not unsubstantiated, they are facts. Demavrian was the last person to see Veradeus. Demavrian was the last person to see Athenia alive, and then he ran. He left the citadel without explanation. They are all facts."

"Veradeus was alive when Demavrian left. Athenia had been attacked and left for dead when Demavrian found her on the steps. Demavrian did not leave the citadel voluntarily. They are all also facts," Felather replied.

"Enough." Serenia flicked her fingers. "You will remain

silent until Roland has laid out his evidence, then you may refute them. Roland, continue."

Felather hissed his breath out, and Mav grabbed his arm. "Don't," he murmured. "You are no good to me dismissed for contempt."

"Contempt? This is a farce."

"I know. But our turn to speak will come."

"Are you sure about that?" Felather grumbled, but he relaxed enough for Mav to release his arm.

The man droned on, but the only part Mav deciphered was that the charge was based on the fact that only an archdeus had the power to restrain and remove Averdeus.

Icy cold fingers of dread clawed at his core. If his father wasn't on this plane and it wasn't a challenge then it was either Amaridin or Serenia who had done it, because he hadn't forced his father to go anywhere. "Are you serious?" he asked, his gaze skimming the ranks and back to the dais to fall on Serenia and his brother. "I've never heard a more stupid accusation in my life. What is going on? Are you throwing seraphim's lives away?"

"Answer the charge," Serenia snapped.

Mav turned back to the seraphim and then glanced back at his brother. "Amaridin, did you not instruct your scribe to frame his accusations better? Did you not prepare him at all?"

Amaridin stiffened and slowly rose. "The accusations are as stated. Defend yourself or accept the consequences."

"But they are not even accusations. You say our father has been missing for as long as I have and is presumed dead? And I killed him?" He glared at his brother. "And what has been done to find him? If you are so concerned for his health, what steps have the citadel taken to reassure themselves that he is well?"

"We are not here to scour the citadel's actions; we are here for your defence," Serenia stated.

"Really? Well, I could say I have no idea. He was here on his throne the day the captain of your Heavenly Host knocked me out. Averdeus planned to visit the Isle of Clouds for a few years as it was Amaridin's turn to rule. When did you realise he was not relaxing but was missing?"

"Why don't you tell us?"

Mav shrugged, and paced again, only stopping when his knee twinged a warning. He had always thought better when he was moving. "If my father had died, the citadel would stop sparkling." He glanced around the tiers. "It's a pretty obvious sign. Has it? No? Then he must still be alive. I expect you didn't even have to check the isles as you knew he wasn't there. You know where he is. Don't you?" He glared at Serenia and then Amaridin. "I don't understand why you waste your time accusing me."

"We don't know where he is, that's why you are accused. He disappeared the same day you fled."

"Do you seriously think I woke up in that cell, walked through the locked door, and avoided the guards, all the way to my father's rooms, and then did my dastardly deed before escaping the citadel?"

Kyrill spoke up. "So it was you! You know where he is. He has proven his own guilt."

"Are you really that obtuse?" Mav demanded, disbelief curdling his veins.

Kyrill flushed.

"The citadel still breathes; its heartbeat drives the time-piece. My father lives, which you all know as Amaridin has not ascended to replace him. So I am unsure why you would spread that rumour unless you meant ill will."

"There is no proof that he lives," Kyrill shouted.

Mav arched his eyebrows and smiled. "My brother is proof enough. He does not sit on the golden throne."

"I don't sit on the throne in deference for father. Until we know, one way or the other," Amaridin said, his jaw so tight, he barely forced the words out.

Mav inhaled and gritted his teeth. "The citadel glitters, its heart beats, therefore my father lives. If he is not on this plane, then he accepted a challenge. That is the only explanation for his absence."

"There is no heartbeat," Amaridin's scribe declared. "You are making it up."

"Can you not hear the citadel's heartbeat?" Mav asked. Staring around the room, his eyes widened in surprise. "What none of you?" Reaching for Xylvin he asked, *"Can you hear it?"*

"The heartbeat hasn't been heard since you left."
"That's not possible!"
"They have forgotten their purpose. I told you the citadel needs you."

Mav exhaled, fear clearing his vision, bringing all his senses to alert. "What have you done? Have you cast aside the very heart of the citadel and banished it from daily life?" he asked. Spreading his arms wide, palms facing up, he closed his eyes.

"Stop him," Serenia screamed. "Stop him before he calls down some ungodly wrath upon us."

Mav ignored her. Concentrating on his own heartbeat, faint but steady, he reached for the citadel. Admittedly, he should have tried to reconnect to the citadel before now, but it hadn't been at the top of his list. He hadn't wanted to face another rejection, not after all the rejections he had faced the previous day.

Light and dark shadows swirled around him. Cool air wafted and metal clinked as the host entered the hall. The beat of his heart thumping in his chest echoed through his body, vibrated in his bones. Thump, thump, thump. It resonated through him. The air rippled and the beat grew louder; it was all he could hear. He opened his heart and mind and drifted. His blood hummed with anticipation, pulsing down his veins, thump, thump, thump.

Serenia's voice was muffled as she continued to shout.

Skin tingling, he folded into the citadel's embrace. Overwhelmed by the effusive welcome, tears leaked down his cheeks as unadulterated love consumed him. Love, compassion, concern, and relief swirled around him. Battering him in its enthusiasm, the citadel poured its fears into Mav, cut off for too long and eager to reconnect.

Images flashed past in quick succession, images of people he knew in dire distress, incarcerated and left to die. Mav shuddered at the image of Athenia's body lying on the steps, a grey-robed woman hovering over her with raised arm, a knife glinting in the candle light. A fledgling?

Crystals tinged off each other as the chandeliers vibrated, a chiming counterpoint as a single heartbeat resonated throughout the building. Candle flames wavered, making the chamber walls shimmer. Angels rose in shock, faces upturned as the citadel throbbed, louder and louder, and then the connection was gone, slipping through his fingers, leaving him bereft.

Desperately trying to reconnect, Mav didn't see the guard who barrelled him to the floor, nor the hilt of the sword that bashed into his temple, and he slid into the dark shadows surrounding him. Adriz's snarl of anger was the last thing he heard.

A single heartbeat resonated through the citadel. Angels covered their ears, but it didn't stop the vibrations pounding through them, realigning their heartbeats to the citadel, so that all beat in time. Xylvin's roar shook the building, and the echoes lessened, calmed, and then faded away. Archangels and seraphim collapsed back into their seats, dazed and shocked, their fledglings milling around them in confusion. Councillors and officials peered about them, unsure what had just happened.

Serenia rose, face pale, eyes wide and stared down at tableau in the middle of the hall. Her guards surrounded Mav's limp body and his furious oathsworn. The absence of the heartbeat was shocking in the silence. A silver ball swished through the glass tubes of the timepiece on the wall, a reminder of the endless symbol of life. Her gaze swept the chamber of shattered angels, all in degrees of distress as their brief connection with the citadel was cut off, many having connected for the first time.

Serenia cleared her throat. "Apologia is in recess for two days. Count two to be reviewed. Until a proclamation is made, Demavrian Deusson is to be restrained in a cell. Continuation of Apologia will be determined on our return."

"You have no right to detain him whilst Apologia is in session," Felather protested.

"It isn't in session, and until it is, restrain him," Serenia said and swept out of the hall.

15

DEMAVRIAN

Mav awoke with his head in Adriz's lap. Her fingers combed his hair, long soothing strokes, a counterpoint to the ache that pounded behind his eyes. Cold seeped into his body, the stone slabs beneath his legs hard and unyielding. Only one candle lit the dim space, illuminating Adriz's pinched face and not much else.

"Adriz is worried about you," Xylvin whispered, her voice a soft susurrus in the back of his mind.

"What happened?"

"Don't you remember?"

His heart beat in his chest, loudly, as if he had been recharged and operated at full strength. Though the rest of his body didn't agree. Deep within, his bones ached and a fleeting memory still hovered just out of his reach.

"Don't fight it."

Sighing, he closed his eyes. *"Why doesn't Serenia want me to reconnect to the citadel?"*

"I don't think she expected you to try, and for some reason she was afraid when you did. For that alone you need to reconnect, but you need a

SoulBreather to bind your soul into the citadel for it to work, and we no longer have one of those."

"That's why I was so affected when I landed in Eidolon. I not only lost my soul but the connection to the citadel as well?"

"I'm so sorry, Mav. I think when Athenia took your soul, she also severed the connection."

"It's not your fault."

"But Mav, you need to be bound to…"

"Mav?" Adriz's voice was hushed as she leaned over him.

"Yes?"

"Are you alright?"

"I'm not sure. Did I defend the count?"

"It is in review. Felather is trying to argue your case. What did you do, Mav?"

"What my brother should have done years ago."

"And what was that?"

"Recharge the citadel. The citadel guards us all but only if the angels within are in tune with it, in alignment with its objective to protect all. Amaridin and Serenia have allowed that principle to dwindle and die over the years. I bet some of those seraphim have never felt the citadel before. Never felt the true connection, been one with the purpose." Mav chuckled. "I just undid five decades worth of brainwashing. Someone is really going to be upset."

Adriz hissed her breath out. "It will make little difference if we can't get you out of here."

"Where are we?" Mav lifted his head and groaned.

"Lay still for a moment. Your body is still waking up. Serenia had you placed back under arrest; you are in the cells."

Mav eyed her. "And you are here because…?"

"I didn't trust them, and I can't protect you if I'm not with you."

Gritting his teeth, Mav sat up. A growing sense of anger

stirred in his gut. His brother had much to answer for. Why had he allowed the citadel to become dormant? He should have sustained his connection. Mav was sure one archdeus connecting would have been better than none. "I can't stay here. There will be questions. Those angels need explanations, otherwise this was all for nothing. Why would Amaridin and Serenia stifle the citadel? What are they afraid of?" Mav paused and rubbed his face. "Was that really only the second count? Feels like it should be more."

"Apologia is in recess due to your actions, and Serenia is using it as an excuse to detain you on the grounds that you are a threat to the citadel."

Huffing, Mav ran his fingers through his hair. "A threat? When I am the one who woke it? I would suggest she is the threat for trying to subdue it. What about Amaridin? How did he react?"

"All colour drained from his face; I thought he was going to puke. Didn't move a muscle. He was still sitting there with Eodan standing behind him when we carried you out."

"I am surprised Amaridin chose Eodan to stand in for his scribe as well as his captain. Not that Valerian was just a scribe; he was Amaridin's partner for life." Mav scowled up at Adriz. "I don't care what you say, Valerian would never have left Amaridin. They were devoted to each other. I don't believe Valerian would have left of his own free will. Did anyone go after him, check he was alright?"

Adriz stared at him. "Why would we? Amaridin said they had parted ways amicably."

Frowning, Mav rose to his feet and stretched, his back cracking as he rotated. "Anyone else in the chamber react?"

"Difficult to tell. Everyone looked stunned." Adriz's lips curved into a small smile. "I'd forgotten we used to hear the heartbeat. It felt good, but it's gone again."

"I couldn't hold on to the connection. The citadel was

trying to tell me something, but the images flashed by too fast for me to grasp them. It must have known we wouldn't connect for long. It seems I need a SoulBreather to bind me back into the citadel as well as return my soul. And I let her slip through my fingers."

"Shhh. Don't say that too loud."

"God, what a mess." Mav peered through the bars into the empty corridor. "Why are we locked up? We need to get out of here."

"They will kill you on sight if you try to escape. We have to wait for Apologia to be in session. They can't touch you unless you fail to defend a count."

Lips twisting, Mav spun and leaned back against the metal barrier. "Can't touch me? They seem to be doing a good job of preventing me from defending myself."

"Then use the time to plan your next move. Once Apologia is in session, if they ratify count two, which they will have to as the citadel's heart beating is proof that your father lives, you will have to defend count three immediately. Which count are you going to choose next?"

"Good question. But we've only proved my father lives, not where he is." Mav scowled. "The only reason he would not intervene in this mess is if he is beyond the plane and cannot return." Mav rubbed his chin. The only possibility he could think of for his father's absence was that someone had posed his father a puzzle to solve. Something that he hadn't seen an immediate solution to, and he had gone off to one of his retreats to study it. With the connection to the citadel being severed, he had been unable to return. "I told him he should stay here, but he was bored. There is always a risk when he travels beyond our world. Maybe he accepted a challenge, but I have no proof of that either, nor who may have challenged him. When I last spoke to him, he had no intention of challenging anyone."

"When *did* you last speak to him, Mav?"

Pushing himself off the bars, Mav limped over and sat beside her, back against the wall, legs straight out before him. He began repeating the conversation he'd with Xylvin.

"You should've told us," Adriz said, her gaze boring into him. She had been growing gradually stiffer as he spoke, but Mav had kept going and told her everything he knew about his father's plans.

"I had intended to. But events overtook me before I had the chance. When I woke up in Eidolon. I was confused, disoriented. It took a few years just to regain my balance, as it were. I do not recommend you ever have your connection to the citadel severed and your soul removed at the same time. It is the most debilitating sensation."

"But if you don't have a soul, then what do you have?"

Frowning, Mav contemplated the far wall. "Something that is equally acceptable to the citadel, I assume. It didn't reject me when we briefly connected; it was pleased. Though seeing as it has been absent for so long, maybe that doesn't mean anything anymore." He chuckled. "Me surviving that first day was a farce. The citadel hasn't been checking for souls for decades. It's funny how everyone assumed that it still was."

Adriz inspected his face and then nodded. "But it didn't reject you when you *did* connect, therefore whatever you have for a soul is acceptable. If we can identify what you have, how you got it, then it could be possible to redeem the soulless. Do you know how to help them?"

"I'm not sure how to give others what I have when I have no idea what I have become. Until I met Solanji, I didn't even know I had these shadows." Mav fidgeted. His bottom was getting cold. "We need to get her out of Kyrill's clutches. She is part of the answer, I'm sure of it. Not only can she help me understand the shadows, but I think she can help me remember who I saw in the hall. The citadel shared some memories, but I can't quite grasp them. They are at the tip of my fingertips, but it's like they are just out of reach, as if they weren't transferred over to me properly or something. I am positive I know who it was; I must be suppressing it for some reason. It's got to be someone I know, someone I like, otherwise why can't I remember?"

"Maybe don't try so hard. If the citadel gave them to you, they will come back to you," Adriz suggested.

"I don't have time to wait. We need to solve this now."

"So, assuming Felather ratifies your second count, you've got two left. Either flare your wings or prove you didn't kill Athenia. Which is it to be?"

Mav sighed his breath out and lowered his voice. "I haven't flared what's left, but I don't know how I'm supposed to prove I'm not Athenia's killer if I can't prove who is. I need Solanji to help me remember. We need to get her away from Kyrill. He's claimed her as a fledgling, so unless we can make him reject her, we can't touch her."

Adriz stiffened and her eyes widened. *"Oh my god. You can't flare your wings?"*

Mav shrugged. "I don't know."

"I didn't say that aloud. Has your mind speech returned?" Adriz whispered. *"You heard me? Can you hear anyone else? Can you reach Felather?"*

Mav sat up. "I thought it was Xylvin amplifying my ability. I don't know. Let me try. *Felather? Can you hear me?"*

There was a startled silence, and Mav grinned as Felather spoke. *"Mav? Thank goodness. Are you and Adriz alright?*

"As well as can be expected after a night in a cell. I need a bath." Mav sagged in relief as he realised his ability to speak to his oathsworn had returned. Maybe his brief connection to the citadel had helped. Solanji, as his oathsworn, should also be able to hear him. *"Solanji? Can you hear me?"*

There was no answer, and Mav grimaced. Seeing as it was the middle of the night, she must be asleep.

"Count two has been struck." Felather said. *"Golaran and I managed to convince Amaridin that the citadel's response confirmed your father is still alive. As there is still some question as to your father's whereabouts, Amaridin instructed his scribe to withdraw the count and the charge has been struck. Serenia was not happy. I must admit, it was touch and go for a while. I didn't think Amaridin was going to stand up to her, but he did. You'll have to defend count three next."*

"Well that's something, I suppose. Does that mean they will release us now?"

"I've spent the day arguing for it. Serenia has finally agreed as long as you stay in your rooms when Apologia is not in session. She wants to speak with you. I think she wants you to swear you'll be on your best behaviour and abide by her rules."

Adriz spluttered beside him. *"They are the ones who need to behave with honour."*

"You should be set free momentarily. I'll come down and meet you."

16

DEMAVRIAN

Archangel Serenia stood with her back to the room, gazing out of an arched window that was open to the afternoon sun. Straight-backed, her blonde hair plaited into loops currently hanging unadorned, she was as unyielding as the stone framing her. Golden sunshine bathed the room, and Mav relaxed into the warmth. He knew it wouldn't last long. Serenia's summons had been brief and to the point.

"Serenia," he said after the door had closed behind him.

She finally turned and inspected him. A slow perusal that would have had him squirming in his younger days, but he stood still and waited. Serenia had been his father's trusted advisor for centuries before Mav was even born. She had been a close friend of his mother's. She had stepped in to help when his father, overcome with grief at his wife's passing, had retreated from their world. It had only been within the last few centuries he had returned, but even so he had left the running of Angelicus in Serenia's capable hands.

Growing up under her steely gaze, Mav had learnt to survive her scrutiny and her interrogations. An elegant eyebrow rose as she met his eyes. "Where have you been, Demavrian?"

"You must know where I've been."

Serenia shook her head. "No, I don't. No message, no explanation. Just decades of silence."

"Did my father not share his plans with you?"

"No, he did not. Did he share them with you?" she snapped back. Her voice was so sharp it could draw blood.

"I do not believe my father would exclude you from his plans. You are his most trusted aide."

"Not as trusted as you, obviously. Please do tell what he told you and not me." There was bitter resentment in her voice, quickly hidden. Mav inhaled in sudden doubt.

"Did Amaridin not tell you?"

"Tell me what? He blathered on about a ridiculous idea of his to reunite Eidolon and Angelicus. I mean, how silly was that?"

"So silly you've never acted on it," Mav said.

"Of course not! Whoever heard such nonsense. I soon put Amaridin straight. But you. Running away. I never thought it of you, Demavrian."

Mav glared at her. "You had me arrested for Athenia's murder. Why?"

"You were caught, red-handed as they say."

Mav winced. "In no lifetime is that amusing or appropriate."

A muscle in Serenia's cheek twitched, and her shoulders dropped. "I suppose not, my apologies. I didn't mean to be facetious. But you ran without telling me why."

"There was nothing to tell."

"There is always something to tell. An explanation would be helpful."

"I found Athenia on the steps. She just kept urging me to leave her. I think she knew she was too far gone."

"Did she tell you who attacked her?"

"No, but I couldn't leave her, not to die on her own."

"What did she say?"

"Nothing, just to go."

"That is not helpful, Demavrian; didn't you ask her?"

"Of course I did, but she told me to go."

Serenia wrinkled her brow. "Told you to go? Or was she trying to say Golaran?"

Mav stared at her. "That is a bit of a leap. Why would you assume Golaran was involved?"

"You are saying it wasn't you, so it has to be someone else, someone powerful. If not you, then who? The only word Athenia said, according to you, was 'go'. It doesn't take much intelligence to make that connection. You mean to say you haven't?" Mav stiffened at the contempt in Serenia's voice.

"I don't believe Golaran would hurt a hair on Athenia's head."

"Someone did."

"Are you calling my judgement into question?"

"I wouldn't say it is particularly trustworthy at this time. You've been missing for a long time, and only now, when Amaridin has finally given up on you, you decide to return."

"You sound like you would have preferred I never came back."

"Oh, I wouldn't say that, but unless you start explaining, you may well end up back in that cell. You still have to prove your innocence."

"To whom? The citadel accepted me, allowed me entrance."

"To me. To Amaridin and the rest of our brethren. You cannot expect to be welcomed back when you are the only named suspect."

"Did you even bother to look for another culprit?" Mav

asked, walking across the room to join her at the window. Looking out over the golden city, for a moment his heart squeezed so tight at the familiar view that he thought he might pass out. He waited for Serenia's reply, and when it didn't come, he turned to face her. "Well? Were you so determined to believe it was me?"

"Of course we considered others, though you running didn't help. The host were more interested in searching for you."

"You mean Julius was."

"And he was the one to find you in the end."

"And yet he didn't bring me here. Why?"

"The case was given to the host to investigate. I trusted Julius to do what was needed."

Mav stared at her in disbelief. "You trusted the man who lost his beloved to be fair and just in his dealings with those he thought to be the cause?"

"But you said you were innocent. If you could prove that to Julius, then you could prove it to anyone."

Mav exhaled. "He never gave me the chance."

"The chance to do what?"

"Prove anything."

"Don't be ridiculous. Julius is a captain of the Heavenly Host. He has no choice but to uphold the law."

"You don't think his personal feelings may have clouded his judgement?"

"No."

At such a bald response, Mav bit his lip. "Do you know where I have been for the last year?"

"I haven't seen or heard from you in fifty years. Why would I know what has been happening in this last year?"

"Are you even interested?"

Serenia drew herself up. "May I remind you that you are

the one under suspicion. If you wish to be heard, I suggest you consider your words more carefully."

Mav almost laughed. "Or what? I have just spent decades in the depths of Eidolon and the last year in a personal hell and you want me to consider my words?"

"Demavrian." The way she said his name was a warning.

"What, Serenia? If you won't believe my word, then what will you believe?"

"I expect you to tell me who *did* murder Athenia."

"I don't know."

"That is not good enough."

"Why do you assume I would know? Don't you think I would have said before now?"

"I thought you were out there searching for proof. I didn't expect it to take so long, nor for you not to report back." She took a steadying breath. "Why did you run, Demavrian?"

"I didn't."

"You expect me to believe that, after all these years?"

"Yes, I expect you to believe me."

"I can't."

"Why not?"

"Because you were caught covered in Athenia's blood and kneeling over her lifeless body."

"I told you, I found her like that."

"Why didn't you go for help?"

"I couldn't leave her to die on her own."

"You might have saved her."

A pulse beat under Mav's eye, a tiny flutter like a bird's heartbeat. "She was dying."

"According to you. You don't know that." Serenia gripped his arm and stared at him. "How did you get out of the cell?"

"I don't know."

"How can you not know?"

"Julius knocked me out. When I awoke, I was in Eidolon."

Serenia pinched her lips. "I don't believe you."

"Why not?"

"It doesn't take five decades to return from Eidolon."

"Eidolon is bigger than you think."

"Mav!"

Slowly exhaling, Mav was relieved she wasn't using his full name anymore. "I'm sorry, Serenia, I truly don't know. When I awoke, I was in a bit of a mess. One of my dearest friends had just died in my arms, her lover had just accused me of killing her, and I was in the middle of nowhere. I didn't know where I was or what had happened and I had gained these." Mav pulled the vendetta stones out from under his shirt. Athenia's death wish, the red stone, and his father's blue stone a constant reminder of his loss and his failure to discover who had caused it.

Serenia covered her mouth with her hand as the blood drained from her face. Her hand shook as she touched the blue one. "Vendetta stones? Mav! What did you do?"

"I didn't do anything!"

"But, to have two?" Her voice was a mere whisper, her eyes wide, pupils distended as she looked at him in horror.

"Maybe you should sit down," Mav said and guided her to a nearby chair before she collapsed.

"Mav!"

"I swear, Serenia, I did not kill Athenia." He raised the red stone. "This was her death wish."

Serenia jerked her head up. "No, she wouldn't."

Mav blew his breath out. "It is a vendetta stone. I cannot lie."

"I thought you said she didn't say anything."

"She wanted me to avenge what had happened to her.

There is something …" Mav hesitated, "a shadow, as if it is hovering in my peripheral vision, just out of sight. I feel that I should know who it is." His voice strengthened. "It is a person I know."

"Who?" Serenia asked, leaning forward in her eagerness.

"I don't know. It's as if I need one more puzzle piece to click into place."

"Can you tell if it is male or female?"

"No, it's just a hazy shadow."

Serenia tapped her lip as she frowned in thought. Her gaze was drawn to his vendetta stones. "What is the blue one?"

"That I don't know."

"You must know."

Grimacing, Mav sat in the chair beside her, easing his leg straight. "Well, I don't."

"It seems even after all this time there is a lot you don't know. That will not be accepted by the council. You need to find some better answers." She fidgeted and then stood, paced away, and returned, looking down at him with her direct gaze. "Where is Averdeus?"

"Now, I did not expect that one to still be laid at my door," Mav said after a breathless moment, working to keep the waver out of his voice. That Serenia thought he could raise a hand against his own father made his blood run cold. That they even thought he was capable of such an act was frightening. Could they really believe he was a monster? One that could bring down a god?

"Where else would it be laid? Your attempt to trick the assembly into believing you woke the citadel and subsequently the connection to your father was in poor taste."

"Trick?" Mav stared at her as his gut churned. She knew the citadel was dormant, and she had not worked with Amaridin to wake it? Why not?

"Of course. Amaridin has confirmed the citadel is inert and that there is no sign of your father. What did you do to him?"

"Why did you not reconnect to the citadel?"

"We tried and failed. That's why we know your father is not here. Your parlour trick earlier only taunted those who have no opportunity to know what the full connection should be like. I forbid you to try again. You'll only do damage."

"How do you know I wouldn't have reconnected? The heartbeat was heard until your men knocked me out."

"That was not the citadel. That was you. You do more harm tempting them with something they can't have."

Sheer frustration tightened Mav's muscles. Did Serenia even hear the words she spouting? Did she really believe what she was saying? "How do you know they can't have it? You didn't let me finish."

"You will not attempt again. If you do, Apologia will be deemed proven and your life will be forfeit. I mean it, Demavrian. You are under Apologia and tainted. You try to distract from the bigger issue, as you do now. Where is Averdeus?"

Throat dry, Mav had difficulty swallowing. "You still think I know where my father is? I would tell you if I knew."

Serenia's face was unyielding. "The only reason you are free is because Amaridin wants to believe you. More fool him. Your father disappeared the day you were accused of murder. If you can commit one murder, why not two? No one has heard anything from either of you. Not a coincidence, don't you think? You have two days until the next council session. You had better have your arguments ready. I will not allow Amaridin to intervene for you again." She turned to stare out of the window, and Mav rose, knowing she wouldn't speak again, and returned to his rooms.

• • •

"They think I am guilty without hearing a word I have to say," Mav said, pacing back and forth across his room, his limp pronounced. "Serenia wouldn't even listen."

"Mav, sit down," Adriz said.

"She didn't even ask."

"Ask what?"

"What happened to me."

"If you don't stop pacing, your leg will collapse. You need to rest it, Mav. Now sit down." Adriz blocked his way, gripped his arms, and shook him. "Sit down."

Mav hesitated and then deflated. His aches and pains rushed back to plague him as he collapsed into the chair allowing Felather to prop his leg on a stool. He closed his eyes and leaned his head back. "If my own family doubt me, so will everyone else."

"Serenia supported you this morning," Felather pointed out.

"Apparently, Amaridin intervened, not Serenia."

"She has to seem impartial. Her situation can't be easy. On the one hand she has Julius calling for your head, on the other she has to keep the council happy."

"She jumped at the chance to blame Golaran," Mav said.

"Because she doesn't want it to be you, Mav," Adriz said.

Mav gritted his teeth. Her tone was soothing, as if he needed calming. "You wouldn't know it by her behaviour. Golaran is already an archangel. He had no motive to murder Athenia."

Felather's voice was accompanied by the clink of glasses and liquid being poured. "He is busy creating his projects in Eidolon. His rehabilitation plans. He has uses for the soulless. Maybe his plans have grown."

"I don't believe it. He has only ever done good."

"People change."

"Not angels."

"Even angels. Here, drink this."

Mav clamped his lips shut and tried to calm his racing thoughts. Opening his eyes, he took the glass Felather was offering. "What is it?"

"Just drink it, Mav." Felather stood over him, and Mav knocked the liquid back, grimacing at the acrid taste of the draught. For the millionth time he wracked his brain as to who could have harmed Athenia and why. There had been no one in the hall, no bloody footprints leading away, no voices. He knew it wasn't him, so it had to be someone else. The question was who? And where had his father gone? He fingered the blue vendetta stone; it had something to do with his father and Eidolon, but he didn't know what.

The draught started working, and he relaxed, his mind calming. He needed Solanji to help him remember.

"We need to get Solanji away from Kyrill. Do you have any idea how we can extract her from his clutches? Can you find out where he took her?"

Felather shrugged. "She'll be with his other fledglings, I expect. I'll find out. But Mav, unless he casts her out, you won't be able to help her."

17

SOLANJI

Solanji tossed and turned in her narrow cot as she waited for the other girls to stop talking and go to sleep. She had screwed up her courage to go and search Kyrill's office, and the longer she waited the more her nerve wavered. At last silence fell and one of the fledgling's gave a low snore. Rising, she skirted the beds and padded over to the door that led into Lormin's office, and after a quick glance around she crossed the room.

She inhaled sharply as she stubbed her toe on a chair leg. Clamping a hand over mouth, she suppressed her grunt of pain as she squirmed round to grip her toes. Tears sprang into her eyes, and it took a moment for her to calm down. Her little toe was now numb, and she thought she might have broken it. Opening the door to the corridor, she peered down the dark hallway.

Kyrill's rooms were at the other end of the corridor, and she scuttled down the hall, glad of the carpet beneath her bare feet. Before she could change her mind, she listened briefly and then opened the study door.

Moonlight lit the room, a room of dark shadows and

sharp edges. She searched through the papers on Kyrill's desk, lifting what looked like a letter, and tilted it towards the uncurtained window to read it more easily.

The writing was terrible. Solanji's heart beat rapidly as she glanced at the chamber door and then back to the letter. Something about the need for more supplies for a compound. She continued riffling the desk and then moved onto the drawers.

Silently easing the draw open, she pulled out a rolled-up piece of parchment, which she hurried to lay out on the desk. It was a map of Eidolon, with a scattering of squares with numbers annotated next to them.

After a moment, she rolled the parchment back up and slid it back into the drawer. Continuing to search, she froze, her heart rate ratcheting as she suddenly realised there was a soft yellow glow emanating from under the door to Kyrill's bed chamber. What was he doing up in the middle of night? Had she disturbed him?

Enough. Her heart couldn't cope with any more. She had to get out while she still could. A low conversation tempted her to creep back across the room, and she couldn't resist pressing her ear against the wood and straining to listen.

"What happened today?" Kyrill's exclamation was oddly muffled. "Years of work, lost."

"You underestimated him," a deeper voice replied. The accent was very similar to Kyrill's. Solanji didn't know if he had a brother or a relation in the citadel. "I told you not to let emotions interfere. You toyed with him, let him slip through your fingers, and now…now he is even more of a risk. Now he is a problem."

"What did he do?"

The deeper voice hardened. "He has gained confidence from winning two counts. I wanted him despairing, helpless, ready to fall. He has to give up, else I can't take him." A fist thumping the wall made Solanji start, and her heart raced. "I need him defeated, desperate."

Solanji swallowed, her throat suddenly dry. Ready to fall? Only Kaenera waits for the soulless to fall, and he wasn't supposed to leave the Oblivion Gate.

"What do we do now?" Kyrill asked.

"Target his oathsworn. He depends on them. Remove his supporters and he'll blame himself. Get rid of any loose ends. Nothing must lead back to us."

"We should have killed him when we had the chance." Kyrill's voice faded for a moment as if he had walked away. "We had him crushed. Taken everything from him. He was defeated! You said all we had to do was bring him back here and humiliate him in front of his peers. Make them sentence him to death. We had four chances, and he's already wriggled out of two of them."

"Then we can't waste the other two! It's the only way I can collect him. You can see what he's like. The way he draws people to him without even trying. We have to smash him, destroy his reputation, squash all his hope. He must go down, through the gate, and never rise again."

"I'll kill him properly this time."

"I've waited a long time for him. Nothing else can go wrong. Follow the plan."

Solanji frowned. The malice in the deep voice made her shiver. She rubbed her arm as the hairs rose. Whatever could Mav have done to earn such ire? She had pushed her luck already, it was time to leave, and she hurried over to the door and slid back out into the corridor.

Relief rushed through her, making her knees weak as she leaned against the study door and breathed deep. The silence of the citadel embraced her, soothing taut nerves. What a waste of time that had been.

The door suddenly gave way under her back and she fell

through the opening, sprawling on the floor in an ungainly heap. "Well, what do we have here?" Kyrill snarled.

Solanji caught a brief glimpse of swirling shadows, black as the deepest night, and then she was being dragged up by her hair. "A loose end, and we know just what to do with loose ends." He struck her face, open-handed, and she sucked in her breath against the shock. Clawing at him, her nails scraped his skin as she tried to fend him off, but he hit her again, letting her fall to the floor with the force of his blow, dazed and disoriented. His ring had caught her cheek, ripping the flesh, and warm blood oozed down her stinging face.

"Don't get blood on my carpet." Kyrill kicked her in the ribs, shoving her across the floor until she hit the wall. Solanji tried to breathe. Carefully. Pain spiked in her side, and she curled her fingers until her nails bit into her palm. Breath hissed out as Kyrill jerked her up towards his face. Solanji dangled in his grip, her heart stuttering, chest constricting as Kyrill narrowed his eyes. Flashes of vivid red streaked through his golden soulmist, roiling as angrily as his thoughts. He wanted her out of the way. She was a loose end. "You think you can spy on me? I own you. I can do what I like to you. Didn't you learn that lesson in the mountain?"

Solanji slid her palm down her thigh, fumbling for the dagger concealed under her shift.

Kyrill laughed, harsh and cold. "Your family are all dead and now you can join them. I will kill you slowly so you feel every moment of pain, and then," his voice dropped, "Kaenera will embrace you, seeing as you are so eager to see him. Did you think we didn't know how you helped Demavrian?"

Solanji's breath hitched as her mind spiralled into shock. Extending her soul fingers, she skimmed his thoughts. She had little to lose now. He knew about her and Mav? She had failed her family? There were no images of her family in his thoughts, though, only glimpses of Mav hanging limp and bloodied in the torture chamber under the mountain and a sense of complete and utter exultation. The man was revelling in the memories, gloating even, at his power over Demavrian, and yet he had never managed to defeat him. Images of dreary compounds and downtrodden people were interspersed with flashes of intense satisfaction at the control he had over others. He held their lives in his hands and he loved it.

Kyrill dragged his fingernail down her skin. "Such a pretty throat. Shame it only speaks false and betrays those it loves. I knew you weren't trustworthy. I should have just killed you."

Gritting her teeth, Solanji eased her dagger out of its sheath. If she could take him with her, she would at least have achieved some retribution for her family. Engulfing pain almost incapacitated her, burning through her veins and spiking in her temples, whiting out her vision.

"Mav? My love? I'm so sorry." She threw out the desperate thought.

Embracing the memories of her elder brother, she thrust with all her strength, twisting her blade as her brother had instructed. The dagger sank in deep and Kyrill grunted. She hit something solid, jarring her wrist. *"I made a mistake. Mav! Please. Can you hear me? Kyrill's working with Kaenera. He's going to kill me. Help me!"*

Kyrill hissed his breath out and gripped her wrist with one hand and her throat with other. A spike of pure agony shot through her arm as he twisted her wrist and disarmed her. Her gasp was cut off as Kyrill tightened his grip around her neck and rammed her against the wall.

She extended her soul fingers, grabbing his soulmist, and

the dragon slithered down her arm, formed in the air between them, and began to suck it in, and then, she choked and spat it back out again. She dissolved into a fine mist and disappeared.

"You think you could ever harm one such as me? You are nothing but vermin." Spittle sprayed her cheek, and her sight blurred as Kyrill squeezed tighter and tighter. Hissing filled her ears as she struggled in his grip, her arms were getting heavier, she couldn't release his hold, black spots marred her vision, expanding as they spread and connected together. She was drifting. Why was she struggling? She couldn't remember. Her hands dropped, and he threw her limp body to the floor.

From a long distance away, she heard the seraphim speak. "Get rid of the whore. It's not needed any more." And she slid into the consuming darkness and knew no more.

18

KERRIS, EIDOLON

It took two days for Kerris to reach the crossroads. Leaning over the wooden rail of the bridge which stretched over the wide river, he stared at the dark, slow-moving water as it flowed south into the depths of Eidolon, and he wondered if it would lead to his friends.

He had followed the wagon's tracks which had joined the main road leading north to the mountains or south towards the crossroads and then who knew where. The muddy wagon tracks had turned south, so Kerris had followed, seeing as it was the same direction that led to the divide.

He had lost the trail amongst the other carts and cattle hooves that had churned up the mud, but he assumed they had continued south. He was torn, desperate to follow them, but he knew he wouldn't be able to rescue them on his own. He needed help, and that meant crossing the divide and finding Mav's contact in the city of Puronia.

Gripping the railing, he considered his options. He wouldn't be able to cross the divide on his own. Without papers, he needed a patron of some sort. Someone who would be returning the same day, otherwise, he would be stuck in Puronia and he would die there. He shivered as a flash of cold sped down his spine. Could he risk it? Should he?

He rested his face on his hands and squeezed his eyes shut. He could do this. For his friends, he *would* do this. Slowly, he became aware of raised voices and the bleating of many sheep. Straightening, he glanced around and frowned at the woolly bundles aimlessly blocking the bridge.

A short, stocky man dressed in drab robes waved his crook at a much taller man. He jutted his face forward, his small goatee beard prominent, and spat something, and the taller man jerked back and then shook his fist in the air. The voices became shriller and the sheep continued to mingle, caging in Kerris and other travellers trying to cross.

Kerris grinned and then hopped up onto the bridge wall and ran across the narrow railing, oblivious of the horrified stares of the trapped people, one of whom peered over the edge at the slow-moving water and visibly shuddered.

Jumping off the wall, he whistled loudly, and spreading his arms, herded the sheep across the bridge. "Where do you want them?" he yelled over the bleating, and the short man broke off from his argument and pointed to the corrals opposite the tent market lining the crossroads.

"B3," he replied, and Kerris gave him a thumbs up, and chivying the sheep in the direction the man had indicated, he chased them down the street.

Kerris caught the last stubborn stray and bundled it into the corral as the shepherd arrived. The man observed him for a moment. His face was creased with many lines, his hair grey and straggly, but his black eyes were bright. "You looking for work?"

"Depends," Kerris replied. "I need to cross over to Puronia and return within a day. Does your business take you there?"

The man pursed his lips. "It didn't. I hadn't intended on going to Puronia as I can't take the flock on my own." He inspected Kerris. "But I'll consider delivering my sheep to Puronia if an offer comes in and you're available. Soulless, huh? Where will I find you?"

"Unless you'll pay for a meal, right here, I suppose."

The man's sharp eyes flitted around the other pens. He rummaged in his pocket and produced a coin. "Go get something to eat, you'll need it if you're coming with me. Let me see who's interested. If I haven't come and found you by the time you've finished your food, return here. Ask for Avery. We'll be going tonight, if we go at all." He flipped the coin at Kerris.

Catching the coin, Kerris nodded. He would wait and see if the job came through. If not, at least he'd got a meal out of it and he could check out who else was intending to cross. As the day progressed, corrals slowly filled with other livestock and men and women bickered as if their lives depended on it, and for many, it probably did.

The inn took up all of the north corner of the crossroads, a large rambling building which was the only permanent structure in the constant tide of humans and animals that passed through.

"If you haven't got the money, you don't come in," a stern voice preceded the heavy hand that grabbed Kerris' shoulder. Kerris quickly displayed his coin, and the hand let go of him. "Hmrph," the man snorted and then peered a little closer. "That will only get you a bowl of the stew."

"Stew, bread, and a mug of water," Kerris replied.

"Nothing else, and you leave once you've finished."

"Fair enough." Kerris handed over his coin and found a small table in a shadowed corner. When the food arrived, he inhaled the rising steam and his mouth watered. He hadn't eaten properly since the day before he went to the market.

Three days of borderline starving made his stomach ache and his head a little floaty. So he sat quietly in the corner and tried to eat his stew as slowly as possible, revelling in the heat created by so many bodies and the relief of warm food in his belly.

He looked up in surprise as another dish replaced his empty one. A plump woman smiled down at him. "A slice of my berry pie. On the house." She winked and wended her way through the tables. Kerris dug in before anyone could take it away.

Sighing, he patted his very full stomach. He wasn't sure he could move. A pleasant sense of satisfaction suffused him as he observed the room. It was getting busier as farmers concluded their business. He would be turfed out soon, but he lingered, pretending he was part of the community for just a moment longer.

Memories surfaced of sunny fields and glossy livestock. The lush smell of sun-warmed grass and his older brother's happy face as they mock sparred. He forced the memory away and stood up. They were best forgotten.

Wending his way back towards the pen, the gloom thickened as the clouds darkened. A chill wind whipped the canvas tents causing them to creak and groan, and he hurried past.

An unacknowledged fear eased as he saw the sheep still penned. It had felt a little too easy. With everything that had happened, he'd expected to have trouble trying to cross the divide. He crossed his fingers, hoping against hope that the man had sold his sheep to someone in Puronia.

"Ah, well timed. I was about to come and find you. Five coppers and passage to and from Puronia for your assistance to get this flock to the abattoir in the south of the city. You'll have at least six turns in the city before we need to return. Suit you?"

"Yes," Kerris replied, and then he wondered if he should have negotiated the price. The shepherd needed his help; he might have paid a bit more. But really, he wasn't doing it for the money, he just needed a legitimate excuse to cross.

"Excellent. Let's get going then."

Slave camp, Eidolon

Shandra flinched as the door slammed shut. Nothing in this place was quiet. Voices were loud and abrasive, commands were yelled, whips cracked and fists flew. Questions were never asked, only assumptions made with the worst possible outcome for the unfortunate soulless cowering in the mud.

Slamming doors were the least of her worries, but it was the one aggravation out of everything that set her on edge. The one thing she couldn't ignore with her usual insolent glare. Muntra had warned her to tone it down, but she couldn't. She was the only person who stood between the girls and *them*. If she wasn't strong, if she wasn't prepared to fight then who would?

The boys were all in a different barracks with their own issues to face. Wishing for a saviour to descend from the skies was not going stop those filthy, conniving slavers from grabbing her kids.

Sure that no one was coming for them, Shandra returned to shaving the end of a wooden splinter into a point and smoothing the edges so she could grip it. Kiara knelt beside her, sorting through the various items she had managed to dismantle or pilfer.

"Look, what about this? You could slot it in the end like an arrowhead." Displaying a thin piece of metal in her hand, Kiara tilted her hand back and forth to show the sharp edge.

"What would we fix it with? We have no string."

"I got some of that paste they used to…to shut that man's mouth."

Shandra glanced at the young girl beside her. She had thought none of the youngsters had been in the yard that day. The images still haunted her as the guards had made an example of a slave who had dared to speak out. He wouldn't speak again or breathe.

Ragged and begrimed, Kiara looked about eight years old, but she was one of the older children Shandra had tried to protect, on the cusp of becoming a teen. Fortunately, her slight build made her look more like a boy and had kept leering eyes off her—so far.

Greasy hair hung in disgusting clumps around her face, and Shandra knew Kiara deliberately smeared herself with grease to help disguise the delicate features hidden under all the grime. That she knew enough to hide herself without being told to made Shandra want to spit and curse.

Shandra deliberately kept herself cleaner, not only to draw attention away from the others, but also to make them all look different. If they were all greasy lumps, the overseer would get suspicious.

"Be careful with that stuff. You don't want to stick your fingers together. Keep it away from the younger kids. And anyway, where did you get it from?"

"Better you don't know. This would be easier for a littley to use. Easier for them to slash than stab. Give them time to get away."

Dear lord above, see what you've reduced us to? Out loud, Shandra said, "You should get some sleep. Aren't you on early shift?" and stretched her aching back out. She had spent the day standing at a machine taller than her, feeding in lumps of rock that came out ground into a powder. Shandra had no idea what it was used for, but she had to fill so many sacks a day otherwise they docked her pay. Some of the smaller kids had to push the wheel to rotate the grinding stone. They all choked on the fine dust constantly hanging in the air and coating every surface it touched.

Keeping an eye on some of the smaller children as well as her own workload was beginning to wear her down; the younger kids never made quota and never got their full food ration. Even sharing her food didn't put any meat on their bones, and they were all already listless and slow after just a few days.

One blow from the overseer would break them, and she thought he knew it too, because he always blamed her for any lapses. She had the welts and bruises to prove it. But she never flinched; she just stared him in the eye until he grunted and moved off again.

"I said I'd make one for Bailey. He is too pretty for his own good. Even smeared in grease they can't take their eyes off him. I'm worried, Shandra. I don't think he's gonna last. If they take him…"

Shandra gripped her arm. "Don't. Don't say it. If you say it, it'll happen."

Eyes wide, Kiara nodded. "So I'm making him a blade."

"You know if they catch him with it, it'll be worse for him? And could get you into trouble too."

"I don't care. We look after each other." A mulish expression spread over Kiara's face as she worked. After a moment she said, "I was thinking of sabotaging the railing system."

Exhaling, Shandra cast a worried glance at her. "Won't they be suspicious?"

"Nah, they know it's about to collapse; they're waiting for it to fail."

"I'd rather you didn't. You are taking too many risks."

"What else is there to do? We can't sit around and do nothing. It's only going to get worse. We have to plan a way to escape. None of us will survive here. Do we just wait for the littleys to die one by one?"

"Kerris will find Mav, and he'll find us."

Kiara huffed her breath out. "You don't know if Kerris is even alive, let alone whether he will find Mav. He would have to cross the divide, and you know none of us have been near that place. He would have no idea how to get there or who to speak to."

"He's our only hope," Shandra admitted, her voice almost a whisper.

"If I can disrupt the mine, what little organisation they have will disintegrate. It will be easier for us to search for a way out. We have to get out of here, Shandra, before it's too late."

Bending her head, Shandra squeezed her eyes shut. "Wait. Just another day. Let me see if Muntra has any ideas."

A soft snort was her only response, but Kiara scooped up her treasures and disappeared into the gloom of the girl's sleeping area.

19

DEMAVRIAN, CITADEL

av startled awake, gasping against the constriction in his chest. A shrill scream lingered in his ears, cut off abruptly. Solanji's voice calling for him. A bad dream? Feeling unsettled, he got out of bed and went to pour a glass of water. Sipping his drink, he tried to calm his fluttering pulse.

"Solanji?" He threw her name out into the dark night on a whim, but nothing came back.

Heart thumping, he quickly dressed. Something wasn't right. Grabbing his sword and sliding his knives into his belt, he flung open the door and paused on the threshold of his empty rooms. Adriz and Felather would be asleep, knowing he was safe in his chambers.

His breath stuttered as a swirl of golden mist formed into a small glowing dragon and hovered in the air before him. The dragon flew towards the door, and as it glanced back at him, Mav followed it. The SoulBreather's familiar had come to find him. Solanji must be in dire trouble.

He hurried out of his study and down the adjoining corridor and banged on Adriz's door, moving on to Felather's and doing the same. The dragon hissed in agitation beside him. "We need more help," he murmured as the little creature settled on his shoulder and nipped his ear.

"Did you hear her?" he asked as Adriz rushed out her door, already dressed with a sword in her hand.

Adriz stared at him, took a steadying breath, and said, "Hear who?"

"Solanji. She called for help. But I can't reach her."

"You heard Solanji call you for help? That's not possible, unless…" Adriz hesitated, her eyes widening. "You didn't," she breathed.

"We did. Thank my dear father, we did. We exchanged oaths, and Kyrill won't know she's immortal. He'll just try and kill her the usual way."

"I doubt she'll enjoy that any better," Felather muttered as he joined them, buttoning up his shirt.

"Why didn't you tell us she's your oathsworn?" Adriz growled.

"You let her be dragged off by Kyrill when he has no claim?" Felather interrupted her, shock darkening his face.

"Solanji suggested it. A way to get someone on the inside."

"You should have said no," Adriz hissed as she led the way towards Kyrill's rooms. "And you should have told us. You promised you wouldn't keep secrets from us."

"We weren't ready to share the news." Mav shrugged. "It felt special, ours. I didn't want you treating her any different in case anyone noticed."

"We know how to conceal knowledge, Mav. You deliberately put your, what is she? You said 'we'. Did you both swear to each other?" Felather inhaled sharply. "You allowed your wife to go into danger, alone?"

"I know. You don't have to beat me over the head with it," Mav bit out in response. His gut was already churning with guilt, he didn't need Felather piling more on. The dragon hissed in his ear as he rushed through the corridors, not caring if anyone saw him, until Adriz jerked him to a stop.

"Think, Mav. You can't just storm into Kyrill's rooms and accuse him of attacking Solanji. We need to be more discreet." She glanced around them. "And you are not supposed to be roaming the citadel. Let me go and check; you and Felather keep out of sight."

Chewing his finger, which Adriz slapped away from his mouth, Mav heaved a sigh. The dragon darted down a side a corridor, returned, and hissed again. "Alright, I'm coming." Mav trailed after the glowing creature, glancing back over his shoulder at Adriz as she paused outside Kyrill's door and braced her shoulders.

Felather drifted down the passage after him, his head cocked. "Someone else is out and about tonight," he breathed as he joined Mav in a darkened alcove. Drawing the velvet curtain around them, Mav listened. Disgruntled voices and heavy footsteps lingered in the empty corridors. The dragon hooked a claw in his shirt and pulled on it. "We need to follow them," Mav said, and they slipped out from behind the curtain and hurried after the little familiar as the echo of Adriz rapping on Kyrill's door disturbed the thick silence of the night.

"How do you know where to go?" Felather huffed as he tried to keep up with him.

Mav threw a glance over his shoulder. "The dragon."

"What dragon?"

"Solanji's."

"Solanji has a dragon?"

"The SoulBreather's dragon."

"Wait, what? You mean Athenia had one too?"

"The same one."

"Since when has Solanji had this dragon? I thought you were going to tell us everything?"

Mav smiled at the whine in Felather's voice. "I thought you knew. The tattoo was pretty obvious."

"What tattoo?"

"You can't see the tattoo?"

"Obviously not."

"It covers her forearm. And it's currently a rather petulant, glowing ball of gold leading the way."

"Well, I'm glad you can see it, otherwise, we'd never find her. Why is it upset?"

"You're not running fast enough."

"Pshht! I'm keeping up with you! Where are they taking her?"

"The midden, if I'm not mistaken."

Felather cursed and hurried after him.

Mav halted at the end of the corridor outside the entry to the citadel's midden and watched in molten fury as Kyrill's men turned away from the gaping maw that led to an enormous pit of refuse and waste.

If they had dumped his wife in that stinking cesspit, he would hunt them down and make them pay. How dare they. He vibrated with burning anger, ready to kill the next person he saw as he rushed to the entrance. The stench was vomitworthy. A bit like the blue cheese he hated, he thought, trying not to heave.

"She must be unconscious," Felather said as he peered into the darkness, listening for any movement.

"That would be for the best," Mav agreed. How the hell were they supposed to get her out of there? At least there could be no argument about Kyrill rejecting her. A slither of muck shifting drew his head around. And again, a soft mumble. The tiny dragon darted across the midden and hovered, casting a yellow glow. Moving without realising it, he shinnied down the iron loops in the wall.

"Mav, wait! Let me go." Felather's voice was urgent above him.

"You can't see the dragon," he growled, slogging through the soggy mess of discarded vegetables, slop, and worse. "Solanji?" he called as his boots sunk into the muck. Making a mental note to charge Kyrill for a new pair of boots, he waded through the putrid waste, pushing away untold horrors. The stink made him retch, though fortunately he had nothing in his stomach to add to it. He hadn't eaten much; he hadn't felt like it after the sheer petty ministrations of the day before.

Another mumble. The voice was muttering a constant stream of words, none of which made any sense. He battled his way across to her. She was half submerged in a sea of muck, a tangle of limbs flailing as if she was drowning. When he grabbed her arm, she convulsed and groaned in pain. "All lost. I'm sorry, so sorry. I failed you."

"What? Solanji? Where are you hurt?"

"Demavrian? I called, but you didn't hear me. I'm sorry I let you down. I didn't mean to, don't hate me," her words dribbled off into mere sounds.

Mav pushed away the muck, smoothing it off her face, hissing at the metallic smell of blood mingling with riper scents. "Dearest one, you have never, nor will you ever, let me down." He scooped her up, and her bone-deep moan of pain shuddered through him. She had injuries aplenty. Staggering back towards the metal ladder, he cursed as each step caused her more pain. Solanji was delirious now, a constant stream of nonsense, interspersed with names, said with such shocking loss that he knew they must be dead.

"Demavrian's got you now. You're safe. Please forgive me

for not protecting you," he whispered, repeating it over and over in her ear.

He reached the ladder and took a deeper breath. "Solanji, this is going to hurt. I am so sorry."

"I deserve everything I get," she said clearly and then dropped back into nonsense.

He peered upward and then shifted her over his shoulder. Balancing her, he grabbed a rung with his other hand and began the slow and painful climb to the top. Stopping halfway, he gasped for breath. Her deadweight was heavier than he'd thought. His arms and shoulders were shrieking with pain; he would pay for this later.

"Felather?"

"I'm here, just a little further."

Gritting his teeth, he grasped the next rung and moved up a step. He grabbed the next one, one more step. Slowly working his way up the ladder. He reached the top and had a momentary panic. How was he supposed to get her over the lip?

Felather hung over the edge and pulled Solanji out of the midden.

Mav hauled himself over the side and scrambled over to Solanji. "Is she alright?" he gasped as he tried to control the trembling in his limbs.

"Ribs, I think," Felather said as he gently ran his hands over Solanji's limp body.

"You stink," Sero said, as he appeared out of the gloom and hovered above them.

"Sero, now is not the time," Mav replied as he clasped Solanji's hand. The dragon had returned to her arm and glistened in the dim light. He smoothed her matted hair off her bruised face. "I'll kill him," he growled.

"I'll help you," Sero offered as he peered at Solanji.

"You don't know who he wants to kill," Felather muttered

as he scooped Solanji up and marched off before Mav could protest.

"Whoever did that to Solanji deserves a beating, if not worse," Sero replied.

"Cherubs are not so sweet and innocent these days, huh?" Mav muttered.

"Oh please. Don't be so trite." Sero flitted off down the passage ahead of them.

When they arrived back at Mav's rooms, the bath was already running. Sero had been before them and flitted off. "Use the shower," Adriz commanded Mav as she directed Felather to the bathing room.

"What happened to you?" Felather gasped as he took in her reddening eye and split lip.

Adriz's smile was feral. "Kyrill might be making a complaint."

"I thought you said I had to be discreet?" Mav asked mildly as he stripped of his stinking boots and then his clothes. He dived in the shower, rinsed off, and was back out before Adriz had finished peeling off Solanji's clothes. Wrapping himself in a towel, he helped Adriz gently lower Solanji's limp body into the bath.

"Kyrill is an insolent moron and deserved everything he got," Adriz said with a smug smile.

"Mind her ribs, her whole right side is bruised. I'll hold her while you rinse the worst off her. Don't want her drowning," Mav murmured. "Felather, use the shower. You're stinking up the room."

"I am not! It's your clothes," Felather protested, though he did shed his soiled clothes and entered the shower.

Mav cradled Solanji's shoulders as Adriz rinsed her down and then washed her hair.

"What did Kyrill say?" he asked.

Adriz's lips tightened. "It's not worth repeating. That man has an ego the size of Eidolon. He acts as if he is an archdeus, not you."

"That's his goal, I think."

"Well, he won't achieve it if I have anything to say about it, and he is well aware of my opinion of him."

Mav stared at her. "Was that wise? You make yourself a target."

"We're already targets. We support you." Adriz held up her hand, soap suds dripping off her fingers. "And don't say anything. It's not your fault. It's our choice. Family sticks together." She gently smoothed a strand of wet hair off Solanji's swollen face. "We're all in this, as your wife will tell you when she wakes up." Adriz lifted Solanji into Mav's towel-draped arms and wrapped the material around her body. "You chose well," she said, lightly kissing Mav on his cheek, and before he could respond, she turned her attention to Felather in the shower. "You alright?" she asked as he squawked and told her to go away. "I'm already wet, so stop being such a baby."

Mav grinned, as he heard her clucking over him like a mother hen, demanding to see his shoulders and offering to massage them. The door closed behind her, and he could imagine they might be a while, his sweet cherubim and his gentle scribe.

Carrying Solanji into his bedroom, he laid her on his bed. Smoothing her damp hair away from her forehead, he scowled at the vicious cut and the bruising that marred her beautiful face. He gently rubbed her down, drying off the worst, and then smoothed the salve that treated all ills over the bruising on her body and the cut on her face before wrapping the blanket tightly around her. After dressing in clean clothes, he settled himself on the bed and leaned against the headboard as he cradled her head and shoulders in his lap, as she had once done for him.

A turn passed before Solanji stirred in his arms and groaned. A deep, instinctive groan which made him cringe as he remembered the feeling. He held her a little more firmly. "You're safe now. I've got you. You're a little banged up, but nothing that time won't heal." He winced at the understatement. He'd had plenty of time to inspect her injuries, and his wrath bubbled just under the surface.

Her long lashes fluttered on her cheeks and then lifted, and her inky black eyes were gazing at him. One was bloodshot and already discoloured with the dark bruising that would cover half her face. He smiled at her. "Hey."

She stiffened and moaned.

"Relax. You're safe now. Try not to move too much. Your ribs are banged up a bit."

She licked her lips, and he reached for the glass of water he'd had the forethought to pour. "Here, drink." She swallowed eagerly. "And this," he murmured, reaching for a second glass of clear liquid. "It will help with the pain."

Her hand wormed its way out of the blanket and grabbed his damp shirt. "Mav? Why are you here?"

He grinned and kissed her nose. "Well, you see, this is my bed. So, I have every right to be here."

Her eyes began to glaze, and her lashes fluttered. "I need to tell you something."

"It can wait, you need to rest."

"No, s'about Kyrill. He's got a plan t'take you out." Her lashes closed and she was asleep.

"Shit," he said as he laid her on his bed. He stared at her and his heart clenched. That bastard would pay for hurting her.

He walked into the outer chamber. His oathsworn were nowhere to be seen, though they had vacated the bathroom.

Which bit of 'they didn't have much time', did neither of them understand? They'd had fifty years to roll about. He took a deep breath and slowly exhaled. Patience. There was a time for everything, or so it seemed.

He moved around his rooms, letting his mind drift as he tidied up, touching familiar items until he was finally seated behind his desk with a pen in his hand. Making a note of the angels, and the liaisons he could remember, he mapped them to the list of Kyrill's known associates that Felather had provided. He was interrupted by the arrival of Felather, no longer smelling, and in clean clothes. His gaze roamed the room and avoided Mav. He sidled up beside Mav and peered over his shoulder.

"What are you doing?"

"Kyrill's friends."

"Hold up. Palent, Mort, and Groller? Solanji said those names. I thought it was just nonsense."

Mav circled them. "Unfortunately, I dosed her with the sedative you gave me before she had a chance to tell me. That's fast-working stuff. She managed to say, 'Kyrill has a plan to take you out,' and she was asleep."

"Shit," Felather said, and Mav grimaced in agreement.

"See anyone else you remember her saying?" He twisted the paper round so that Felather could read it more easily.

"No, but those two, Laener and Dorne, aren't they the ones supporting that new initiative to redirect the soulless?"

"I don't know, you tell me," Mav replied, a slight edge to his voice.

Felather winced, and then clearly reordering his thoughts, he started reeling off the latest notices. Mav leaned back in his chair and listened, parsing the information for something that resonated.

"There are a lot of unfamiliar names in the seraphim.

Since when has there been a recruitment drive?" Mav asked, staring across the room.

"You're right, I hadn't noticed. It's been a slow trickle, but when you take them all at once, there's enough to swing a vote."

"So, that is one thread. The other is what initiatives are they are supporting."

"They want the soulless to man the new production sites in Eidolon. Make some use of them, I suppose."

"It is not their place to use them," Mav said. "They seem very eager to create more soulless. What are they producing in those sites?"

Felather rubbed his chin. "I don't actually know. I'll look into it."

"Do that," Mav said. He frowned at his list and then drew an arrow and added a question mark. "We need to find out what they are up to. My father wanted to reunite Angelicus and Eidolon, and I believe he is right. We have to remove the divide and restore some equality between our people. Whether you have a soul or not should not decide how you live. And removing a soul should not be a legal punishment, it should be a crime. It is inhumane."

Felather blew his breath out. "Not all would agree with you. That could be a motive for removing Averdeus. It stopped his plan in his tracks, didn't it? Amaridin and Serenia have not suggested any motion like that."

Mav considered for a moment. "And Athenia and I were just collateral damage? I don't think so. It is all too convenient."

"If anyone is behind this, it's got to be Kyrill, hasn't it? If he intends to replace you?"

"What makes you think a seraphim has the power to coordinate this?"

Felather stilled. "Serenia would never…Golaran? You think Golaran is behind this?"

"Maybe he's grown used to his new position and doesn't want to give it up," Mav suggested.

"Using Kyrill is too obvious though. His own seraphim? It would lead you straight back to him." Felather rubbed his eyes. "Golaran has a few charity projects running in Eidolon, but if anyone, it's Amaridin who's been most interested in what's happening; he's had Eodan sending his host into the depths of Eidolon for years."

"Amaridin knew our father's plan. I expect he was still trying to build relations with the border folk."

"Or he was looking for you," Felather said.

"Probably." Mav heaved a sigh and pushed the pad away.

"Kyrill's been jealous of you for years. Once it was amusing, but now…" Felather hesitated. "He wants you dead, Mav."

"How can he be jealous of me when I wasn't even here?"

"He wants your seat."

"He can't kill me, but he can weaken me," Mav mused. "Maybe he thinks he's weakened me enough to challenge me outright. He is brash enough. I suppose seeing me powerless and vulnerable, he thinks it will be easy to remove me."

"Well, at least he knows it won't be *that* easy after yesterday."

"But now, I'm on a clock to prove my innocence."

"What are we going to do about that, Mav? Which count are you intending to defend next?"

"I'm not sure," Mav said, frowning in thought. Was Eidolon the new battleground? Were the angels hoping for a piece of that unclaimed land? Mav straightened. Could that be possible?

"You need to be bound to the citadel to fight this fight."

Solanji's slurred voice came from the doorway of his bedchamber, and Mav struggled to his feet.

"What are you doing up? You should be resting," he said as he crossed the room to her.

Solanji cupped his cheek, her eyes gleaming with tears. "Mav! I'm so sorry. I didn't find out anything that would prove…"

"Hush, tell me later. We don't need to do this now."

"I do." Solanji scowled at him. "I heard him talking to someone. I think it might have been Kaenera. He wants to smash you to pieces, defeat you so you would fall into his arms. The only person waiting for a soulless is Kaenera. He doesn't just want to kill you; he wants to destroy you."

"Solanji," Mav whispered her name, and she stilled. "This can wait. You are sore and hurting, and you need to rest."

"You said it yourself. You're on a clock. You don't have time for me to sleep. And don't ever knock me out again without warning me."

"Never," he promised, steering her back to the bed.

"You have a large bed," she murmured as she lay back down.

"I like to stretch," he replied.

"Ah, yes." Her hand wandered up past his shoulder, and he shivered as she caressed the shadows roiling around him.

"You can see them?" he asked.

"Pretty wings," she breathed. And her eyes drifted shut. "Kyrill is running the slave compounds in Eidolon. I saw them in his thoughts. He has a map."

"What? When? Solanji? Wake up." Mav watched her for a moment. Her bruising had already darkened, her skin black and swollen. The ugly cut under her eye looked crusted and sore. He looked across the room at his oathsworn standing by the door. "Felather, did you hear what she said?"

"Yes, and she hasn't left the citadel. So for her to know this, Kaenera must have come here."

Mav stared at him. "Or she skimmed Kyrill's thoughts."

Feather shook his head. "Something must have happened last night for Kyrill to cast her out."

"What if it is Kaenera behind all this? What if he is the one who wants to ascend the throne?"

"Is that what you think he challenged your father for?"

"If he did, he shouldn't be here. Why would he jeopardise that? It doesn't make sense." He sighed out a deep breath and massaged his temples. "None of this makes sense!"

"Why don't you get some sleep? You've got another day before Serenia reconvenes the Apologia. You can talk to Solanji tomorrow." Felather tapped his lip. "I have that map of Eidolon I found in that newly built compound. I'll go and get it and leave it on your desk."

"Can you treat that cut and her ribs first?" Mav asked as he made himself comfortable on the other side of the bed. He wondered if Solanji even realised she had been awake. Her pupils had been wide and dilated, still under the influence of the sleeping draft Felather had provided.

Felather hesitated before looking across at Mav. "If I do, I won't be able to heal you again until later tomorrow."

"Who knows what tomorrow will bring. She needs help now."

Grimacing, Felather smoothed his fingers over Solanji's face, and Mav closed his eyes.

20

____

KERRIS, EIDOLON

Kerris stared up at the sheer escarpment rising above them, lost in the shadows of the night. It would take them most of the night to climb up the steep trail. He swallowed as unease stirred in his belly. He wouldn't have much time to try and find Mav's contact. That's if the person was still there. The paper crinkled under his fingers. He had memorised the name and address, but uncertainty filled him.

The shepherd, Avery, was busy arguing with the guards at the base of the divide. Kerris stayed with the sheep, kept his head down, and waited as patiently as he could. The sheep milled about, bleating mournfully, as if they knew it was their final journey.

At last, Avery waved his arm and Kerris herded the flock forward. His mule was tied to Avery's and docilely followed the shepherd towards the winding path. Eyes downcast, he concentrated on keeping the flock together. The guards inspected him as he passed, but they didn't question him, and he relaxed as they started up the incline.

The trail was wide enough for a single cart and lined

with a rope strung fence. Not that that would help anyone. Deep ruts worn into the hard packed mud was proof of how many wagons travelled up and down the escarpment. Kerris scowled, taking more produce out of Eidolon than bringing it in, no doubt. He glanced at a man waiting in one of the passing bays. Sure enough, his cart was empty for the return trip.

The night passed and Kerris was exhausted, having had to strong arm stupid sheep who tried to launch themselves off the edge of the trail. His arms trembled with fatigue, and he was covered in road dust.

A dense mist swirled around them as they reached the layer of cloud cover near the top of the escarpment. The clouds were thick and damp, coating man and sheep alike with droplets of water, and then they were through, and Kerris stopped, staring up at the starlit sky. His mouth dropped in shock at the unending expanse of sparkling pinpoints and the radiant ball suspended above him casting a silver sheen over everything.

"Kerris. Pay attention!"

Kerris jerked. The sheep were trying to scatter. He grabbed a handful of soggy fleece and tried to force the escaping animals to turn around, but he couldn't stop their momentum as he was pushed towards the edge. He teetered for a moment over the sheer drop and the rope fence gave way under his weight. The contents of his stomach rose into his throat as he scrabbled for purchase against the crumbling edge of the trail.

"Avery," he yelled as his foot slipped, and as he lost his balance, his gaze returned to the endless expanse above him. It never seemed to end. It just went on and on. A sudden spurt of self-preservation made him hold on tight to the rope as he fell, tangled with the sheep which bleated its horror as he released it. The rope fence strained under his weight and then the rope snapped, and he dropped, his body slamming into the unyielding rock face. Pain screamed through his shoulders, his palm burning at the sudden descent. One of the metal staples holding the rope in place popped out of the cliff face and then another. He fell, skin scraping across the rock, and, jerked to a halt. He hung for a moment, gasping for breath as sparkly lights spread across his vision.

The wave of nausea faded, and Kerris wedged himself in a crevice and just breathed. His racing heart thrummed in his chest and he concentrated on his slow breaths to calm himself down. He was surrounded by a thick swirling mist; he had dropped into the edge of the cloud bank. Gingerly wrapping the rope more tightly around his wrist, he hugged his burnt hand to his chest and fought the darkness crowding his vision.

Deep breaths helped. The darkness receded, and Kerris peered up. Would Avery help him? Or would he herd his sheep up the rest of the trail?

He squeezed his eyes shut against sudden tears as Avery shouted his name.

"Avery?" he yelled back.

"Son? How far down are you?"

Kerris exhaled and braced himself against the rock as he tugged the rope. "I'm in the cloud cover."

Cursing drifted down to him, but the rope went taut. "You've a ways to climb then. Think you can do it?"

"Is the rope secure?"

"As secure as it's gonna be."

Kerris' worn shirt tore easily as he ripped a piece off to wrap around his sore hand, and then, gritting his teeth, he began the slow climb back up the escarpment. He had to stop as waves of pain from his wrenched shoulders took his breath away, and he clung to the rope and moaned.

"Not much further, son," Avery's voice coaxed from just

above him, and in the end, Avery pulled him most of the way the last few feet and grabbed him close as Kerris belly-flopped over the edge in a shuddering heap.

"I've got you, lad," Avery murmured as he rocked him back and forth.

"You helped me!" Kerris gasped after a moment.

"Of course I did. You promised to help get my sheep to Puronia." His voice roughened with concern. "You hurt?"

"Only bruises." Kerris winced as he sat up.

Avery watched him with knowing eyes. "More than that, I think. You took a bit of a battering, as well as the not knowing."

Kerris tensed. "The not knowing?"

"That's some fall. You must have thought you were done for."

Kerris swallowed as the fall flashed through his mind. He wouldn't forget the rushing of the wind as he fell. A worse thought was that he had almost failed his friends. At that, he moved out of Avery's embrace and hissed his breath out as his shoulders throbbed.

"Thought as much," Avery said as he rose and went to rummage in one of his mule's saddle bags. He had strung the mules across the trail, preventing the sheep from fleeing back down the divide. Some straggled up the rise, but Avery didn't seem concerned. He was more worried about Kerris. Avery handed him a small pot. "You've not seen the sky before, eh, lad?"

"No." Kerris took a moment to open the pot and sniff it. Dipping his finger in, he found it was quite greasy but it smelt sweet, a familiar aroma he couldn't place. He smoothed it over his palm and sighed as it soothed the burn. Wrapping the piece of cloth back around his hand, he focussed on his shoulder muscles, wincing at the red flare of strained tendons.

"Thought not. You wait until the sun rises. Now that is a sight. Be glad you're still here to see it."

Kerris exhaled and with Avery's help stood up and swayed. "Only because of you. I don't know how to thank you."

"Just because you're from Eidolon, doesn't mean you're not worth saving," Avery muttered.

"Still, I should have been paying more attention to your sheep."

"Lad, nothing beats your first sight of the sky. If I'd known, I would have been more prepared." Avery chuckled. "At least you won't forget it, eh?"

Kerris twisted his lips in agreement.

"We'll be in Puronia by the time the sun rises. Much safer! Come on, not far to go, and then you can rest for a bit."

Kerris didn't have time to rest. He needed to find Mav's contact in the city.

Herding the sheep onwards, Kerris followed Avery, trying to ignore the ache in his shoulders and his stinging palm. They soon reached the top of the escarpment and approached the tall walls which surrounded the city of Puronia. Moonlight gilded the walls with a subtle glow, a magical glimmer that permeated the stone and seemed to set the whole city alight.

Stunned at the buildings rising around him, Kerris struggled to focus on keeping the flock on course. He had never seen so many houses collected together in one place, some even built off the one next to them, lining the street like a stone tunnel. It was huge; he would never find one person in this maze of streets.

Kerris numbly followed Avery until they reached the structures that made up the hostelry. The sheep were herded into a pen behind the collection of buildings, and Avery disappeared into the largest one.

Kerris held on to the rope around his mule's neck and stared up at the sky. Avery had called the pin pricks of light, 'stars'. They were fading as the sky lightened to a steel grey and then a pale blue. A vibrant ball of fire rose from behind the building, a brilliant glare that turned the sky yellow and made Kerris shield his eyes. Such colours! He winced at the stabbing pain in his shoulders as he moved, the ache a sullen reminder that he hadn't stopped long enough to treat his injuries.

Avery spoke from behind him. "Don't stare at the sun, lad; it will take away your sight."

"The sun?"

"Yeah, that ball of fire can burn your eyes dry if you're not careful."

Kerris closed his eyes and raised his face to the warmth and couldn't agree more as he smiled. "It is warm."

Avery chuckled at the wonder in his voice.

"How do I find the Minstrel's Rest tavern?" Kerris asked.

"The Minstrel's Rest? That's up near the citadel. What are you wanting up there?"

"I need to get a message to a friend. He said to leave it at the Minstrel's Rest."

"Well, that's the other side of the city. Make sure you keep your eye on the time. You need to be descending the escarpment before the sun begins to set.

"How long is that?"

Avery shrugged. "The time it takes the sun to travel across the sky. Once it dips behind those buildings…" Avery pointed to his right, "and it begins to get dark, you need to be on the trail back down. Don't loiter, Kerris. If you don't get down the divide in time…" Avery's voice trailed off and he frowned. "I don't want to hear you left it too late."

"Why can't we exist here too?" Kerris asked, failing to hide the whine in his voice.

"I don't know, lad. It's not fair, I agree, but don't waste your life for it. Don't forget, be on your way back down before the sun sets and get your hand treated."

"I will, Avery. Thank you." Kerris watched Avery disappear back into the building and flexed his shoulders. They wouldn't heal in one go, and he couldn't treat himself standing up in the middle of a courtyard. It would have to wait. He needed to find the inn and send a message to this Ryvalin person.

It took him most of the morning to reach the citadel. The city was a maze of streets, leading him in the wrong direction. He was hot, sweaty, and weary by the time he found the Minstrel's Rest. The large tavern dominated the street and backed into the yellow citadel walls.

A loud roar, so close Kerris imagined it blew his hair awry, rattled the buildings, and he struggled to control his terrified mule as a huge man shot out of the tavern and shook his fist in the air. "Xylvin! Will you belt up?" He disappeared again.

Xylvin? Were they anything to do with Ryvalin? Kerris darted down the road, tugging his mule after him. He tied it to the railing in the courtyard and hesitated on the threshold of the Minstrel's Rest. The interior was dim and much cooler out of the glare of the bright sun.

"Yes? What do you want?" The large man who had shouted at Xylvin, whoever that was, loomed out of the shadows and Kerris took an involuntary step backwards. This man was built like an oak tree, with a broad chest and massive limbs.

"Are you the t-tavern keeper?"

The man stepped into the light and Kerris gulped. The man had a patch over one eye and a jagged scar down his face. "Yeah, and who might you be?"

"M-Mav sent me."

The man burst into laughter. "Am I supposed to know who that is?"

"He sent me with a message for Ryvalin. O-only I don't where to find Ryvalin."

The man peered closer. "You expect me to believe you know Ryvalin?"

"N-no. Mav said to go to him if we needed help."

"Her."

"Her?"

"Ryvalin is a woman. The dragonair up at the citadel. Just follow the roars and you'll find her." The man laughed and walked back into the interior.

"D-dragon?"

The man laughed louder and Kerris stumbled out of the tavern. He stared up at the golden walls and swallowed as his gut fluttered. Gritting his teeth, he untied his mule and walked back down the street. At the end, he turned left and followed the curving road up the hill towards the citadel. The road widened, the surface smooth with flagged stones, the houses grew bigger, and the last butted up against the rising walls.

The road continued through tall iron gates and became a large open courtyard with a fountain in the centre before continuing onwards. Water misted in the air and coated the dragon's scales in a gleaming multicoloured sheen, and Kerris froze. A dragon?

A low rumble vibrated down its throat as its huge head lay on the decorative cobbled stones surrounding the fountain, face pointed towards the gate. The rest of its massive body was curled around the fountain and its tail thumped the ground, the finger-like fronds tapping one at a time in a ripple effect.

Two guards, dressed in full armour and white tabards, blocked the gate, their pikes angled towards each other. They stood at stiff attention, staring straight ahead, until the dragon hissed and wisps of smoke drifted across the flagged stones, wrapped around their ankles and they twitched.

"Move on," the guard on the left shouted, waving Kerris away, and the dragon raised its head, its scaly eyelids sliding up, revealing large faceted eyes. The lids blinked and the black pupils narrowed as the enormous head swung towards the open gate and stared at Kerris. A long thin tongue flicked out as the dragon tasted the air, and Kerris stumbled backwards before he stiffened his knees and straightened his back.

Ryvalin was a dragonair, therefore she must be wherever the dragon was. He took a step forward, ignoring his thrumming heart and dry mouth. He licked his lips, but it didn't help as the dragon watched him as if he might be its next meal.

"And who might you be?" a whispery voice slithered through his mind, and he shivered against the intrusion. The dragon's eyes narrowed, and it rose to its feet, filling the courtyard, its tail curling around the fountain as the dragon stepped towards him, and he tilted his head up to watch it as his stomach churned. *"I recognise you."*

Kerris couldn't quite believe the dragon had noticed him, let alone talked to him. He rubbed sweaty hands on his trousers and stuttered, *"Y-you can't know me."*

The dragon rumbled as it moved towards the gate and the guards scattered. *"Why not? I know who I know, and I know you."*

"I-I'm looking for Ryvalin." Kerris stared at the dragon, mesmerised by its glistening scales.

"See, if you know Ryvalin then I know you."

"That doesn't make sense." Kerris stepped back again as the dragon stretched her head through the gate. His mule brayed with fear as he shuddered. He was talking to a dragon in his head.

"My name is Xylvin; What's yours?" she asked, steam curling out of her nostrils.

"Kerris." Please don't eat me or my mule, he thought. He cringed as the dragon glanced at his mule and huffed out a puff of smoke.

"Kerris. And you know Demavrian. I see his mark on you."

"D-Demavrian?"

"You have his shadows."

"I don't know what you are talking about. I need to speak to Ryvalin. It's urgent. I don't have much time. Please, can you tell me where I can find Ryvalin?"

"She is on her way. Come inside and I'll introduce you."

"I can't stay."

"Yes, you can. I assure you I don't eat visitors."

Kerris flushed. "I need to speak to Mav."

"And so you shall."

"You know where he is?" Kerris caught his breath and took a hesitant step forward.

"Of course. I am his, as are you."

Kerris blinked up at the enormous beast. *"Mav owns a dragon?"*

The dragon chuckled, more smoke curling out of her nostrils. *"No one owns a dragon."* She withdrew her head from the entrance as a stocky woman hurried into the courtyard and climbed over Xylvin's tail. She slowed as she reached the gate and saw who Xylvin was talking to.

"I'm Ryvalin," she said, slightly out of breath. "Xylvin said you're looking for me and Mav?"

Kerris' stomach churned. "How do you know that? I only told the dragon I was looking for Mav."

Ryvalin grinned and tapped her temple. "We can speak mind to mind, just like you have been with Xylvin."

"How is that possible?"

"It's too complicated to explain now, but if you are coming in to see Mav, he can explain."

"Mav is here?"

Ryvlin beckoned for him to enter. "Yes. Come with me and I'll take you to him. He doesn't have much time before the next session of the assembly commences."

"Nor do I. I can't stay. I am from Eidolon, and I have to return before the sun sets." Kerris hurried forward, dragging his reluctant mule and the guards barred his way.

"He can't enter the citadel without permission," the guard said.

"I just gave him permission, you idiot, let him through," Ryvalin snapped as she pushed his pike up and out of the way. The guard resisted.

Xylvin growled and the guard visibly swallowed and after a moment stepped back.

"I can't stay. I need to see Mav straight away," Kerris repeated as he allowed Ryvalin to drag him inside as she called for a lad to deal with his mule.

21

—————

SOLANJI, CITADEL

Later that morning, Solanji awoke in a soft bed, wrapped in warm, strong arms and streams of shadows. They curled and caressed, assured and seductive, much like their owner, who was a solid presence at her back. She was wrapped in a blanket and Mav.

Reluctant to move in case she woke him, his steady breathing proof enough that he still slept, Solanji trawled back through her memory, trying to understand how she had ended up in Mav's bed. She stiffened as memories of Kyrill and Kaenera returned.

Twisting in Mav's arms, she hissed as her body complained and pain spiked through her side. Mav's eyelashes fluttered open. His gaze was unfocused for a moment, and then his face firmed as he fully awoke. His lips curved into the most gorgeous smile. "Good morning," he said.

Solanji couldn't help smiling back, and she winced as her face ached. "Why am I sleeping in your bed?" she asked as she wriggled a hand free to cup her cheek.

"Ah, well, you see, I only have one bed in my rooms, and

seeing as your last mentor cast you out, I thought, as your husband, I ought to keep a closer eye on you."

"Did you now?" Solanji asked, trying not to squirm in his embrace. She frowned. "Did he throw me in the midden?"

"Yes, you can thank your dragon for alerting us. It seems Kyrill has no further use for you. He never did appreciate your talents."

"And you do?" Solanji asked. "Wait! Did you say *my dragon* showed you?"

"You know I do. And yes, your dragon manifested and led us to you. Felather also healed your cracked ribs and a nasty cut under your eye, but you might still be a bit sore."

Solanji was glad to have her aches explained, but she was still stuck on her dragon appearing. There was so much she didn't know. It was a tattoo. How could it appear of its own volition? It hadn't appeared before anyone except Sero before now. "You saw the dragon?"

"I did. Felather couldn't though. He was most upset."

Suddenly remembering what had happened, she grasped Mav's shirt and realised he was fully dressed, while she…was just wrapped in a blanket. Shaking off her sudden embarrassment, she met his amber gaze. "Kaenera was in Kyrill's rooms. I'm sure it was him. He wants to see you crushed."

"You mentioned him last night before you passed out."

"Next time, let me tell you what happened before you knock me out."

"I will, I promise. But let's hope there is no next time." He shuffled up the bed and made himself more comfortable, tugging her against him. "Tell me what you remember. Kaenera is not usually welcome in the citadel."

Solanji snuggled into his embrace. He was safe and comforting. His shadows were wrapped around both of them and she sighed as she stroked them into submission.

"If you keep doing that, I won't be responsible for what happens next," Mav said, his voice edged with tension.

"Sorry, I can't resist them, they are so responsive."

"Well, they've completely surrendered. Now tell me what you remember from last night before Felather and Adriz turn up."

Solanji giggled but started talking. When she finished, Mav was staring across the room, his gaze distant. "You're sure it was Kaenera?"

"Kyrill didn't call him that by name, but it has to be. They were so...I don't know, aligned. It was like they finished each other's thoughts."

"He is not supposed to be able to enter the citadel. The fact that he has, and he knows that he can, means some of the protections are down." Mav frowned. "And that means someone must have told him."

"Wouldn't it have been Kyrill? I mean he was the one who dragged me to your torture chamber. Oh, and he also said he deliberately let us escape. Why would he do that?"

"Because they still need something from me. I wasn't going to last much longer after they took my wings. I was as low as I could get. If he wanted to physically crush me, he had. And yet, Kaenera let me return here, why?"

"He said crushing you wasn't enough." Solanji's grip tightened as she met his eyes. "Mav, he wanted to humiliate you as well, take every last shred of hope from you. When you were executed, he wanted you to fall through the Oblivion Gate."

Mav hissed his breath out. "That's the only way he could get me. But why does he want me so badly? With Kaenera you can never tell. There is always some twisted plan he is trying to feed."

"Kyrill also said to target your oathsworn. He wants to whip Felather like he did you."

"He'll regret laying hands on any of you."

Tears welled, and Solanji pushed the words out. "He said my family were dead. My mother and my brother."

Mav hugged her tight. "You know you can't believe anything he says."

"But it could be true." Solanji's voice wavered.

"I'll ask Ryvalin and Xylvin to go and check for you. I highly doubt Kyrill would have bothered to do anything. He is all bluster."

"He hurt you," Solanji whispered.

Mav kissed her. "Only because he had me in chains. Little effort on his part. Love, let Ryvalin check before you give up on them."

"Alright." Solanji hugged him back and inhaled his comforting scent.

Mav looked around them. "You ought to get dressed."

"In what? I own nothing here."

"I'm sure we can find you some more of those delightful fledgling tunics."

"So I'm *your* fledgling now, am I? What if I don't want to be a fledgling?"

"You are not a fledgling, though we might still disguise you as one; you are so much more. If you feel up to it, I need you to take me back to my memories of Athenia's death. I know who did it. Between us, we'll have to tease it out of me."

"Of course I'll help." Solanji scrunched up her blanket and carefully shuffled off the bed. "Find me some clothes," she said as she scuttled to the bathroom.

When she came back out, tunic and trousers and a silver-grey robe lay across the bed, and Mav had disappeared. Stroking the soft material, she smiled. Mav hadn't skimped on the clothes like Kyrill had; that was just another proof point of Kyrill's lack of thought for others. She hurriedly dressed and, finding a comb on the dressing table, tried to bring her unruly curls under control, but they just sprang back into her usual messy mop. Shoving her hair pins back in the sides, she gave up and just tied it back off her face before she ventured out of Mav's bedchamber and froze on the threshold as she found Mav had a guest.

Mav watched his former friend from across the room. Julius' face was stiff and cold. His pale blue eyes blazed with years of anger and despair.

"Why return now? Why couldn't you have just stayed in the hole you buried yourself in?" Julius demanded.

"I probably would have, except someone kept hunting me down, and I got fed up of being blamed for something I didn't do. I thought it was time to clear my name."

"Blamed? More like tortured," Solanji said through gritted teeth as she walked out of his bedchamber and scowled across the room at captain of the Heavenly Host. He was immaculate. Larger than life in his white finery. The fitted dress jacket nipped in at the waist, the figure-hugging trousers accentuating his muscular legs. Silver brocade curving over his shoulders glinted and twinkled in the candlelight.

Mav's lips twitched as Solanji inspected his former friend as if he was putrid slime she had found on the base of her boot.

"What is she doing here? Kyrill claimed her." Julius physically growled as he stared at her.

"Kyrill tried to kill her. I'd say his rights are forfeit. She is under my protection now," Mav replied.

Julius curled his lip. "You can't protect yourself, let alone anyone else."

"That is only because you betrayed me."

"You got what you deserved."

"I thought the host stood for justice, existed to protect the innocent. Your actions tarnish all that you stand for," Solanji hissed.

"You know nothing."

"I know enough to recognise personal revenge in place of justice."

"I know a murderer when I see one."

"You don't know him very well, obviously." Solanji smiled sweetly.

"Solanji," Mav said.

She ignored him.

"I was tutored with him, grew up with him. You've known him, what? A few days? How would you know who he is and what he is capable of?" Julius snapped.

"If that is so, then you should be ashamed of yourself. I've known him a short while and I already know him well enough to know he would never, ever do whatever it is you are accusing him of."

"Solanji," Mav said again, a warning in his voice.

Solanji whirled on him, her finger pointing. "You know you wouldn't, so shut up."

Julius' lip curled. "She has you well trained, does she?"

Snarling her breath out, Solanji strode up to Julius and stared up into his face. "A true friend would listen, not need proof. A friend who needs proof is no friend at all."

Julius stiffened. "You don't know what you are talking about."

"Mav held Athenia, held her until she bled out. She died in his arms, even though she told him to go. She knew he would be blamed. But he wouldn't leave her to die alone."

"Solanji, enough!" Mav's voice was sharp.

"He needs to know, though why you won't tell him is beyond me," Solanji replied, her lip curling as she glared at

Julius. "Does it comfort you to blame your oldest friend? Does it make you feel better? Instead of finding the real culprit?"

Mav limped across the room and pulled Solanji away from Julius. "Dear one, enough. It is history. Athenia is gone. It won't bring her back."

Solanji leaned against him, letting him calm her. She suddenly lurched away from him. "They all believe that, don't they?" she whispered. "How do you live with that? Knowing people believe you could do such ill? When it is all false."

"Sweetheart, I am fallen. The fallen are capable of anything."

"But you are not fallen."

Mav placed his fingers over her lips. "Hush, no more."

"What does she mean you are not fallen?" Julius snapped.

Mav met his glare. "In her eyes I am not fallen; it is just semantics."

Julius laughed, his expression ugly and harsh. "Semantics? You think you can lie your way out of this and you call it semantics?"

"I am not lying," Mav replied and ran his hands through his greying hair. Julius followed the movement, and then his eyes widened as he actually looked at his friend. "Mav? What's happened to you?"

Solanji leapt out of Mav's embrace. "What do you think has happened to him? Your friend, Kyrill, half kills him whilst you watch and *do nothing to stop him*, everyone shuns him or blames him for anything that is unexplained, and you accuse him of killing your girlfriend."

Mav covered his mouth with his hand trying not to laugh. Considering the topic, it wasn't really amusing, but Julius' slack-jawed expression was priceless. When Solanji said she'd defend him, she meant it. He limped over to a chair and sat, easing his leg. Solanji drifted over to another chair, her gaze never leaving them.

When he looked up, Julius was standing in front of him. "Mav?" he said, five decades of unanswered questions in his voice.

"You never gave me a chance to explain," Mav said.

"You ran."

"I didn't."

"Mav, how can you say that? You betrayed us."

A shaft of pain pierced Mav's chest at the words, and he had to stop a moment to control the flash of anger that followed. "I didn't betray anyone."

"I'd say Mav is the one who's been betrayed," Solanji said, a bitter edge to her voice.

Mav heaved a deep sigh. "It wasn't my choice."

"What wasn't?"

Mav closed his eyes. "Leaving."

"You expect me to believe you didn't voluntarily escape the cells?"

Mav nodded, his eyes still shut, exhaustion hovering on the edge of awareness, waiting to ambush him.

"What happened then?" Julius demanded.

"I'm not sure of all the details, but my father asked Xylvin to dump me in Eidolon."

"Why?"

"My best guess? To follow up on his concerns about who was exploiting the people of Eidolon."

"That has never been proved."

"Not yet."

"And you're not going to tell me what you found out." Julius raised his hands. "I don't blame you," he said, blowing his cheeks out. "Xylvin?"

"You can ask her yourself."

"Don't worry, I will."

He collapsed in the chair beside Mav and stared at him as if seeing him for the first time. Mav knew he was readjusting his thinking.

"Why didn't she say anything?"

"She tried to, but apparently, no one would listen to one of *my* oathsworn."

Julius winced. "If it wasn't you, who was it?"

"I don't know."

"You must know. You were the first on the scene. How can you defend against the count without proving who did it?"

Mav observed Julius for a moment, debating whether to trust him. No. He couldn't trust anyone, not anymore. He bit his lip, keeping his words behind his teeth with difficulty. His natural inclination was to share, hash out his ideas, but he could tell by Julius' slight withdrawal that he knew Mav wasn't going to tell him.

Julius gave a moue of resignation. "I suppose I can't blame you."

"Did you never consider it could be someone else? Not once? Was our friendship worth so little?"

Julius winced. "I was distraught."

"Then you were the last person that should have been searching for me."

"Maybe." He heaved a sigh. "Serenia had all the answers. I never questioned her. Xylvin should have persisted. I would have listened to her."

"Would you? I think you all did a good job of discrediting my oathsworn for some reason. She searched for me instead."

"Not that she found you." Julius ignored his jab, and Demavrian's anger coiled a little tighter.

"No, only you managed that."

"I wish I hadn't. But you are so predictable, even now." He dropped his eyes to hands. "I didn't know that Kyrill would torture you."

Solanji sat upright.

"You expect me to believe that? Really? Especially as you didn't try and stop him. Not once did you question his motives." Mav gritted his teeth against the flash of memories, the unease in his gut.

"Julius gave you up to that bastard?" Solanji asked, making sure she heard right.

"Yes."

"You should have killed him in Eidolon. I regret stopping you."

"Blood-thirsty wench, isn't she?" Julius said.

"You have no idea," Mav said with a tired grin as he met Solanji's eyes. "But really, Julius. A mere seraphim. What made him the judge and executioner? What gave him the right to hold me for so long? Shouldn't you have handed me over to the citadel?"

Julius squirmed. "I don't know what I thought. I just wanted you to pay for what you did to Athenia."

"Without a trial? How is that justice?"

"What justice did Athenia receive?" Julius lurched to his feet, his eyes flashing with anger.

"So Mav shouldn't get any either? Some Heavenly Host you are," Solanji said with a growl.

Julius deflated and rubbed his eyes. "Sorry. It riles me whenever I think of her and that it was you who killed her."

"But it wasn't me," Mav said gently.

"There was no one else."

"That doesn't mean it was me. You *know* me, Julius. Did you really believe I would ever hurt Athenia?"

Julius stared at him, pain etched on his face. "I didn't want to believe it was you."

"Then why did you?"

Shrugging, Julius exhaled. "Because there was no alternative."

Solanji broke the extended silence. "How can you say that? How could you believe that of your best friend?"

"What made you so sure there was no one else?" Mav asked.

"There was no one else at the scene. You must have stabbed her; you were covered in her blood."

"Having compassion doesn't make him a murderer," Solanji said. "And Mav knows he didn't kill Athenia, therefore it must be someone else."

Julius stared at her and then slowly moved his gaze to Mav. He swallowed, his throat bobbing. "It truly wasn't you?"

"What can I say that will make you believe me? I swear, I never hurt a hair on Athenia's head. She was like my sister. You know that. I could never hurt her." Mav's anguish finally penetrated Julius' thick layer of conviction, and he sat back, turning the possibility that he had been mistaken over in his mind.

After a long period of silence he looked up. "If it wasn't you, do you have any idea who did kill her?"

"Why should he trust you?" Solanji asked.

"I suppose you wouldn't tell me even if you do know who it was," Julius grumbled. After another short silence he said, "I'm sorry." He raised his face and met Mav's eyes. "I know it's too little too late, but for what it's worth, I *am* sorry."

Mav twisted his lips. "For what?"

"For believing you would ever hurt Athenia. It will take a while for me to accept that. For too many years my only thought was making you pay."

"Have you ever wondered why Serenia was so quick to blame me?" Mav asked.

"No. You were covered in her blood."

"Because I comforted her, Julius. Don't you think I would have had more sense than to stay at the scene of the crime if I had attacked her?"

Julius exhaled. "Of course you'd have more sense than that. God, I've missed you." Julius ran his hands through his hair again, leaving it in disarray. Solanji drifted over to another chair and sat, watching him as she chewed her nail.

"I've missed you, too," Mav said.

"Why didn't you tell me? All these years. If you had explained, we could have cleared your name by now. And I wouldn't have wasted years hounding you."

"You were convinced I was guilty. You never listened to me. Your mind was already made up, and then you gave me up to Kyrill."

"Shit, Mav. I thought you killed her. And there was nothing saying otherwise. Everything pointed to you." Julius paused as if a thought had struck him, but he continued, his mind obviously elsewhere. "And then you ran, and that was final proof."

Mav rubbed his temple.

Solanji rose and came over to sit on his lap. Extending her soul fingers, she soothed away his distress until he relaxed, resting his head against her chest. She wrapped her arms around him, and he closed his eyes.

Julius leaned back in his chair and considered them. "I supported Serenia's proposal to call Apologia," he said abruptly, and Mav stiffened. Solanji's arms tightened as Mav sighed into her neck.

They were interrupted as the door opened and Felather slid in. "Mav, you're not going to believe what I'm hearing." He froze as he saw Julius. "Julius," he said, nodding stiffly.

Julius returned the nod.

"Julius was just telling me," Mav said.

"Julius was telling you? That he proposed one of the counts, and you're just sitting having a chat?" Felather was almost beside himself.

Mav stilled, his heart dropping. The pain sliced through him, making him breathless. Still, his friends believed the worst of him. He thought he had accepted their betrayal, but he realised deep down that he had still hoped. "That sure, are you? You really want to see me dead?"

"Mav." Julius was pleading. "You have to understand what it looked like from our side."

Mav inhaled Solanji's soothing scent, letting the aroma of clean cotton and violets ground him. "You could have at least spoken to me first. You've never heard my side of events. I'm surprised you are even here. Did you propose yourself or is it via a proxy like the others?"

"I stand behind my word."

"More fool you then," Felather snapped. "You'll find out you are wrong the hard way."

"I think you'll find my defenders are less forgiving," Mav said with a sharp smile. "But you should note, I do intend to prove my innocence."

"I hope you do. Thanks be to your father, wherever he may be, that you have some defenders, because your friends failed you." Julius' voice was rough with emotion. He suddenly stood. "Is Adriz on her way?"

Felather smiled, his eyes glittering. "Anytime now."

"Mav, I'll see you tomorrow."

"Not afraid of my cherubim, are you?" Mav said with a faint grin.

"Everyone is afraid of your cherubim," Julius replied frankly.

"Good," Solanji breathed in Mav's ear as the door snicked shut.

22

DEMAVRIAN

rowning at the door, Mav absently took the proffered glass from Felather. "If you are going to try and retrieve your memories, this might be the best time, Mav. I can keep everyone away for the next few turns. Adriz will guard your door when she gets here. No one will interrupt you."

Mav sighed and rubbed his temple. Exhaustion hovered, draining his energy, but he knew it was reluctance really. In his gut he knew who he was expecting it to be.

Solanji slid off his lap and grabbed his hands, tugging him out of the chair. "Come on, let's see who is behind all of this."

Mav quirked an eyebrow at her. "You think it is only one person?"

"No idea, let's find out."

"I'll scribe for you," Felather said. "Solanji, do you think you can narrate what's happening? Describe as much as you can. You'll need someone to break you out of the trance if it's anything like last time. Let me just warn Adriz not to let anyone disturb us." He darted back out the door.

"Very well," Mav said and followed Solanji into his bedchamber. He lay on his bed and shuffled onto his side, facing Solanji, who lay beside him. He inspected her face as Felather re-entered and quietly shut the door. A soft fluttery sensation shivered through him and he knew she had caressed his shadows.

"There are more. They seem to be getting thicker."

"Is that a bad thing?" he asked.

"I don't know. They are shot with silver threads and they sparkle like soulmist, so I don't think so. They are just a variation of a soul; a shadow soul."

"Let's see if we can understand what happened and put a face to a murderer." He shivered in apprehension but relaxed as Solanji smoothed her fingers over his cheek and stroked his beard.

"So soft," Solanji murmured as she extended her soul fingers and gently trawled them through his shadows. Mav sank back into his pillows, his eyes fixed on her.

Felather spoke softly from behind him. "Mav, do you remember the last time you saw Athenia alive?"

Mav twitched, and Solanji soothed his agitated shadows. He took a deeper breath and then began speaking. "I was in a meeting with my father, Athenia, and Amaridin, the day before she died. We were discussing the need to redeem Eidolon and my father's plans to reunite the two countries. Amaridin was in support, in fact, he was quite eager. He was a little put out that I was going to explore Eidolon and not him. I think he saw it as a break from the citadel." Mav's brow wrinkled. "He left when Valerian arrived. They were going out for dinner at sunset. Athenia was about to leave when my father said he had one last topic he wanted to discuss. He wanted Athenia to take and hold my soul so I would blend into Eidolon better."

"And did she?"

"I said it wasn't necessary." Mav couldn't help the edge of tension leaking into his voice, but Solanji soothed him again, leaching away his fears and his voice softened. "The thought of letting her take my soul, even if it was temporary…" Mav's eyelids drifted lower, and Solanji took up the narration.

"He refused to begin with. He argued against it, quite eloquently, but his father persuaded him to agree." Her eyebrows rose. "It took some time, until full dark. Athenia said to wait until it was light again, Mav would need the sunlight to help him adjust, and then Mav left, leaving Athenia still speaking with his father. He didn't see either of them again until he found Athenia sprawled on the steps later that night. He had been to see Xylvin and was returning through the citadel. He didn't see anyone; the corridors were empty, which he thought odd, but he continued to the grand hall. There was quite a large pool of blood. I think she had been laying there for a while.

"Hold on…" Solanji scowled and tilted her head. "This doesn't make sense! He's seeing something different." Solanji fell silent, and Felather leaned forward, his quill at the ready.

"Solanji? What do you see?" he whispered.

"It's a different view of the hall." Solanji bit her lip. "From above? No, sideways?" Her head tilted further and her eyes narrowed as she tried to make sense of what she was seeing. "It must be an earlier vision because Athenia is still alive." Solanji wrinkled her brow. "This can't be Mav's memory. Athenia was already injured when he arrived. She is descending the steps, her golden robes are trailing behind her, she's turning. There's someone behind her. Shadowy grey robes. There's a knife. It's like one of those knives you use to gut fish." Solanji flinched, her face paling. "They just struck her, over and over. Ripping the knife out and plunging it back in again. Athenia didn't have a chance.

Right-handed; the attacker's holding the knife in her right hand."

"Can you see who it is?"

"The face is hidden by the cowl of her robe, but it's definitely a woman. She has slim arms, not muscular like a man's, but she is so strong. Taller than Athenia, blonde hair, there are wisps of it escaping from her hood. Her robes are blood-spattered; it would be difficult to conceal such stains.

"Footsteps, there are footsteps echoing down the corridor. She's hovering over Athenia, feeling her neck for a pulse, I think. She has a ring on her left hand, fourth finger; it has a black stone, no, a purple stone? It's difficult to tell with all the blood. She's running back up the stairs the way she came. She is very fast. She's gone, and Mav is entering the hall. He's rushing up the steps, and the expression on his face…" Solanji paused and swallowed. "He…He's distraught. He's trying to staunch the blood, there's blood everywhere, he's kneeling in it. He can't stop it, it's…it's spurting out of her. All over him."

"Must have hit an artery," Felather murmured.

Solanji didn't hear him. "Athenia is attempting to speak, but it's all garbled. "Go? No… she's trying to say gold. I'm sure it's gold. Oh…!"

"What?" Felather asked. "Solanji? What happened?"

"She took his soul. She took it, even though she must have known she was dying. Why? He was keening over her body, shouting for help, and then he stopped as if she cut him off. The Heavenly Host have arrived, and he's…he looks lost, he's…it's as if…" Tears welled and leaked down Solanji's cheeks. "She took his soul and then she died." She lurched back as if struck, and Felather rose out of his chair ready to steady her.

"What is it?"

"The memory reverted back to what Mav saw. Julius just

knocked him out. It's all gone dark. He didn't even let Mav say anything. Julius just struck him."

"Solanji, you need to reassure Mav. He is really pale. In fact, he looks translucent. Can you do that? Tell him he is fine; it was just a memory. Help him relax, tell him he's safe and we're here for him, then tell him to wake up."

Solanji moulded herself to Mav's cold body. "Get some blankets," she said as she kissed his face and rubbed his arm. "He's freezing. *Mav? Come back to me. It was just a memory. You are safe with me. I've got you. Felather is here. Adriz guards the door. You are safe, loved, and warm. Mav? You need to wake now. We need to dissect your memories and see if you can recognise who you saw.*"

Mav didn't respond. She stroked his shadows, slowly persuading them to relax. They had cinched in tight around him, a protective shield. The sparkles were brilliant, silver and gold and very prickly. *"I'm sorry. I didn't mean to upset him,"* Solanji said to his shadows. *"You know he wanted to remember. He needs to find out who killed Athenia. He said he knew who it was. You need to make him feel safe enough to remember. He was traumatised when she died in his arms. She took his soul; he had no time to adjust."*

The shadows loosened their grip on Mav, and Solanji slid her soul fingers inside. Stroking and caressing, she embraced Mav with everything she had. Her own soulmist inveigled its way into the shadowy strands. *"Let me in, Mav. You're not alone. You'll never be alone again, I promise."*

The sensation of weighted blankets intruded. Felather was piling blankets on top of them until she heard Adriz's voice. "They'll suffocate, you fool. What have you done?"

The weight was comforting, and under the protection of the blankets, Solanji worked the laces of Mav's shirt open and slid her arms around his body and hugged him tight. She kissed his chest, his neck, his chin. *"I'm here, Solanji is here,"* she murmured over and over as her soul fingers caressed and soothed and loved. She plucked a strand of her soulmist and wove it into Mav's shadows. *"Here, this is for you. From me to you, connecting us always."* She shivered as the dragon tattoo slithered down her arm, solidified, and hovered between her and Mav. An exquisite miniature dragon, impossibly shimmering in the air. Peering at Mav, she huffed. She glanced at Solanji and tutted before she sucked in a shadowy strand and then raised a scaled eyebrow.

Solanji plucked another thread of her soulmist and wove it into the space where the shadow had been. The dragon inhaled another strand and Solanji replaced it with her soulmist. The dragon breathed on the connection, and it flared brilliant and scintillating. *"Mav? You need to wake up now."*

"Why?" Mav's voice was distant, as if he had retreated far inside himself.

"Because it's time. We need to talk."

"It hurts so much."

"I know it did. But it won't hurt so much anymore."

"It's never stopped hurting."

"I know," Solanji whispered, soothing his shadows. She only knew an inkling of what Mav had suffered and already she was amazed at his resilience, his tenacity. He had pursued his father's dream, even though he had been ambushed by some unknown person and brutally tortured by Kyrill. She loved the man he had become. There, she had admitted it; she loved him as he was. She wondered what he had been like before his father's necessity had changed his life forever.

The dragon slithered back up her arm, leaving the impression of a self-satisfied smirk hovering in the back of Solanji's mind. Mav's heart thumped under her ear, and she eased back to watch him. He was warming up, in fact, heat was radiating off him, and she pushed the blankets off them. Mav's eyelashes fluttered and Solanji held her breath.

"Mav?" she whispered.

"What?" he breathed.

"It's time to wake up."

After a moment he sighed and opened his eyes. They gleamed gold in the dim light.

"Are you alright?" Solanji asked.

"I have no idea what alright means," he said, and Solanji winced. He hugged her. "Sorry. That was facetious. I feel fine, if emotionally drained."

"I'm not surprised. It wasn't a nice memory, but we need to talk it through with Felather and Adriz if you feel up to it."

"As long as I don't have to move."

Solanji chuckled and peered over the mound of blankets. Felather and Adriz stood beside the bed with worried frowns on their faces.

"He's awake," she said. "Any chance of a hot cup of bannoe?"

Adriz hissed her breath out and Felather rolled his eyes, but he scuttled off to make the bannoe whilst Adriz dragged off a blanket and began folding it. She stacked it on the chair and started folding another one. She didn't speak until Felather returned, and Solanji enjoyed the brief respite being sheltered by Mav's arms. He didn't seem keen to let her go either.

"Well?" Adriz demanded.

Felather checked his notes. "A woman. Taller than Athenia, blonde hair, right-handed, strong, knew how to wield a gutting knife. Ring on left hand, probably amethyst."

"Golden robes under the grey ones," Solanji added. "That was what Athenia was trying to say."

Adriz froze and stared at Mav.

Mav exhaled. "Serenia."

Solanji frowned. "How does that identify her?"

"Only an archangel can wear golden robes," Adriz said.

"Someone could have stolen them and worn them under their fledgling robes. It could have been a fledgling pretending to be an archangel," Solanji argued.

"Then why did Athenia try to tell Mav if it wasn't important?" Felather asked.

"Only one archangel wore an amethyst ring, and that was Serenia," Mav said. "My father gave it to her when she ascended to the upper echelon. She couldn't be an archdeus but she was as close as she could be. She always wore it. Like a badge of honour. No one else was allowed to wear purple."

"She doesn't wear one now." Solanji frowned. "I'm sure her ring was an opal. There was an inner fire to it; it was all colours."

"It never used to leave her finger, but now you mention it, you're right; she was wearing a fire opal when I met with her," Mav said.

"It's not enough to prove it was Serenia," Felather said reluctantly. "We would need to find the amethyst ring and a cherub prepared to reveal its history. But why would she kill Athenia? What was her motive?"

The room was silent.

"What did Athenia have that Serenia wanted?" Solanji asked. "She was vicious in her attack."

Mav exhaled. "What are the typical motives? Greed? Wrath? Envy?"

"Maybe she was jealous of Athenia's position in your father's inner council. She was his SoulBreather, something Serenia could never be," Adriz said.

"Jealous of what? Serenia was high as she could go! She ruled in my father's name, for goodness sake."

"Maybe that was no longer enough. She's ruled for centuries. Maybe she wanted it all. I thought...I thought once that your father would marry her, once he got over your mother's death," Adriz said.

"Unlikely," Mav replied. "My father has never stopped loving my mother. No matter what Amaridin and I said, even after all this time, he wouldn't listen. Company would be good for him."

Felather dragged his hands through his hair. "This proves nothing. It's all conjecture."

"At least you know it has nothing to do with your soul. When Athenia was struck, she hadn't taken your soul yet," Solanji said.

"Why did she still take it?" Felather mused.

"Because my father told her to," Mav said, deep in thought. "Just my bad luck that she died."

"But Kyrill wanted it. He wanted me to take it in the torture chamber," Solanji said.

"My soul seems to be in great demand."

"Why?" Solanji asked. "What is different about your soul?"

"Apart from it being missing?"

Solanji hugged him. "You know that is not true. Why does everyone want it?"

"No idea."

"Not helpful."

Mav released his breath. "I am an archdeus, one step away from a god. Maybe they think my soul will give them divinity."

"Will it?"

Mav smiled. "No."

"Why not?"

"Divinity is only for those pure of heart."

"Kyrill has no chance, then," Solanji said with a small smile.

"Probably why he was so desperate," Mav said.

Solanji frowned. "You know, maybe that is it. Serenia knew she would never be 'good' enough. Good being the operative word. Maybe she believed she had found a way to change that."

"How?" Mav asked.

"By stealing your soul. If she had your soul, she thought she would be as good as you." Solanji tapped her lip. "Maybe she was working with Kaenera? She could steal your soul, use it to ascend and could then step into your position and finally be an archdeus. By killing Athenia, no one could stop her."

"But by killing Athenia, there was no one left to bind my soul into her."

"Maybe Athenia refused."

"Still conjecture," Felather said. "This is getting us nowhere. And why would Kaenera help her?"

"He wants Mav," Solanji said quickly. "Serenia gets Mav's soul and his seat. Kaenera gets Mav. A partnership made out of greed."

"Serenia would never stoop so low," Mav said, his jaw tight.

"Why not? She must be getting desperate. Amaridin has made it clear he is not interested in her, as has your father. You've been absent for five decades; no one will miss you now," Adriz said.

"Thanks, I think," Mav murmured.

"No, seriously, Mav. This is making sense the more I think on it." Felather's voice was rising. "If it's true Kaenera is after you."

"I overheard him speaking to Kyrill about it, here in the citadel," Solanji said.

"Still no proof. You didn't see him, and Kyrill didn't say his name," Mav said.

Felather grimaced as Solanji rolled her eyes. "If Kaenera is involved then it has to be Serenia. No one else would dare! He wouldn't stoop to work with anyone else."

"He's working with Kyrill," Solanji said.

"Kyrill is a lackey. Kaenera must have an agreement with Serenia. Amaridin is already an archdeus; he has no need to bargain with the devil."

"But trying to use my soul would not make Serenia an archdeus," Mav insisted.

Felather shrugged. "Maybe Kaenera convinced her otherwise. Desperate people are more likely to believe what they want to hear, and Kaenera is an expert manipulator. You know he wouldn't be able to resist getting one over Serenia or your father."

Mav collapsed back on the pillows and covered his face with his arm. "Enough," he said, his voice harsh. "You're giving me a headache. Why should anyone go to such an effort over me?"

"Mav, you are a good person." Solanji leaned over him, her hands on his muscled chest. "Never think that you aren't," she whispered, and then she kissed him as she caressed his shoulders and then his shadowy wings.

He sighed out his breath and his arms snaked around her.

Felather jerked his head at Adriz. "We'll be in the outer room if you need us," he said and all but dragged Adriz out of the room with him, ignoring her protests.

Solanji carded her fingers through Mav's hair and her soul fingers through his shadows, and under the double onslaught all thoughts of self-doubt flew from his brain and he melted into her embrace.

Desire thrummed through him, heightened by the soft caress of Solanji's fingers through his shadows. They writhed under her touch, sending an exquisite shiver across his skin. She peeled his tunic off him and he nearly jerked off the bed as her gentle touch smoothed over his chest, tingling shadows and sensitised skin almost his undoing.

He hurried, fumbling in his haste, to rid her of her clothes, tossing them on the floor and then stroking her warm body in return. As he slid against bare skin, heat flared through him where they touched, melting away his reserve, his protections, and he ached. He traced her cheek, her jaw, and brushed her hair from her face, dipping to taste her lips, her skin, her body.

Stroking and caressing, he writhed under the sensations and preened as she moaned his name, shivered at his touch, and deepened his kiss. Soulmist and shadows danced on the verge of sight, tangled and entrenched, a glowing darkness that expanded, encasing them, subsuming them. Deeper and deeper he quested, pursuing the moment when all thought ended and exquisite sensations cascaded through him, one after the other, and they fell over the edge, together.

He was drowning in lust and desire. Toe-curling pleasure that had him shivering in delicious agony. His core tightened as he tried to hold himself together, but another delicate caress had him shuddering his release, crying out as Solanji clenched him tight, throbbing all around him, encasing him in sheer delight.

23

DEMAVRIAN

"That was not fair," Mav murmured much later as he hugged Solanji close to his heart.

Solanji chuckled into his chest, trailing soft kisses against his damp skin. "I said you were good. Do you believe me now?"

Mav hesitated, and she raised her head and peered at him. "If I say no, will you do that again?" he asked, raising a hopeful eyebrow.

She laughed. She couldn't help it and snuggled back into his embrace. His shadows curled around them, twining with her soulmist, and she shivered as exquisite sensations rippled through her. "That's not fair," she said as he smoothed his hand over her warm skin, followed by shadowy nips that made her toes curl.

"Who said we were playing fair?" he muttered against her neck as his hand swirled her breast and the shadows teased her nipples. She gasped as he moved down her body. Solanji stiffened as someone knocked on the outer door of his chambers, and Mav cursed under his breath and rested his face on Solanji's stomach.

Soft voices in the outer chamber abruptly ended, and then there was a tap at the door.

Reluctantly raising his head, he called, "What is it?"

"Message from Ryvalin. She said it was urgent," Felather replied.

"I will be having words with her about what is urgent," Mav said, as he dropped a kiss on Solanji's belly and swung his legs over the side of the bed. Pulling on his robe, he tied the belt around his waist and smiled as Solanji rushed into the bathroom and shut the door.

"Well?" he asked as he opened the bedchamber door.

Felather twisted his lips and thrust a sealed letter at him.

Shrugging, Mav closed the door and slid his nail under the blob of red wax sealing the document. He quickly skimmed the note. "What the fuck?" he gasped. He tossed the parchment on the bed and hurriedly began dressing.

"What is it?" Solanji asked, peering out the door.

"Kerris is here. No idea how or why." Mav eyed Solanji for a moment. "If necessary, do you think you can give him that spare soul you've got?"

Solanji stared at him. She had been thinking of the soul as his last resort. "I'm not sure."

His lips pinched. "What is he doing here? He should know better."

"He must have had a good reason."

Mav nodded. "Which makes it even more worrying."

"Did the citadel let him enter?"

"Looks like it."

"That child has guts," Solanji said as she tugged on her grey fledgling tunic.

Mav slowly smiled. "That he does. There're spare clothes in the wardrobe; we'll disguise him as a fledgling, though if the citadel let him in, he's already proved himself enough for me."

"You aren't supposed to leave your rooms."

Mav ran a hand through his hair and scowled. "*You* can, though. Felather will escort you. Kerris knows you. Bring him back here."

Solanji's smile widened, and she pulled open one of the tall wardrobe doors. Snagging another grey robe, she crossed the room and gave him a quick hug.

Mav led her out of the room. "Felather, please escort Solanji to Xylvin's lair. There is someone you need to bring back here. Don't let anyone stop you. I'd come with you, but I don't want to draw attention to him."

"Xylvin?" Mav extended the thought, more in hope than belief. He hadn't spoken mind to mind in years, and now his reach was pathetic. *"Xylvin? Can you hear me?"*

"Mav?" Xylvin's replied.

"I got Ryvalin's message about Kerris."

"The boy is brave, if foolhardy," Xylvin said as Mav paced in his chamber. *"He actually faced me down. There's not too many who'll do that these days."*

"*He's one of mine,*" Mav replied without thinking.

"So I see. His heart is pure, and I see your mark on him. That's why I kept him here. He has your shadows."

Mav's heart leapt. He remembered Solanji saying something similar back in Eidolon.

"I don't know how he got them. I don't know how I got my own."

"You need to find out. I'm sure they are important."

"Felather and Solanji are on the way to collect him."

"We'll be waiting."

Rubbing his aching head, Mav grimaced. Hopefully with practice it wouldn't be such an effort. He hovered by the door of his chamber, pacing impatiently until Adriz opened it and let them in. He swooped on the boy as soon as he crossed the threshold, dragging him into his embrace. "What are you doing here?" Mav's voice shook.

Kerris laughed, a tremulous warble, but a laugh all the same. "I could ask the same of you," he said, his returning hug just as ferocious.

Adriz observed them for a moment and then shook her head and closed the door. She turned her back to it and took up guard, a smile tugging her lips.

Gently grasping Kerris' neck, Mav hugged him tight. "He's my fledgling," he said to Felather, meeting his eyes over Kerris' shoulder. Felather's mouth rounded in an 'O' and he silently nodded.

Mav chuckled into Kerris' neck. "As much as I am pleased to see you, why *are* you here?"

Kerris shuddered. "Mav, you need to come back. We need you."

Mav pulled back. "What's happened?" he asked as he inspected the boy. His mop of brown hair was overlong and he looked ragged and destitute. He wondered how he had even gained entry to the citadel looking like a skinny street beggar. He was so dirty you couldn't tell his skin colour, which was a warm brown like Solanji's. In the candlelight, he looked grey and old before his time. "Who does?"

Kerris stilled. He glanced around him, fear in his eyes.

"You can trust all in this room," Mav said. "They are sworn to me."

Kerris nodded and his lips quivered. "Mav, they took them all."

"What? Who?"

"Shandra, Muntra, and the kids. They've all gone. The homestead is empty." He raised fearful eyes, his bony fingers fidgeting at the dried dirt on his clothes, dislodging lumps of mud onto the floor. "I found wagon tracks but nothing else."

Mav frowned. "Start at the beginning. Come and sit down and tell me everything."

"There isn't much to tell. I went to the market to get

supplies. When I came back, they were gone. All of them. I don't know who took them or where they went." Kerris twisted his fingers, his face tight.

Mav gripped Kerris tighter. "It's alright. Let's get you cleaned up. You'll feel better after a bath."

"I will?"

"I promise you will. After your bath, you can tell us how you got here."

Kerris caught Mav's arm. "Mav you need to come h-home with me. We have to rescue them. They're just kids!"

Mav hugged him. "We will. Don't worry, we will. But Kerris, you took a grave risk. You know the soulless shouldn't cross the divide."

"*You* did. So why can't I?"

Mav huffed out his breath on a laugh. "How did you know where to find me?"

Kerris dropped his eyes and squirmed. "You gave me that bit of paper with Ryvalin's name on it. So I went to the Minstrel's Rest. I didn't know where else to go."

"Good. I'm glad you did."

"Mav, you have to understand. You are important to us," Kerris began.

"You are all just as important to me," Mav replied, and Kerris jerked his eyes up.

Xylvin's voice echoed around the room. "Don't say that too loudly, Demavrian. You'll get the boy killed."

Solanji gasped and covered her mouth as she peered up at the ceiling. "I didn't know Xylvin could speak to us across the citadel!"

Kerris stiffened in Mav's embrace. "Demavrian? You really are Archdeus Demavrian?" He tried to pull out of Mav's grip.

"Xylvin!" Mav hissed. "She doesn't usually do that, and there was no need for her to speak now!"

The dragon was unapologetic. "The boy needs to know who you are."

"Mav?" Kerris' eyes were huge.

Mav exhaled. "Yes, I am Archdeus Demavrian, though my status is currently under question."

"But…" Kerris began.

"Have your bath first," Mav said, pushing him towards the bathroom.

"Do you still not know?" Xylvin asked.

Mav scowled. *"Know what? What's that supposed to mean? Stop being so cryptic."*

"Demavrian! You are not usually so obtuse."

"I'm not at my best at the moment," Mav replied.

Xylvin snorted. *"I suppose not. Mav, you must know, your father left Eidolon in your hands, to protect and to sustain."*

"No," Mav gasped.

"Of course he did. How could you think otherwise? You've lived amongst them, learnt to love and understand them. No one knows Eidolon better than you. Who else would you want to protect them?"

Mav froze. *"I can't protect them. I can't even protect myself."*

"But you will," Xylvin said. *"How else was Kerris able to cross the divide? He has no soul, and yet…your mark is on him…and here he is."*

Mav was relieved when she fell silent.

"Everything went to pot when you left," Kerris said.

Xylvin's chuckle was like grinding stone. "Why am I not surprised?"

"Mav, you're rich?" Kerris' voice trailed off as he took in the opulent room.

"Not really. I'll explain later. Go have your bath." Mav leaned over the tub and pulled out the plug to release the water. He smiled as Kerris gaped at the steaming water flowing into the tub and started shedding his clothes. Mav poured a handful of salts into the bath. "Don't worry, Xylvin is another sworn to me. You can trust her."

"You have a dragon?" Kerris asked, his eyes huge.

"She's not mine; she's a friend."

Kerris inhaled. "Smells nice, but I don't know what it is."

"Lemon," Mav said and offered him a bar of soap. He picked up another bar. "Solanji? Could you order us some food? Nothing too rich."

"Of course," Solanji came to the door. "I'm not looking," she said with a laugh as Kerris yelped. "Here are some towels."

Mav scrubbed Kerris' back and then washed his hair, twice as his busy mind turned over Xylvin's words. Kerris complained he was shrivelling up by the time Mav let him out of the bath, but he soon burrowed into the warm towels and groaned with pleasure.

'I'll leave you to dress. Food will be ready when you come out," Mav said and entered the main chamber. He joined Solanji, Adriz, and Felather at the table.

Mav glanced up as the bathroom door opened and Kerris peered out. He beckoned the boy over and patted the chair seat next to him. "Come and eat, you must be starving."

Mav inspected him as he settled. He looked like any other fledgling in the grey tunic and trousers, though his knobbly wrists stuck out at the ends of the sleeves.

Smiling, Mav ruffled his hair. "You need to stop growing."

Kerris smiled back shyly and accepted the plate of roasted chicken and vegetables. He was soon eating, his eyes flicking around the room. Mav sipped his bannoe and let the boy eat in peace. He and Solanji chatted quietly with Felather and Adriz, and Kerris gradually relaxed. "Have some more," Mav said, ladling more vegetables onto his plate.

Kerris eyed it. "I don't think I've eaten so much at once, ever," he said.

"I know the feeling," Mav said, rubbing his stomach. "I haven't got used to it either."

"Stop playing with your food," Solanji said. "If you don't want it, leave it."

Mav realised she was speaking to him and grimaced. He laid the cutlery to the side and pushed the plate away. Kerris copied him, and Mav suddenly felt guilty for making the lad think he had to eat it all.

"Let's move to the armchairs, they're more comfortable," Mav suggested. "And you can tell us what happened."

Kerris sighed as he smoothed his hand over the plush material and curled his long legs under him. "You have nice rooms, Mav," he said a little wistfully.

"Wherever I am, you will always be welcome," Mav said carefully. He still had two counts to disprove and he was beginning to doubt he would be able to. It was all very well remembering what had happened, but it was proving it that would be the difficulty.

"You mean you'd let me stay here? With you?" His face fell. "But I can't, I don't have a soul. I have to leave before dark."

"It seems that you might have a soul. Where you would normally have soulmist, you have shadows, like I do, which is why the citadel allowed you entry. I have been here for more than a day and I only have shadows. Solanji believes I gave them to you in place of your soul."

Solanji nodded. "They behave like a soul, so you should be fine."

"Looks like I'll have to reinstate my fledgling hall," Mav said with a smile.

"Fledgling hall?"

"Each angel trains their own fledglings to become scribes, cherubim, or seraphim. Some may even achieve archangel. We are responsible for housing, feeding, and clothing you. In return you learn as best you can and then if you want to, you swear allegiance to your angel and enter his or her service, or you can choose to take your skills elsewhere. The hall is where you sleep whilst you are training."

"How many fledglings do you have?"

"None at the moment. I've been away for many years. You can be my first if you want to."

"Isn't Solanji one?"

Mav gave Solanji a slow smile. "Solanji is much more than fledgling, but we don't want anyone to know so we are disguising her as one. So you must remember to treat her as a fledgling."

"I would like to be your fledgling." Kerris made a funny bob of his head and the matter was settled. "I need to know how to heal you. You're always getting hurt. You need someone to look after you."

"He can heal?" Felather lurched out of his slouch in surprise.

"Yes, though he has no training. I want you to train him, Felather," Mav said, an unexpected warmth spreading through him at Kerris' eagerness. "But first I need you to tell us what happened to Shandra and the other children."

Kerris straightened. "Although I have no proof, I bet the dybbuks took them. It couldn't be anyone else! Kiara first brought word that they were still in the area and causing trouble. You know how she's always fixing things. She started staying late at the smithy in the village, helping mend some of the tools and such. She got friendly with some of the villagers. They got used to her being around. Forgot she was there, you know?

"She overheard some of their conversations. They had recently been given some money for a weaver's project. Their woollen goods were in demand, but they were worried that the village funding would dry up. The targets they had to meet kept being reset, and they never seemed to be able to hit them. Then they kept losing people and they were struggling to get enough people on the lines. Stuff like that.

"Later, she heard them talking about some other projects being set up in the same district. New competition for the funding, but the conditions were much worse, so they could undercut their costs and make them seem more profitable or something."

"Did they say who was in charge of these new projects?"

Kerris shook his head. "I don't know. But there were more of those guards around. Like the ones who hunted you down."

"The Heavenly Host?"

"The soldiers in the white uniforms. So stupid in muddy Eidolon," Kerris said with a laugh. "You'd think they would dress better."

Mav grinned. "Their sense of righteousness goes to their head sometimes and there's not enough room left for common sense. Makes them easy to spot though."

"But that does mean angels are involved in some of the projects," Solanji said.

Mav thought for a moment. "Golaran and Amaridin have been setting up most of the projects, so it's not surprising, but I doubt either of them would deliberately set out to make the workers' lives worse. I think this is another example of a good idea being twisted by someone."

"So who controls the host? Who do they report to?" Solanji asked.

"There are usually three captains. Julius is Serenia's captain. Eodan is Amaridin's. Ryvalin is mine. Golaran is the senior archangel after Serenia. I expect he has a captain in my stead."

"Will you get your captain back?"

"Ryvalin will always be my captain. No one would deny her and Xylvin, but if I can't defend the next two counts then I don't know." Mav shrugged.

"Counts?" Kerris asked.

Mav quickly changed the subject. "Felather, did you bring that map of the compounds?"

Felather rose and went over to Mav's desk, riffled through some papers, and brought the map over to the table. "Where was your farm?" Felather asked as he spread the scroll out. Mav and Kerris scanned the map and both pointed to a spot to the north-east. "And the tracks went south?"

"Past the road to the divide I would say."

"So, we've got at least ten possible compounds to search, then." Felather said, sweeping his hand across the map.

"Xylvin and Ryvalin can go check them out. They'll recognise the shadows now they've met Kerris. I can give Xylvin the images of Shandra, Bailey, and the others."

"And I can provide Brennan's image," Solanji added.

"I could go with them," Kerris offered. "I need to leave by sundown anyway." He looked around nervously. "I can't stay any longer."

Mav rubbed Kerris's back. "I told you. I think you'll find there is no issue with you staying longer. Solanji can see your shadowsoul."

"What does that mean? A shadowsoul?" Kerris asked, his eyes gleaming with interest.

"It means you have a soul and you won't expire after a day," Solanji said with a grin. "Just as Mav hasn't."

"Wow!" Kerris breathed. "You mean it? You want me to stay here and be your fledgling?" His face fell. "Are you sure? I mean it's not like I don't believe you or anything, but how do you know I'll be alright?" He glanced around him wistfully. "Much as I'd love to stay Mav, I don't think I should risk it."

"If Solanji says you'll be fine, you will be. You've got the same shadowsoul as I have, so if we're not going to survive, we'll go together." Mav grinned. "But we won't, so don't worry. The citadel is not rejecting people at the moment."

Kerris frowned at him. "What do you mean?"

"What I said. The citadel is dormant. It won't reject you, so don't worry about it."

"But how? Will it change its mind?"

Mav chuckled. "No, I don't believe it will. But we have more important things to worry about." He ignored Kerris' concerned expression and tried to redirect his thoughts. "Although you are my fledgling, you will be Felather's apprentice. Felather is my scribe and he will introduce you to the role of a fledgling and a scribe, and he will help you learn to control your healing ability.

"I need to deal with some business here at the citadel, but after, once Ryvalin and Xylvin confirm where Shandra and the others are, we will go to Eidolon and rescue them, I promise. We will find them and bring them here as well. In the meantime, I want you to tell Felather everything you can remember about your journey here, the dybbuks, and what you've heard."

Rubbing his eyes, Felather leaned forward until his elbow rested on his knees. "If we have time! We need to prepare for tomorrow. Do you think we have enough to accuse Serenia?"

"No, we have no proof! I will not be accepted as a witness. My word is suspect. They will not believe anything I say."

"That they dare question your honour." Felather scowled at the floor.

"I think…I think I might have to try and flare my wings.

Ever since I've been back here, it feels like I have wings. I can feel them pulling on my back."

"You do have wings, Mav. They are beautiful and elegant. Deepest black shadows, shot with gold and silver," Solanji said.

"My wings were made from pure white feathers," Mav said, catching his breath as the memory of their loss filled his mind. He shivered as the chill and aroma of the blood-drenched cavern overwhelmed him, reminding him once again that he was unable to prevent the loss of his wings. Anguish tore through him as they went up in flames.

"Mav?" Gentle hands rubbed his shoulders, soothed his shadows, and he exhaled, flexing his neck. He tried to remember what he had been saying. Wings, they had been talking about his wings.

Solanji continued, "They may not be the same, but they are still wings. I can see them. I swear."

"But will anyone else be able to see them?" Mav asked.

24

____

DEMAVRIAN

Ryvalin arrived and Mav was glad to change the conversation back to how they were going to rescue his fledglings. Felather spread another scroll out on the table, and positioned the map of the compounds beside it.

"Kerris said the tracks went south, so the compound where the kids are being held must be south of this line." Felather drew a line across the map of Eidolon and began to annotate the locations of the compounds.

"It's got to be one of these," Mav said. "You're just going to have to work your way down and check them all."

"If I find your fledglings, what do you want me to do?" Ryvalin asked.

"Use your judgement. If they are at risk, and by that I mean in danger of injury or death, get them out. But there are about twenty of them, if they are all still together, so you won't be able to transport them all at once."

"And the younger kids don't have souls, so you can't bring them straight here," Solanji added. "I only saw Shandra,

Bailey, Muntra, and Kiara with shadowsouls like Kerris'." She hesitated. "My brother, Brennan, won't have a soul."

Mav rubbed his face. "Let's find them first. Then we can worry about getting them somewhere safe. I'd prefer it if you came back for more resources. You alone may not be able to extract them."

Ryvalin shrugged. "I don't know. I'm sure Xylvin can scare a few dybbuks away." She held her hands up at Mav's worried expression. "But we will look out for a farmstead nearby where we could take them, if necessary."

"Be careful, Ryvalin. We have no information on how well these camps are guarded or what they are even using the people for."

Felather pointed to one of the compounds to the north. "The one we burned down had a couple of watch towers in the perimeter fence, but not much else, and it was more for keeping the prisoners in than worrying about an external attack."

"And that was where you found this map?" Ryvalin asked, tapping the parchment.

"Yes, along with a letter from Seraphim Kyrill."

Ryvalin wrinkled her nose in thought. "So Kyrill is known to be involved? Could you write out some orders for me to collect these specific slaves? And sign it like Kyrill? The dybbuks won't know the difference."

Mav exhaled. "Great idea, and a peaceful solution, which would be safer for the children. I was thinking we'd have to fight our way in."

"I'll use it as way to get inside. Otherwise, I'll have no chance of identifying them."

"To that point, Kerris and Solanji can share the images of Brennan and the others with Xylvin, so she can share them with you."

Ryvalin nodded and began folding up the map. "I don't

know how long this will take, and I have no way of getting a message back to you."

"I trust you to do what's best for them. If you find them but need help, then return and we'll come back in force."

"Get this ridiculous Apologia resolved and then you can focus on more important matters," she said as she glared at him.

"Don't worry, I will. Good hunting." Ryvalin clasped his arm and then led Solanji and Kerris out of the room, Adriz following close behind.

Felather rolled up the map and hesitated. "Mav. We've got this extra recess day. Don't you think you and Solanji should try and reconnect to the citadel?"

"I think Sero needs to explain a little more about Soul-Breathing to Solanji first. I don't want her sucked into something none of us can get her out of. Imagine how overwhelming it would be for her if she connects to all those souls?"

"We're a bit short on time, Mav."

"I'm not risking her, and if I try to connect, it will be noticeable. You heard the citadel's response last time. Serenia will send the host to lock me up again. Let's make sure Solanji has some basis to work from before we try to bind me back into the citadel."

"Wouldn't Averdeus be able to return though? If you reconnected?"

"I don't know. It depends on what trouble he has found."

Felather exhaled. "I'll go and write out those orders for Ryvalin and then see if I can find Sero."

"Thank you, and if you could spend some time with Kerris, make sure he's not over reaching himself. He heals instinctively, but he doesn't know his limits."

"Of course," Felather murmured as he left the room.

Mav stood still for a moment. The room was silent,

expectant almost. It was the first time he had been alone in his rooms since he had returned. Slowly rotating, he inspected the bookshelves, the desk, the mirror on the wall. He stared at himself in the reflection and realised he was the stranger here. His room was unchanged; he was the one changed beyond recognition.

He still didn't fully understand what had happened to him or why. They had to find Serenia's ring to see if it would reveal its history to Sero. Provide some of the proof he needed. And for that he was dependent on Sero's help. The little cherub had been an unexpected boon. They had never really interacted that much previously. Mav had always seen the cherubs as aloof, unapproachable. He understood why they were like that, he just hadn't realised that it was a front. Self-preservation against all the stories every person carried about with them.

Choosing one of his favourite books from the shelf, Mav sat in one of the more comfortable chairs and, stretching his legs out, began to read. The peace seeped into his muscles and he relaxed. The timepiece swished in the corner, a gentle reminder of time passing, but nothing more urgent.

His eye lids drooped and then closed, and the book slid from his fingers as he drifted and fell asleep.

Felather halted on the threshold to Mav's chamber, a hand raised to hush Sero as he saw Mav sleeping in the chair. Sero flew across the room and hovered in front of him. "He looks exhausted," Sero said in a hushed voice.

"Then don't wake him."

"He'd sleep better in a bed."

"But if you wake him, he won't go to bed."

"Stubborn archangels," Sero muttered and returned to the table where Felather sat.

"Tell me about this book you found," Felather said.

Sero cast a glance back towards Mav. "Will he regain his youth when he reconnects, do you think?"

"I don't know. We are on unknown ground here. An archdeus has never lost his soul before."

Sero sighed and produced the book. "Solanji found the phrases in here. It mentions Mav is the cornerstone. But we don't know what it means."

Felather began flicking through the pages. "They are just drawings of flowers."

"That's all I can see as well."

Looking up in surprise, Felather raised his eyebrows.

Sero nodded. "The messages were left for a SoulBreather."

"So there's no point me reading it then," Felather said with a huff as he leaned back in his chair.

"Reading what?" Mav asked as he stirred.

"You woke him up," Sero said.

"I did not."

"You so did."

"I wasn't asleep," Mav said as he closed his book and put it on the side table.

Sero laughed. "Oh you so were. You were snoring."

Mav rose and stretched. "Whatever," he murmured, and Sero chuckled again.

"Solanji and I found a book in the library."

"When were you in the library with Solanji?" Felather asked.

Waving his hand as if it wasn't important, Sero said, "We almost got caught on a midnight jaunt, but that reminds me, two seraphim entered plotting a land grab. Felather you should check the submissions for Eidolon during Apologia. They seemed to think everyone would be distracted and the request would be passed."

"They'd probably be right," Mav said as he sat opposite Felather. "Sero, would you be prepared to go on another jaunt with Solanji to search for Serenia's ring?"

Sero exhaled. "Why do you need me?"

"I was thinking you could search her rooms while I'm in Apologia defending the next count. Everyone will be in the assembly hall."

"Let me guess. You want to know its history."

"It would help prove my innocence if you can attest that the ring was on her hand when she killed Athenia."

Nodding, Sero twisted his lips. "To be honest, I was expecting something like this. I suppose I can help."

Mav grinned at his utter lack of enthusiasm and changed the subject. "Let's see the book, then."

Felather slid it over and Mav swivelled it around and stared at the page. "Those flowers are familiar. They were engraved on the north tower. My mother used to love the trailing vines."

Sero snapped his fingers. "I thought I recognised them. I just couldn't place where I'd seen them."

Mav leaned closer. "This is Athenia's handwriting," he said.

"Yes, that is Athenia's book; she left some messages for Solanji. Or not Solanji specifically, but the next SoulBreather."

"What messages?" Mav began turning the pages more quickly.

"Solanji copied them down, but she didn't get the chance to finish the book, so I don't know if there is anything else in there. I thought Solanji could check, seeing as she is the only one who can read it."

Mav smoothed a hand over the page. "I miss her," he said.

"We all do," Sero said softly and shuffled over to pat his shoulder.

Mav looked up, and Sero rubbed his back. "Do you think you can help Solanji to find a way to connect to the citadel?"

Sero smiled. "With Athenia's help, I hope so."

"Good," Mav said and closed the book.

Solanji and Kerris returned in high spirits, both convinced that Xylvin and Ryvalin would find the others within the day. Adriz trailed behind them with an amused smile on her face. Solanji hurried over to the table when she saw Athenia's book lying there. "Oh, were you allowed to take it out of the library?"

"Probably not, but what they don't know won't harm," Sero replied. "You need to finish reading it so we can figure out how to connect to the citadel."

Solanji exhaled in a rush. "Oh."

"Felather and Kerris, you have work to do." Mav shooed them off, and Adriz followed them.

"Solanji, tell your husband he needs to go to bed and sleep. He's exhausted. And he'll only distract you while we work," Sero said.

Solanji looked at Mav in concern.

"He fell asleep in the chair. Go," Sero ordered as he pointed his finger to Mav's bedchamber.

Solanji laughed and tugged Mav towards his room. "I'll leave the door open so you can hear us. You won't be alone," she said as she kissed his cheek.

Mav gave in and went to bed.

"Right, now he's out of the way, what else does the book say?" Sero asked as he patted the chair next to him.

Solanji pulled the book closer as she sat and started flipping the pages. "No matter what we find, I think we'll still need Mav to help connect. If he is the cornerstone, then all else is built on him."

"Possibly, but the SoulBreather needs to protect the souls. You must be able to access the souls, even without connecting to the citadel."

Solanji frowned, her tummy fluttering at the thought. "Why do you think I can connect?"

"Because the SoulSingers can. They continue to remove souls and store them in the citadel, even though the citadel is dormant."

"What makes you believe the souls are stored in the citadel?"

"Because the SoulSingers could not hold that many souls within them, and," he twirled his fingers, "I checked."

Solanji stared at him. "You checked."

"Yep. I have a tongue in my head, you know."

"How do the SoulSingers pass the soul to the citadel?"

"Much the same way as they take it."

Solanji frowned down at the page she had just turned. *"Inhale and exhale. Breathe a soul into being."*

"Exhale. That's right," Sero said.

"But…to where? Do I have to touch the citadel?" She couldn't do this; she had no idea where to start.

"The building is not the citadel. It's *called* the citadel. That's different. The citadel surrounds us. It's in the air we breathe, the wind that passes, the presence in the silence. Each of us connect in our own way. Demavrian was bound to the citadel. When his connection was severed, the cornerstone, as Athenia calls him, was lost, and the citadel fell dormant." Sero pursed his lips. "I believe you can connect to the citadel through your SoulBreathing; it's a more personal connection. A bit like meditation. You have to feel the citadel, recognise what you are feeling. But you need to bind

Demavrian back into the citadel to wake it, which I fear is more complex."

"So if I find the connection, I just exhale and the soul will go into the citadel, and if I inhale a soul will come out?"

Sero chuckled. "I think you may have to search for the soul you want." He shrugged. "Try it. See if you can feel the citadel and look for your brother's soul. You'll recognise it when you find it."

"Let me just check there aren't any further messages first." Solanji hurried through the final pages and paused. *"Believe,"* she said.

"Self-belief is the starting point for most challenges," Sero said.

"Belief," Solanji murmured and closed her eyes. Silence fell and Sero waited patiently.

"Nothing," Solanji said as she opened her eyes.

"Practice," Sero said. "Practice every chance you get. It will happen. The more you practice, the easier you'll find the connection. Athenia didn't even have to think about it."

"If you say so," Solanji said, closing her eyes again and trying to relax. The citadel surrounded her, she just had to find it.

She opened her eyes as Sero rose into the air. "I'll return this book to the library. Keep practicing."

Solanji scowled at him as he flew to the door and opened it. Once the door clicked shut, she slumped back in the chair. The soft swish of the time piece was soothing, the knowledge that Mav slept in the other room comforting. She rose and went to check on him. He was stretched out across the bed, the blankets tangled in his legs. Tutting, she went to untangle him and then couldn't resist laying down with him.

His arms immediately found her and hugged her tight as he mumbled against the back of her neck. She closed her eyes and relaxed, concentrating on trying to discern what he was saying.

"Imagine the citadel is like soulmist. How do you touch that?" he asked, his voice a soft whisper against her skin.

Pushing up on her elbow, she searched his face, but he was still asleep. Like soulmist? Was it that easy? Solanji relaxed back into his embrace, closing her eyes and extending her soul fingers, letting them quest in the air, drifting without purpose until they snagged on something. A door. The door was ornate, exquisitely detailed with carvings of cherubs and angels.

Tentatively, she ran her fingers over the carvings, and her heart stuttered. The door was solid and cool to the touch. Lifting the metal latch, she pushed the door open and entered a long corridor filled with sunlight. As she peered through the blinding light, she saw that there were wooden doors all along the hallway, each painted a different colour and adorned with a shiny brass plate. She stopped at a pale blue door with the letter 'B'. "Brennan," she breathed.

The door opened easily under her hand, and she was engulfed in a swirl of souls, all clamouring to be returned to their hosts. "I'm sorry," she exclaimed, "but I don't know who you belong to."

Solanji pushed her way in, sweeping the soulmist aside as she searched through the scintillating swirls of gold, hope a lump in her throat as she waded in deeper. The room seemed never-ending as flashes of memories, a moment in time, bombarded her, and she struggled to keep them separate, to not inhale them and carry them with her.

She caressed the soulmists dancing in the air, people's names ringing in her mind as she left the room, her shoulders slumping as she closed the door.

The spare soul, which had resided in her since she had killed the soldier all those weeks ago in Eidolon, rippled with distress, and Solanji wavered. "I am so sorry. I didn't mean to kill you, but you were going to hurt me. There is no host to return you to."

A sudden need to exhale overwhelmed her, and the soldier's soulmist streamed out of her and drifted further down the passage. A forest green door stood open, and the soulmist was sucked inside, and she knew it was a place to wait until Averdeus returned to guide them on their onward journey.

Releasing the image, the corridor faded as Solanji let the connection slip and Mav's arms solidified around her. Tears drenched her lashes as she snuggled against him, craving the comfort he so instinctively offered her. So many souls lost, so many people's lives disrupted or destroyed. How was she supposed to find Brennan's soul in all of that chaos?

25

MUNTRA, EIDOLON

The soulless were woken by the clashing of metal against metal. Muntra groaned as he rolled out of his thread-bare blanket and slowly rose to his feet. His hands were wrapped in strips of cloth, but that didn't prevent his skin from being covered in nicks and cuts which stung when he plunged them into an ice-rimmed bucket of water to scoop up a handful to drink.

The water was so cold it hurt, but he sucked it down through his broken teeth. He hissed in his breath as his jaw protested, a sharp ache that had him cupping his cheek.

He had picked the wrong fight with the wrong man, trying to protect some of the kids taken from Shandra's place. All of them had been abandoned in Eidolon without souls and without families. No hope until Shandra swept them under her wing and provided a roof and food and the freedom to play. Only five of them had been older than ten; all the other children were younger. Shandra was afraid they would be sold off to soulless families desperate for kids. Muntra thought that might be a good thing. He was more afraid they would be used for other purposes.

He was shoved out the way by a larger man, and although he gritted his aching teeth, he backed away. Any more injuries and he wouldn't be able to work. Staying strong was the most important task he had, according to Shandra. Ready for when they would escape.

The other men were all meaner and stronger than him, and although he tried, he only distracted them long enough to give Shandra enough time to insert herself and whisk the child away. He swore he would be the meanest and the strongest one day and they would all pay for what they were putting them through.

Just because they didn't have a soul didn't mean they could be sold like a piece of meat. Eidolon was a land of gloom, shadows, and laughter, if you knew where to look. Shandra's place had been a good home until they'd lost it all. He was the largest of the kids who had sheltered in the rundown house she had maintained, and that came with responsibilities. With that thought, he searched for Bailey.

Shuffling over to stand next to the boy, Muntra offered him a grubby woollen hat to pull over his blond curls, though his vivid blue eyes could not be so easily disguised. "Don't smile," Muntra growled. "Keep your eyes on the floor and remember to scowl. How are your hands?"

"Fine." Bailey displayed his grimy hands which were wrapped in blood speckled strips of cloth. "Stop growling at me. You'll only draw more attention."

"You don't need me to do that."

"One more day, Muntra. We need to survive one more day."

"And then what?"

"We survive another."

"What if we can't survive?"

Brilliant blue eyes flashed up at him. "We will."

Muntra wanted to believe him. He was so assured, so

determined. Yet, Bailey didn't realise his days were numbered as the guards watched him with greedy eyes. *Too innocent for a place like this.* "One more day," Muntra muttered under his breath as he and Bailey joined the crew line for the mines. Another day in the dank gloom of the rock face. Another day of watching the ceilings for rock falls and the threat of flooding. Another day of keeping an eye on Bailey.

As they shuffled down the path to the mine entrance a slight figure darted out and joined the line. Muntra barely heard the low whisper. "Here, keep it with you at all times." Bailey stiffened as something was shoved in his hand, and the figure was gone. Bailey knelt briefly as if to fiddle with his boot and stood again. Kiara? Had that been Kiara? How had she gotten into the men's section? They hadn't heard from the women's quarters. He hoped they were all well. Or as well as they could be.

Muntra wanted to watch where she went, but he kept his eyes down and tightened his grip on Bailey's arm. It took them longer to reach the rock face than he remembered. Stumbling over the uneven ground, crawling through tunnels barely big enough for him, they were exhausted by the time they arrived to start work. A crippling fear of his was getting stuck in the narrow tunnels. An even greater fear was that he would be deemed too big for the kid's mines and drafted into the men's section. He wouldn't be able to protect Bailey and the others if that happened.

He collected one of the crude pickaxes out of the barrel. The tools were blunt so they couldn't be used for weapons and as a result took twice as long for them to make any useful impression on the rock face.

Bailey took another pick and headed off down a side tunnel. Muntra soon heard the dull thud as he attacked the rock. Muntra entered a narrow tunnel dragging a truckle box behind him. The square boxes were on runners, supposedly to make it easier to push them back out once loaded, but Muntra didn't think they made much difference with the uneven rocky floors.

The scent of tangy water infused with hidden minerals pervaded the damp air. The constant trickle down the walls was a counterpoint to his rhythmic swings. Drip, thud. Drip, thud. As a pile of rock fragments collected by his feet, he dropped to his knees and began to shift it into the truckle. His fingernails were ripped and torn as he shovelled up the rock. Sweat ran down his face as he bent and scooped, over and over, ignoring his stinging fingers. Lifting his head, he frowned as the thuds stopped from the adjoining tunnel. Was that a cry? He leapt to his feet and ran down the passageway towards the entrance Bailey had chosen.

Skidding to a halt, he gaped as a boy stumbled out of the tunnel, clutching his face, followed by a Bailey whom Muntra didn't recognise.

Bailey's eyes flashed with fury, and he held a tiny blade in front of him. His face was pale and strained under all the grime, his blue eyes wide and hard. "You so much as come near me again and I swear I'll cut your fucking dick off."

Muntra stared in shock as Bailey faced down the older boy. He had never heard Bailey use such language before.

"You'll pay for this," the boy snarled, clasping his face as blood seeped through his fingers.

Bailey's hand was steady. "No, you will, you sadistic bastard. I swear, you ever touch me again, you'll regret it."

The boy stumbled away and Muntra went to grasp Bailey's arm, but he flinched away. "Sorry," Bailey mumbled, crouching down to hide his precious weapon down his sock.

"What happened?" Muntra asked.

"Nothing. I don't want to talk about it." Bailey turned his back on Muntra and strode back down his tunnel.

Muntra hesitated for a moment, concern for his friend

locking him place. He had never seen such a ferocious expression on Bailey's beautiful face before, nor did he ever want to see it again.

Brennan hit the wall so hard he snapped the wooden handle, and he whimpered as pain shot up his arm. He was no better than a snivelling coward. He had seen that boy follow Bailey and he had done nothing. After all the kindness Bailey had shown him, he had chickened out and left him to fend for himself. But he was as shocked as the older boy who attacked Bailey, when Bailey proved to be no push over.

Brennan didn't think he had the guts to stand up for himself like Bailey had done. And even so, had it only made it worse? Was Bailey going to be even more of a target? Brennan didn't know. This place was only full of bullies.

Stomping back towards the junction to get a new pick, he ignored the mutters of a group of boys who passed him in the tunnel. Damp air swirled around him, and he shivered, his thin shirt no protection against the cold. It never seemed to be warm in Eidolon. Everything was damp and dreary.

"What are you doing here?" a rough voice snapped, and Brennan was jerked out of his thoughts.

"M-my pick broke," he stuttered.

"That will be docked from yer pay. Name?"

"Bren."

"Get yerself another, then. What you waiting fer?"

In the dim light of the lantern hanging from a hook in the overhead beam, he selected a new pick, and the guard snarled at him to get a move on.

Brennan was relieved the man didn't follow him as he hurried back along the rough passageway. Time away from the rock face meant less ore in his box, and that meant no pay. He would starve today if he didn't hurry up. Especially if he was docked for the pickaxe. It was so unfair. His stomach grumbled at the thought of no food.

A sharp cry echoed down the tunnel and he froze.

And then, before he could think twice, he rushed towards the entrance where Bailey had gone. Arriving at the end of the tunnel, a large boy, Muntra he thought his name was, swung his pickaxe at another boy, and the boy jerked back, revealing Bailey pinned down by two other lads, his clothes torn and bloody, his pale skin glowing in the dim light.

Brennan gritted his teeth and rushed in, swinging his axe like Muntra, and the boys scattered. Bailey curled up in a ball and hid his face. Brennan swung again and made contact, more a thumping bruise than chopping off a limb, but satisfaction flooded him as the boy yelped in pain and ran away.

Muntra had chased away the other two boys, his fury leaving them battered and bleeding, and was now kneeling next to Bailey. He tentatively extended a hand. "Bailey? Are you alright?"

Bailey shook and huddled into a tighter ball.

Glancing up, Muntra gave Brennan a tight smile. "Bren, isn't it?"

Brennan nodded.

"Do you think you could go and find some new clothes for Bailey? They ripped his to shreds."

"Did they hurt..." Brennan stuttered to a halt. Of course they had hurt him. He wouldn't be clenched so tight if they hadn't.

"He'll be fine once he's dressed," Muntra replied, but Brennan didn't believe him.

"They'll come back."

"I'll kill them if they do," Muntra growled.

Brennan hurried away. He had no idea where to get clothes that might fit Bailey. Nor did he want to bump into the lads who'd attacked him. They could be waiting at the tunnel entrance.

He darted back into his tunnel and dropped the axe against the wall. There had been a small crevice in the shadows at the bend. He had felt a draft earlier and had intended exploring. Maybe it had been a sign and now was the time to investigate. If it kept him away from the other boys then he was fine with that.

As he worked to make the hole larger, fresh air flooded the passage, and crawling through the gap, he scurried on hands and knees towards the flow of air, the rough rock scraping his skin. Breathing out a sigh of relief, he crawled down the tunnel, the light brightening at the end.

He wracked his brain, trying to remember where the store rooms were. One of the dybbuks had come out of a windowless hut with a pile of blankets. That building might be a store room. It couldn't hurt to look.

The tunnel came out on the eastern side of the compound, near the part of the fence which butted up to the cliff face. No one was watching, that he could see, so he parted the bush and squirmed out. Trying not to run, he scuttled towards one of the buildings without windows next to one of the sleeping huts. Crossing the yard and creeping around the side of the building, he crouched in the ditch and watched the dybbuks harrying kids from one place to another.

They all seemed too busy to notice him.

One of the planks at the bottom of the building was bowed, and Brennan tugged it, and then he loosened the one above so he could peer inside. It was too dark to see, so he squirmed through the gap and stilled, listening.

The air was musty and dry, so Brennan crawled further in, feeling for boxes or shelves in the dark. The scant light from the loosened boards only revealed the wooden floor and shelving. He began feeling his way down the shelves until he found material. Grabbing what felt like a blanket and maybe trousers, he froze as the door rattled. His heart jumped into his throat as sweat trickled down his spine.

Muffled voices spoke outside the door and then moved away. Brennan exhaled and then froze as he kicked a box and it clinked. Recognising the long dark shapes in the dim light as knives, more than one stacked in a box, he grabbed a couple and then made his escape, his heart still thrumming as he squeezed out the gap and pushed the planks back together.

After a quick check that no one was watching the yard, he darted back across the muddy ground into his concealed tunnel entrance and breathing heavily, he hurried back to Bailey and Muntra. As he approached the end of Bailey's tunnel, he heard a low voice, soft and soothing, and although Bren couldn't hear the words, the tone was comforting.

Muntra broke off and looked up as Brennan hesitated in the shadows. Muntra had given his shirt to Bailey, who was in his arms, curled up on his lap, and Muntra had been whispering in his ear.

Brennan dropped to his knees and wrapped the blanket around them both. In the light of the lamp, he realised he had grabbed a shirt. Far too big for Bailey, but it might fit Muntra.

"I found these as well," he said, showing Muntra the knives. "I don't know how to use one, but I thought you might. If-if they come back."

Bailey shuddered in Muntra's arms, and Muntra soothed him again, tightening his embrace. "We have to get Bailey out of here," he said.

"There was a guard near the junction. He was walking through the tunnels."

"Making sure no one is slacking. I'm surprised he hasn't

come to check why we are not working." Muntra stared down the tunnel. "But I didn't mean out of this mine, I meant out of this compound. He's not safe here. If it's not the other boys, it will be the dybbuks."

Bailey whimpered.

"But why? He wouldn't hurt anyone."

Muntra scowled. "There is always someone who wants to spoil whatever is more beautiful than them."

Brennan clenched his jaw. "I'll help, if I can."

Muntra smiled at him. "It's safer if you distance yourself from us. We really appreciate your offer, but there's no guarantee we'll succeed."

"I don't care. I'm not staying here. I'd rather go with you."

Bailey wormed a hand out of his blanket and briefly gripped Brennan's arm before disappearing under the cover again, though his face remained tucked in Muntra's neck.

Raised voices, deeper in the mine, had Muntra rising, Bailey still in his arms. "We can't stay in here, it's a dead end."

"There's a crevice off the tunnel where I was working. I found it yesterday. It comes out near the stores shed. Only, I don't think you'll fit, Muntra."

The voices came closer, and Muntra came to a decision. "If we can hide you and Bailey in there until dark, then I can meet you by the stores shed. They won't notice we're missing until roll call in the morning. We need to be gone by then."

"What about Shandra and Kiara?" Bailey whispered.

"I'll try and get word to them. We won't be able to take all the kids, but if we can get out, we can at least tell others what is happening here."

Brennan led the way to the crevice, and Muntra scowled. "I never thought I'd regret my size, but it does me no favours in here." He set Bailey down, who clutched at him. Muntra kissed his head. "I promise I'll meet you at the stores shed. I'll cause a diversion on the other side of the compound, draw them away, and then we all get out in the confusion."

Bailey looked up at him, eyes wide, pupils blown, and after a moment, he nodded. Squaring his shoulders, he hugged the blanket tighter.

"Lead the way, Bren. Take one of the knives just in case," Muntra said.

Bailey took it, his knuckles gleaming white at the strength of his grip, and then he ducked into the crevice and was gone.

26

DEMAVRIAN, CITADEL

Early the next morning, Sero arrived with the breakfast trolley. He flew in the open door and pirouetted above Mav. "It's a beautiful day to go ring hunting!" he trilled.

Mav glared at him. "Shout it a little louder, why don't you?"

Sero laughed. "No one takes us cherubs seriously, except for you. You always did."

Huffing his breath out, Mav pulled up a chair and offered to pour Solanji a cup of bannoe. She smiled her thanks and buttered a piece of toast, slathering it with a tangy conserve. She offered it to Sero, who swooped in to grab it and stuffed it in his mouth.

"More fool them," Mav muttered.

Solanji buttered another piece of toast, slowing as she realised Sero was watching her.

"Don't stop. You need more butter."

"You're not a butter baby, are you, Sero?" she teased.

Sero blushed, not taking his eyes off her plate. "I can't help it. I just love it. Don't bother with the conserve." He accepted the toast and closed his eyes as he bit into the crunchy bread and sighed out with pleasure as he dropped to the table and sat down. He savoured the buttery flavour, and then as he sucked the melted deliciousness off his fingers, he opened his eyes and blushed an even deeper red as he saw Mav and Solanji both watching him in amusement. "It's my guilty pleasure. Don't tell anyone, please."

"I wouldn't dream of it," Mav said, placing his hand over his heart.

"Me neither," Solanji promised.

"I knew you could be trusted," Sero said happily, eyeing another piece of toast. Solanji began buttering again.

"This is so homely," Sero said as he rose into the air, his golden wings fluttering as he hovered above them. "I'll sing you a song." A small golden harp appeared in his hands.

Leaning back in his chair, Mav sipped his bannoe and watched the little cherub. "Much as we would love to listen to you sing, we don't have much time," he said.

"No one ever wants to listen to me these days. But you haven't finished your meal yet. It won't take long."

"In that case, we would be honoured," Mav said, setting his cup down and reaching across the table to clasp Solanji's hand. "What would you like to sing to us?"

Sero's blue eyes gleamed. "A love song, of course."

"Of course," Mav said, his lips twitching. "Cherubs can't resist jumping to conclusions when they see a man and a woman seated together."

Solanji chuckled and caressed his knuckles. "I've never heard a cherub sing."

"Then I will be quiet and let you enjoy." Mav grinned at Sero, and the cherub ran his fingers over his harp and began singing. Solanji and Mav sat mesmerised as his pure tones encased them in his magic. They were silent, staring into each other's eyes as Sero finished singing and plopped onto the table.

"Is there any butter left?" he asked with a satisfied smirk as he watched them.

Mav stirred and blinked. "What?" He relaxed his grip on Solanji's hand and gazed at Sero.

"You're a lost cause, my dear archdeus!" Sero said with a laugh as he dipped his finger in the butter dish, and Solanji flushed as he gave her an insinuating smile.

Solanji cleared her throat and released Mav's fingers. "Umm, so Sero, you can get us into Serenia's rooms?"

"Easy, once Mav starts his show. They'll all be watching him."

"You're not going to have that long to search for the ring, though. Any thoughts on where she'll have stashed it?" Mav asked.

"If she always used to wear it, it should be easy to get to. Maybe it's still in her jewellery box," Solanji suggested.

"That's too simple, surely?"

Solanji shrugged. "After fifty years, she'll not be thinking anyone remembers it, and if she likes to keep it close, the jewellery box makes most sense."

"Depends how guilty she is feeling," Sero said, licking his fingers. "Not very, I expect, so she may not be hiding anymore. That's if she ever did hide it."

"I don't like it," Mav said, rolling his shoulders as tension threatened to seize him up. He hated being so helpless.

"If it helps prove your innocence, it will be worth the risk." Solanji rose and began kneading his shoulders. "Let us help, Mav. You can't do everything on your own."

"Listen to your young lady," Sero said as the chamber doors opened and Felather and Kerris entered, followed by Adriz.

"Ready?" Felather asked.

. . .

Mav walked into the council hall as the timepiece struck nine. He had deliberately worn his ceremonial blue robes, denoting his station, and they felt heavy on his shoulders; the weight of expectation heavier than the gold-embroidered material. He ignored the buzz of gossip, not caring what they thought. His mouth tightened as he thought of his fledglings and what they were up to. Sero had better make sure they came back. Adriz and Felather followed him down the hall, and as his footsteps slowed, they strode past him to their positions behind his seat on the dais.

Mav walked up the steps and made a show of sitting in his chair next to Serenia. As soon as he sat, Serenia was on her feet calling for silence. "Apologia is back in session. Archdeus Demavrian stands accused of four counts." She scowled at him before continuing. "The first count, that Demavrian is soulless, was successfully defended." She twisted her lips as she gestured at Mav. "As you can see, he is still here and very much alive."

It sounded very much like she wished he wasn't, and Mav lifted his chin as he stared down the hall.

"The second count has been struck. The council accept that Demavrian did not murder his father. The citadel confirmed that Averdeus still lives, even if his whereabouts are unknown. As such, Demavrian will still be confined to his rooms when not in Apologia until the council is fully satisfied that Demavrian was not involved in Averdeus' disappearance.

Demavrian stiffened. He had disproved the count, so now they had reverted back to the original accusation? He ground his teeth and said nothing.

"Which count do you choose to defend next?"

Mav rose and descended the steps.

"Count three. I will flare my wings. Who accuses and what is the real question?" Mav asked, his deep voice echoing around the silent chamber. "You know who I am. You know I have wings, so what are you really asking?"

"We haven't seen your wings since you returned," a bored seraphim stated from his seat in the front tier, not bothering to rise. He brushed the wrinkles out of his sleeve and didn't even look at Mav.

Mav stared at him, the silence lengthening until the seraphim looked up, met Mav's eyes, and slowly rose to his feet. "I am Seraphim Lianderis. I restate, we haven't seen your wings since you returned."

"Are you the accuser?"

"I am."

"Is that it? I flare my wings and you accept that I am an angel? An archdeus no less? And the count is discharged. Which of course you already know. Or is there some ulterior question lurking beneath your exquisite feathers?"

Lianderis hissed his breath out.

"So, I repeat, I demonstrate I have wings and that is the end of your accusations?"

"Yes. Show us your wings and we accept that you are truly Archdeus Demavrian Deusson. Returned and forgiven."

Mav stiffened. "Forgiven for what precisely?"

"For leaving."

"Shit," Felather muttered under his breath.

"What?" Adriz breathed.

"If he accepts that he needs to be forgiven then it is a tacit acceptance that he did something wrong."

"But I didn't leave voluntarily," Mav replied and Felather relaxed.

"Yes, you did. You deserted us in our time of need. Your

father gone, our SoulBreather lost, last seen dying in your arms. You ran."

"I was unconscious. You incarcerated me in a cell, or so I am told," Mav said, strolling down the hall to the point where the ceiling was highest. "With the threat of execution hanging over my head."

"What's he doing?" Adriz whispered.

"I have no idea," Felather breathed back, his face tight.

Adriz stepped out of formation and strode down the hall to stand behind Mav. She slammed the butt of her spear down on the marble floor and stiffened into a ceremonial stance. Armour gleaming, sword honed sharp, a statement. Validation.

"Oh, god," Felather muttered and followed Adriz down the steps and across the hall until he stood behind Mav's right shoulder.

"You think your cherubim and your scribe can validate your right to stand in this chamber?" the seraphim sneered.

Mav raised his eyebrows, not having acknowledged the arrival of his cherubim or his scribe. "Of course," he replied. "Their provenance is not being challenged."

Amaridin spoke. "I confirm their provenance, should anyone question it."

The word *dare* hovered in the air, and the seraphim backed down. He bowed to the throne and formally declared, "The cherubim and the scribe are accepted."

"Noted," Amaridin said. "Continue."

Lianderis hesitated and glanced at Serenia, who stood immobile before her chair.

"So," Mav said, his voice low and sharp as a blade. "We return to the question."

Lianderis glared at him. "Which question?"

"Are you unable to follow the discourse, Seraphim Lianderis?" Mav raised an eyebrow, observing the seraphim.

Lianderis laughed, though he sounded a bit hollow. "My colleagues and I have discussed many more complex issues than you and your wings, I can assure you."

"I would hope so." Mav murmured and faced the rising tiers of the council seated to the left. Many faces he recognised, but there were many he didn't, and they were all avidly watching him.

Lianderis drew himself up, his robes swirling around his legs. "You delay. Flare your wings or accept your sentence."

Mav pursed his lips. "That you dare to pose such an accusation makes me doubt your sanity, or maybe your longevity," he said, his voice soft as his shadowy wings flared behind him, and the occupants of the hall gasped, seraphim and fledglings alike rising to their feet at the sight. "My wings are mine," he declared as he rotated, his glorious wings extended, sparkles of silver and gold accentuating their sleek power and strength, "and unless I deem it necessary, this is the only time I will display them to you." He glared at the standing seraphims who stared at him, at his impossible wings, with mouths agape, until he met Serenia's shocked gaze.

"No, they are not true wings," Lianderis protested. "They are not white! How did he get them?"

"Since when do wings have to be white? I trust I have proved my point," Mav said.

"Yes, I believe you have," Serenia replied, her face tight, her lips thinning with displeasure, and then she said, "Count dismissed." And a gravel slammed down in the recesses of the hall and echoed through the chamber. The host grabbed the protesting Lianderis by the arms and escorted him out.

"Good," Mav said, and he flexed his glistening wings and then folded them away as he strode out of the hall. The chamber exploded into discussion, voices raised in shock and disbelief.

27

SOLANJI

ero led the way through the dim back corridors towards the wing where Serenia had her rooms. "Are you sure everyone will be at the Apologia?" Solanji asked as she scuttled after him.

"Anyone who matters will be. They can't resist a bit of drama. We've probably got a turn, maybe two, so no time wasting," Sero replied.

"That's not long enough!"

"It will be," Sero chuckled. "I'm with you.

"Are all Cherub's as big-headed as you?" Kerris asked.

Sero spun and wagged his finger in front of Kerris' nose. "Are all fledglings disrespectful of their elders?"

"How old are you?"

Sero raised a golden eyebrow. "A scribe should be more subtle in their information gathering, but I like your direct-ness, surprisingly," he added and flew off.

"Stop distracting him. You can ask him after, if we don't get caught." Solanji paused and then shrugged. "Or even if we do get caught, it will probably alleviate some of the sheer terror we'll be feeling."

"We'll be fine," Kerris said.

"I like your confidence," Solanji murmured as they hurried after Sero down corridors lined with huge oil paintings. High ceilings rose over head, the carpets were soft and spongy under foot and Solanji hunched her shoulders against the sense of being in the wrong place. The citadel was a treasure trove of exquisite decorations and she felt like an intruder. Lifesize marble statues of angels, cherubs and the Heavenly Host peered at them from sheltered alcoves as they passed. Solanji had never seen the like before and shivered as the blank eyes followed them as if they knew they were up to no good. They reached Sero as he hovered outside a gilt-adorned set of double doors. "There's no one inside, so in you go."

"Are you not coming to help us search?"

"I'm on guard," Sero said, pretending to march back and forth in the air.

"You won't fool anyone doing that," Solanji said as she tried the door. It was locked. She sank to her knees and pulled out an ornate pin from her hair. The pin was intricately grooved and connected to a flexible rod that flexed as Solanji squeezed them together.

"That's an interesting tool for a young fledgling to have," Sero whispered in her ear and Solanji bit her tongue trying not to squeal out loud.

"Don't do that," she growled, her heart in her throat.

"Well, it is. You have hidden depths, my dear," he said as the lock clicked and the door swung open.

"I did have a life before I became entangled with angels," Solanji replied as she and Kerris slid into the room. The door snicked shut as she leaned on it, trying to control her racing heart. She glanced around Serenia's room. It was exquisitely impersonal. Pale blue rugs covered the floor. Elegant statement pieces of furniture were strategically positioned to entice you in, but there were no personal items. Kerris hovered near the door, his face a picture. He looked like he expected to be berated for daring to enter such a *clean* room.

Solanji took a breath and stepped onto the rug. Her boots sank into the plush pile and she resisted the urge to drop to the floor and scrunch her fingers through the thick strands. She jumped as a ball dropped with a clink into a shallow glass jar on the mantelpiece above the fire. A miniature timepiece tracked the time. It was a quarter after the ninth turn. "You search this room and I'll search the next," Solanji hissed and forced herself to walk across the rug to the other side of the room. She paused with her hand on the door handle. "Kerris," she snapped, and Kerris visibly flinched and swallowed before taking a step forward. "We don't have time to gawp. Just get looking!"

Kerris nodded and moved over to the roll top desk made of dark brown wood. He slid the ridged cover up, slowing at the loud clack of the slats as they folded away, revealing cubby holes filled with papers. Perching on the edge of the chair, he exhaled and began rifling through the contents.

Solanji opened the door to the inner chamber and halted on the threshold. If she ever had a room of her own, she imagined it would be something like this. A four-poster bed took up most of the space, festooned with drapes of cloth in dusky rose and the pale blue matching the outer room. A soft, plush chair sat in an alcove that would get plenty of sun, and shelves of books surrounded it. An ornate mirror stood on a table, with a bank of drawers underneath. Solanji hurried over to the dressing table, her fingers fluttering over pots and jars.

She pulled out drawers and halted when one revealed a wooden box with a cloudy white flower design inlaid on the surface. Dropping to her knees, she lifted it out and raised the lid. A jumble of beads of all colours and a mess of golden chains greeted her eyes. They were all knotted together, and Solanji doubted they could ever be untangled. She lifted the mass out, but there was no ring lurking beneath it or within it. She shoved the box back in the drawer and continued searching.

Solanji's heart stuttered as a tingling chime rang around the room. A turn had passed; they were running out of time.

She was crawling about in the depths of the wardrobe when Sero's voice came from the outer room. "Quick, hide, the maids are coming."

She poked her head out the door. "What? You're supposed to divert them!"

"No time," he squeaked, pushing Kerris before him and into the wardrobe with Solanji. He shut the door behind him, and they all huddled beneath Serenia's robes.

"We're not all supposed to hide in the same place!" Solanji exclaimed.

"Hush," Sero hissed and they fell silent as the chamber door opened and someone entered. The maid moved around the room, though Solanji had no idea what she could be doing. The room was immaculate. The wardrobe door swung open and Solanji shrank back from the dim light. She gripped Kerris' arm, and she knew he held his breath.

The maid swept the robes apart and stilled. "What the…?" Her lips parted and a faint blush tinged her cheeks. "You do know this is a lady's chamber and men are not allowed?"

Solanji froze, her heart in her mouth.

"Then it would be best if she didn't know," Kerris replied, a faint tremble in his voice. "The others will rib me rotten if I'm caught."

"Lil? Who are you talking to?" another young voice called.

"No one, just myself," Lil replied and swept the robes back together. "I am going to pretend I haven't seen you. I suggest you find another room; this one will get you killed, and that would be such a shame." And then she shut the wardrobe door.

After a few excruciating minutes, Sero poked his head out. The rooms were silent and he flitted to the door and rested his hand on it. "They've gone," he said.

"Will they raise the alarm?" Solanji asked, finding it difficult to breathe.

"I don't think so, thanks to Kerris' quick thinking. Well done, lad. But we are running out of time. Have you found anything?"

"Nothing. I was about to start on the books."

Sero nodded and flitted over to the book shelves and trailed his fingers along the spines. Kerris inspected the wood panelling that ran around the bottom half of the walls and then started tapping.

"Weren't you supposed to be guarding the door?" Solanji asked.

Sero shrugged. "You were right, I wouldn't fool anyone. Anyway, we'll search quicker with the three of us. These books are just for show. She hasn't read them."

"Why does she have so many, then?" Solanji asked with a frown.

"Ow!" Kerris yelped as a wood panel swung open and bashed him in the face. He held his cheek and grabbed the panel before it could slide back into place. Sero rushed to his side and peered into the opening.

"Well, what do we have here?" the cherub murmured, and he squeezed into the hole.

"Sero? What are you doing?" Solanji demanded as she inspected Kerris' reddening eye. Tears streaked his swelling cheek, and he flinched away as she tried to dab his face. "You are going to have a lovely black eye."

They froze as the outer door clicked open. "It is untenable," Serenia's cold voice echoed in her perfect room. Solanji let the panel snick shut, and she dragged Kerris back towards the wardrobe, shoved him inside and dived in after him.

Barely breathing, she listened intently as Serenia entered the room, moments later the bed creaked as she sat and the dull thud of her shoes hitting the floor followed. "Amaridin, darling, this is your fault. You were too lenient on him. I told you he would twist everything. He is not an archdeus anymore, even you should be able to see that."

"Just because his wings have changed doesn't mean he isn't an archdeus."

Serenia sighed loudly. "You must see they change everything!"

"Why?" Amaridin's response was sharp and cold.

"Because his wings are black. He must have fallen to Kaenera's influence. He has been tainted by his time in Eidolon. He is no longer the man he was; it is quite obvious. You can't allow that in the citadel."

Solanji silently exhaled as the bed creaked again as Serenia rose. "You will hold it all, Amaridin. It's what you've always wanted, don't you remember?" Her voice dropped to a whisper.

"That is what you want, Serenia. Prove his guilt or let him go. False accusations will get you nowhere."

"Dear boy, your attempts to assert yourself are pathetic. You will do as I say or pay the consequences."

"Eodan is overstepping the line," Amaridin protested.

"You are overstepping. Be careful, Amaridin. Now I need to change, so be off with you."

Serenia tutted and then closed the door. The swish of her

robes dropping to the floor preceded her sweeping a gown off the bed.

Struggling to keep her eyes open, snuggled in the dark wardrobe, Solanji exhaled in relief when Serenia finally left the room. Solanji eased her way out from the wardrobe. One eye on the chamber door, she tugged on Kerris' arm. "Kerris?" she breathed, and gave the boy a shaky smile as his pale face appeared between the silk dresses. His pupils were huge in his terrified face, and putting her finger to her lips, she crept to the bedroom door and listened.

"Let Sero out," she mouthed.

Kerris' nod was a bit jerky, but he carefully pressed the wood and rotated the panel. He peered inside. "Sero?"

There was silence.

"Where is he?" Solanji whispered.

"He's not there."

"We need to go. Maybe he slipped out." Solanji frowned. She wasn't sure when he would have had the chance. They were out of the bedchamber and nearly across the outer chamber when the door to the corridor began to open.

Solanji's heart stuttered, and she grabbed Kerris and pulled him behind the opening door. His face was salt white and he looked like he was going to faint. She clutched him tight and peered through the gap between the door and the door frame, his heart thrumming as fast as hers.

A woman shut the door, her back to the corner where Solanji and Kerris stood like statues, and crossed the room, grumbling under her breath. Solanji watched her disappear into the bedchamber and then yanked the door open and dragged Kerris with her, as they fled down the corridor.

Behind the wooden panel, Sero listened intently as Serenia's voice grew louder. He wrinkled his brow, disbelief curdling his veins as she denounced Demavrian. It was only since Demavrian's return that the citadel had felt anything like its former self. The one time the heartbeat had pulsed through the building, revitalising all within it, was all down to him.

With renewed determination, Sero touched the wooden panel, letting its history seep into his mind. The tree it had been cut from, the carpenter who had shaped and polished it, the builder who had set it in place, the archangel who had hidden her treasures within.

Sero dropped to the floor and smiled as the memories of Serenia levering up a plank and hiding a bundle beneath, scrolled before him. Following the ghostly hands, Sero pulled up the dusty wood, and brushing cobwebs away, he rummaged below and almost laughed out loud as his fingers touched soft material.

Sealing the plank back in place and unravelling the cloth, Sero froze as he touched the ring, and its last memories became his. His heart stuttered, and he felt light-headed as the memories seeped into him, his to hold forever. After a moment of deep breathing to control his rapidly beating heart, he slid the ring on his middle finger. Rotating the large amethyst gem to be hidden within his palm, he gripped it tight and followed the dark passageway towards the faint glow at the end.

He ignored the cobwebs trailing through his hair, the dust griming his usually pure white tunic. He needed to find Demavrian.

Arriving back at Mav's chambers Solanji slammed the door shut behind her and leaned against it as she scanned the room. "Is Sero here?"

"I thought he was with you," Felather replied, raising an eyebrow. "Did you find it?"

"No, we were nearly caught." Solanji flung herself into a chair. "It's impossible! We found a secret hidey-hole. Sero got locked inside it when Serenia returned to her rooms and we all had to hide. But after she left, we checked again and he was gone. We kept getting interrupted by the maids."

Kerris collapsed on the chair next to her and clasped his head in his hands. "That was scary as shit!"

"And Sero was useless," Solanji said. "Where *is* he?" She looked around and narrowed her eyes. "What happened in Apologia? Where's Mav?"

Felather shrugged. "Mav flared his wings; the count was rescinded."

Solanji exhaled. "Thank goodness."

Kerris frowned at her. "You said he had wings; you knew he would flare them."

"Yes, but he didn't completely believe me. There was always a chance…" Solanji's voice trailed off as she rose and began pacing. She couldn't keep still. Pacing back and forth, she chewed her lip as Felather and Kerris watched her. "Was he alright?" Solanji asked pacing again.

"He'll be fine, Solanji."

"I'm worried about Sero. We shouldn't have left him. What if Serenia finds him?"

"Unlikely, don't you think? She was more likely to discover you or Kerris. And it would be worse for you than a cherub."

"We still shouldn't have left him! I feel terrible."

"Don't be. Sero must have found another way out. Worst case he just has to wait until the maid finishes."

Solanji huffed. She clenched her fingers into fists, wishing she could thump someone. She was sure she had lost a few years from sheer fright. Kerris was hunched over by the fire. At least he had a little colour in his cheeks, though that may have been the bruising from by being bashed by the wooden panel. His prowling skills were little better than hers. "Where do you think Mav went?"

"It's probably the first time he's flown in centuries. It will take him a while to come back down."

"But his wings…"

"What about them?"

"They are…"

"Perfect," Mav's voice came from the doorway. He limped inside, shutting the door behind him, and Solanji was across the room, a tentative hand reaching for him.

"Mav," she whispered as she brushed his silver-streaked hair away from his beautiful face.

"Solanji," he replied.

"Are you truly alright?"

"As well as can be expected," he murmured against her fingers as she caressed his lips.

"What do you need?"

His breath sighed out, exhaustion in every line of his body. "Apart from some sleep, I have no idea."

Her fingers smoothed over his cheek; soft shadows gilded the edges, giving him an inhuman beauty, and he leaned into her palm. Extending her soul fingers, she caressed his shadows, and his shoulders dropped, his eyelids lowering. She pressed against his body and his arms slid around her waist as he exhaled, his breath hot on her neck.

"Did you find the ring?" he asked.

"I don't know," Solanji whispered back, combing her fingers through his hair. "Sero is trapped in Serenia's rooms and we're waiting for him to escape. We found a hidden space, but we don't know what's in it, except for Sero. Mav, I'm so sorry, we left him there. Serenia came back and we had to escape when we had the chance."

Mav shuddered and she tightened her grip on him.

Felather cleared his throat, and Mav tensed. "We'll let you two talk. Kerris, we can use the time to discuss healing. Mav should rest. Don't let him do anything too strenuous...I mean, umm...sleep. He needs to sleep. I'll send some food up later." Felather bobbed his head, his face bright red, and grabbing Kerris, he ran. The door clicked shut behind them.

"Sleep? Is that what you need?"

"It may be what I need, but it's not what I want," Mav replied, kissing her. "You were saying?" He nudged her hand.

She laughed and snuggled into his golden-shot shadows as they circled around her, drawing her into him, and they shuffled over to his bed chamber. She helped him lift his leg onto the bed and he groaned as he relaxed. "My back. I've been using muscles that haven't flexed in decades."

"Let me help you with that," she murmured as she began to undo his buttons. Her lips followed her fingers, soft and moist, leaving a hot trail across sensitive skin. Mav shivered under her touch and she unbuckled the straps, pulling them out from under him, aware that his gleaming eyes followed her every move.

Pushing his shirt over his shoulders, he shrugged out of it, and she flung it over her shoulder, smiling as his lips twitched. "I might need that," he said.

"Not for now, at least," Solanji whispered against his skin as she kissed her way down his chest, her soul fingers stroking the edge of shadowy wings, and he melted into the bed as she rubbed her cheek against the soft, dark hair on his chest and dropped gentle kisses on his stomach. He shuddered beneath her. His eyes, more golden than amber, closed as she caressed all of him. She worked the buckles loose at his waist and snapped the belt away, jolting him back to his senses. She didn't want him so ensorcelled that he wouldn't remember.

Soothing him back down on the bed with long, sensuous strokes of his shadows, she straddled him as her nimble fingers loosened the trouser fastenings, smiling at the heat of his arousal beneath her hands. A similar heat was building within her, though he hadn't touched her yet, he just watched her with a lazy smile on his face. A smile that sent her brain spiralling out of control. He reached for the ties of her shirt. His slender fingers were cool and pale against her darker skin. She trembled at the gentle sensation as his touch slid across her ribs and down her side, tickling, and she shuffled back, pulling his trousers with her.

He raised himself on his elbows. "We've been here before, I think. Though I'm sure you had fewer clothes on." His voice was low and gravelly, at odds with the flames burning in his eyes.

Solanji stripped the rest of her clothes off and paused for a moment for him to look his fill. After all, she had seen him naked more than once. She flushed as he slowly inspected her, his smile widening and then she climbed on the bed and slid her cool body the length of his heated one, and he groaned as she kissed her way up his neck and across his gritted jaw which tightened as she ground against him, stoking the fires. She worshipped the sharp angles of his cheeks, breathed into the shell of his ear and then back to his sensuous lips, where he took control and plundered her mouth as he flipped her over and covered her with his body.

She was burning. His heat was exquisite; it was torture as he explored her face in turn. Too slow, he was too slow. She arched her neck and his laugh was soft and sexy, but he skimmed down her neck to her chest and then stopped at one of her breasts and she groaned as he throbbed between her legs.

"Exquisite," he breathed against her skin. "You are so beautiful."

Solanji chuckled. "You're blind."

"No, my love, you are." He nuzzled her breast, sucking, teasing, and planting a trail of kisses that ignited her skin. A wave of heat swept through her, and she gasped as she arched off the bed, chasing his amazing lips.

He continued kissing his way down her body as heat pooled in her core, and she gripped his hair as she writhed under his touch. More, she needed more. His tasted her, tongue teasing, and she went up in flames, scorching desire rippling through her as she tried to hold herself together.

"Please…" she whispered. "I need you…now!"

Mav raised his head and peered at her over her belly, and she met his blazing eyes as he slid up her body, his erection hot and pulsing against her skin, and then kissing her, he slowly pushed his way inside.

Solanji devoured his mouth, her questing tongue plundering deeper as she clenched around him. She swallowed his groan as he thrust again, and she arched against him, taking him all the way as he shuddered. He tried to pull out, but she followed him, keeping him embedded to the hilt as she clenched around him, relaxed, and clenched again. He pushed with her, a sensuous motion that took them both to the peak, and they both stilled, questing after that moment of sheer exquisite pleasure, before they began breathing again and shuddered in unison as they came, waves and waves of sensation and tingling desire rippling through them.

Breathing heavily, Solanji hugged Mav tight, preventing him from moving. He was seated deep inside her, and she never wanted him to leave. His heat flooded her, his body was limp and heavy on top her, and she had never felt better in her life.

"I love you so much," she whispered.

Mav raised his head and met her gaze, his amber eyes molten with desire. "I love you just as much," he replied as he gently kissed her. "You are absolutely perfect, and I love every bit of you."

Solanji chuckled, and he groaned. "Don't laugh, I can't take any more." She let him ease out and flop next to her. Snuggling into his arms, she inhaled the delicious scent of his sweaty body and then couldn't resist kissing his shoulder, his neck, tasting his salty skin, inhaling deeply.

"You sound like you want to eat me," Mav murmured. "We should get dressed and have some lunch."

"I want to devour you," Solanji replied, "every single day of my life."

Mav relaxed in her arms. "That can be arranged, my darling."

28

XYLVIN, EIDOLON

Xylvin spread her wings and glided over an area of thick forest which was split by a muddy track, leading to the first compound on their list. She tasted the damp, pine-scented air and said, *"There is no way we can tell if Mav's fledglings are in there from up here."*

"Which is why we land and see if they'll let me in," Ryvalin replied. *"We have no time to waste. We have nine more compounds to check."*

"Hopefully, we'll find them before we have to search all of them. I get the feeling we have days not weeks."

"Me too, and we've wasted half of one getting here, so land here Xylvin, and let's see what we can find."

Xylvin banked and then back-winged as she carefully descended through the trees and onto the road leading up to the main gate. A flurry of activity in the compound had the gate creaking open, and a shabby looking guard squinted at them. Someone shoved him in the back, and he scowled at the person behind him, stepped through the opening, and slowly approached, his eyes wide as he stared at the dragon.

He peered up at Xylvin and visibly gulped as he halted a

good distance away. "Yes? What do you want?" he called. His voice shook, and he instinctively took a step back as Ryvalin dismounted.

Waving her papers in the air, she walked towards him. Xylvin hissed out her breath, curls of smoke drifting around Ryvalin's ankles. "We're here on Seraphim Kyrill's orders. He had some of his fledglings delivered here by mistake and he wants them back," Ryvalin said.

The guard shook his head. "Not had any new slaves arrive for at least two weeks. They're not here."

Ryvalin frowned. "You're sure? It would have been a wagon of youngsters from up north."

"No kids here. You've been told wrong."

"Seraphim Kyrill doesn't get things wrong."

The man shrugged. "You can come and look if you want, but there are no kids here. Must have been taken to one of the other compounds. There's a couple of camps further south that use kids for mining. They can fit in the small spaces."

"They're not here," Xylvin murmured. *"Let's not waste our time."*

Ryvalin scowled. "Very well. Do you know which compounds use the children?"

"The ones near the ridges. That way, I think." The man waved vaguely in the air and retreated. Ryvalin let him go.

"Do you know which compounds are near ridges?" Ryvalin asked, as she climbed back up onto Xylvin.

"There were some hills to the southeast. I think there was a compound on the other side. Let's try that one."

"As good as any." Ryvalin clipped the straps on her harness. She held on as Xylvin leapt into the air and manoeuvred herself around the over-hanging trees.

"Let's hope it's a bit more open," Xylvin said as she banked sharply and slid through a gap, rising into the cloudy sky.

"It really is beautiful," Ryvalin said as she looked around her. *"Except for those compounds."* She peered down at the people watching them from below.

"It may be beautiful, but it looks like we might be flying into a storm."

Ryvalin patted Xylvin's shoulder as she observed the bank of black clouds on the horizon. *"We won't melt."*

"I won't, but you'll get waterlogged."

Laughing, Ryvalin scanned the terrain as they passed, noting the snaking roads, the gleam of water, the isolated villages and farmsteads. Small patches of land around the dwellings were cultivated, but the vast majority was covered in thick vegetation and forests.

The untouched forest gave way to rising hills. Rocky outcrops perched on green-coated slopes peeping above the tree tops and then disappeared back into the tree line and down onto flat plains before rising into higher ground in the distance, a ridge of craggy cliff faces, weatherworn back to the underlying red-tinged rock. A wide river wound its way through the hills, a road following its route.

Ryvalin leaned forward as she spotted a muddy track wending its way towards the cliffs. *"There's a track to our left."*

"I see it," Xylvin replied and banked to follow it as a low rumble vibrated through the air.

"Let's try and get in and out before the rain starts," Ryvalin suggested.

"Agreed."

There was more room to land this time, the road opening into what looked like a turning circle for wagons to be loaded and unloaded. Xylvin dropped onto the waterlogged area, raised her leg for Ryvalin to dismount, and flipped her wings back as she watched her rider approach the gate, skirting the many muddy puddles. It seemed the storm was circling back around the hills for another deluge.

Ryvalin rapped on the gate with the hilt of her dagger. "Open up in the name of the citadel."

"Whaddya want?" a voice hollered.

"To speak to whoever is in charge," Ryvalin yelled back.

"The overseer ain't here, and we have orders not to open the gate."

"Well, you can either open it or my dragon will land in your yard and flatten anyone in the way. Your choice," Ryvalin replied.

Xylvin roared, making the fencing the rattle, and Ryvalin grinned at the yelps that came from the other side of the gate. A muted argument filtered thought the wooden slats.

"We ain't supposed to open it."

"That there's a dragon; she could burn it down."

Ryvalin doubted that, the wood was too wet, but Xylvin could, no doubt, knock it down. Maybe that would be a good idea, help these poor people escape. How long would they be free, she wondered. As soon as she and Xylvin left, the guards would just round them up again. These people had nowhere to go, and were probably far from home.

The argument continued. "If we open it, she'll eat us."

The guards had no sense between them. "You can either let me in and talk to me, or my dragon will bust open your gates and eat you all," she declared.

"Yuck! I'm not eating them," Xylvin muttered.

Ryvalin grinned back at her, but the gate did finally open, the hinges squealing.

Drably dressed men peered around the gate and jerked back at the sight of the dragon now standing behind Ryvalin.

"Seraphim Kyrill has mislaid some of his fledglings. Did you have any youngsters delivered in the last week or so?" Ryvalin snapped.

"Fledglings?" One of the guards repeated, looking blankly at the others.

"Children," Ryvalin clarified. "Have you had any children arrive recently?"

"Kids?"

"Yes, kids."

"A few."

"Show them to me."

"What, now?

"Yes now. Seraphim Kyrill is expecting me to find them."

"Kyrill?"

Ryvalin gritted her teeth. "Show me the kids that recently arrived."

"Only two left, t'other two died. Kids no good, not strong enough."

Ryvalin wanted to ask why they used them then, but there was no point. "Show them to me."

Xylvin growled deep in her throat, and the man jerked back, his eyes widening. "Wait here," he said and slammed the gate shut.

Ryvalin tapped her leg with her knife as she waited. *"I don't think these are Mav's kids,"* she said. *"Not enough of them."*

"Possibly not, but still, we should take them away from this terrible place."

"We can't rescue every child we find, Xylvin."

"It's not right."

Ryvalin sighed. *"I know."*

Spots of rain began to fall, and Xylvin extended a wing over Ryvalin's head. *"We're not going to get away before that storm gets here,"* Xylvin murmured as a flash of lightning lit the darkening sky and another rumble of thunder followed it. *"And I won't be able to fly in that if it gets much closer."*

Before Ryvalin could answer, the gate opened and the guard shoved two emaciated kids forward. "These them?"

Stomach clenching at the forlorn sight, Ryvalin said, "Yes," and pulled the terrified children towards her.

The guard snorted, "Good riddance," and slammed the gate shut.

Xylvin chuckled. *"Can't save them all, huh?"*

"Shut up," Ryvalin replied. *"We need to find somewhere dry and feed them."* She knelt in the mud, ignoring the icy water seeping through her trousers, and smiled. "You're safe now. We'll look after you."

The girl stared at her, and then she looked up and saw the dragon and all colour fled her skin as she crumpled to the ground. Gasping, the boy dropped beside her. "Beth?" he shook her shoulder, and then he too looked up. "Tha' beast won't eat us, will it?"

"No," Ryvalin soothed. "See, she's using her wing to keep the rain off us. Would a child-eating dragon do that?"

"S'pose not."

"Is Beth your sister?"

"Nah. We met here." His lip trembled. "My brother died. He were only tiny."

Ryvalin wrapped an arm around his thin shoulders and hugged him. "I'm sorry. Why don't we leave this horrible place and make camp before the storm really hits?" Large plops punctuated her words, and she grimaced.

"Alright."

"My name is Ryvalin. This is Xylvin." Ryvalin waved at the dragon. "What's your name?"

"Tam."

"Well, Tam," she said as she scooped Beth up into her arms. "How do you feel about riding a dragon?

"Cor, really?"

"Yes, really."

29

—————

SOLANJI, CITADEL

Sero flew into the room as Mav and Solanji finished their leisurely lunch.

"Sero! What happened to you? I am so sorry we left you, but we didn't know where you'd gone," Solanji exclaimed as she rose to her feet.

Grinning, the little cherub perched on the back of a chair opposite them. "There was more in that cubby hole than you would think."

"And?" Mav asked, tapping his knife on the table.

With a flourish, Sero waved his hand in the air, the amethyst ring on his middle finger glinting in the lamplight.

"You found it," Solanji breathed as she leaned forward for a closer look at the faceted gem. "It's beautiful."

"And tells us the whole sorry story." Sero frowned and then rubbed his face. "It was Serenia. This ring is covered in blood and was on the hand that struck the blow. Serenia would not allow any other to wear it, and no one else has until now." He twisted the ring on his finger. "Athenia didn't have a chance."

"And will you testify to that?" Mav asked, his hand stilling on the table.

Sero nodded. "Of course. I am your proof." He slid the ring off his finger and offered it to Mav.

"Keep it. You should present it to the council in support of your testimony. If any cherub is asked to corroborate your words, I would prefer not to be in the ring's memory."

Snorting, Sero returned it to his finger. "That they should dare."

"They dare to accuse Mav, the Archdeus General," Solanji pointed out.

"True," Sero replied. He hesitated a moment. "There's more."

"Like what?" Mav asked as Solanji sat down with a thump.

"More? Of what?" she asked.

Sero sighed. "There was a passage behind the panelling, not that it had been used in years; there were cobwebs on the cobwebs." Staring off into the distance, he twisted his lips and flicked his gaze back to Mav. "I don't think Valerian left voluntarily."

Mav lurched forward. "What?"

"Who's Valerian?" Solanji asked, rubbing Mav's back in concern as tension vibrated off him.

"Amaridin's life partner. Or that's what he used to be. Valerian was his scribe, but their relationship was more permanent. I never thought they would part but Felather said they had split, amicably enough, but still I never thought they would separate."

"I don't think he ever left," Sero said.

"How do you know?" Solanji asked.

"Sero, just say what you know," Mav said, a trace of exasperation in his voice.

"It's funny, but I keep seeing your mother's flowers, those

trailing vines she used grow. In Athenia's botany book, engraved on the north tower where your mother kept her wine cellar, and as a memory in this ring." He waved his hand, displaying the amethyst. "Your mother used to keep a stock of mountain wine in the cellars under the tower. Do you remember?"

"Good lord, yes. Amaridin and I used to play hide and seek in the tunnels while she checked her stocks. There were plenty of hidey-holes and alcoves."

Seri nodded. "Your mother had exquisite taste. She shared a bottle on occasion."

"I will give you two bottles of mountain wine if you get on and tell me why this is so important," Mav growled.

"You would?" Sero squeaked in anticipation. His chubby cheeks blushing a rosy red. "No one else has ever offered!"

"Is it a deal?"

"Yes! The memory in this ring, is of Serenia meeting with Eodan in the cellars. It seems Eodan was more than Amaridin's scribe. He spent time with Serenia in a more… how shall I say it…intimate manner?"

"In a cold and drafty wine cellar?" Mav asked.

"Well, not in this memory, but they did elsewhere in other memories. But in this memory," Sero continued hastily before Mav could suggest taking back his wine, "Serenia instructed Eodan to remove certain people and to hold them in the catacombs below the cellars."

Sero preened a little at the silence that followed his announcement.

"And you believe Valerian is one of them?"

"I know; the ring says so."

"You're saying Valerian and some other unfortunates have been locked in the catacombs for years?" Mav asked in disbelief. "Someone would have noticed."

"Why? The catacombs were sealed years ago, the north

tower closed on the grounds that it was derelict and needed renovating. Not that anyone has ever bothered to check."

Mav rose and began pacing. "But surely the people would have been missed!"

"Like Valerian has been?" Solanji asked with a wry twist of her lips.

"Amaridin must know," Mav whispered. "How could he allow his partner, his *lover*, to be incarcerated all these years?"

Sero perched on a chair. "Maybe Valerian was the ransom for Amaridin's silent acquiescence to whatever Serenia's been planning?"

"Now that could be possible," Mav agreed, staring at Solanji. His chest clenched at the thought of her life in the balance. Considering how little time they had been together, she was melded to his heart, and he couldn't imagine existing without her loving presence, which constantly embraced him. He took her hand and kissed her knuckles.

His shadowsoul shivered as she caressed the strands and he kissed her on the lips. Sero cleared his throat, and Mav straightened, a grin tugging his lips. "How do we save them?"

"Not you, us. You're not allowed to leave your rooms," Sero replied.

"Alright, how are *you* going to rescue them?"

"I'm going to need Solanji and Adriz."

"Why?"

"Adriz because we need a guard with some strength, and Solanji because we might need to contact the citadel to let us in."

"What makes you think the citadel is involved? I thought it was dormant," Solanji said.

Sero shrugged. "Just a feeling."

"Would it not be better to take Felather as well? In case you need a healer for those poor people," Mav suggested.

"I think they are long past the need for anything a healer could do, and we would not leave you unprotected," Sero said.

"I am not completely helpless," Mav snapped.

"No, but I don't trust Serenia to stand by her word. Not after what I've seen in this ring. She cannot be trusted." Sero folded his arms, a determined expression on his face. "The sooner you defeat her the better."

"Very well. Adriz and Solanji. But you are only searching. If you find them, and there's nothing you can do for them, you return immediately."

"Agreed. Call Adriz. The sooner we leave, the sooner we'll know what we have to deal with."

30

SOLANJI

Solanji scuttled down the corridor after Sero, exchanging worried glances with Adriz. "Sero? Do you really think we are going to find Valerian?"

"Shh, keep your voice down." He hovered in an alcove, waiting for some servants to pass, and then said, "I'm positive. Though for them to have been kept secret all this time, I am concerned about what we'll find."

"It's been twenty years since Valerian and Amaridin parted ways. Twenty years!" Adriz exclaimed. "To have hidden this for so long…how could he?"

Sero sighed. "You are assuming that Amaridin knew what happened to Valerian, though I agree he must have at least suspected."

"He must have known," Adriz said, a hard edge to her voice.

"I think we'll find that Amaridin has suffered just as much as Demavrian has, if in a different way." Sero shook his head. "To have both Archdeus compromised at the same time. No wonder the citadel fell dormant."

"And you're sure we can get in the North Tower?" Adriz asked.

"With a bit of your brute strength, I'm sure we will," Sero said as he flew down the corridor and out into the courtyard. They skirted the fountain and passed through an arch that led into another smaller yard. The clash of swords echoed from the training yard and they turned into a side passage lined by sheer golden walls. The passageway curved around a white stone tower, and Sero beckoned them on.

"The old entrance is concealed by the vines. That's why I remember them so well. Malena, Demavrian's mother, always said the flowers held her secrets. The front entrance is boarded up and too easily observed. We'd never get in that way."

Solanji was breathing heavily by the time the passage wound around the tower, and Sero came to a halt and hovered in front of a vine-covered wall. Green leaves were interspersed by pale pink flowers in a curtain of colour against the white stone walls.

Adriz pushed the mass of greenery aside and revealed a wooden slatted door, sagging on its hinges.

"It's probably rusted tight," Sero said.

Adriz tugged the metal ring. It didn't budge. "Worth a try," she said. "Alright, keep a look out. This is not going to be quiet." She unsheathed a dagger and began digging around the hinges, rotten wood falling to the ground.

Solanji peered back around the curve of the passage as Adriz grunted behind her, and the hinges squealed. The screech echoed down the passage, and Solanji shifted from foot to foot as she looked over her shoulder.

Adriz muttered under breath and heaved again. The door gave underneath her and she lurched forward, her curses muffled as she disappeared into the tower. Solanji hurried back to where Sero hovered holding up the vines, and she darted in the black hole.

Solanji nearly tripped over Adriz who crouched on the floor. "Hold this," she instructed and shoved a torch into Solanji's hand. She struck a flint, and a spark flew through the air and then another. Adriz breathed on it and the ember glowed and the torch flared into flames.

The sunlight from outside dimmed to a soft green glow as Sero released the vines to cover the door and fluttered inside. "There may be a guard, so be quiet."

"Now you say," Adriz snarled as she shielded the torch and inspected their surroundings. The stone tower was perfectly cylindrical and empty except for the stone stairs that led up in a spiral and also down into deep shadows from the landing they stood upon.

"They are probably bored to death, but best we take care. No silly injuries."

Adriz's voice was acidic. "Did Mav threaten to take your wine away if we came back battered?"

"He'd better not," Sero growled as Adriz led the way down the spiral staircase.

After what seemed an endless descent, as Solanji's shins began to ache, a glow began to grow down below. Sero held up his hand. Let me go and check how many guards there are. If there is only one or two, I'll deal with them."

"How?" Solanji whispered.

Sero flourished his harp and grinned at her before flying into the darkness. After a short while, Adriz laughed as soft strains of music drifted up the stairwell. "Well, let's see if his claims about his music are true or not."

Solanji crept down the shallow steps behind her. The aroma of dry stone and lingering fruit grew stronger along with the faint scent of musty cellars. Torches threw flickering shadows at the bottom of the stairs, and two guards lay slumped in their chairs, cards splayed out on the barrel between them.

"Hurry," Sero called. "They'll only stay asleep for a few minutes."

"Can't you keep them asleep? It would be better if they didn't know we were here."

Sero narrowed his eyes. "A case," he said, pursing his lips. "Mav owes me a case of wine."

Adriz huffed out a laugh and nodded before hurrying into a shadowy tunnel. Snatching a torch from the wall, Solanji raised it to chase away the darkness. Empty racks lined the first alcove on either side of the passageway, and she continued walking down the stone-flagged floor. The second alcove was filled with a wood pile consisting of broken up crates.

More cobwebs draped the curved arches, drifting fronds of grey webbing crisscrossing the ceiling. Dust motes swirled in the dank air, attracted to the flame like death-defying moths. Adriz kept going, waving the torch in front of her as if it would cut through the thick silence.

"There wouldn't be guards if there wasn't something to hide," Adriz said. "Keep looking."

The light from Solanji's torch revealed more stone paving as she followed Adriz into the depths. Reaching a fork in the tunnel, they took the left-hand passage and started down another staircase.

"There's nothing much down here. Certainly no wine," Solanji said as she rotated, raising her torch to peer into the dimmer corners. The sudden clatter of wings made her start. Heart racing, she stumbled back into one of the alcoves, tripped over a raised slab, and dropped her torch as a stream of bats swarmed past her. Her torch snuffed out and smoke trailed into the air and eddied in a cool breeze.

Solanji frowned. How could she see the smoke? And where was the breeze coming from?

"Solanji?" Adriz screeched her name, and it echoed down the tunnels.

"I'm fine. I just disturbed some bats," she called as she scrabbled around on her hands and knees. She followed the draft and stubbed her fingers on the raised stone slab on the floor. Hovering her palm over the edges of the slab, she felt a definite stream of cold air. Feeling along the edge, she found a divot and forced her fingers into the groove and strained to lift the heavy stone. The slab rocked, and she thought she heard the echo of a voice.

"Adriz? Where are you? I've found something," Solanji called. "Look, there's a draught."

Adriz stuck her torch in a sconce on the wall and, straining, managed to lift the stone enough to get her shoulder under it. A blast of putrid air struck her in the face, along with the stench of dirty bodies, and she choked. Resting for a moment, she let the air clear, and then she shuffled round and stared down into the hole. "How many people have gone missing?" Adriz asked, her voice tight as she scanned the dim cavern below him.

"I don't know, at least one?" Between them they rotated the slab so that it leaned against the wall, and Solanji gasped as she peered through the opening. "There's more than one," she whispered as she inspected the faces of the men and women sprawled on mats on the floor. They all lay in some sort of stupor, eyes half slitted, gleaming as they stared straight ahead. She shuffled to the edge of the hole, reaching for the first roughly hewn step.

Adriz grabbed her shirt. "You are not going down there," she said.

"These people need help. Sero said Valerian is down here. We have to get him and the others out."

Adriz pushed her out of the way and leaned through the opening. "Valerian? Where?" She squinted. "Isn't that Councillor Neralon's wife? I heard she ran off with another man; Neralon wouldn't have her name mentioned."

"I would suggest she didn't have a choice. I believe we have found the leverage that Serenia is using to control the citadel," Solanji said.

"Leverage?"

"How the council is being controlled. And why Amaridin is not standing up to Serenia and her machinations," Solanji replied.

"There has got to be another entrance. This one has hardly been used. There must be an easier way to get to them. At a minimum they need to be fed and watered every day."

"Are you sure they are alive? They're not responding to our voices, and we haven't been quiet. You'd think they'd be clamouring to be let out." Solanji glanced behind her. "Sero? We've found them," she called and then started down the roughly hewn stairs. Stone ceilings arched overhead in graceful curves, and Solanji would have stopped and admired the stonemason's work if not for the poor people trapped within the catacomb.

"What the..." Sero gasped as he arrived and peered down the hole. "How are we supposed to get them out of here?" he asked when he flew into the room. He gazed at the rows of unmoving bodies and, landing beside a middle-aged woman, lifted her wrist. Breathing a sigh of relief, he moved on to another cold and unresponsive body, but at least they lived.

"How long will those guards sleep, Sero?" Adriz asked.

"We ought to be leaving. We've been here long enough." Sero cut himself off as he fluttered over to blond haired man dressed in blue robes, shackled to the wall. "Valerian," he whispered. "It's true! How dare they." Sero shook Valerian's shoulder. "Valerian, wake up."

"They are not asleep. It's like they're in some sort of stasis. Alive but not. Valerian looks just as I remember him, yet you would expect him to be aged or emaciated," Adriz said. She suddenly looked up. "Solanji, they still have souls, don't they?"

"Yes, they're sluggish and muted, but still present."

Sero ran a hand through his hair. "We need to leave before those guards stir. I'll go and make sure they are still sleeping; you replace the slab."

"We can't leave them here," Solanji protested, gazing around in horror.

"We can't take them with us, and they're not going to know any different. There is no reason for Serenia to harm them any further; she doesn't know we found them. We need to tell Mav about this." He fluttered off, and Adriz tugged Solanji out of the cavern.

"Mav will rescue them as soon as he defeats count four," Adriz said as she pulled Solanji up the stairs. "Help me with this slab." A dull thud echoed through the cellars as the slab fell back into place. "Let's get out of here." Adriz grabbed her hand and rushed through the cellars.

"They cast the Ensatra on them," Sero hissed as soon as they were all in Mav's chambers and Felather had shut door. Solanji bent over, panting. Adriz hadn't stopped once, rushing her back through the citadel, as if someone knew what they had been up to.

"What?" Mav stared at him in shock.

"It was Eodan. I saw the memory when I touched Valerian. Serenia told Eodan to cast the Ensatra. I didn't think of it at first, it's not something you come across often, certainly not in the mortal world." Sero frowned. "I recognised it as soon as Adriz said it was like they were frozen, in a stasis."

"But how did Eodan cast the Ensatra? Only a god can perform the Ensatra. And only a god can remove it. My father isn't here, so he couldn't have, so that only leaves…Kaenera."

"Kaenera?" Adriz said in an explosion of breath.

Sero shrugged. "He's the only other god I know of in this world."

"But what does Kaenera have to gain by doing this?" Adriz asked.

"I don't know," Mav said slowly. "Maybe it's what he gains from the bigger picture. This is just another piece of the puzzle, giving Serenia full control of the citadel. Another reason to remove my father from the board." Mav fell silent and then said, "Another favour that he will demand payment for."

"Another favour?" Adriz asked.

"Yes. Serenia is racking them up. Let's hope she has the tally correct or she may find she can't pay the final reckoning."

31

MUNTRA, EIDOLON

Muntra lugged his box of rock out of his tunnel and evenly distributed it between Bren's and Bailey's boxes. At least it made it look like they were working. Then he hurried towards the entrance, cudgelling his brain for the best way to get word to Shandra that they were going to break out tonight. They also needed a diversion to draw the guards away from them.

He paused near the end of the passageway and watched the bustle in the cavern, sorting out who was doing what. Three dybbuks stood around watching, their sticks hanging from their belts. A team of men, were heaving beams of wood towards another smaller tunnel. As they got in a tangle, drawing the dybbuks eyes, Muntra walked out of the cave, trying not to rush, though it was difficult. Every minute he wasted, Bailey was in danger of being found.

Skirting the compound and continuing past the sleeping huts, Muntra scanned the perimeter fence. It was too high to climb and too difficult for the smaller kids. Sheer wooden panels were unclimbable without a rope and he had none of that. There was a section of chain link fencing between the end panel and the cliff face, plugging the gap, but he had nothing to cut a wire fence either.

Desperation clawing at his gut, he grabbed a bucket, half filled it with water, and continued deeper into the compound. He had last seen Shandra near the larger grinding shed, where they ground the ore out of the rock. Smaller kids were harnessed to a large mill stone, which they walked around in place of a mule, which would have been much more efficient in Muntra's mind.

"Muntra."

Muntra spun at the sound of the familiar voice, and he let Kiara tug him through a darkened doorway. "Kiara, I was looking for Shandra."

"She's in the shed, but what you are doing out of the mines?"

"Bailey was attacked. I need to get him out of here."

Muntra was shocked at the spew of foul language that fell out of Kiara's mouth. "I told Shandra he wouldn't last long in here."

"It wasn't his fault; the boys ganged up on him."

"I didn't say it was his fault. Here, take these. I made some wire cutters. You'll be able to cut through that fence by the ridge face. Just don't cut the base wire; there's some sort of circuit set up and it'll set off the alarms. Don't ask me how, it just will."

"When did you make these?" Muntra asked, examining the sturdy metal clippers.

"During a break from washing my hair! When do you think?"

"I don't think we'll be able to take all the little ones, Kiara. It'll be hard enough surviving as it is."

"Then make sure you steal enough food to take with us. Shandra won't leave any of them behind, you know that."

Muntra groaned. "We'll be lucky to get out, let alone steal food."

"Wait until dark. I'll start a few fires; they should make a nice diversion. We'll meet you at the fence."

Muntra swept her up in a fierce hug. There was nothing of her, she felt so fragile in his arms. "You're the best, you know that, right?"

Kiara laughed and hugged him back. "Go on, and Muntra, make sure you make a hole big enough for you to get through as well. If we leave, we're all leaving. I'll tell Shandra." She disappeared before he could say anything more.

Stuffing the clippers down the back of his trousers, he peered out of the doorway. He needed to hide until it was dark. The best place would be to hide where he was supposed be, working at the rock face. So he made his way back to the mine. It took a lot longer to return as he was more aware of the cutters down his back and the need not to get caught.

Shandra stretched her aching back and glanced round the grinding shed. Her lips tightened as she watched the smaller kids, roped to a wheel, constantly walking in a circle. Their little legs stumbled as exhaustion sapped what little strength they had.

She bashed a rock extra hard and hissed as a splinter sliced her knuckle. Sucking the cut, she repositioned the rocks and more carefully ground them together. Anger helped no one here, it just drained your energy.

They had to escape. None of them could last much longer, least of all the tiny ones. Her heart ached for them. They'd had such a terrible start to life, through no fault of their own. She would make Kiara tell her what she was planning tonight. It was obvious Kiara had been working on something, even being as secretive as she was. Sometimes that child was too clever for her own good. What was the world coming too, when youngsters were hatching escape plans? She really didn't know.

The bell rang for lunch. They were only half way through the day! She wasn't sure she could keep going, let alone anyone else. Painting a bright smile on her face, she called out, "Come along then, my lovelies, time for something to eat. You can stop now."

The children waited, their drab clothes hanging off thin shoulders. They stood, lifeless, staring at the floor. Then a little girl collapsed in a heap.

"Tannie," Shandra exclaimed as she rushed to unharness her and scoop her into her arms. Blank eyes stared up at her, and she shuddered as she hid her face in the child's chest and rocked back and forth.

"No wasting time, get yer food now or starve." A dybbuk hauled Shandra up, and after a glance at the child, dragged her out of Shandra's arms.

"No! Leave her be, you beast." Shandra beat him with her fists, fury flaring through her, and the dybbuk lashed out, back handing her across the face. She stumbled back, tears streaming down her face, mingling with the blood from her split lip. "You murderer!"

"Get back to work or you'll be next!"

"They can't work without food." She gestured at the body in his hand. "We'll all end up like her, and then who will you use?"

"You'll eat while you work," the dybbuk said. "Get yer grub now and dish it out."

He glared at her until she followed his orders and went to the sacks at the end of the hall and dug inside for the dried strips of meat that took forever to chew, and the nearly rotten apples. The dybbuk left the hut, and Shandra beckoned the children over.

"Put some in your pocket for later, that's right," she encouraged. Rummaging through the sacks, she filled her pockets with more chunks of dried meat and hard biscuits.

Gnawing on a biscuit, she dipped a mug in the bucket of water and took a deep drink, then filled it again and handed it around the kids. "Back to work, my sweets," she whispered, dropping a soft kiss on their heads. "Tonight we'll have a feast! So don't let anyone see what you've got in your pockets."

Dull eyes brightened for a moment before they faded as the children began walking again. Shandra watched them. At least she had most of her little crew together. Only the smallest had been carried off, which she supposed was one blessing. Tears welled again as she thought of the children the dybbuks had selected to be sold to childless families.

Muntra said maybe they were the lucky ones; at least they would have a home. But they were her children, her family. She went back to grinding rocks, ignoring the tears that leaked down her cheeks.

"Shandra?" Kiara whispered, appearing at her side. She gripped Shandra's arm. "What's happened?"

Shandra wiped her cheeks with the back of her hand. "Tannie died."

Kiara hissed her breath out as she counted the kids. "We're getting out tonight. Once it's dark."

"How? Do you have a plan?

"I saw Muntra. Bailey was roughed up. Muntra agrees that it's time to get out of here."

"Is Bailey alright?"

Kiara sighed. "Are any of us alright? At least he's alive. I gave Muntra the wire cutters I made. He's going to cut through the fence tonight. You need to get the kids and any food you can find to the wire fence in the far corner. I'll create the diversion to draw the dybbuks away and meet you there."

"Be careful, Kiara." Shandra hugged her and kissed her cheek. "We all leave together, right?"

"Of course. I'll see you there. Wait for full dark, Shandra."

32

DEMAVRIAN, CITADEL

The morning dawned all too soon. Especially after a sleepless night trying to tie all the information they had discovered into an argument that would make sense to the assembly. It wasn't only Serenia that Mav had to convince, it was the administrators and the other angels as well.

If Mav didn't reinforce each point, he would lose them and any chance of disproving the count. Mav wiped his damp hands down his trousers as his gut fluttered, and he was glad he hadn't had much to eat that morning.

Adriz and Felather had accompanied him to the assembly hall and stood behind his shoulder, their presence comforting. Solanji and Kerris were seated with Sero amongst the tiers of angels.

Standing at the side of dais, Mav twisted his lips at the sight of his brother entering the hall; he did not look well. He was pale and distressed, though his blond hair was perfect. He obviously had his own problems, and Mav was certain he knew what one of them was. Valerian was a glaring absence, and now he knew why.

He wasn't sure how his brother would react once he found out what had happened to Valerian, if he didn't know already. Mav wasn't sure he could forgive Amaridin for not trying to save those people if he did know. The space behind Amaridin's shoulder was filled by Eodan, who would never be Amaridin's choice.

Eodan's arrogant stare was out of place. Mav shivered at the covetous gleam in his eye. What did he want? Something Amaridin wouldn't give him?

Serenia arrived beside Amaridin, her hand on his arm as if she was his consort. Was that it? She wanted to rule Angelicus with Amaridin? He was momentarily aggrieved that she hadn't chosen him, but he laughed at himself, his tension easing as he watched them mount the steps.

Adriz leaned forward. "What?" she whispered.

Mav shook his head, and Adriz straightened. Mav would never have agreed to rule with Serenia. They were too alike, both used to command, whereas Amaridin was softer, more pliable, except for when Valerian bolstered him and gave him the courage to stand his ground and voice his beliefs.

He adjusted the sword belt under his robe. Adriz had been determined that he would not enter the hall unarmed. Count four would be the culmination of the Apologia, and Serenia would be getting desperate.

Serenia faced the assembly. "Apologia in session, Count four. Archdeus Demavrian Deusson is accused of Archangel Athenia's murder. Accuser Captain Julius Teravin. Julius, state your count."

Julius stepped forward, a thoughtful frown on his face. "It's been fifty years since Athenia was murdered. For all that time Demavrian has been the only name considered for her murder. He was caught at the scene of the crime and never defended himself against the charge, until now.

"I don't believe it is as simple as accusing Demavrian of

murder. I never believed my best friend would kill Athenia. Demavrian and Athenia were as close as brother and sister, a fact I lost in my grief and anger in the aftermath of her tragic death.

"For five decades I have hunted Demavrian, never letting him rest, never giving him the opportunity to defend himself. And all that time, I thought I was doing the right thing. I believed Demavrian killed Athenia, but since his return I have begun to doubt, to question my blind belief. For there is no real proof to substantiate that accusation."

Serenia shifted in her seat, a scowl beginning to crease her perfect complexion.

Mav spoke into the growing silence. "You set Julius up as inquisitor, and every time he faltered you reminded him of how Athenia died by my hand. Reinforcing his anger. You expected him to kill me before I ever had a chance to return, didn't you, Serenia?"

"Julius is a captain of the Heavenly Host. Who else would I appoint?" Serenia asked.

"I couldn't understand why he held such vicious hatred for me. That he would believe so ill of me, even after all this time. As if there was no other possibility. It was you, wasn't it? Brainwashing him all these years?"

Serenia slow clapped. "And here is the Demavrian we know and love, finally putting the pieces together and coming up with the wrong answer. If Julius believed the worst of you, it was because he was jealous of how Athenia looked at you."

"That's not true," Julius said, his expression horrified.

"Of course it was," Serenia said, the scorn in her voice making Julius flinch. "Why else would you be so quick to believe an archdeus guilty?"

"Because I believed *you*, Serenia. You said you had seen Demavrian with the gutting knife, hovering over her on the stairs. Stabbing her, over and over, ignoring her screams, covered in her gushing blood, his hands stained red...blood everywhere."

Mav drew in his breath against the vivid image, one he knew he hadn't seen, but Serenia had. "I know it wasn't me, and there wasn't a knife next to her body. No one knew what type of weapon was used."

"It was obvious from her wounds what type of knife had been used," Serenia said.

"But you said you saw it. You didn't go to Julius for help; you went to make sure he would accuse me whilst you got rid of the evidence."

Serenia curled her lip in disdain. "You were caught red-handed. You ran. I had no need to accuse anyone."

Mav laughed. "Me? What about you, Serenia? I've noticed you no longer wear the amethyst. You swore it would never leave your finger. What happened to it? Afraid the cherubs might glean its story? That it would incriminate you just by existing?"

Serenia's face paled and she clamped her lips tight. "Getting desperate, Demavrian? Throwing wild accusations about will only undermine your own credibility."

Mav raised his hand, and Sero fluttered down and landed beside him. Sero held the amethyst ring up. "Did you think it would stay hidden forever?" Sero asked, scorn lacing his voice.

"Who allowed you into my rooms? You had no right stealing my things!"

"You admit this is your ring?" Mav asked.

Serenia hesitated, and Mav smiled. If she admitted it was hers and the cherub revealed its bloody history, she was condemned by her own word.

Sero didn't wait for her response. "Your ring holds a very interesting history. One drenched in bloody murder."

Julius swallowed, his face paling. "No…" he whispered. "It was you?" His voice strengthened. "You killed Athenia? But why? Athenia never harmed anyone."

A ripple of horrified exclamations passed through the chamber.

"Don't be silly, of course it wasn't me." Serenia glared at the tiers of angels. "I am the only one holding this citadel together. Demavrian is desperate, accusing anyone he can. Julius, you must state your accusation for the Apologia."

Julius pursed his lips. "I believe you should state the accusation, as you are the one determined to find Mav guilty of the crime."

"It is not my place to accuse. I have stood at the head of Angelicus for more years than you can count. I *am* Angelicus."

"No, you are not," Mav said, his shadows swirling around him as he turned to face Serenia. "This world is not only composed of Angelicus; you are forgetting Eidolon."

Serenia wrinkled her nose. "Only you would champion the soulless. Eidolon is a punishment. A half-life. It should be cleansed on a regular basis. There is no need for it; those undeserving should go straight through the Oblivion Gate."

Mav took a step back at her cold dismissal. "Is that your agreement with Kaenera? Those you deem unworthy to live in your world should be forsaken and handed over to him?"

"Don't be ridiculous! Nothing good comes from the shadows," Serenia hissed. Her gaze flitted around the chamber as the mutterings grew louder. "Oh, grow a set," she snarled. "None of you have ever gone out of your way to help them. You've been eager to take advantage of them at every opportunity."

"That is not true." Golaran heaved himself to his feet. "At least I now understand why you continually try to block my initiatives to help the people of Eidolon."

"People? They are not people! They are all miscreants, criminals, and beggars."

"Showing your true colours at last, Serenia?" Mav drawled.

Serenia snapped her mouth shut and glared at him. She drew in a deep breath. "My word is law. You are accused of Athenia's murder, as well that of your father. How dare you stand there and accuse me of your sins. Accusing others does not negate your guilt." She waved her hand at the guards. "Take him."

"Hold," Julius commanded as his men bracketed Mav.

"Be very careful, Julius," Serenia warned, "or you will be joining him."

Julius laughed. "Since when did you become God, Serenia? You seem to have forgotten that Amaridin is also an archdeus and no charge has been declared." Julius faced the silent archdeus up on the dais. "What do you have to say, Amaridin?"

"It is Archdeus Amaridin to you, Julius, and he agrees with me," Serenia said. She looked at the guards. "Take Demavrian to his cell where he will await our sentence."

Mav twisted his lips as he faced Serenia's fury. For some reason, he didn't think he would make it to the cell.

"I think I would prefer to hear Amaridin say that," Julius said, his voice sharp.

Amaridin glared at Julius and then rose. He met Serenia's eyes and stiffened before he nodded at the guards. "Take him," he said.

"Over my dead body," Julius growled and drew his sword.

Serenia climbed the steps to stand beside Amaridin and placed her hand on his arm. He tensed, his discomfort clear as Serenia gazed out over the chamber. "That can be arranged," she said, regaining her composure. "Arrest them both."

"But this is not all the ring tells us," Sero said, his sharp voice slicing through the tension. "There is more yet to share. For instance, the unexplained disappearance of those near and dear to many people in this room. What do you have to say about that, Serenia?"

Serenia paled and flicked a glance at Eodan.

"Nothing? Not of how you instructed Eodan and his men to…what shall I call it?" Sero tapped his lip. "Abduction? Kidnapping? Extortion? Which word would you prefer?"

"This is ridiculous," Serenia snapped. "Eodan, arrest them."

"What about your agreement with Kaenera?" Sero's voice rang through the silent hall.

The assembly stirred, voices exclaiming.

"Your agreement to deliver him more soulless, oh! and Demavrian on a plate, and in return he would cast the Ensatra over your unwanted guests."

Gasps of shock interrupted him. Amaridin lurched forward, his face a travesty of hope and fear.

"Enough! Eodan, stop him talking. They spread lies and innuendo; they have no proof."

"A cherub cannot lie," Mav said, stepping in front of Sero as Eodan descended the steps and called his men forth. "And you should know better than to threaten the life of one bound to speak the truth."

"Kill them!" Serenia commanded, and the council chamber erupted. Mav drew his sword as Eodan retreated back up the steps, a manic grin on his lips and Sero was barrelled over by rushing guards, the ring skittering across the slick marble. Mav jerked Sero upright, and he fluttered out of reach. Someone kicked the ring, and Mav lost sight of it as angels scrambled out of the way. The Heavenly Host drew their swords and charged towards Mav and Julius, only to be abruptly halted as Adriz and some of the host about turned and met the charge.

Solanji worked her way through the confusion to Felather's side and gripped his arm. Kerris close behind her. "I don't understand. Didn't she just admit to…?" Solanji frowned. "I'm not sure what she admitted too, apart from holding the citadel together."

"She is very clever. She managed to deflect every accusation, even though it is plain as can be that she must have killed Athenia," Felather replied as he dragged Solanji and Kerris back against the wall. Fledglings and angels alike fled the chamber. "Can you see the ring?"

"No, but I thought it went towards the dais." Solanji peered through the heaving bodies.

"Circle the room. You go that way and I'll meet you at the dais. We need to find that ring. There's nothing else we can do until things calms down. The chamber needs to hear all that Sero can tell them. They will believe a cherub; he cannot lie in a telling."

"That's if Serenia allows him to speak," Solanji said, flattening herself against the wall as battling guards careened past her.

Mav parried a strike and wondered how he always managed to get into such a mess. Felather dragged Solanji away from the chaos and Mav's tension eased. Julius fighting back-to-back with him was an unexpected comfort as he had lost sight of Adriz in the melee.

A flailing sword catching his arm had him tightening his guard, and he concentrated on the matter in hand. Serenia would not go down lightly; her guards would have overwhelmed him, if it had not been for Julius and his men.

"This feels just like old times," Mav muttered under his breath as he and Julius grasped forearms and swung themselves around to face the next threat.

"Old times, would mean I'd have you flat on your back," Julius growled.

Mav laughed. "In your dreams," he said as his sword slid down his opponents, and he gripped the man's wrist as he twisted inwards and followed by thrusting his sword into the man's stomach.

Mav spun to meet the next attack and raised his eyebrows as Kyrill glared at him from across the hall. Mav made an elaborate bow, flourishing his hand as he held Kyrill's eye, inviting him forward. Did the seraphim really believe he could best him? Was this Serenia's hope? Kill him off regardless.

Kyrill turned to search the room, and finding what he was looking for, he smirked at Mav and then began making his way towards the dais. Following his progress, Mav caught his breath as he saw Solanji and Kerris skirting the hall, their attention focused on the floor.

Hissing his breath out, he began fighting his way through the host, desperate to reach Solanji before Kyrill did. He didn't, but Solanji darted away just as Kyrill tried to grab her, and she slid along the floor, rising triumphantly with Serenia's ring in her hand. Her expression froze as Kyrill bore down on her, and Mav spread his wings and launched himself across the room. Shadows writhed around him as he landed beside Solanji and he tossed her out of Kyrill's reach. Solanji flailed, grabbing at the ropes that held the flaming chandeliers aloft.

He spun to face Kyrill, who flinched as his saw Mav's

expression. "You've already tried to kill her once; you don't get a second chance," Mav growled.

Kyrill bared his teeth. "Then it will have to be you."

"You can try," Mav replied as he met Kyrill's charge.

Kyrill forced Mav back, raining heavy blows on him with sweeping overhead strikes that Mav barely deflected. Sheer fury masked Kyrill's face and Mav suddenly realised he may have underestimated the seraphim.

Kyrill yelped as a flaming candle bounced off his chest, followed by another. He flinched away from the burning missiles, and Mav attacked, taking advantage of the distraction and driving his sword home. He planted his dagger in Kyrill's chest and held his eyes, wide with disbelief as Mav followed him down to the ground.

Kyrill's blue eyes darkened as shadows filled his eyes. Bile rose in Mav's throat, and he swallowed. Kyrill had been led astray; by whom was the question. Plotting and secrecy may be rife in the citadel, but the taking of another's life for personal gain was unheard of until now. No more! He gritted his teeth as he stared at Kyrill's slack face. Immortality was a gift, not a weapon to be used to subjugate and outlive all others.

Adriz strode towards Mav, her face hard and her eyes sparking with anger. That citadel guards had attacked them was beyond belief. That Serenia was still advocating her innocence, laughable.

Fledglings and seraphim were falling over themselves to clear the floor, forming a loose horseshoe around the man slumped on the marble flagstones and the archdeus hovering over him like an avenging angel in truth.

Julius and his lieutenant stood either side of Serenia and Eodan at the base of the dais; his men controlled the room. Amaridin stood to one side, pasty-faced and trying to distance himself from Serenia. Adriz curled her lip. He had ordered the men to arrest his own brother. She would never forgive him for his treatment of Demavrian.

Unease stirred in Adriz's chest as Serenia stood straight and tall, head held high, eyes flashing with contempt as she watched Mav rise from the floor, his blade dripping with blood. Mav's face was stark, as if hewn from the stone beneath his feet, and he swayed before he stiffened. Adriz cast about for Solanji, his ever-present shadow, and her heart fluttered when she couldn't find her; she was not next to him. As she hurried up to him a chink of crystal drew her gaze upwards, and her brows rose as she observed Solanji perched in the chandelier.

"Why is Solanji swinging from the chandelier?" she asked, her voice loud in the stunned silence.

"Where have you been? We've missed you," Mav replied, wiping his sword on the body.

"Oh, I don't know, looks like you needed the practice," Adriz said, inwardly releasing a sigh of relief. He seemed unharmed. "Though that doesn't answer my question."

Glancing around, Mav sheathed his sword, and hissed his breath out as he shifted awkwardly to greet her. Adriz was beside him in moments, her hand steadying him. He was not alright. *Are you hurt?*" she asked.

"*Wrenched my knee, nothing new,*" he replied as he gave her a hug. Out loud he said to Solanji, "You can come down now."

"I don't know how," was Solanji's reluctant reply.

Mav chuckled. "You got up there, I'm sure you'll figure a way down."

Solanji huffed down at him. "Don't you leave me up here."

"Adriz, are you unhurt?" Felather was patting her down, and she fended him off.

"Not here," she growled and pushed him away. Seeing the hurt in his eyes, she softened her voice as she gripped his arm. "I'm fine," she promised as she looked up at Solanji. "How did you get up there in the first place?" Adriz asked, scanning their audience. Her gaze stopped on the corpse. "And since when do seraphim attack archdeus?" she asked, using her foot to roll the silver-robed body over. Her breath hissed out as the blond perfection of Seraphim Kyrill was revealed.

"Kyrill thought he could best me," Mav said. "He was mistaken."

"He thought by attacking me he would distract Mav long enough to sink a blade in," Solanji said from above them.

"He didn't touch you, did he?" Adriz's stomach dropped as she checked Mav over. That had been her worst nightmare, that someone would penetrate Mav's defences in her absence. But she should have trusted him. He had survived without her for fifty years; why should it be any different now?

"Nowhere close," Mav said.

Solanji cleared her throat. "By the way, I'm just wonderful, thanks for asking, but how am I supposed to get down?"

Adriz grinned up at her, relief making her feel lightheaded. "Let yourself drop, and I'll catch you."

"Really? Just drop."

"And I'll catch you." Adriz laughed at Solanji's expression of disbelief. "How did she get up there?" she asked Mav.

Peering up at the chandelier, a good ten feet above them, Mav shrugged. "Not sure."

"You threw her up there," a wide-eyed fledgling said.

"No he didn't, she flew," another said.

"Not possible, she doesn't have wings."

"It doesn't matter how I got up here, it's how I get down that I'm interested in." Tightening her grip on the rope, Solanji scowled down at them as the crystal chandelier swayed and tinkled.

"Well, if you got up there you should be able to get back down. Most cats will wail all night, but when they get hungry, they find their way down in the end," Mav said.

Solanji glared at him. "Are you comparing me to some stray cat?"

"Your kitten is flexing her claws," Adriz murmured.

Mav rotated his neck to relieve the tension and Adriz sighed. "I'll get her," Mav said as he flared his gold-shot wings, glorious and strong, and he smoothly rose before Adriz could protest. He ignored the murmurs of the watching angels and, avoiding the remaining candles, scooped Solanji off the chandelier. She hugged him tight and hid her face in his neck. He was soon back, landing beside Adriz, and Solanji slid out of his arms.

Mav dragged her back into his arms. "I'm never letting go of you again," he murmured into her hair.

Solanji lifted her face, and he gently pushed her dishevelled curls away from eyes. His head dipped as if to kiss her, but he was interrupted by a mocking laugh, and Mav spun to face Serenia once more.

33

DEMAVRIAN

"Darling Demavrian to the rescue, and for a fledgling as well. Haven't you got more important things to be doing? Like defending yourself against Apologia, which is still in session? You haven't proved anything except your lack of respect for the citadel and Angelicus. I demand that you yield and allow me to restore order."

"There is nothing for you to restore, Serenia. You've betrayed everything my father stood for. After all these years of supporting him, what changed, Serenia? What made you decide you wanted it all for yourself?" Mav released Solanji and spread his arms as he rotated, glancing around the silent tiers. "Why don't you tell your colleagues what you have been doing?"

"Demavrian, you are the one being tried. Not me."

"And yet, you are the hand behind each of these evil deeds. It is quite obvious, even to Julius, one of the captains of the Heavenly Host, that you killed Athenia."

"I refuse to declare the count," Julius said from behind

him. "Count four of the Apologia is null and void and the charge against Archangel Demavrian Deusson is struck."

Serenia hissed her breath out. "You can't withdraw your claim. As you are under arrest, you are no longer a Captain of the Host."

Julius laughed, a deep rumble that should have been joyful and hearty, but instead it made Mav shiver with the hidden threat. "You can't just dismiss me by your word alone, Serenia. Especially when you stand accused of Athenia's murder."

"You have no right to accuse me."

"We have every right," Mav snapped, his voice breaking as the anguish hit him. "You wanted to see me executed, based on lies and false accusations. You betrayed me, and my father, and Athenia. Why?"

Serenia straightened and gazed around the hall. Her throat bobbed as she took in the narrow-eyed stares, the silent accusations. She raised her chin. "I would never do such a thing. After everything I have done for Averdeus, for *you*, how dare you make such an accusation? I am Deus in all but name. I run Angelicus for him. I do all the work, make the decisions. I don't need his ratification." Serenia's eyes were hard as she glared down at Mav. "You have been absent for years, Demavrian; how dare you return and accuse me!"

Mav's gaze remained riveted on Serenia as she climbed back up the steps and sat on the throne. "You knew my mother. You knew what she meant to my father. He would never replace her, and you knew that. Her death only gave you more power as he stepped back to grieve." Eyes widening, Mav stared at her superior smile. He clenched his fists as the realisation formed. Acid burned the base of his throat, and his stomach cramped. "My mother?" he whispered. Clearing his throat, he tried again. "It was you?" Mav swayed. How many people had she killed to get her way?

How had she managed to hide her disdain for them all, her innate greed and drive to achieve her diabolical plans? He took a deeper breath. How long had she been planning this?

Serenia ignored him. "Poor, poor, Demavrian. So busy running away that he's lost track of his responsibilities. And Amaridin, so weak and afraid. Always needing his father's reassurance. Remove you two and what is left? Just your father, and, well, we all know his weak spot. He always believes in the good of people, and then where are we? You need me and you know it."

"You knew!" Mav raised the blue vendetta stone and climbed a step. "You knew what this was all along, didn't you? The only way for my father to return was to weave my soul back into the citadel." Mav gasped. "You deliberately let the citadel go dormant. Amaridin was the only one who could have kept the connection going, so you had to nullify him, too, so you took Valerian. Didn't you?"

Serenia's smile hardened.

"*That* was what you were so worried about when I tried to reconnect to the citadel. You thought my soul would be rebound. Three souls to bind the plane and open the portal for Averdeus to return. If I had been bound to the citadel, my father could have returned and called foul.

"Averdeus trusted you. He told you about his plan, that he was sending me to Eidolon, that Athenia would hold my soul so Kaenera wouldn't suspect anything. And then you killed Athenia so the portal would never be reopened. All this time you knew."

"At least I still have my soul," Serenia said. "I don't know how you manufactured what you are calling a soul, but whatever trick you used, it won't last. I *know* Athenia took your soul. The citadel will cast you out. It won't accept you."

"You could only know that if you had been there," Mav said, his voice loud and strained in the echoing hall.

"It doesn't matter. My word is law. Yours is tarnished with blood and lies. You have no soul. You shouldn't be standing here at all."

"I think you'll find you are mistaken. I have a soul. Maybe not the same as yours, but the citadel accepted it or I wouldn't be standing here." Mav ignored the hiss of whispers from the galleries. "Neither the council nor the citadel will forgive your actions."

"The citadel can't be reached because you murdered the last SoulBreather, and for what? So you could come back with your tail between your legs begging for mercy?" Serenia sneered at Mav.

"Your imagination runs away with you, Serenia. I have no need to beg because I committed no sin. The sin was done unto me." Mav straightened. "But you have sinned not only against me but many others. You preyed on others' weaknesses. Instead of supporting and nurturing, you wrecked and destroyed. Families, lives, and memories. All because you wanted something you had no need of."

"How do you know what I need?"

"You already ruled Angelicus, what more could you desire?"

"She wanted a consort," Sero replied as he flew across the room. "A consort with heavenly blood flowing through his veins. If not Averdeus, then you; if not you, then Amaridin. She wanted the family Averdeus once had."

"You lie," Serenia hissed.

Sero smiled and pointed at the ring in Solanji's hand. "It's all in there. The lies, the deceit, the murder. All of it. You are guilty, Serenia. May God in his mercy forgive you."

Mav climbed the rest of the steps until he reached Serenia and she stiffened as two of the Heavenly Host moved to stand behind her. "You saw your chance to betray my father and then you bargained with Kaenera."

Serenia's gaze flitted around the hall, and then she swayed. "No," she whispered. "Eodan…"

"It's too late, Serenia. Eodan can't help you now," Mav said. "That was why you had to kill Athenia. You knew my father's plan. You attacked her so she couldn't take my soul because someone else wanted it. Unfortunately for you, she still took it. You had intended on using a SoulSinger to take it instead. Were you going to steal it while I was unconscious, Serenia? Once you had taken my soul, she was the only one who could possibly bind it back into the citadel and release my father, so you had to be sure she was dead. What did Kaenera want in return? What is it he is so desperate for that he would help you?"

Serenia laughed, a harsh, strangled sound that she cut off abruptly. "He wants you! Everyone wants you. It is always Demavrian everyone looks to."

"That isn't true."

"Of course it is. Even Amaridin is jealous. He was easy enough to sway. He knew you would rule in his stead if you had the chance."

"That isn't true either. Amaridin is the elder, that has never changed, and he knew I didn't want his position; that was just some vicious seed you planted. The only reason he stands beside you is because you threatened that which he valued the most." Mav glanced over at his brother slumped in his seat, his hand covering his eyes. Mav raised his voice, though he knew Amaridin could hear him. "Since when did Eodan advise you, Amaridin? Valerian is obvious by his absence. I'm surprised no one has been searching for him."

Amaridin jerked up in his seat as if a puppet master had pulled his strings. His face was pasty, and he shook as he rose. He worked his mouth as if he was about to speak, and then he collapsed back in his chair as Serenia laughed at him.

"Amaridin is too weak to rule on his own. That is why I agreed to stand by him when his lover left him."

"What did you say, Serenia? Keep silent, rule with me and you'll let Valerian live? That you wouldn't hurt him?"

Serenia curled her lip in derision.

"Once you had abducted those you needed, you let Kaenera enter the citadel, and he cast the Ensatra on them," Mav said as anguish swept through him, followed by a wave of exhaustion. He just wanted to curl up in a ball, go to sleep, and block out the sight of Serenia's disdainful face.

"Demavrian, your accusations become more extreme every time you open your mouth."

"That an archangel could fall so far. Someone with the trust of the people, responsible for the wellbeing of all." Mav rubbed his face; he was so tired. His knee was throbbing and he needed to sit down. Just a little bit longer. He needed to keep Serenia talking. Seeing Serenia still sitting in her chair as if she was supreme and untouchable galled him. He had to finish it now, while the council were listening to him.

"I accuse you. Four counts, Serenia." Mav declared. "One, Athenia's murder. Two, conspiring to falsely accuse me of murder and banishment. Three, abducting Valerian to control Amaridin and many others to control the council. Four, consorting with Kaenera to betray Averdeus, and that doesn't include the murder of my mother and countless other poor souls."

"You can't accuse me. You are still under Apologia yourself; your sentence hasn't been ratified," Serenia snapped.

"You convict yourself by your words. There is much we don't know, but the citadel remembers all, and Sero has spoken, the truth has been heard." He turned and descended the steps. He couldn't stand to be near her.

Eodan suddenly twisted out of the guard's grip and dashed down the steps, a sword in hand. He launched himself at Mav, and Mav flinched back, where had the sword come from? Mav raised his own sword and parried the blow, backing away from such ferocious rage. Sheer fury emanated from the man, and Mav wondered why.

He gave way under the pressure. "Eodan, please. Don't throw your live away. It's over."

"It's not over. I should have killed you when I had the chance."

"But why?"

Eodan grunted as he struck again, and Mav braced as the shock vibrated through him. He needed to finish this and finish it fast. Help came from an unexpected quarter as Sero shot Eodan with one of his golden arrows. It bounced off his skin, but it was enough of a distraction as Mav ran him through, and Eodan howled and swung around like some maddened beast as Julius ran up behind him and disarmed him.

"No!" Eodan shouted, his voice a high-pitched keen as he fell to his knees, his hands clasped to his stomach. He began to shudder, and a shimmering black mist rose out of his body, coalescing into a shapeless form above the dying man, and Mav lurched away. Eodan's body toppled over in an inanimate heap.

Exhaling in shock and retreating towards the dais, Mav watched the mist solidify into a familiar form. Kaenera stood in front of him, a roar of anger on his lips, his fingers curled in vengeance. His beautiful face, savage.

"You constantly ruin my plans," Kaenera hissed, rising to his full height. His black eyes glinted with banked fury. "Centuries spent preparing for this day and still, you manage to disrupt, to destroy." He clenched his jaw, his expression murderous. "You will submit before me now or all you love will be lost."

"I will never submit to you." Mav stiffened at the implied

threat. "What is it you actually want, Kaenera? How are you here?"

Kaenera's smile was visceral as he casually surveyed the horrified assembly. "Looks like you've been having some trouble." He hesitated as his gaze fell on Kyrill's body, and then he moved on. "The citadel not capable of doing its job?"

"The citadel is more than capable, as you will soon find out."

Kaenera waved his hand. "Seems a bit impotent to me. After all, here I am and yet your father is missing."

"He's not missing, just absent," Mav replied.

"Ah, absent," Kaenera repeated as he inspected his nails. His black robes drifted around his ankles likes shadows. "That happens when you step away for a moment and can't return."

"You drew him away while Serenia killed Athenia."

"So easily deceived. Averdeus always wanted reconciliation." He shrugged. "Shame she took your soul. I was so looking forward to taking it myself. But enough talk, your submission will fulfil the need."

"No."

"You can't have him," Sero said from above them. "Demavrian was never yours to have."

Kaenera snarled at Sero and then stiffened. Unnoticed, Solanji had crept up behind him and attempted to take Kaenera's soul. "You dare!" he screamed as he battered Solanji away. Kaenera flared his wings, spinning fast, reaching for her as she recoiled from the lash of his fury.

Solanji raised her hands in a futile attempt to protect herself and Mav didn't hesitate. He swung his sword with all of his strength, and Kaenera roared in anger. Unable to avoid the blade, he faltered, fury gleaming in his black eyes. "You'll regret this," he hissed as he dissolved into a sinuous mist and disappeared as Mav cleaved the remaining shadows.

Piercing screams filled the citadel. The assembly collapsed with their hand overs their ears as the building shook, chandeliers clashed, and candles snuffed out, leaving the hall in darkness.

Writhing shadows flew up the blade, eager to find a new host. Mav tensed as power flowed through his body, visions of death upon death nearly suffocated him as his breath stuttered and he fell to his knees on the bottom step of the dais, struggling to absorb the mantle of the Gate Keeper, the Keeper of the Oblivion Gate, and all the soulless he was now responsible for.

34

DEMAVRIAN

Time stood still as everyone held their breath and then Serenia erupted out of her seat, dashed down the steps and struck Mav in the back, and before anyone registered what had happened, she wrenched the knife out and stabbed again, embedding the knife in his side.

Mav huffed out a breath and reared up, stiffening as burning pain engulfed him. Fire tore through him as he twisted and blood erupted from his mouth as he continued rotating. He staggered trying to right himself, but he had no strength, and he crumpled to the floor. Roaring filled his ears and drowned out thought, all-consuming and deafening. His body wouldn't respond as he gasped for breath, choking on the blood that filled his mouth.

Shadows swirled in panicked agitation, still adjusting to the influx of power. Simmering power which flexed, blocking ruptured blood vessels, staunching wounds, but not fast enough.

Voices rose around him, fearful and sharp, but strangely muted. Serenia's voice cut through the noise demanding something, and Julius replied from above him, his voice cold and edged with glittering emotions he couldn't identify, ordering his men to hold her despite her shrill protests.

Solanji's fear pierced the fog of pain and confusion. She needed to bind his soul back into the citadel, that was his only chance. His ability to heal himself would be restored, strengthened by the citadel. He tried to speak. "Ta… Ta…" and he choked on the blood filling his mouth, thick and suffocating. Someone raised his head, and he groaned as pain shot through his body and hands clamped against the wounds. So much blood. Where was it all coming from? His vision was beginning to grey around the edges, and he realised how Athenia must have felt, trying to tell him who had killed her. It was impossible. His sluggish healing powers were overwhelmed, they couldn't keep up with the damage.

He strained to reach Solanji. Where was she? There was something he needed to tell her, only he couldn't remember what. Shivers rippled through him. *"Solanji?"*

"Mav? Stay with me, please, Mav."

"Solanji?" Mav wasn't sure if he imagined her voice or not.

"Mav? Please, hold on, Felather is here, and Kerris, they will heal you, but you have to do your part."

"I love you." Had he said that out loud? He wasn't sure.

"I love you too, Mav. And I promise I will show you every day, only you must stay. Stay with me, Mav."

"M-my soul, bind it…"

"I don't know how!"

"D-do it…" Red bubbles frothed in the corners of his mouth. *"N-now."* He convulsed as his body shuddered. Cold, he was so cold. He struggled for breath, clinging to Solanji as darkness engulfed him.

• • •

"No. You can't leave me. Mav, noooo!" Solanji keened over Mav's limp body. She clung to his shadows, but they were lost, aimless, as if they no longer had a purpose. She weaved her soulmist into the strands trying to liven them up, to make them react. They suddenly snapped tight, as if realising they needed to protect him. And Solanji snatched her soul fingers back, hissing at the shock of separation.

"Solanji!" Sero clapped his hands in front of her face, before he traced her cheek with gentle fingers. "You must bind him to the citadel."

"I don't know how!"

"Use the dragon," Sero said, and Solanji jerked upright, her fingers still trying to find a way into Mav's shadows.

"How do you know…?"

"I know everything, remember?" he said, tapping her cheek.

Solanji ran her soul fingers over Mav's shadows and searched the surrounding space, reaching for the citadel and not finding it.

"Help me," she pleaded, fumbling about in the dark as Mav's blood soaked into her robe. Desperation drove her to reach for the citadel itself, her soul fingers questing, though she wasn't sure what she was searching for.

The dragon tattoo glowed and swirled around her arm and then rose into the air. Hovering over her head, it peered down at the dying man in her arms and roared. It was more of a squeal, and the little dragon huffed out a few sparks and shimmered.

The deep crimson pool of blood, so vibrant against the lifeless white stone, grew larger as Mav faded, and Solanji didn't know what to do. She was watching his vitality drain out of him. His shadows were so tightly wrapped around him, she couldn't find an opening. His wings were absent, no sign of them; it was as if they didn't exist.

"Help me!" she cried as she hovered over Mav's limp body. His skin was grey and clammy to the touch as she smoothed her fingers over his cheek. Felather and Kerris had their hands clamped to his wounds, their clothes soaked in his blood as they tried to stem the endless flow.

Solanji jerked when vice-like hands gripped her shoulders. "Help him," Adriz snarled, shaking her so hard Solanji's head snapped back against her golden armour.

Ignoring the growing ache in her head, Solanji stuttered. "H-his soul is wrapped so tight I can't grasp it."

"Solanji," Felather gasped, his face pale and strained. "You have to weave his soul into the citadel. Solanji, you have to! Once his soul is rebound, he'll be able to heal himself. The citadel will restore his powers. It will also open the portal and allow Averdeus to return. Solanji, hurry."

Serenia cackled as the guards pinned her against the wall and shackled her wrists. "It's too late. Neither Averdeus or Kaenera can have him now. It's far too late!"

Solanji stiffened and reached for the soulmist dragon. She would not allow Serenia to win. *"What do we need to do to save him?"*

Xylvin's roar made the chandeliers' tinkle, and the tiny dragon began to grow. She solidified into a shimmering golden dragon. A dragon which was elegant, ethereal, and as tall as Solanji was.

"Do you accept the bond?" The dragon asked in a light and feminine voice.

"Yes, yes, I accept, tell me what to do."

"Does he accept the bond?"

"What? Mav? He's unconscious; he can't accept anything!"

"Then you'll have to accept for him."

"Whatever it takes to save him," Solanji replied.

"Say the words."

"I accept on behalf of Archdeus Demavrian, now tell me what to do."

"My name is Ellaria, and you need to wrap your soulmist around Demavrian and weave wherever you touch. We are about to become one."

Solanji shivered at the tinge of excitement in the dragon's voice. In Ellaria's voice. But she focused on plucking a bright strand and weaving her soulmist into whichever shadows she could grip.

"Raise him up off the floor," Ellaria said. *"We need to wrap him in soulmist and us."*

Solanji didn't waste time arguing. "Stand him up," she snapped, her fingers busy, forcing Mav's shadows open. She wasn't taking no for an answer, and she trampled all over the strands, forcing them to submit to her.

"What? Solanji, no. He'll bleed out faster," Felather protested.

"I need to embrace him; I can't do that whilst he's on the floor. Lift him up."

Julius and Adriz raised Mav off the floor, holding him upright between them. Solanji cupped Mav's face and kissed him lightly on his cold, grey lips. "This is for us," she murmured as she hugged him tight. Ellaria's coils slithered around them both, and Julius and Adriz gasped as the golden dragon manifested before them. They stepped back and gaped at the iridescent dragon coiled around Mav and Solanji. The three of them began to glow and then they began to rise, and shock rippled through the chamber. The dragon flared her membranous wings, and they hovered a few feet off the ground. A glowing golden dragon with outstretched wings, wrapped around an archdeus and a Soul-Breather.

Sero fluttered above them, drinking in the otherworldly

radiance. An awestruck expression spread over his face as the citadel throbbed.

Solanji reached for the citadel. Her soul fingers danced, moving of their own accord as she searched for the connection. Glinting threads of Mav's shadowsoul and her own golden soulmist quested with her. Ellaria's hum buzzed through her veins, joining Mav's heartbeat, faint and thready but vibrating through her body. Even with her eyes closed, she could still see the glow emanating from their dragon.

But there was more. The air thickened as she carded her fingers through empty space, searching for an impossibility she wasn't sure she would find. Flicking her eyes open at the unexpected texture, she peered through the mist, discerning pale strands of lifeless thread, limp and twisted, colourless and transparent, drifting aimlessly towards the floor.

Was this the citadel's heart? Languishing without its link to the archdeus?

She grasped a thread, frowning at the tacky sensation against her finger tips. The strand clung to her skin and twitched as she bound a piece of Mav's glittering shadowsoul to it.

"That's right," Ellaria crooned. *"Take your joint soulmist and bind it into one with the citadel."*

Solanji twisted her soulmist into the shadowsoul, heat running through her body as Mav's soul absorbed hers and shimmered more brightly as it seeped into the citadel's heart.

The citadel throbbed and consumed the scintillating combination of soulmist and shadowsoul, and then as the pale strands flared to life, the purest tone chimed through the building.

"No," Serenia screamed. She began to struggle against the guards restraining her. "No, it's not possible."

More strands solidified and flared into colour, glowing golds and yellows, sparkling silvers and greys, shadowed blues and greens, warming reds and oranges. The colours morphed as they spread and flowed down the complex weave at the heart of the citadel.

A beat resonated through the hall, through the whole citadel, and then beat again; a vibration felt deep in the bones, and yet at the same time it filled the air around them. In time, it would settle, diminish to a subtle throb in the background, forever present. Bound to the Gate Keeper, the SoulBreather, and a dragon.

Amaridin stumbled down the marble steps. Raising a hand towards his brother, he hesitated as a flash of light blinded him, and a slender man dressed in white tunic and trousers edged with gold stepped onto the dais and surveyed the room. His gaze lingered on the glowing dragon still hanging in mid-air with her burden, and he exhaled.

His face was classically handsome, unlined, with high cheekbones and a straight nose; golden hair was swept back off his face in elegant layers and vivid blue eyes saw all in a glance. He walked down the steps, his wide-legged trousers flaring. Staring around the room, he took in the ranks of open-mouthed councillors on the front benches, the angels rising behind them, and the bodies on the floor. His mouth tightened for a moment, and then he turned his back on them and inspected his dragon-bound son.

"Amaridin," he said, not raising his voice, though it reached every corner of the citadel.

"Yes, father?"

"Do you understand what you are seeing?"

"No, father."

"I thought not. You need to pay attention, because there is much that has gone wrong here, and I expect you to put it right."

"How?"

"That is your problem, but I suggest you take counsel

from your brother when he has recovered from this," Averdeus said, gesturing at the spectacle. He glanced around the room. "And of Valerian, whom I believe you will now find in the healerie, along with those others recently reported missing and who suffered a similar fate."

There was a brief flurry as concerned councillors rose, staring at Averdeus, and at a flick of his fingers they rushed out of the hall.

He sighed and faced Serenia, still held between two of the host.

"You have a choice, Serenia, which is more than you have given others. You can pass through my hands or you can pass through Deus Demavrian's, but you may not remain here."

A wave of voices exclaimed at his words, angels staring at them in shock as they realised that Demavrian was no longer an archdeus; he was the new Gate Keeper, a god.

"Kaenera. Help me!" Serenia wailed.

"Is that your choice?" Averdeus asked. Turning back to his youngest son, he observed the golden dragon wrapped around him. "Though Demavrian is in no fit state to accept you right now. For now, restrain her. Demavrian will deal with her later. Ellaria, can you return my son and his wife to Demavrian's chambers?"

"Of course," Ellaria replied and disappeared with her burden in a flash of golden light.

35

MUNTRA, EIDOLON

As soon as night fell, Muntra shuffled out of the mines with the other men and dropped his pickaxe in the box by the entrance. His back ached, his hands were sore, but he had managed to fill his, as well as Bailey's and Brennan's, boxes. The guard checking they had met their quota ticked them off his list and moved on without question. Muntra tried to brush off the white dust coating his clothes but it rose into the air, choking him. The weary men didn't notice when he ducked into the shadows, they just marched on, heads down, like ghostly apparitions drifting across the ground.

An unusual silence blanketed the compound, and Muntra observed more than one dybbuk milling about aimlessly, with other guards trying to get them to return to their posts. The silence was broken by a rumbling growl of thunder, and large splats of rain began to fall.

The dybbuks turned and stared as a dull thud was followed by a loud 'whump' as one of the out houses roared into flames. Muntra stopped and gaped as the dybbuks seemed mesmerised by the dancing flames, and then he jerked back into motion. He had no idea how Kiara had done that, assuming it was her work, but he wasn't going to put it to waste.

Bending low and keeping to the darker shadows, he made his way towards the perimeter fence. Two small children huddled in the deep shadows behind a small outhouse, and he nearly tripped over them. He exhaled in frustration. Shandra was determined to bring everyone. He wouldn't be able to protect them all. She appeared with two more kiddies in her arms, faces streaked with tears, and he kept his opinion to himself.

"Just keep them quiet," he whispered and knelt by the fence and started cutting the chain links. Shandra didn't answer but disappeared again. He glanced over to the cliff face, but he couldn't see the concealed entrance where Bailey and Brennan were hiding. He just hoped they were paying attention. The snap of the metal was a high 'plink' on the night air, but Muntra kept working, shaking his hand out against the pinch of the clippers. Kiara had done an amazing job, considering the tools she had to use.

"Muntra! Down!" Bailey's voice reached him, and he dropped flat to the ground as footsteps thudded past, headed for the fire. Cold rain pelted his back and he shivered.

"All clear," Bailey whispered. Heart thudding, Muntra glanced around before rising, but he returned to the fence, flicking the rain out of his eyes. The huddled children whimpered, but Shandra was back hushing them.

Muntra peeled back the fence and continued clipping. He froze as a flash of lightning lit the compound followed by another growl of thunder. "Bailey, do you think you can fit through this gap? I'll send the kids over to you if you can."

Bailey crawled out of the tunnel, followed by Brennan, both stretching stiff joints, and crept over to Muntra. They wriggled through the gap, clothes snagging on the sharp edges. Muntra unhooked them, knowing he wouldn't fit.

"Hide in the trees. I'll send the little ones over to you."

"I'll take them," Brennan offered. "They'll be scared on their own."

Muntra beckoned two of the kids over, and they crawled through the gap, and Brennan grabbed their hands and ran through the pelting rain.

Another deep whump shook the ground, and a second building went up in flames. Voices shouted, raised in fear. A woman's voice penetrated the confusion, decisive and commanding, ordering the guards about, and Muntra wondered who she was.

"Hurry up," he whispered as he beckoned two more children over as Brennan returned. Shandra deposited two more in their place and gave Muntra an exultant grin. "Isn't Kiara amazing?" she whispered before she hurried off again.

Muntra grinned and began snipping a few more links. He hissed his breath out as the clippers crunched, pinching his skin and drawing blood. They had disintegrated in his hand. Sucking the wound, he directed two more kids through the fence. He inspected the hole he had made and hoped he would fit.

Night was descending as Xylvin flew over the third compound of the day and circled down to land by the main gates. The search for a homestead to take in the children from the last compound had taken longer than they had expected and a sense of urgency nipped at their heels as they continued their search.

Each compound they visited seemed worse than the one before. The conditions were appalling and the people little more than slaves. Eyes dulled with despair barely acknowledged Ryvalin's presence as she walked through the enclosure, checking the empty buildings they called sleeping huts and peering into dank caverns.

Kyrill's name opened the gates, though the dybbuks barely glanced at the papers she waved at them. Ryvalin didn't think she could cope with seeing much more depravation and hopeless acceptance. These people had given up and were ready to lay down and die.

Face tight, Ryvalin waited for the gate to open as thunder grumbled around the valley. Darkness was descending swiftly, no sunset to speak of in Eidolon, just grey and then full dark. No real transition. After this compound, they would return to the small camp they had set up last night for the children further north. Ryvalin had had enough for the day.

This compound nestled up against another stone ridge which rose majestically above them into the night sky. Dust thickened the air, and Ryvalin wrinkled her nose. Muted noises came from the enclosure, and Ryvalin tried to identify them and failed.

"They're digging up rock," Xylvin murmured.

"To do what with?"

"There's an ore in it they want."

They were interrupted as the gate creaked open and a large man filled the gap. Behind him, Ryvalin could see a torchlit yard and shadows scurrying across the open space.

Waving her papers, she said. "I'm here on behalf of Seraphim Kyrill. He's mislaid some of his fledglings. Have you had any recent arrivals?"

"Kyrill's not been here in months. He owes us some supplies."

"I'm not looking for Kyrill. Have you had any children delivered?"

"What if we had?"

"I need to check them. Kyrill wants his fledglings delivered to Puronia."

The man shrugged. "We need them here. We have quotas to deliver."

"I doubt these children add much to your quota."

The man assessed her. "You would though."

Xylvin stepped forward out of the shadows, her massive head peering over Ryvalin's head as the rain swirled in the rising wind. The man tensed and cursed under his breath.

"I am not here to slave for you; I'm on Seraphim Kyrill's business." Whispers rose behind the gate, and Ryvalin caught the word 'dragon' and smiled grimly. "Now show me these children and I'll be on my way."

The man opened the gate just as a building exploded into flames. Guards cowered back in fear, voices raised in bewilderment. Dark shadows flickered across the ground as the yellow flames spread, eating through the wood and hissing as they met the damp outer frames.

"Where do you keep your water supply?" Ryvalin yelled. "Form a bucket chain."

The guards milled about, uncertain what to do as slaves poured out of the huts, adding to the confusion.

Ryvalin searched the open yard, but there were no obvious barrels or vats. Before she could question anyone, another building went up with a loud whump, sucking the air around it into the fire, and Ryvalin frowned in suspicion. Was this an escape attempt?

"Xylvin, keep the gates open, I don't think this is an accident."

Xylvin moved her bulk between the gates. *"I think I may be more of a deterrent than the gates. I'll just tear them down and move out of the way."*

Moving further into the yard, Ryvalin continued to order the guards to get water. They did set up a basic bucket chain, but the guards were more interested in herding the slaves back into the buildings. They made little impact on the fires.

Across the yard, a young girl with two kiddies holding her hands ran towards the ridge face, *away* from the open gate, and Ryvalin frowned as she watched. *"Xylvin, go east around the perimeter, I think some of our resourceful kids are trying to escape."*

"On my way."

Ryvalin hurried deeper into the compound and stopped as she heard a girl scream, "Muntra! Help me!"

She couldn't see where the voice came from, but a large lad came barreling past and was about to enter one of the still standing buildings when it exploded, blasting the lad and Ryvalin across the yard.

Before Ryvalin could react, the lad was up. "Kiara!" he yelled and dived back into the burning building. Another girl came running, and Ryvalin grabbed her around the waist and managed to stop her. The girl was strong, but Ryvalin was stronger. "Shandra, is it?" she asked, and the girl gasped and stopped struggling.

"My name is Ryvalin. Demavrian sent me."

"Demavrian?"

"Mav."

"Oh," the girl swayed. "Where is he? We're trying to escape. But Kiara and Muntra are in there. We can't leave them behind."

Xylvin roared as a scream pierced the night air, and Ryvalin exclaimed, "What now?"

"The others were escaping through the fence. The kids are with Bailey and Brennan."

"Xylvin? What's happened?" Ryvalin asked as she peered into the burning building. "Stay here," she said curtly to Shandra and dashed around the side. The far wall had been blown out, and planks of wood stuck up in all directions. The fire burned fiercest on that side of the building. Ryvalin

didn't hold out much hope for Kiara as she saw the splinters of wood piercing the wall of the neighbouring building.

She started shifting debris, lifting smouldering planks, trying to clear a path through the wreckage. She saw movement and called, "This way." A large shadow moved in the darkness. "Muntra? Over here. I can help."

Muntra staggered out of the building, a small body in his arms. He was smoke-blackened and his voice was husky as he said, "She's not breathing."

"Let me see her," Ryvalin said, kneeling in the mud beside him as he collapsed to his knees and began rocking.

"She's not breathing," he repeated as Shandra came rushing up.

Ryvalin pulled Kiara out of his arms and searched for a pulse. The child was pale, her eyes fixed and staring, gleaming in the light of the flames. Her clothes were torn and bloody, pierced by splinters of wood. Ryvalin couldn't find a pulse, and she shuddered as she pulled the thin cloth away; a splinter had pierced her chest.

"She got snagged on a pipe," Muntra said, his voice emotionless. "She always had to do one more than she needed to."

Ryvalin exhaled and leaned back on her heels. *"Xylvin? I need you! I have a child who is mortally injured."*

"Busy right now! I also have an injured child!"

"Who?"

"No idea. But he's one of Mav's fledglings."

"We're going to lose this fledgling if you don't get here right now. She's not breathing."

Xylvin's voice was soft. *"Then you've already lost her, my dear. Let me try and ensure we don't lose another."*

36

DEMAVRIAN

av opened his eyes and stared up at the ceiling of his bedchamber. Inhaling a careful breath, he stilled. An unfamiliar hum throbbed through his veins, sheathing him in comfort and warmth. He considered for a moment and gave up trying to identify it. He was alive, though he wasn't sure how. Serenia's blade had hit something vital, that much he knew with the amount of blood he had pumped out over the floor.

He shivered, remembering Athenia, and then Kaenera. Had he killed him? Was he now the Gate Keeper of the Oblivion Gate? Something had definitely changed. Underneath this thrumming contentment was a heavy darkness waiting for him to acknowledge it. Warm arms embraced him, and he inhaled the scent of Solanji's skin and relaxed. The citadel's heartbeat thumped, and he smiled, the familiar vibration shimmering through his bones, soothing.

"How am I alive?" he murmured.

"Ummm, I bound you to the citadel, and your father returned."

"You did what?" Mav exclaimed, trying to rise, but Solanji held him down.

"You need to rest. Your body is still recovering." A tear dripped on his face, and he tugged her tighter as she murmured, "It was the only way to save you. I nearly lost you, Mav."

"But you didn't. I'm still here." He kissed her nose. "And my father? He was able to return?" Relief flooded Mav as he relaxed back on his pillow. "Is he is well? I bet his arrival shocked everyone."

"Yes. He is fine, and there is much you need to catch up with, but Mav…" Solanji faltered.

"What?" he asked dreamily, basking in her delightful embrace and a sensation of utter contentment. Trying to figure out why he felt so good seemed like too much effort.

"You did say you loved me."

"I do."

"Well, I…umm…Mav."

"Spit it out, what did you do?"

"I've bound us to each other, Ellaria and the citadel."

There was a short silence. "Ellaria?"

"Our dragon."

Mav stiffened. He was bound to a dragon? The contented thrum vibrating through his body increased, and he relaxed as he began to chuckle. He couldn't help it. He had bonded with a dragon just as Xylvin had predicted. "Is that why I feel so good?"

"I don't know. I'm still learning what it means."

"I expect we have much to learn about a lot of things. How long has it been since you bound us to Ellaria and Averdeus returned?"

"It's late afternoon of the same day."

"And he's left us alone?"

"He did visit briefly, but he said you would wake when you were ready and he would speak to you then."

"So, you've dragon bound us? What does that mean?" Mav asked as he pulled her down on top of him and kissed her.

"Well," she said on a gasp when she came up for air, "my tattoo changed into a real dragon who we now share a soul with; a golden dragon called Ellaria. She is beautiful and much larger, though not as large as Xylvin. All three of us are bound as one, with the citadel."

"How did you manage that?"

"I have absolutely no idea."

Mav burst out laughing, though he soon stopped as he gasped for breath and his chest ached.

"You need to be careful for a few months. Your injuries are healed, but your lungs need time to recover. Serenia managed to do a bit of damage. You will get tired easily. Ellaria will keep an eye on you."

"She will, will she?"

"Yes, I will. I have permission to sit on you if necessary," Ellaria purred as she landed on the bed, having shrunk to a third of her size. *"You're known to be stubborn."*

"Who gave you permission?" Mav demanded, staring at the absolutely gorgeous, ethereal dragon sitting on his bed. The wooden frame groaned, and Mav wondered if his bed would collapse.

Ellaria's laugh rumbled deep in her chest, and he shivered as her happiness glissaded through him. *"Do you want a list? Solanji, Xylvin, Felather, Adriz, even young Kerris has had a word, your father, the citadel, Sero, the list goes on."*

Mav smiled. "Really?"

"Yes, really," Solanji said. "Everyone has been worried about you. Serenia nearly killed you. It shocked all of Puronia. Your father has been really concerned."

"Yes. So you will do as you are told. Averdeus did what he could, but he was shocked at the damage you had suffered. I think he feels guilty about making you so vulnerable," Ellaria said, stretching out on the bed. The soft sound of her coils sliding against each other was comforting. She rested her head on Mav's chest. *"We nearly lost you,"* she murmured, her ashy breath warm on his cheek.

Mav was convinced the bed was going to collapse.

"And that is not acceptable," Solanji added.

Sensations flooded through Mav, and he gasped, trying to sort through them. *"Don't fight it,"* Ellaria said. *"It will settle, and you'll understand which emotions are yours and which are mine or Solanji's. Together we will work it out. Solanji is worried you didn't have a choice, but we didn't have much time, and we believed you'd rather be alive with us than dead."*

"I think you made the right choice," Mav said, rubbing Solanji's back and Ellaria's eye ridge. Ellaria's inner eyelid dropped as she purred. Her contentment covered them like a warm blanket, and Mav closed his eyes, exhaustion and Ellaria lulling him back to sleep. Solanji cuddled him on one side and their dragon curled against the other.

Mav woke later that evening with a start, a sense of loss flooded him making his chest ache. Solanji was wrapped around him, and he frowned, trying to identify what was wrong. Pain spiked in his chest and he gasped as he tried to rub it away.

Power simmered under his skin. More power than he knew what to do with. Images of tall, imposing gates which swung open as he approached filled his mind, and he was standing in an empty room lit by a soft green light which emanated from the walls.

Open stone archways led off the vestibule, leading to

large halls with vaulted ceilings. The halls were empty, silent, waiting. He walked across what he assumed was the entry hall, peering through the open archways, but he was drawn further down the passage, towards an iron gate, which was embedded with lattice work and trailing vines. He touched the flower buds and the petals opened as the metal work vibrated beneath his fingers. Muted voices rose and someone thumped on the gate.

He opened the gate and anguish ripped through him, taking his breath away. His heart stuttered as Kiara flew into his arms. "Mav, we need you!"

He hugged her tight. "Kiara! What are you doing here?"

"We were trying to escape, but it's all gone wrong. I blew up one building too many and I couldn't get out in time."

"You blew up a building?" Mav repeated, stunned.

"Three of them," Kiara said proudly, and then her smile faded as she looked down at herself. She shimmered, her solidity wavering. Tears gleamed in her eyes as she looked back up at him. "Muntra ran into a burning building to rescue me. But I don't feel right…uh, I think I might be dead." She wavered, her form undulating. "Am I dead, Mav?"

"I don't know," Mav whispered. Though the ache in his chest increased as he realised he did know. "You're standing at the Oblivion Gate."

Tears dripped down her cheeks. "Why are you here? Are you dead too, Mav?" Kiara asked as she reached for him. "It won't be so lonely if I'm with you."

"You'll never be alone, my darling girl. I will always hold you in my arms," he said as he hugged her again. She solidified in his embrace.

"This is so weird," she muttered. "Why do you make me feel more solid?"

"There is much I don't know and much I have to learn,

but I believe I am the new Keeper of the Oblivion Gate," Mav said.

Kiara grinned through her tears. "Wow! The Gate Keeper? Does that mean you're a God?"

"I suppose it does."

"Can you make me alive again? I never got to say goodbye to Shandra or Muntra or the others."

"I am so sorry, but that is one thing I cannot do." Kiara's face fell, and Mav rubbed her back. "You have a choice to make," he said gently.

"What choice?"

"To stay or go. You can stay here with me or you can pass through the gate."

Kiara jerked upright. "I can stay with you?" She frowned. "I wouldn't be a dybbuk, would I?"

"No, I have no need of dybbuks. They were puppets, mindless bodies for Kaenera to control, and I would not treat anyone in that way." Mav realised he would have to deal with those poor people lost once again without Kaenera's direction. "But Kiara, if you stay, you will be bound to the gate; you wouldn't be able to leave it. The Oblivion Gate is a complex portal that needs maintaining. If you would like, you could be my Gate Wraith and help me look after it."

"A wraith?"

"It's the only way you can exist here. Over time, I think you will be able to control who can see you, become more solid, I think." Mav shrugged. "We could find out how together."

"Will you live here?"

"Yes. This will be home, with Solanji, you, and the others if they choose to stay with me."

A sad smile spread over Kiara's face. "Well, in that case, count me in. I get to look after the gate?"

"You don't want some time to consider it? It may sound

good now, but not being able to leave may become untenable over time. I would not keep you here if you didn't want to."

"Mav, stop. I would never leave you, and I know you would let me pass on if I chose to." She glanced back through the gate and then gasped. "Mav, you need to go, Bailey's approaching the gate. You mustn't let him through. Not Bailey, please Mav." She pushed him away and slammed the gate shut.

A loud knock on the door of his bedchamber jerked Mav awake, and he blinked away the images of the Oblivion Gate and Kiara's desperate face as his father appeared in his room.

Lurching out of bed, Mav staggered as he reoriented himself to his bed chamber. Kiara's words ringing his ears, he grabbed his clothes. "Not now, father, I've got to go. Solanji, wake up."

"Demavrian, my boy. You make your old father proud."

"You can tell me how much tomorrow."

"We need to talk. My apologies for the inconvenience. But I had to take the moment when it arose."

"Inconvenience?" Mav growled. "Fifty years you let me suffer."

"It's not my fault you were slow on the uptake." Averdeus held his hands up as if to fend off Mav's antagonised expression. "What?" he asked in an injured tone.

"When?" Mav was rigid, his anger palpable. 'When did you give me a clue?"

"Mav?" Solanji said from the bed.

"When?" he demanded. "It wasn't until Solanji arrived to rescue me that anything changed."

"Yes, well, best laid plans and all that. They don't always work the first time, but we got there in the end, didn't we?"

Mav teetered on the edge of exploding, except he didn't have the energy. *"I do,"* Ellaria murmured, and Mav growled.

"I don't have time for this. Solanji, get dressed quick; we need to leave."

Solanji rose and hurriedly began to dress. "What's happened?"

"Emergency." Mav glanced back at his father, fidgeting as he waited for Solanji. "Where have you been?"

Averdeus grimaced, fine lines creasing around his mouth. "I found myself in a situation I had never experienced before. It was enlightening."

"Oh?" Mav said, trying to keep the impatience out of his voice.

"Yes. I was stuck."

"You don't say."

"Mmm. I hadn't expected Serenia to strike out at Athenia. How she kept her anger and greed hidden all these years, I don't know. I had no idea she was capable of such atrocities."

"We can discuss this tomorrow."

"You need to know that Kaenera is not dead. You stole his powers when you defeated him, but you didn't kill him."

"Did I defeat him?"

"You wouldn't now be the Gate Keeper if you hadn't," Averdeus said.

"So, I am the Gate Keeper? Don't I get a choice?"

Averdeus laughed. "Is there anyone else you would trust with such a responsibility?"

In truth, Mav had to accept that he didn't. The people of Eidolon were his. "Maybe not. Where did Kaenera go?"

"I don't know. Somewhere to regroup, lick his wounds. He will be even more dangerous now."

Rubbing his temples Mav frowned. "So he can return?" He waved his hand. "No, don't answer. I don't have time for this; we'll talk tomorrow. Solanji, do you trust me?" Mav asked as he pulled her close.

"With my life," she said as Ellaria coiled around them. Mav's wings flared, and they disappeared.

Averdeus stared at the place they had been standing and smiled. "A fast learner." His smile faded as he exhaled. "He'll need to be."

Slave compound, Eidolon

Mav and Solanji appeared in the midst of a compound in chaos, Ellaria still curled around them. She blinked out of sight as rain splattered in heavy drops, cold and uninviting. Soot and ash thickened the air and caught the back of their throats as hissing smoke billowed around them. Dybbuks wandered aimlessly as if not sure what they should be doing, oblivious to the slaves fleeing out of the open gates. Mav ignored them all as he tugged Solanji towards a small group of people gathered around a body on the ground.

Ryvalin looked up in shock. "Mav? How did you get here?"

"I'll explain later," Mav said, his gaze drawn to the lifeless body lying in the mud. He hugged Shandra. "I'm so sorry, my dear," he murmured into her hair as she sobbed against his shoulder. He gripped Muntra's shoulder in sympathy as tears streamed down the lad's soot-covered face.

"I couldn't save her," Muntra said, his voice thick.

"I know," Mav replied as he released them and sank into the mud, lifting Kiara into his arms. "My sweet Kiara," he murmured as tears stung his eyes, and he hid his face in her soft hair and curled his wings over them in a protective shield.

He imagined a safe and peaceful arbour with graceful trees and colourful flowers deep in the halls of the Oblivion

Gate; a safe place for Kiara to rest until her family could say their goodbyes. When he rose and folded his wings, his arms were empty and his heart was bleeding as grief threatened to overwhelm him. "Where's Bailey?" he asked, forcing words out through a tight throat as he walked deeper into the compound.

"Mav? Are you alright?" Solanji lay a soft hand on his arm and he tensed.

"Sorry, my love. We need to find Bailey before it's too late."

"Xylvin is with him. Outside the perimeter fence with the other children," Ryvalin said.

"We were escaping through the fence," Shandra said as she hurried up beside them. "Kiara," she faltered and cleared her throat. "Kiara made some wire cutters so Muntra could cut the fence. We pushed the little ones through the hole with Bailey and Brennan, but then Kiara screamed for help and we rushed to help her."

"Brennan? Did you say Brennan?" Solanji gasped. "What did he look like? Where is he? Is he alright?" She spun away and screamed, "BRENNAN?" into the night.

A faint "Solanji?" floated from behind the huts, and Mav grabbed Solanji's hand and they disappeared.

Solanji stumbled as they landed. "Sorry," Mav murmured as he steadied her and ran towards Xylvin who was sheltering a group of children under her wing.

"Mav, thank goodness you're here. I've done what I can, but he's not responding."

"I know," Mav said, sinking to his knees and stroking Bailey's blond hair. He was vaguely aware of Solanji dragging another boy into her arms, but he ignored them and concentrated on Bailey.

He closed his eyes and extended his senses, searching for the injuries still draining Bailey's life. A puncture wound in his side and one in his leg. A vicious strangulation mark around his neck was the most probable cause, he thought, as he soothed inflamed muscles and widened swollen airways. He bent over him and breathed air into his lungs, watching Bailey's chest rise and fall. As he repeated the motion, over and over, he drifted, leaving his body. Returning to the Oblivion Gate, he walked through its silent halls until he found Bailey sitting outside the lattice work gate. He looked so young and vulnerable, clothed in a grimy, blood-streaked shirt far too big for him, and not much else.

"This is not the place for you, Bailey," Mav murmured as he sat on the onyx bench beside him.

"I'm tired," Bailey said, his blue eyes dull and lifeless.

"I know, but you can survive these wounds if you want to. It's up to you."

"I'm tired of people expecting me to be more than I am. That just because I'm pretty they can choose what they do to me." He sighed. "I'm tired of being weak and dependent on others to protect me."

The brief altercation flashed through Mav's mind. Of Bailey stepping in front of Brennan, protecting him with just a dagger. He had held his own for a brief moment but slid to one knee as the guard threw a knife and it embedded in his leg. The guard cinching a wire around his throat as another blade penetrated his ribs. Xylvin roared, and the guard flinched back and then screamed as Xylvin pounced and Bailey fell to the ground, blood pouring from his wounds.

"You are not weak and you are not defenceless. If it wasn't for you protecting Brennan and the other kids, they would have been hurt too. You fought off a man much larger than yourself."

"But he still hurt me enough that I ended up here." There was a pause. "Kiara's here, isn't she?"

"Yes. I'm sorry, but she is."

"She was shouting at me to go back, but she shouldn't be here alone."

"Oh, Bailey." Mav swept him into a hug, dragging him onto his lap. "Kiara will never be alone, for she will always be with me. But you, it's not your time yet, my dearest boy. You have much to give to this world yet, in the land of the living."

Bailey leaned into him. "Really?"

"Yes, with me here in Eidolon, if you want to. I am the new Gate Keeper, and I have much to do."

Bailey shifted in his arms. "The new Gate Keeper?" he asked as he peered up, a spark of interest in his vivid blue eyes.

Mav smiled. "Yes. Kiara is going to help me, and I want you to help me, too. But you have to help from the other side, the side of the living."

"Kiara will still be with us?"

"For as long as she wants to be."

"And I can stay here with you and her?"

Mav nodded and the rain-splattered glade returned to his awareness. Icy droplets penetrated his clothes and trickled down his neck.

Bailey's chest rose and fell of its own accord, and Mav heaved a heartfelt sigh of relief as he leaned back on his heels. He waited and Bailey's chest rose again.

"Xylvin, can you and Ryvalin take Bailey back to Puronia? Ask Felather to care for him and then return here?"

"Of course."

Mav rose and pushed his hair out of his face, weariness tugging at him. *"Solanji?"*

"Here, my love."

"Was it your brother, Brennan? Is he alright?"

"He's a little traumatised, but he will be well."

Rubbing his face, Mav smiled at Brennan, a smaller

version of Solanji. "Hi, Brennan. It's nice to finally meet you. I'm, Mav, Solanji's friend." His smile faltered as Brennan shrank away from him, pressing into Solanji's side. "I'm glad you are safe. I think it's best we return you along with Shandra and Muntra to the homestead for now, let the kids return to a little normality. Solanji can stay and look after you all while we figure out what's best for everyone. Xylvin and Ryvalin will take you when they return from taking Bailey to Puronia."

"I want to go where Bailey goes," Muntra said, a determined expression on his face.

"Very well. Xylvin is taking him back to the citadel to recover. My scribe, Felather, will meet you there, along with Kerris."

"Kerris? He's in Puronia?" Muntra gasped.

"Yes. He crossed the divide to find me. I am sure he will be really glad to see you."

"He stayed in Puronia? But how? We are all soulless."

Mav smiled, certainty spreading through him. "Because he is my fledgling, just like you, Shandra, and Bailey are."

Expressions of anguish and hope warred on Muntra's face. "You can't want me," he whispered. "I failed them all."

"Oh, Muntra. You never failed anyone." Mav hugged him tight. "Without you, none of them would have survived. Bailey needs you, so get yourself on that dragon and make sure he arrives safely."

Mav stared out over the burning compound, blind to the chaos and destruction. There was much in Eidolon that needed fixing. But for now, he would make sure his family were safe. He hugged Solanji tight, wrapping his arms around her and Brennan.

Given time, Solanji would master SoulBreathing and return Brennan's soul. His fledglings would be given the choice of staying with him or leaving, and he needed to learn what being the Oblivion Gate's Keeper meant. He intended on taking up the mantle and protecting these people. He had no doubt that was more easily said than done.

Instinctively, he recognised his connection to the Oblivion Gate. The Gate in return was tentative, uncertain of its regard. He would have to earn its respect.

And then there was Kaenera. The God would be incandescent with fury, weakened, and out for vengeance. And his target would be Demavrian.

EPILOGUE

Mav walked through the silent halls of the Oblivion Gate. Torches flared with green-tinged flames as he passed, casting eerie pools of light. His fledglings were scattered and in disarray. He needed to collect them all and speak to them, reassure them, offer them the choice. A new life in Puronia or a life with him in Eidolon. He hoped they would help him build a new home. There were many secrets the Oblivion Gate had yet to reveal; their company would be a blessing as they attempted to unravel them. There was even more work to be done in Eidolon.

Kiara's cool presence embraced him, and he smiled as she briefly manifested, her cheeky grin undiminished. "Thank you, Mav," she whispered. "I'll be the best Gate Wraith ever." Cold lips kissed his cheek.

"You're the only Gate Wraith there's ever been," he replied as he tousled her hair.

"Low bar to cross then! I'm already the best," she laughed as she spun away. "I'm the world's best ever Gate Wraith to the world's best ever Gate Keeper."

"Of that I have no doubt," Mav said with a grin, as he followed her through the halls of the Oblivion Gate. The new Gate Keeper surveyed his domain and smiled.

THE END

Sign up to my newsletter to find out first when book three of the SoulMist series is released.

Mav learns the secrets of the Oblivion Gate Keeper and discovers why Kaenera wants revenge. Solanji tries to find her brother's soul and Mav's fledglings decide whether they want to take up residence in the Oblivion Gate.

BOOK THREE OF THE SOULMIST SERIES

Due to be released in 2024.

OblivionGate, Book Three of the SoulMist series

Having defeated four counts of Apologia, Demavrian has every right to be feeling triumphant, but the threat hanging over his head from the vengeful god, Kaenera, is enough to snuff out any celebrations.

His fledglings are distraught and in disarray. Solanji's brother is still without a soul and she has no idea how her soul-breathing works. He has no idea how to manage the Oblivion Gate and even with his Gate Wraith's help, the burden of the soulless banging on the gate may be his undoing.

If Demavrian doesn't learn the secrets of the Oblivion Gate fast enough, he may be the shortest lived Gate Keeper in history.

GLOSSARY

Angels

    Demavrian (duh-MAV-ri-un) Archdeus

    Amaridin (a-MA-RI-din) Archdeus

    Veradeus (v-AIR-ad-ay-us) God, father of Demavrian and Amaridin

    Malena, (Mah-Lain-ah) Veradeus' Wife

    Kaenara (k-nair-a) Veradeus' brother

    Serenia (s-REN-i-a) Archangel

    Athenia (a-th-eh-ni-a) Archangel, SoulBreather

    Goloran (go-law-ran) Archangel

    Capt. Julius Teravin (t-air-a-vin) Captain of the Heavenly Host

    Eladriz/Adriz (el-a-driz) Cherubim

    Felather (fell-a-th-ur) Scribe

    Sero (s-air-ro) Cherub

    Ryvalin (riv-a-lin) Captain of the Heavenly Host

    Xylvin (SHIL-vin) Dragon

    Kyrill (k-i-rill) Seraphim

    Valerian (Val-AIR-ian) Amaridin's partner

    Dalruan (Dal-rue-an) Seraphim

Lianderis (Lee-an-dare-iss) Seraphim

Councillors

Neralon (N-AIR-ah-lon)
Palent (Pay-lent)
Mort (Mor-t)
Groller (Gruh-ler)
Laener (LAY-ner)
Dorne (Door-n)

Mortals

Solanji (so-lan-j-i) Mortal
Brennan/Bren (bren-an) Solanji's younger brother
Georgi (j-or-gi) Solanji's elder brother

Kerris. (k-air-riss) Orphan
Shandra (sh-an-druh) Orphan
Muntra (mun-truh) Orphan
Bailey (bay-li) Orphan
Kiara (key-ar-a) Orphan
Tannie (Tan-ee) Orphan

Locations

Angelicus (an-zh-el-i-cus) country
Puronia (p-roh-ni-a) Capital city of Angelicus
Bruatra (bru-ar-tra) Town in south Angelicus
Eidolon (Eye-d-oh-lon) Country
Merapol (m-air-a-pol) town
Jinnel (j-in-eh-l) town

Apologia (ap-o-low-gee-a) Formal process to prove innocence
of charges or forfeit life.

ACKNOWLEDGMENTS

Writing is such a joy and a pleasure. I am so relieved that I put pen to paper that day and started writing and haven't stopped.

DragonBound is the second book in the SoulMist series, the second series I have written, and it is just as exciting to be writing 'The End' in this book, as it has been for any other book.

Writing a book is a labour of love. You create characters you fall in love with, and then you put them through all sorts of pain and anguish, and have to get them out the other end, resolving those situations you put them in and offering them some sense of completion. It certainly gets your brain cells working, but it is such fun!

Thank to my editor, Maddy Glenn, for making me dig deep and split my original story into two books. You wouldn't have been reading DragonBound otherwise. Delving deeper into the world and my characters has made for a much richer story. I hope you agree! The benefit to my readers is of course this series is now at least a trilogy instead of the duology I had planned.

Thank you to Michael, my alpha reader who has been on this journey with me from day one, offers unstinting support, and is always ready to read another one of my books.

My wonderful team of ARC readers continues to grow. Thank you to each of you for joining me on this journey, I really appreciate all your support, comments and feedback.

Click this link to sign up to my ARC team if you are interested in reading my books early.

I love my cover. Seeing my characters brought to life is such a great feeling. The cover was designed by the Ukrainian creative company MiblArt, who have continued to support their authors through very difficult times. My thoughts and prayers go out to all of you.

Thank you all.

Helen

ABOUT THE AUTHOR

Helen Garraway is the USA Today Bestselling author of the award winning epic fantasy Sentinal series which was first published in 2020, followed by the first book of the fantasy romance SoulMist series, SoulBreather, released in 2022 as part of the Realm of Darkness boxset.

An avid reader of many different fiction genres, a love she inherited from her mother, Helen writes fantasy novels and also enjoys paper crafting and scrapbooking as an escape from the pressure of the day job.

Having graduated from the University of Southampton with a Degree in Politics and International Relations, she remains an active member of their alumni. You can find out more at www.helengarraway.com.

<u>Patreon</u>

Join Team Arifel, Team Darian or Team Sentinal and get access to the first chapters of my new books first, free bookish downloads, polls, early sneak peeks.

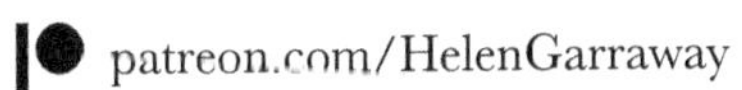

SENTINAL SERIES

Interested in my epic Fantasy Sentinal series? Find out more at www.helengarraway.com
Available in the format of your choice.

- Audiobook
- Ebook
- Paperback
- Hardcover

Sentinals Awaken is the first book in the saga of Remargaren, a vibrant, ancient world of high fantasy suffused with magic and adventure.

Remargaren is a vibrant, ancient world. With Goddesses, Sentinals, Rangers and Ascendants all trying to protect or attain that which is important to them.

Join me on the journey, as we meet Jerrol Haven, a King's Ranger, who is destined to become Lady Leyandrii's Captain. A role lost in the mists of time after her last

Captain spectacularly disappeared with her when she sundered the Bloodstone and banished all magic from the world.

Throw into the mix some magical creatures, magic seeping back into the world, an insidious disease affecting the Watches of Vespiri and the tall sentinal trees, the only reminder of the Lady's Guards, her faithful Sentinals, and we have the Sentinals Series.

We travel deeper into the world of Remargaren as Jerrol grapples with the expectations of goddesses and kings, and tries to stay alive long enough to figure out how he can wake the ancient guards sleeping in their tall trees. They are his only hope to help him protect their world against the wild magic of the shadowy Ascendants.

ONE
THE SENTINAL SERIES
SENTINALS
AWAKEN
USA TODAY BESTSELLING AUTHOR
HELEN GARRAWAY

SENTINALS AWAKEN

Sentinals Awaken is the first book in the saga of Remargaren, a vibrant, ancient world of high fantasy suffused with magic and adventure.

As a three thousand-year-old threat reemerges, only one man has the power to awaken the world's greatest protectors and restore order to the realm. He just doesn't know it yet. When Jerrol Haven, a captain in the King's Rangers, discovers treason at the highest level, he knows immediately that the knowledge puts his life at risk. And indeed, though he expected the ailing king to shield him, the ambitious Crown Prince sentences Jerrol to death.

What hold does the Prince have over his weakened father, and who or what is he protecting?

Now, with signs that her veil is weakening and the Ascendants are creeping back into power, the goddess, Leyandrii, has returned and is in dire need of Jerrol's help. For though he doesn't know it, Jerrol possesses a rare gift: By chance, he touches a revered Sentinal tree and awakens

Birlerion, one of the Lady's personal guard who have been sleeping in the strange, tall trees since they were last called to battle. Aided by Birlerion, Jerrol flees and begins his journey to help Lady Leyandrii save Remargaren once more.

But time is running out: As it was with the king, the old guard lords are everywhere being usurped, attacked, and assassinated. Jerrol must unravel the mystery of the Ascendants' return, stop the sinister force that is dividing good families through bloodshed and betrayal, and rescue the king —and his troubles are only just beginning.

Ideal for lovers of The Witcher, Tad William's Shadowmarch or David Eddings' Belgarion series.

Global Book Award Silver Medal, Wishing Shelf Book Award Bronze Medal, Readers' Favorite Finalist.

www.ingramcontent.com/pod-product-compliance
Lightning Source LLC
Chambersburg PA
CBHW070422170726

48291CB00002B/314